KELROY

broadview editions
series editor: Martin R. Boyne

KELROY

Rebecca Rush

edited by Betsy Klimasmith

broadview editions

BROADVIEW PRESS – www.broadviewpress.com
Peterborough, Ontario, Canada

Founded in 1985, Broadview Press remains a wholly independent publishing house.
Broadview's focus is on academic publishing; our titles are accessible to university and college
students as well as scholars and general readers. With over 600 titles in print, Broadview has
become a leading international publisher in the humanities, with world-wide distribution.
Broadview is committed to environmentally responsible publishing and fair business practices.

The interior of this book is printed on 100% recycled paper.

Library and Archives Canada Cataloguing in Publication

Rush, Rebecca, 1779-, author
    Kelroy / Rebecca Rush ; edited by Betsy Klimasmith.

(Broadview editions)
Includes bibliographical references.
ISBN 978-1-55481-200-4 (paperback)

    I. Klimasmith, Elizabeth, 1969-, editor II. Title.
III. Series: Broadview editions

PS2737.R63K4 2016   813'.2   C2016-900093-1

Broadview Editions
The Broadview Editions series is an effort to represent the ever-evolving canon of texts in the
disciplines of literary studies, history, philosophy, and political theory. A distinguishing feature
of the series is the inclusion of primary source documents contemporaneous with the work.

Advisory editor for this volume: Michel Pharand

Broadview Press handles its own distribution in North America
PO Box 1243, Peterborough, Ontario K9J 7H5, Canada
555 Riverwalk Parkway, Tonawanda, NY 14150, USA
Tel: (705) 743-8990; Fax: (705) 743-8353
email: customerservice@broadviewpress.com

Distribution is handled by Eurospan Group in the UK, Europe, Central Asia, Middle
East, Africa, India, Southeast Asia, Central America, South America, and the Caribbean.
Distribution is handled by Footprint Books in Australia and New Zealand.

Broadview Press acknowledges the financial support of the Government of Canada through
the Canada Book Fund for our publishing activities.

Typesetting by Aldo Fierro
Cover design by Aldo Fierro

PRINTED IN CANADA

Contents

Acknowledgements

I would like to thank my students, colleagues, friends, and family who helped to bring this edition to fruition. I first encountered *Kelroy* as I prepared for my doctoral examinations under the direction of Priscilla Wald, whose mentorship continues to influence and inspire me. I vowed then to write about *Kelroy*, but the novel sat on my bookshelf for over a decade until I decided I should teach it as part of a course on "Reading and Writing the American City." I put *Kelroy* on the syllabus, but soon realized that the 1992 Oxford edition I had used as a graduate student, with Dana D. Nelson's wonderful introduction, was out of print. I decided to keep the book on the syllabus, scanning my copy's pages so the students could read it digitally. Their enthusiasm for the novel sparked this edition, and I thank them here. One of those students, Megan Mitchell, worked for me as a Research Assistant. I am grateful to her and to her fellow RA, Tiril Pollard, for their help finding and transcribing documents for this edition's appendices. I am eternally grateful to my incomparable colleagues at UMass Boston, especially Cheryl Nixon, Louise Penner, Sari Edelstein, Shaun O'Connell, Matt Brown, Libby Fay, and Len von Morze, who have provided intellectual and logistical support for this project. My treasured writing group, Renée Bergland, Laura Saltz, and Sarah Luria, helped me to conceptualize this edition and convinced me to pursue the project. I am so grateful to the people at Broadview Press, especially Marjorie Mather, Martin Boyne, and Michel Pharand for the care, enthusiasm, and support that have made this edition possible. My biggest thanks, as always, go to my friends and family—my children, my parents, my siblings, and most of all, my husband, Bayard.

Revised material from my essay, "*Kelroy*'s Parlor Games," originally published in *Early American Literature* 49:2 (2014): 467–97, appears in the Introduction with the kind permission of *Early American Literature*.

Introduction

When readers encounter Rebecca Rush's 1812 novel *Kelroy* for the first time, they often compare it to Jane Austen's novels of manners, especially *Pride and Prejudice* (1813), and for good reason. Like Austen's novels, *Kelroy* features the interplay of mothers and daughters, marriage and money. Set in genteel Philadelphia drawing rooms, at sophisticated balls, and in urbane Pennsylvania country houses that resemble the settings in Austen's novels and emphasize the Atlantic world connections that structured early American cities, *Kelroy* critiques the economic system that limits intelligent women's influence to the domestic world and marriage market. *Kelroy*'s observant, inconspicuous, and occasionally judgmental narrator, perhaps an analogue to Rush herself, guides readers to understand the powerful but understated forces that move the cosmopolitan Philadelphia society she chronicles, from the unwritten rules of polite conversation to the deathly reverberations of swallowed pride. But Rush's most vivid character, the scheming, ambitious Mrs. Hammond, propels *Kelroy* forward with a powerful anger she can barely conceal, giving Rush's novel of manners a Gothic edge. As one perceptive reader put it, "*Kelroy* is like Austen—with evil."

Kelroy's imperious, conniving protagonist expands our sense of literary roles for women in early American novels. Mrs. Hammond might remind readers familiar with Susanna Rowson's *Charlotte Temple* (1791) of Charlotte's scheming French teacher, Mademoiselle LaRue. But LaRue merely facilitates Charlotte's seduction and then turns a blind eye to her friend's subsequent suffering, while Mrs. Hammond secretly and systematically destroys her own daughter's life. Mrs. Hammond shares the brilliant strategic mind of Martinette, the cross-dressing soldier in Charles Brockden Brown's *Ormond* (1799), although Brown's dashing heroine is more interested in international affairs than in drawing-room intrigue. Mrs. Hammond's tactics, including gambling and letter-writing, may be confined to the domestic sphere, but they are nonetheless as ruthless as Martinette's wartime savagery. Rush's brilliant characterization of an ambitious woman whose own survival depends on manipulating her daughters' marriage plans enables *Kelroy* to transcend generic expectations.

Along with sharply realized characters like Mrs. Hammond, Rush's flair for dialogue and description makes *Kelroy* a gripping read as well as a significant early American novel; as Cathy Davidson notes, "All in all, Rush's novel is one of the best written in America before 1820."[1] Yet *Kelroy* has enjoyed far less critical attention than other novels by early American women, like *Charlotte Temple* or Hannah Webster Foster's *The Coquette* (1797). Perhaps because it doesn't conform to readers' expectations that early American novels were, almost without exception, seduction narratives (which *Kelroy* most definitely is not), Rush's novel has twice fallen out of print. Recent scholarship in the fields of material culture, such as Bernard Herman's *Town House*, and Atlantic studies, including Elizabeth Maddock Dillon's *New World Drama*, however, opens the elite cosmopolitan networks that structured Rebecca Rush's—and *Kelroy*'s—urban world to readers today. This context transforms our sense of *Kelroy*. Though *Kelroy* still matters as a groundbreaking novel by an early American woman writer, it will also resonate for today's readers as a significant American urban novel as well as a text that offers an important "new" voice to studies of the literature and culture of the Atlantic rim.

Rebecca Rush and *Kelroy*'s History

When it appeared in 1812, *Kelroy*'s title page identified its publishers, Bradford and Inskeep, and its printer, Jane Aitken, by name. *Kelroy*'s author, in contrast, was identified only as "A Lady of Pennsylvania." Originally thought to be Leonora Sansay (b. 1773), the Philadelphia-based author of *Laura* (1809) and *Secret History* (1808), *Kelroy*'s "Lady of Pennsylvania" was in fact Rebecca Rush. By 1897, Rush received credit for *Kelroy* in the *Critical Dictionary of English Literature and British and American Authors*:

> Rush, Miss Rebecca, a daughter of Judge Jacob Rush
> ... was the author of Kelroy, a Novel, by a Lady of
> Philadelphia, 1812, 12 mo. Purchased by Bradford and
> Inskeep for $100.[2]

But the novel, like its author, remained relatively obscure.

---

1 Cathy Davidson, *Revolution and the Word: The Rise of the Novel in America*, 2nd ed. (New York: Oxford UP, 2004) 329.
2 Austin Allibone, *Critical Dictionary of English Literature and British and American Authors, Volume III* (Philadelphia: J.B. Lippincott and Company, 1897) 1893.

We still know very little about Rebecca Rush, and as was true in 1897, we know far more about her family than we do about the author herself. As a young unmarried woman, Rebecca's mother Mary "Polly" Rush (née Rench) supported her own widowed mother and a younger brother by painting the miniature portraits then so popular among the eighteenth-century elite class. However, "after her marriage she never could be prevailed on to paint a single picture; ... she only followed the profession of painting to obtain a living."[1] Rebecca's father, Jacob Rush, was a successful lawyer who served as President of the Court of Common Pleas for Philadelphia.[2] Jacob's brother, Rebecca's uncle Benjamin Rush (1746–1813), is far better known today. A prominent Philadelphia doctor who rose to fame during the city's Yellow Fever epidemic of 1793, Benjamin was educated at Princeton and continued his medical studies in Edinburgh and London, thus experiencing the transatlantic mobility so common in this period.

As *Kelroy* emphasizes, even among the wealthiest classes, men enjoyed far greater opportunities than women did; Rush's fictional world seems to have paralleled her life. Henry Simpson's tome *The Lives of Eminent Philadelphians, Now Deceased*, devotes ten pages to Rebecca's cousin Richard Rush (1780–1859), who served as Pennsylvania's Attorney General, filled the post of US Attorney General under James Madison, was named the American Minister in England at age 37, and became John Quincy Adams's Secretary of the Treasury in 1824.[3] As far as we know, Rebecca wrote one novel, published it anonymously, and died without even having her death date recorded in the family Bible.[4] Needless to say, she is not listed in *Eminent Philadelphians*.

We know that Rebecca was born in 1770, the eldest of five daughters. As a teenager she lived with Benjamin Rush's family in Philadelphia while her father worked in Reading, Pennsylvania, as Third Circuit Court Judge. Letters from Benjamin to his wife Julia in 1793 indicate that Rebecca, then 14, escaped the worst of

---

1 John Sartain, *The Reminiscences of a Very Old Man* (New York: D. Appleton and Co, 1899) 152.
2 Henry Simpson, *The Lives of Eminent Philadelphians, Now Deceased* (Philadelphia: William Brotherhead, 1859) 851.
3 Simpson 854–64 *passim*.
4 For the biographical details of Rush's life that follow, I rely on Dana D. Nelson's introduction to the 1992 Oxford edition of *Kelroy* (New York: Oxford UP, 1992) xi–xxi.

Philadelphia's yellow-fever epidemic by moving with her relatives to a country estate called Rose Hill, where Rebecca looked after her young cousin, Benjamin Rush Jr. Dana D. Nelson's extensive research in the Rush family papers turned up no mention of Rebecca after 1820, leaving the question of whether she ever married, and even the date of her death uncertain.

While the historical record remains almost silent about Rebecca Rush's life, her novel contains some important clues about the context within which *Kelroy* was written and published. Let's return to the title page. *Kelroy* was published by Bradford and Inskeep, a Philadelphia partnership with offices in New York and strong ties to the Rush family. Samuel Fisher Bradford (1776–1837) was from a well-connected local family; with his father he had published Benjamin Rush's *Essays Literary, Moral, and Philosophical* in 1798. Bradford and Inskeep, founded in 1808, published Benjamin Rush's *Sixteen Introductory Lectures to the Course of Lectures upon the Institutes and Practices of Medicine* in 1811, along with original work by women writers, including Leonora Sansay's *Secret History, or, The Horrors of St. Domingo* (1808) and *Laura* (1809). Bradford and John Inskeep (1786–1820) contracted with at least one female printer, Jane Aitken (1764–1832), an independent businesswoman who had inherited her father's print shop. She produced the first (and for almost two centuries, the only) edition of *Kelroy* in 1812. As a material object and commodity, *Kelroy* participated in the commercial world of the Atlantic rim, engaging women in this endeavor to a surprisingly great extent. Yet *Kelroy*'s publication history also reveals the limits of women's participation and success in this economic moment.

Reading the title page closely, one can argue that identifying *Kelroy*'s author as "A Lady of Philadelphia" positions that author—whom we now know to be Rush—within the privileged world of elite Philadelphia, at the time a vibrant city that participated fully in Atlantic world trade and culture. Even if her father never achieved the fame that his brother or nephew did, through her familial connections Rebecca participated in a cosmopolitan sphere in which fashion, pastimes, and behaviors moved freely as the people around her incorporated their European experiences into their American lives. In short, Rush's innocuous pseudonym turns out to be a useful identifier that situates her in a world of relative class status and privilege. But even this privilege could not ensure that her novel would succeed in the marketplace.

Kelroy's plot highlights the fragile state of single women's economic position in the early Republic; its publication history simultaneously underlines women's tenuous financial footing. As Karen Weyler notes, *Kelroy* "enjoyed a relatively robust range of circulation for an Early American novel, given that in 1812 in the United States there was no truly national publication industry or distribution network."[1] Yet *Kelroy* did not find a wide enough readership to merit a second print run, despite its vivid characterizations and timely social critique, perhaps because it had the bad fortune to be published in 1812, just as the United States was going to war with Britain. Though it boasted an illustrious clientele, which included Thomas Jefferson, the firm of Bradford and Inskeep folded in 1815. And soon after printing *Kelroy*, Jane Aitken found herself unable to repay the substantial debt she had inherited from her father and brother-in-law. Her printing equipment was repossessed in 1813, and Aitken was sent to debtors' prison in 1819. Aitken, Bradford, Inskeep, and Rush faded into obscurity, leaving *Kelroy* behind as their shared, but equally obscure, legacy.

It is a legacy worth reclaiming. *Kelroy* adds important dimension to our understanding of the early American novel by disrupting the conventions of the seduction tale shared by many novels of the period, including *Charlotte Temple*, *The Coquette*, *Laura*, and William Hill Brown's *The Power of Sympathy* (1789).[2] Indeed, when Oxford University Press released its edition of *Kelroy*, edited by Dana D. Nelson, in 1992, it was one of four novels in Oxford's Early American Women Writers series overseen by Cathy Davidson. The two seduction novels in that series, *Charlotte Temple* and *The Coquette*, have become standard offerings on academic syllabi and are widely available; the two novels in the series that resist the standard seduction plot, *Kelroy* and Tabitha Gilman Tenney's *Female Quixotism* (1801), have since gone out of print again. Clearly, the seduction plot has resonated with readers and critics, but it represents only one genre of the exciting and diverse types of writing that women writers published in the early Republic.

---

1   Karen Weyler, Introduction, *Kelroy* (San Antonio, TX: Early American Reprints, 2014) iv.

2   See Leonard Tennenhouse, *The Importance of Feeling English: American Literature and the British Diaspora, 1750–1850* (Princeton, NJ: Princeton UP, 2007), and Davidson.

Kelroy's Divided Plot

The typical seduction tale has a simple plot: A young naïve girl falls in love with a suitor who promises marriage—or perhaps even marries the girl in a "private" ceremony with no legal power—only to abandon her, with or without the knowledge of the pregnancy that usually ensues. The typical seduction novel ends with the girl's death and often a moral lesson for the readers of the tale. *Kelroy* departs significantly from this pattern. In the discussion of these departures in the sections that follow, significant plot details must be revealed. Readers may therefore wish to read the novel first and then return to this Introduction.

Instead of seduction, money structures *Kelroy*'s plot, which tracks Mrs. Hammond's efforts to keep up appearances so that she can marry her two daughters, the beautiful but coldly materialistic Lucy and her romantic younger sister Emily, to suitably wealthy husbands before her own limited financial resources run out. The novel opens in Philadelphia, but almost immediately the widowed Mrs. Hammond moves her daughters to the family's country house, where she trains them to make brilliant marriages. When the girls are ready for their debut, the family moves back to Philadelphia. Lucy quickly marries Walsingham, an appropriately rich and handsome British peer, but Emily falls in love with Kelroy, a gentleman poet whose shaky family finances lead him to a career as a speculator in international trade. A series of dramatic reversals—including Lucy and Walsingham's departure for England, and Kelroy's pursuit of a speculative business venture in India—culminates in a massive lottery windfall that brings a newly wealthy Mrs. Hammond and an affianced Emily back to the country, where the second half of the novel unfolds.

In *Kelroy*'s first half, Austenian marriage and money plots are intertwined. As Mrs. Hammond oversees her beautiful daughters on the marriage market, the omniscient narrator keeps a close eye on Mrs. Hammond's financial affairs, especially her dwindling savings. The narrator helps us understand and perhaps even sympathize with Mrs. Hammond's motivations: given her meager inheritance and relative powerlessness as a woman in elite society, Mrs. Hammond has little choice but to marry her daughters to wealthy men if she wants to secure for herself a stable financial future. Yet the narrator also exposes Mrs. Hammond's increasingly desperate methods, revealing how she misleads her daughters' suitors, cheats tradespeople, lets her insurance payments lapse, and, as a last resort, gambles in the decidedly lowbrow lottery.

Kelroy's plot slows down considerably in the second half, but the novel is redeemed by its shocking surprise ending. After receiving several rejection letters from Kelroy, Emily eventually renounces her true love to marry a kind man with an illustrious family and a fortune large enough to satisfy Emily's mother. But at the wedding, Mrs. Hammond suffers a stroke that soon proves fatal. When Emily eventually discovers that her mother secretly orchestrated Kelroy's renunciation through an elaborate forgery scheme, she collapses and later dies, leaving her best friend Helen in charge of revealing the truth about her mother's plot to Kelroy. Thus, while *Kelroy* concludes with the seduction genre's typical fatal swoon, Mrs. Hammond's performance as the beneficent mother familiar to readers of seduction tales here obscures the fact that she is her daughter's very worst enemy. Emily is ruined not by a cunning, deceptive, amoral man, but by her cunning, deceptive, amoral mother.

Kelroy's divided plot is made more compelling by its settings; roughly half of the novel is set in the glittering world of elite Philadelphia, while the second half takes place in what the narrator calls "the country"—a wealthy area along the Schuylkill River about six miles from "the city," an easy morning's ride for Rush's urban characters, who frequently appear in the novel's rural sections (see Appendix A5, p. 221). Though city and country are geographically close, Rush rhetorically opposes the city as a site of speculation and sociability to the country as a site of retirement and retreat throughout the novel. Mrs. Hammond loves the "warm comforts of the social city," while faultless Emily's "mind was not of that description which requires the aid of perpetual bustle, and change of scene, to assist in the performance of its functions, and she preferred retreating to the quiet shades" of her childhood home in the country (p. 197). But it is the social Mrs. Hammond and not the retiring Emily who energizes the text, guiding her daughters—and the novel's readers—through the novel's urban practices.

An Urban Novel?

Kelroy is concerned with the domestic affairs of the elite class. Mrs. Hammond is a manipulative and self-absorbed woman more interested in money and creature comforts than civic life. Most of the novel's action happens indoors. Almost half of the novel is set in Mrs. Hammond's country house. So what, precisely, makes *Kelroy* a particularly urban novel?

A better question might be this: What did urban mean in the early Republic? When *Kelroy* was published in 1812, general consensus (and the official US census) asserted that Philadelphia was a city. Though no longer the nation's capital, and becoming a more distant second in population to New York by the day, Philadelphia remained a cosmopolitan urban center, at least in the minds of many who depicted it in writing and in images. Philadelphia's gridded street plan fostered urban growth and made maps look finished, but in the early nineteenth century many of the city's most prominent urban landmarks were still surrounded by grassy fields (see Appendices A1 and A3, pp. 217 and 219). We might think of the early American city as a group of overlapping small towns connected to form a "cityscape defined by qualities of juxtaposition."[1] *Kelroy*'s geography reflects the paradoxical reality of early American cities—perhaps better imagined as *protocities*—where a street address was not enough to convey one's class position, and where urban and rural often blended. In these mingled spaces, interpersonal contact maintained and enforced a social geography of distinction derived from the cosmopolitan norms of the North Atlantic Rim (see Appendix A4, p. 220).

Regardless of whether they are in the city or the country, Rush's characters spend much of their time indoors. Yet this does not make the novel any less urban. As historian Bernard Herman points out, urban domestic spaces, such as those found in town houses like Mrs. Hammond's, offer crucial, and often overlooked, information about the dynamics of early city life: "Town houses, intimate settings for urban life and action, rendered personal and private experience sensible in the larger situation of urban life; town houses exerted presence of place, communicating and enacting the experiences and meanings of the early American city."[2] Urban homes encouraged an intimacy, especially among people of similar classes, that was beginning to disappear from the street. Thus, though facilitated by physical structures, social practices were what made Philadelphia a city and helped Philadelphians remain—or become—part of the cos-

---

1 Bernard L. Herman, *Town House: Architecture and Material Life in the Early American City, 1780–1830* (Chapel Hill: U of North Carolina P, 2005) 21. See also 266.

2 Herman 5.

mopolitan world (see Appendix C1, p. 243). *Kelroy* reflects and is a product of an urban culture simultaneously more localized and more cosmopolitan than the national urban culture of the industrial era.

Recent historical scholarship in the material culture of early American cities allows us to understand *Kelroy*'s Philadelphia as a surprisingly cosmopolitan world housed in a relatively undeveloped urban landscape. The findings in Herman's *Town House: Architecture and Material Life in the Early American City, 1780–1830* and Dell Upton's *Another City: Urban Life and Urban Spaces in the New American Republic* help to illuminate *Kelroy*'s urban dimensions, especially its focus on gambling, the urban home, and Philadelphia's cosmopolitan marriage market. Thanks to painstaking work by these and other urban historians, students and scholars are becoming increasingly interested in early American cities; as this scholarship makes *Kelroy*'s urbanity legible, the novel opens the urban world of early Philadelphia to its readers. Read in this light, *Kelroy* offers readers a subtle form of early urban realism unmatched by other novels of its day.[1]

For readers familiar with later works of American urban realism, *Kelroy* will not seem especially realistic. Unlike the novels of William Dean Howells (1837–1920), Theodore Dreiser (1871–1945), or Edith Wharton (1862–1937), *Kelroy*'s realism is not visible in copious descriptions of material objects. What *Kelroy* shares with these later texts is an interest in the practices and pastimes of city people. One excellent place to see this experiential realism at work in *Kelroy* is at the card table.[2] Indeed, "entertainments" dominate the social world that Mrs. Hammond and her daughters enjoy in Philadelphia, and every entertainment mentioned in the novel features a card game. Mrs. Hammond is a skilled and enthusiastic player, especially at loo, a popular eighteenth-century game involving multiple hands and multiple deals, where short-term losses matter less than long-term gains. In *Kelroy*, loo (see p. 61, note 1) echoes the marriage game Mrs. Hammond is playing on her daughters' behalf. Just as

---

1 Dana D. Nelson connects *Kelroy* to later realism by comparing Mrs. Hammond to Undine Spragg, the powerful but unsympathetic protagonist of Edith Wharton's 1913 novel *The Custom of the Country* (xvi). I see her as closer in kinship to Lily Bart's manipulative mother in Wharton's *The House of Mirth* (1905).
2 For a contemporary image of playing cards, see Appendix C1, p. 243.

Mrs. Hammond keeps her true financial situation hidden from her daughters' potential suitors, when she plays cards she needs to be able to bluff, even at parties that function as semipublic urban spaces. The narrator allows *Kelroy*'s readers to assess Mrs. Hammond's gambles as she makes them, but woe betide the partygoer who tries to look at her cards over her shoulder: one inquisitive guest perambulating around the room receives "a smart rebuff from Mrs. Hammond, over whose chair he had familiarly leaned to peep at her hand" (p. 88).[1] The novel's readers occupy a far more privileged position than the overly familiar peeper; by the time this game of loo takes place we have seen the hand Mrs. Hammond was dealt by her husband, witnessed her expert bluffs, and watched her succeed in winning her first significant gamble: arranging her elder daughter Lucy's marriage to the wealthy British aristocrat, Walsingham.

In late eighteenth- and early nineteenth-century urban society, card games metonymize the speculative capitalism that underwrote the Early American version of cosmopolitan urbanism by taking large-scale gambling to a personal level. In the novel, as in the era, card games are a hallmark of urban space. And unlike the male-dominated spheres of the counting house or even the dining table, seats at the card table were available to women, who otherwise had little access to the world of trade except as consumers. Because "women competed with men as equals," card games regendered the dynamic of speculation.[2] Their players did not just participate in local events; by playing games they enmeshed themselves in a network of connected peers playing the same games, and using the same rules, in cities around the Atlantic rim. Thus when Rush's characters play and we peer over their shoulders, we are not simply gaining information about them that is inaccessible to some of the novel's characters; we are joining the privileged inner circle of the game—and becoming part of the urban culture it represents and facilitates.

Rush's representation of urban life takes a slightly different form in her depiction of Mr. Marney, a character whose impressive financial success is not enough to allow him entrée into genteel society. The narrator explains that Marney masquerades as a gentleman by mimicking genteel people, adopting their clothes and habits so that he can appear to be one of them. But

---

1 See Appendix C2 (pp. 243–51) for another account of a female gamester.

2 Herman 76.

his speech and education remain somewhat unrefined, as we see in a dialogue about art in which Marney mistakes a painting of the judgment of Paris for a depiction of Adam and Eve in the Garden of Eden. "But where's the snake?" Marney asks, "I don't see the snake?—" (p. 102). In this scene, Marney becomes the laughing stock of Rush's more refined characters, who poke fun at his ignorance about fine art, albeit in the most refined manner. From this humiliating experience, Marney, a skilled copyist and forger, learns the lesson that he must imitate the elite class even more carefully if he is to join their ranks. So, after Emily rejects his romantic advances, Marney finds another jilted gentleman and imitates his behavior. The narrator notes of Marney, "he regulated himself by this example so successfully as to occasion a pleasing surprise to Emily, and much astonishment to her mother, who had the address to make herself in a very short time mistress of all his motives" (p. 208). A forger of behavior as well as of penmanship, Marney plays the role of the properly disappointed lover so well that Mrs. Hammond accepts him as her partner and confidant. Emily is completely fooled into welcoming him into her home and domestic circle. And because the narrator does not reveal Marney's deception to the novel's readers until much later, we are fooled as well. In depicting Marney's exterior transformation from rude to genteel, Rush shows her readers that he can change his class position by changing his behavior, even as she transforms us into gullible elites through the experience of reading *Kelroy*.

Kelroy and Atlantic Rim Culture

In this era, part of an American's sense that he or she was a city person came not from his or her built environments, but from connections to more established urban practices circulating around the Atlantic rim. *Kelroy* depicts and participates in this culture by emphasizing Philadelphia's—and Philadelphians'—connections to cities as far flung as Savannah, London, and Calcutta through trade, luxury goods, the bodies of cosmopolitan people (whether British peers like Walsingham or American speculators like Kelroy), and the letters they send. Marney's financial rise, or the similar rags-to-riches tale of the Gurnet family introduced later in the novel, seem like prototypes for all-American success stories, but in *Kelroy*, as in elite circles throughout the Atlantic world, manners, not money, definitively mark a person as genteel.

Indeed, *Kelroy*'s Atlanticness is more immediately visible than its Americanness. Elizabeth Maddock Dillon calls the eighteenth-century Atlantic world "a field imaginary that is not organized by the nation-state."[1] The same is true of *Kelroy*. From the very first page of the novel, Rush emphasizes that her American characters are closely connected to England. Though we are told nothing of Mrs. Hammond's origins, we learn that Mr. Hammond, "an Englishman by birth, and nearly related to a noble family ... had emigrated early to America" (p. 33). The Hammonds' British ties are reinforced when Lucy marries the noble Englishman Walsingham and moves with him to London. Though Kelroy is American, he too is a citizen of the Atlantic world; he meets and befriends Walsingham "on board the packet in which we sailed together from England" and, when he is told that he must make good on his father's speculations if he is to marry Emily, he promptly sets sail for England and then on to India (p. 63).

Many of the elements that characterize *Kelroy* as an early urban novel also make it a novel of the Atlantic world. As such, *Kelroy* might be productively read with—and against—Jane Austen's novels, as well as works such as Frances Burney's *Evelina* (1778), Susanna Rowson's *Reuben and Rachel* (1798), and Charles Brockden Brown's *Ormond* (1799). As in those novels, *Kelroy*'s characters and settings are enmeshed in connections among the English nobility, American cosmopolitans, inheritance, marriage, and lineage in the context of global cultural and economic exchange. Its setting in an Atlantic-rim city characterized by cosmopolitan cultural practices like card games, entertainments, and fashion enables *Kelroy* to make explicit early Americans' connections to, and stakes in, the elite circles of America, Europe, and beyond (see Appendix C, pp. 243–54).

Early American urban culture was distinct from a more European urbanity, however, not so much in its practices but in the ways in which those practices spread—through personal connections rather than through a sort of *zeitgeist*. For instance, Mrs. Hammond's townhouse, furnished like other Atlantic world interiors, silently signals to her privileged visitors that she is one of them—that they occupy the same position of class privilege—and more importantly implies that marriage to either of her daughters will join partners in economic strength.

---

1   Elizabeth Maddock Dillon, *New World Drama: The Performative Commons in the Atlantic World, 1649–1849* (Durham, NC: Duke UP, 2014) 15.

A Mother's "Most Diabolical Schemes"

Ironically, though she is barely eking out an existence by playing her creditors, including her son-in-law Walsingham, against one another, Mrs. Hammond must act as if her expensive possessions—diamonds, furniture, silver plate—are not special luxuries but merely the everyday items that *should* surround a woman of her wealth and position. She hides things from sight, like the lottery tickets she is purchasing on the sly, that might undermine the appearance of effortless wealth she is attempting to cultivate. Inhabiting the world these objects help create means acting as if she can take them for granted—which may help explain why Rush refuses to fetishize Mrs. Hammond's things through excessive description. At the same time, Rush's narration allows us to travel behind the scenes to see the tensions that strain Mrs. Hammond's capacity to improvise wealth.

When her money *is* gone, Mrs. Hammond's house opens to us; for the first time, Rush describes the objects Mrs. Hammond has used to practice an elite urban lifestyle. By the time Mrs. Hammond performs her last reckoning, in which she decides to sell her possessions, including her horses and town house, and move back to the country, readers have spent more than half of the novel in the urban setting these goods populate and mark as elite. As readers, we have lived the elite cosmopolitan life along with the Hammond women, attended entertainments, sat in on card parties, and come down for breakfast. Possessions have been props for social practice, but Rush's narrator has not described the objects in great detail. In contrast, at the close of Mrs. Hammond's urban career Rush presents an inventory that resembles the lists of property that probate courts would assemble after a person's death.[1] And Rush further emphasizes the objects' symbolic value by setting them alight.

Late one night, Mrs. Hammond is sleeping deeply when a fire breaks out in the kitchen, destroying the house and almost everything within it:

> ... it was too late to attempt saving any thing of value; and except a carpet which chanced to be rolled up, a small trunk containing papers, and a few chairs, not

---

1 See Herman, Chapter Seven, for an expert use of probate records, tax inventories, and wills to reconstruct everyday material practices in early American cities.

a single article of either plate, furniture or wearing apparel had been rescued from the merciless element; and before ten o'clock, of those splendid apartments where so lately taste had shone, and beauty triumphed, nothing remained but melancholy black walls and smoking ruins. (p. 147)

Mrs. Hammond's elite possessions—the silver plate, furniture, and clothing—go up in smoke. The items that are left—a rug, some chairs, and a box with personal papers—are exactly the items that crossed class lines in this period.[1] The fire at once levels the house along with Mrs. Hammond's class pretensions. In the moral universe of the sentimental novel, the fire's destruction would aptly punish Mrs. Hammond for her acquisitive, manipulative ways. But in *Kelroy*, Mrs. Hammond wins the lottery.

Unlike Mrs. Hammond's card-table gambles, which tie her to the cosmopolitan Atlantic world, the lottery ticket—which actually changes her life by making her financially secure—ties her to a network of gamblers of class, race, and regional backgrounds far different from her own.[2] Rather than allying herself with the lottery's broad clientele, Mrs. Hammond has her mulatto servant buy the tickets for her. To maintain her class status, she tries to hide both the fact that she has purchased the ticket and the fact that the lottery is the source of her windfall. "'For really,' continued she, 'people might fancy it wore a strange appearance for *me* to seem so very solicitous about the fate of one poor, solitary lottery ticket'" (p. 153). Here, Rush exposes the preposterousness of a system that allows the brilliantly scheming Mrs. Hammond to attain wealth only against overwhelming odds in a lottery that has nothing to do with skill and everything to do with luck. At the same time, we see how deeply disturbing it would be for Mrs. Hammond to admit that she has gained her wealth by crossing class lines. Revealing that she has engaged in an almost democratic form of gambling would so deeply undermine her performance of elite cosmopolitanism that she opts for an extended hiatus in the country rather than out herself as a class-crossing lottery player.

During *Kelroy*'s first half, Rush makes clear distinctions between the novel's city and country settings. While people move between the two settings, the narrator carefully distinguishes

---

1 Herman, Chapter Six, *passim*.
2 For a range of contemporary sources on gambling, see Appendix D.

between city and country by emphasizing their distance and difference. But during the second half of the novel, when Mrs. Hammond and Emily retreat to the country for good, we learn that the "country" is far more connected to the city than it seems to be in the first few pages of the novel, when Mrs. Hammond secludes her daughters in the country before their urban debut. We are told, for instance, that Mrs. Hammond's country house is located a mere six miles from Philadelphia. Friends from the city frequently drop by. When Emily and Mrs. Hammond move back to the city for a winter season, the transition is barely noted by the narrator. Thus the distance and distinction that Rush so clearly delineates in the first city/country cycle begin to erode. Yet for Rush's characters, a deceptive sense of safety associated with the country remains, obscuring whatever dangers it might hold. We see this after Kelroy leaves for India, when Mrs. Hammond allows the distraught Emily to decide where the two will spend the summer. Emily refuses her mother's suggestion that they travel to one of the fashionable European watering holes that were hotbeds of urban sociality. Emily chooses to retire to the country to protect herself at home, little imagining that her country house harbors her greatest enemy: her own mother.

After Mrs. Hammond's death, the novel reverts from realistic recreations of urban practice to swooning and tears. In the face of irrefutable evidence that her mother has masterminded a campaign of forgery aimed at removing Kelroy from Emily's life, Emily collapses. "Lying senseless on the floor," Emily finally resembles the heroines of the seduction novels with which *Kelroy* has often been classed (p. 206). The events that follow, including Emily's and Kelroy's premature deaths and Helen's recuperative marriage to the widowed Dunlevy, enact sentimental conventions. But after the swooning is over, Rush adds a conclusion, and this climactic chapter, presented as a revelatory flashback, ruptures the novel's brief turn to sentiment.

With Mrs. Hammond dead and Emily's death neatly foreshadowed, the conclusion turns the clock back to describe "one of the most diabolical schemes that envy ever planned, or malignity executed" (p. 207). Described as a "hazard" that only succeeds "by chance," Mrs. Hammond's evil plot is doubly linked to the card games that structure and mimic urban experience in the novel. The forgery scheme and the destruction it causes read as Mrs. Hammond's last and deadly gamble, a game from which the rules and oversight—both the ungentlemanly peeping and the omniscient narration—that structure cosmopolitan society are fatally absent. Breaking away from the expectation of gracious losing that urban sociality demands, Mrs. Hammond refuses to let the old score die and nurses her rage at Kelroy to a dangerous pitch. When Mr. Marney offers to forge letters from Kelroy to Emily breaking off their engagement, Mrs. Hammond readily agrees, even correcting Marney's egregious spelling errors before the final copies are "sent" to Emily from Kelroy's ship. Initially, Mrs. Hammond bets that distance, ensured by the business voyage to India Kelroy must take to untangle his business affairs, will terminate the engagement. But Emily remains attached to Kelroy, and when it seems that she will be on the losing end of that gamble, Mrs. Hammond cheats using the forged letters. Sadly for Emily, neither a random partygoer nor the narrator is present to ensure that her mother plays by the rules. Unlike the novel's other gambles, the forgery scheme becomes deadly because it operates in secret, outside the boundaries of drawing-room oversight. Thus the move to the country that sounds like a sentimental happy ending instead marks the novel's grimmest reversal.

In the city, our knowledge of *Kelroy*'s characters' actions is vast. In the city chapters of *Kelroy*, semi-private encounters, such as Emily's with Kelroy or Mrs. Hammond's with her creditors, are often overseen and overheard by other characters, by the narrator, and by the reader. Sometimes in the urban setting the narrator makes readers privy to clandestine encounters about which some of the novel's other characters remain ignorant. We are told the terms of Mr. Hammond's will, the changing amounts of money Mrs. Hammond has at her disposal, and her plans to manage that money, information that is never made clear to the novel's characters. The Hammonds' final move to the country draws a veil over Mrs. Hammond's nefarious activities. The narrator, busily recounting the quotidian events of country life, doesn't reveal the forgery plot until long after it has done its deadly work. Like that of the other characters, readers' knowledge of Mrs. Hammond's plot is limited. That the scheme is kept secret from *Kelroy*'s readers—that we are bluffed along with Emily—is potent evidence that Rush has successfully incorporated her readers into the novel's world.

Kelroy's Future

Like *Charlotte Temple*, *Kelroy* is a transatlantic novel named for a transatlantic figure. Stephen Shapiro argues that the early

American novel is itself emblematic of the evanescence of nation in this period. The early American novel's "motivations," he writes, "are overwhelmingly not those of either nationality or statehood, but the expression of concerns by a particular set of middle-class interests, a bourgeoisie, rising with the tides of change within the circumatlantic world-system."[1] Shapiro's focus is on the novels of the 1790s; though *Kelroy* grows out of these motivations, it is better read as a harbinger of what Shapiro calls a "new long wave" of British-dominated global relations that emerged in 1800, at the end of the Napoleonic Wars, characterized by "the reshaping of imperial contours away from the Atlantic" and toward South Asia.[2] In *Kelroy*, this shift registers in Kelroy's off-stage actions as he tries to recoup his father's investments in India. His distance and involvement in ventures unimaginable to Emily find material form in his letters to her, which Mrs. Hammond diverts and which Emily reads only after her mother's death. Significantly, we never see Kelroy in India; we merely hear from him through his letters and of him from travelers who return to Philadelphia.

Rush narrates what she knows: the Atlantic world culture in which her Philadelphia played a particular part. That world, she suggests, may die with Mrs. Hammond and Emily (and perhaps even Kelroy), but there are at least three new worlds on the horizon: one that is global and British-oriented, visible in Lucy's marriage to Walsingham; a more egalitarian American future, at least in terms of gender, symbolized by the marriage of Emily's plain but intelligent friend Helen to Emily's worthy widower; and a future of class disruption propelled by families like the newly rich, déclassé Gurnets. Although Rush can't narrate these futures, she intimates that change is in the air.

Predating Catharine Maria Sedgwick's 1830 novel *Clarence* by 18 years, *Kelroy* is one of the earliest urban novels written by an American woman and set in an American city. *Kelroy* recreates early Philadelphia's elite cosmopolitanism, adding exciting dimension to urban landscapes depicted in other early Philadelphia novels, such as Brown's *Ormond* and *Arthur Mervyn* (1799) or Sansay's *Laura*. Freed from reading it as a bad seduction novel, we can now understand *Kelroy* for what it is: a

---

1 Stephen Shapiro, *The Culture and Commerce of the Early American Novel: Reading the Atlantic World System* (University Park: The Pennsylvania State UP, 2008) 4.
2 Shapiro 301.

brilliant and unprecedented novel of urban realism by a talented but nearly forgotten American author.

Kelroy amplifies current notions of the development of the novel in America and is a significant text for teaching and scholarship in the growing fields of early urban literature, American women writers, and Atlantic studies. It is both an American novel and an urban novel; but the Atlantic-world lens allows us to see *Kelroy* in yet another light: as a text that functions beyond "particular, discrete national formations."[1] The characters' international connections assert that *Kelroy*'s geography extends beyond Philadelphia, beyond the city/country binary, and beyond national boundaries. As Toni Bowers and Tita Chico assert, "During the long eighteenth century, ... few inhabitants of any metropole, worldwide, were exempt from the changes brought about by an Atlantic that was being constantly and variously reimagined—not as an endpoint, but as a newly transformative place and experience."[2] With this edition, I hope that new and returning readers will see these contexts as similar jumping-off points for their own engagements with Rebecca Rush's ever-engaging *Kelroy*.

---

1   Toni Bowers and Tita Chico, *Atlantic Worlds in the Long Eighteenth Century: Seduction and Sentiment* (New York: Palgrave Macmillan, 2012) 2.
2   Bowers and Chico 6.

Rebecca Rush: A Brief Chronology

1779   Born 1 January in Philadelphia, to Mary (née Rench) and Jacob Rush, an attorney.

1781   Birth of sister Sarah Rush.

1783   Birth of sister Mary Rush.

1784?   Birth of sister Harriet Rush.

1786?   Birth of sister Louisa Rush.

1791   Jacob Rush named Third Circuit Court Judge in Reading, Pennsylvania. Family moves to Reading. Rebecca spends some of this period living in Philadelphia with the family of her aunt Julia and uncle Benjamin Rush, an eminent physician, helping to look after her cousin Benjamin.

1793   Yellow-fever epidemic strikes Philadelphia. Rebecca, still caring for her cousin Benjamin, moves with her aunt and uncle to Rose Hill, a country estate outside of Philadelphia.

1798   Harriet Rush dies by drowning in Delaware River.

1804   Rebecca again visits Julia and Benjamin Rush.

1806   Mary Rush, Rebecca's mother, dies. Jacob Rush becomes Presiding Judge in the Court of Common Pleas, Philadelphia.

1812   Rebecca Rush publishes *Kelroy* on 3 April. In June, US declares war on Britain.

1820   Jacob Rush dies. Rebecca inherits his Cambridge Bible.

There is no record of Rebecca Rush after 1820. The date of her death remains unknown.

A Note on the Text

This edition of *Kelroy* is based on the original publication: *Kelroy, A Novel*. By a Lady of Pennsylvania, published in Philadelphia by Bradford and Innskeep, 1812 and printed by Jane Aitken. I have relied on the digitized copy of the text held in Early American Imprints, Series 2, no. 26670, from the collection of the American Antiquarian Society. I have retained much of Rush's original spelling; obvious typographical errors have been silently corrected. Brief footnotes clarify terms and references that may be unfamiliar to current readers. Contextual material in the appendices, which has been silently corrected in the same manner as Rush's text, aims to bring to life the worlds inhabited by Rush's characters.

KELROY,

A NOVEL.

BY A LADY OF PENNSYLVANIA.

PHILADELPHIA:

PUBLISHED BY BRADFORD AND INSKEEP.
AND INSKEEP AND BRADFORD,
New York.
Jane Aitken, Printer.

1812.

KELROY.

CHAPTER I.

IN all ages and countries, the legends of that soft passion which pervades creation have ever been cherished with peculiar care. The song of the poet, and the grave pen of the historian have alike been employed to perpetuate its eventful scenes; which seizing the mind with irresistible force, please without variety, and charm in despite of reason. To the youthful heart, they portray in congenial hues, the joys or sorrows of the present hour; and recal to the more advanced the memory of those sweet, early sensations which time has compelled them to abandon; and imagination turns from the cold lessons of philosophy, to contemplate with delight that semblance of impassioned feeling which adorns the narratives of love.

EMILY HAMMOND was the youngest child of a merchant in Philadelphia, who died before she had attained her thirteenth year. He was an Englishman by birth, and nearly related to a noble family, from whom he derived no other benefit, than a portion of their illustrious blood. He had emigrated early in life to America, where his success in trade led him into extravagancies which were better suited to his pretensions than his capital. He had lived in a style which procured him the reputation of immense wealth, whilst his enormous expenses prevented him from accumulating such a fortune as could alone have rendered such blind profusion excusable; and at his death the regret of his widow was greatly augmented by a prospect of comparative indigence, which suited neither her habits nor her temper. She was a woman of fascinating manners, strong prejudices, and boundless ambition, which extended itself to every circumstance of her life, and had prevented her from marrying until she was near thirty; consequently at the time of her husband's decease, she was too much on the wane to hope for a second advantageous connexion of that nature. Still she retained an unabated relish for show and dissipation, which her knowledge of the world, on which she prided herself much, taught her could only be obtained in future, by concealing as much as possible the alteration of her circumstances.

Her daughters were both uncommonly handsome, and to their youthful attractions she turned in the hour of mortifying reflection, as a resource against the evil she most dreaded. She well remembered the power of her own beauty, even when past its bloom; and having revolved in her mind every probable result of the hazardous scheme which she meditated, she at last resolved to carry it into effect, and trust the event to that prudence and circumspection which her previous successes had taught her to consider as infallible.

She took an exact survey of the situation of her affairs, and finding that the debts did not amount to more than two thirds of the property which she held, the greatest difficulty was at once obviated, and by her own dexterity she easily surmounted the rest. Appearances are every thing, whilst they can be continued; and Mrs. Hammond conducted herself with a mixture of cunning and probity, which effectually lulled suspicion, and answered her purposes. She discharged all the demands on the estate to the utmost farthing, after which there remained to her the sum of six thousand pounds,[1] besides the house in which she lived; and having rented that entirely to her satisfaction, she purchased a small, but elegant residence in the country, and retired thither with her children, under pretence that she was incapacitated by grief from enjoying as formerly, the pleasures of society.

The good-natured world, ignorant of her real motives, gave her immense credit for her pretended ones, and praised with disinterested candour the delicate respect of Mrs. Hammond for the memory of her husband; whilst she, secluded from that observation to which she must have remained subject in the immediate view of her large circle of acquaintance, pursued without interruption those measures by which she hoped to continue to her benevolent friends the appearances of undiminished affluence.

She applied herself sedulously to the education of her daughters, and engaged a person to reside with them in quality of governess, who was, in her estimation, fully adequate to the task, since to a variety of accomplishments, she joined an infinity of that species of self-important pride, which teaches its owner instinctively to shun the approaches of the vulgar. She also had

---

1 Estimating the value of Mrs. Hammond's £6000 in today's currency is difficult. Because she would not have earned money by working, her income would have been limited to the four percent interest she would have earned each year on her £6000—£240 per year—to support herself and her two daughters. In England at that time, a member of the genteel class would have needed about £300 per year to maintain an elite lifestyle. In Chapter II Mrs. Hammond estimates that £2,300 will support her family for a year "with a tolerable portion of private economy" (p. 40).

masters from the city, to attend them at stated times: thus uniting in her plan, to real benefit, an air of lofty superiority; and often, whilst contemplating their visible improvements, did her heart expand with delight at the idea of the consequence which she should one day derive from the brilliant endowments of these lovely females. Her affection for them was founded, not on their merits, but their charms and acquirements; and had she been assured that they were unworthy of the admiration which she proudly anticipated, she would soon have lessened her regards, and lamented herself as the most unfortunate of mothers. She was conscious that unless a parent possesses the respect and confidence of a child, all expectations of unlimited obedience must be vain; and she laboured with unwearied assiduity to obtain such an interest in the affections of both her daughters as would subject them in future solely to her direction and enable her to realize the notions of splendid happiness which were eternally floating in her brain.

She professed an utter distaste for her former pursuits, and descanted in flowing periods on her widowed state, and the sweets of that retirement which nothing except anxiety for the gratification and welfare of her children could ever prevail on her to leave; and having impressed them with an idea of the unparalleled sacrifice which she should make of her inclinations, by returning for their sakes to society, she would paint in glowing colours the scenes she had left; and defining beauty to be a talisman equally attractive to all ranks and ages, artfully insinuated the numerous advantages which attended the prudent choice of a partner for life. She spoke of the pleasures of wealth, and described in the most alluring terms that extensive influence, and profound deference which it seldom fails to ensure to its possessor. She warned them against indulging romantic attachments; and ridiculed involuntary love as an unpardonable folly, unless the object of it were gifted with more solid recommendations than mere good qualities of mind and graces of manner; and as a proof of her reliance on their discretion, confided to them the secret that their own expectations in regard to fortune were not quite so exalted as to render such precautions entirely unnecessary. But above all, she particularly inculcated on them as a leading truth, that those persons who were eminently unfortunate, became so wholly through their own imprudence, and deserved thenceforward to be universally shunned and forgotten.

These unworthy counsels, warmly urged, and frequently repeated by a mother who appeared to be actuated merely by a wish to promote their happiness, produced a lasting effect on the mind of one of her children; but to the other, young as she was, they seemed, in a great measure, the result of extreme parental solicitude. And at the expiration of four years, when Mrs. Hammond again removed to Philadelphia, and presented them as candidates for universal homage, she perceived with astonishment the striking contrast of their dispositions, which the seclusion in which they had lived during their approaches to maturity had hitherto concealed from her; and she lamented as a serious evil, those bewitching traits of victorious nature in the youngest of them, which delighted every eye except her own.

Lucy, the eldest, was the very counterpart of her mother, both in person and mind. She was tall, and well made, and her features were regular, and beautiful; but there was a haughty reserve in her manner which prevented her from being generally beloved. She could, when she was so disposed, render herself uncommonly agreeable, and to those whose good opinion she was desirous of cultivating, she displayed an affability tempered with elegance and dignity, which usually ensured their approbation. But her heart was cold, and her understanding warped by the pernicious principles which had been instilled into a mind originally selfish. She was guided in her distinctions solely by a view to her own advancement, and discovered not the smallest preference for any one human being, however amiable, who was not blessed with the requisite passports to her favour, of either fortune, fashion, or connexions.

Emily was one year younger than her sister. Her person was rather below the middle size, but elegantly proportioned; and her fine complexion received singular advantages from a profusion of glossy hair which played round her face, alternately concealing and displaying her large eyes, of a deep blue. Her features were soft and engaging, her teeth brilliantly white, and her hands and arms models of perfection.

Her mind was of the highest order, and her quick feelings, and keen perceptions so happily blended with sweetness and equanimity of temper, as to produce none of those unpleasant variations which are usually attendant on strong sensibility. She had some vanity, but was totally devoid of arrogance, and the consciousness of her attractions served only to increase her pleasantry and good humour. She felt that she had a heart, nor could all the sage assurances she had heard to the contrary, prevent her from believing that excellence was not always the companion of prosperity; and reserving the more lively effusions of her fancy for those who were best capable of appreciating them, she preserved towards all who approached her a gentleness, and amenity which soon rendered her the idol of her acquaintance. Her expressive countenance, her numerous accomplishments, the harmony of her voice, and the peculiar gracefulness of her motions, threw a sort of romantic charm around her, which extended to her slightest word, or action, and rendered her uniformly the first object of admiration wherever she appeared.

Such was Emily Hammond, at the commencement of her eighteenth year; with a heart untouched by love, and a soul which expanded itself to all the generous emotions of innocence and youth.

Sweet season of life! the pensive moralist beholds thy fair blossoms with a sigh!—for seldom does thy Summer keep the promise of the Spring.

CHAPTER II.

AMONGST the few families with whom Mrs. Hammond had judged it expedient to preserve an intimacy in her retirement, was that of Mrs. Cathcart. Her husband was a man of plain manners, and large property; and she was one of those easy, credulous, accommodating kind of beings, who observe little and think less, and approve, in a general way, of all they see, and hear.

Mrs. Cathcart pursued the common routine of life without inquiring into its origin, or suspecting its tendency. She made visits, gave parties, went to the church, and to the theatre in regular succession, not because she believed it to be either right or wrong, but because she saw others do so. She had heard indeed, that a waste of time was criminal, and that christian duties ought to be attended to; but her conscience readily acquitted her of the first part of the charge, as she could scarcely find leisure to fulfil her numerous engagements; and with respect to the second, she satisfied herself with the idea that she performed all that was necessary by giving little charities with a good grace, when they were requested of her, and being very complaisant to her husband, and indulgent to her son, and daughter, whose wishes she never opposed when it was in her power to gratify them; and happy in her own approbation and the enjoyment of the pleasures she preferred, she envied not the most fortunate mortal breathing, but was always ready to bestow praise in full measure wherever it was required.

Such a companion was admirably suited to the occasions of

the designing Mrs. Hammond, who beheld her whole species with disdain, except as they contributed to the gratification of her ruling passion. Mrs. Cathcart had long been her associate in prosperity, and she selected her when a change took place, as one whose want of penetration might, with a little address, be rendered extremely useful.

Flattered by the preference which was shewn her, Mrs. Cathcart had conceived for Mrs. Hammond a sort of regard which she dignified with the name of friendship. In Summer she had frequently visited her, to enjoy, as she said, her delightful society, and the sight of her domestic happiness; but in reality for the sake of the fresh air. She had no country residence of her own, nor could she prevail on Mr. Cathcart to grant her one. It was the only material request which he had ever refused her, and he assigned as a reason for it, that it was inconvenient for him to reside with his family out of town, and he could not consent to deprive himself of their company for a whole season. However he indulged her with an annual excursion with her daughter to the sea shore, or wherever else she pleased; and this, together with riding around the environs of the city, and repeating with thoughtless loquacity to every body she knew, the history of her husband's inflexibility, and her own obliging acquiescence made her quite contented.

In winter, Mrs. Hammond had been in the habit of going frequently to town, to observe the fashions, and learn the prevailing topics of the day, which could nowhere be done with more facility than at the house of Mrs. Cathcart. She was sometimes accompanied by her children, but she rarely took them with her to any place of public amusement, lest by suffering them to be often seen, she would destroy that novelty which is considered as such an essential charm; and on these occasions they commonly remained at home with Helen Cathcart, who although much older than either of them, was the only young person with whom, previous to their entrance into company, they had been permitted to associate on terms of intimacy.

Charles and Helen Cathcart were twins. He was a young man of excellent morals, and sound abilities, and had been bred to the bar,[1] where he was considered as a rising character. The imprudent fondness of his mother had been happily counteracted by the calm, determined measures of his father, and at four and twenty he exhibited no other remains of early indulgence, than

---

1 Educated to practice law.

an occasional impetuosity in argument, which seldom transgressed the bounds of politeness, and arose more from a desire to impress on his opponent a conviction of the truth, than from innate violence.

Helen was not handsome, but she was perfectly agreeable. Her understanding was good, and had been improved by an extensive education; and her constant intercourse with society, had endued her with a degree of ease, and intelligence which prevented the gentleness of her disposition from becoming prejudicial to her; and she displayed her taste in dress, and indulged the sprightly sallies of her humour, without suffering herself to be disconcerted by the sneers, and petty malevolence, which in common with all who mix much with the world, she was sometimes obliged to encounter. She was fond of reading, and well acquainted with literature in general; and books, and music would have constituted her chief amusements, had not her mother kept her constantly immersed in a round of engagements, which she complied with because she knew it gratified her; but had she considered herself at liberty to pursue her choice, she would have been much happier at home. Her heart forbade her to acknowledge even to herself the foibles of a parent who had treated her from infancy with uniform tenderness; but her respect and confidence were involuntarily acceded to her father and her brother, whose affection she returned with enthusiastic warmth. She had had several admirers, but none who was so fortunate as to meet with her approbation; and she frankly dismissed them as soon as their pretensions became known to her. They had all acquiesced in her decision as might have been expected, except one, and he still continued to follow, and profess for her a most obstinate affection; but either from his peculiarities, or those unaccountable causes which sometimes influence the mind, she had conceived for him an aversion little short of enmity. Yet he wholly disregarded it, and made a point of persisting in his addresses to her so publicly, that she was frequently compelled to treat him with the most uncontrouled scorn, which however had no effect, except that of freeing her from his importunities for a short time; and he regularly returned to the attack with renewed boldness, and fresh hopes of success, which had no better foundation than that general disregard of his sex, for which she was so remarkable, that she might have exclaimed with Beatrice, "I had rather hear my dog bark at a crow, than a man swear he loves me."[1]

---

1 Shakespeare, *Much Ado About Nothing*, I.i.122–30.

Helen had caressed and admired Emily as a beautiful child, and as she grew up, and her engaging qualities hourly unfolded themselves, they became the basis of an unalterable friendship between these two young ladies, which the inequality of their ages served only to strengthen. Helen admired the disinterested mind and winning manners of Emily, whilst she, in her turn, was alike charmed with Helen's vivacity, and benefitted by her knowledge, which was a constant resource in every little difficulty that occurred; and in a short time after Mrs. Hammond's return to the city, they became almost inseparable. Lucy too, was sensible of something like an habitual regard for the amiable companion of her childhood, but it extended no further than a transient conversation, or a few compliments expressed with a condescending smile when they met in company; and during the many mornings which Helen passed at their house, whilst she and Emily were busied in works of fancy, or turning over together the pages of a favourite author, Lucy was shut up in her chamber, practising cotillions,[1] and admiring herself in the glass; or studying some mode of dress by which she hoped to exhibit herself to the utmost possible advantage.

While she remained in the country, exclusive of seventeen hundred pounds, which she had paid for her house and grounds there, Mrs. Hammond had expended two thousand more, besides the annual rent of her house in town; so that when she again took possession of it, she had only two thousand, three hundred, left; but she calculated that this with a tolerable portion of private economy, would be sufficient to last her for one year; and if, at the expiration of that time her daughters should remain single, (a circumstance which she scarcely permitted herself to suppose possible) the sale of her country place would support her for at least one more.

Trusting to their beauty, and her own experience, she launched fearlessly into the wide sea of dissipation, and in the incense, and adulation of the giddy multitude, sometimes lost entirely the recollection of the slight means, and uncertain contingencies on which her career depended, and was ready to fancy herself an absolute princess surrounded by her subjects. Nobody's parties were half so crouded, or so fashionable as Mrs. Hammond's; nobody was half so elegant, or so fashionable as her daughters; and by some well timed inuendoes, and the assistance of her echo, Mrs. Cathcart, she circulated a belief that their fortunes would be as immense, as their claims to admiration were indisputable.

---

1   An eighteenth-century "country dance." On dancing see
    Appendices C3, C4, and C6 (pp. 251–54).

Her showy, and expensive style of living, drew to her house an amazing concourse of company; and many gentlemen attracted equally by the charms and reputed wealth of the two young beauties, were tempted to sue for their favour; but the watchful mother soon discovered that their views bore too strong a resemblance to her own, and repressed their advances with a haughtiness of mien[1] and language alike odious to them, and disagreeable to her daughters, who could not divine the necessity of such arbitrary proceedings.

Lucy had too high an opinion of herself, to be in danger from any arrows except such as were headed with gold; yet she took delight in inspiring a passion which she was incapable of returning; and Emily, who had also several lovers, although she entertained no partiality for either of them, was induced from the softness of her temper to conduct herself in some instances, with a mildness which might almost have been mistaken for a warmer sentiment; and they both frequently excited in their mother the most serious alarms. She questioned them on these occasions with jealous anxiety, but the cold negatives of one, and the mirthful denials of the other, usually calmed her suspicions, although neither of them felt internally pleased with her continual lectures and interference.

Thus passed the first two months of the winter, and not one lover had as yet appeared, whose overtures were considered worthy of acceptance. Mrs. Hammond grew rather impatient, and wondered within herself at the indifference of several persons whom she was desirous of honouring with her alliance; but she was particularly vexed at the dilatory temper of Mr. Mangold, a rich bachelor of fifty-seven, whose gallantries she had encouraged with all the art she was mistress of. The coy old gentlemen perceived the snares which were spread for his liberty, and whilst he fluttered round the beautiful Lucy like a dying butterfly over a rose, cautiously avoided any expression which might be construed into an intention of marriage.

The astonishment of Mrs. Hammond at this unaccountable delay of her wishes, was succeeded by indignation, and she was almost beginning to despair, when the approach of Washington's birth-day revived her hopes, and she determined at the annual ball given on that occasion[2] to make one more grand effort.

---

1 Facial expression.
2 An exclusive annual ball was held in Philadelphia beginning in 1791 to celebrate George Washington's birthday on 22 February. See Appendix C5, p. 253.

No sooner had this happy thought taken possession of her, than she imparted it to her daughters, and commenced a consultation on dress and ornaments, in which she was eagerly seconded by Lucy, who anxious both to figure as a bride, and to escape from the trammels of her mother, of which she had latterly become extremely weary, entered with alacrity upon the pleasing task of assisting in the preparations which were deemed requisite to the success of so momentous an undertaking.

Emily beheld all this with a sensation very like contempt. She was fond of amusement and willing to partake of it; but she was in no haste to be married, and could not enjoy the idea of seeking to adorn herself confessedly for such mercenary purposes. Leaving therefore the entire arrangement of the affair to the two persons who were most interested in it, she passed the intermediate space with as much tranquility as if no such scheme had been in agitation.

CHAPTER III.

The eventful evening at last arrived, and after the labours of the toilet were completed, Mrs. Hammond and her daughters, accompanied by Mrs. Cathcart and Helen, and escorted by Charles Cathcart, and Mr. Mangold proceeded to the assembly room.

The numerous lights, and splendid appearance of the company, together with their joyous faces, and the sound of cheerful conversation which met the ear in every direction imparted additional gaiety to the whole party. Mrs. Hammond took a general survey of all the females present, and her eyes returned with increased satisfaction to the two fair objects of her solicitude, whose decided superiority was never more conspicuous; and in the triumph of her heart she listened to Mrs. Cathcart, as to an oracle, ordained to utter the universal opinion.

"Well to be sure, Mrs. Hammond, you are the happiest woman in existence: do but see how every body is gazing on these pretty creatures! and no wonder, for they never looked so beautiful in their lives! Oh, see there! that gentlemen near the fireplace, is smitten already! but no wonder, I expect half the men in the room will be wild. See! see again! but they sit so close together I can't for my life make out which he is looking at. I wish I knew who he was? Helen who is that in the brown coat, talking to Mr. Mangold? Him with the dark hair, that looks so much this way?"

"I do not know madam," replied Helen, "he is a stranger I believe."

"Yes, it is certainly as I said," continued Mrs. Cathcart, "he is speaking to one of the managers and will be here presently I warrant you; and I suspect too, that he is a person of some consequence from his looks. What a delightful thing it would be, Mrs. Hammond, if he was a lord!"

Mrs. Hammond thought so too, but as lords are scarce articles in this part of the world, she had no hopes that it would be the case, and contented herself with a silent wish that he might prove lord of a good estate.

For once in her life, the penetration of Mrs. Cathcart happened to be in the right. The gentleman to whom she alluded, was an Englishman of fortune, who was so much struck with the commanding form, and noble features of Lucy, that he had scarcely ceased an instant from gazing at her since she entered the room; and during Mrs. Cathcart's harangue, was actually employed in seeking to obtain an introduction to her. He had first directed his inquiries to Mr. Mangold, who informed him who she was, and added with an air of exultation which was meant to prevent all further requests, "that he had engaged her for the first dance himself." The young Englishman felt chagrined at the disappointment, and somewhat irritated at the antiquated beau who occasioned it; but entertained no great apprehensions on the score of rivalship and determined by applying elsewhere, to form an acquaintance with her as soon as possible.

The two sisters were dressed exactly alike in white satin and silver. Their fans, gloves and shoes were also white; and the delicacy of their complexions, contrasted with the simple elegance of their attire, and heightened by the bright glow of youthful animation, rendered them lovely beyond description. Lucy was in raptures with herself, and every body around her. The gaze of an admiring croud, and the hum of more than usual approbation exalted her spirits to such a degree, that she actually forgot her system of reserve, and displayed powers of captivation so dazzling, that for the first time in her life, she threw Emily rather into the back ground, who however felt nothing like envy, but enjoyed her sister's gaiety, and the scene before her with perfect satisfaction.

Charles Cathcart with whom she was engaged to dance, had seated himself between her and Helen, and was diverting them with his remarks on the flighty airs, and extravagant compliments of old Mangold, who seemed inspired with new life by the unusual brilliancy of Lucy; when in the midst of their mirth Emily suddenly exclaimed, "For heaven's sake, Mr. Cathcart, who is that object strutting across the floor?"

He looked up, and perceiving the person she meant, burst into an immoderate fit of laughter, whilst Helen, who had seen him before either of them, begged him to be quiet, although she herself was also laughing, and it was some time before Emily could obtain an answer. At length Charles said to her, "You have at last the ineffable pleasure of beholding in that very respectable figure, Helen's faithful swain, the accomplished doctor Blake."

"Hush!" said Helen, "I am afraid every moment he will turn his head this way."

"He is certainly a most singular figure," cried Emily, "but how happens it that I never saw him before?"

"Because," replied Helen, "I was so fortunate, a short time before you came to town, as to succeed in giving him a violent affront, and he has not ventured to come near me since. He is certainly the most ridiculous man alive; and if I were to bestow one civil word on him this evening, he would come to me to-morrow with a parson, and swear that I had promised to marry him."

"Is he a fool?" said Emily.

"No, far from it," replied Helen. "He neither speaks, nor acts like one, except in this single instance; and there he behaves like a perfect idiot."

"Ah! the siege is about to be renewed," cried Charles, "for he has spied us, and is coming in all his glory!"

Doctor Blake now approached them, and after speaking familiarly to Charles, made a formal bow to Helen, who took no notice of him, and another to Emily, who involuntarily returned it from surprise. They were all silent, and the doctor, notwithstanding he had summoned every spark of courage to his assistance, could not help feeling embarrassed at the solemnity of his reception. Helen was too much provoked to speak, and Charles would not increase her vexation by entering into conversation with him; and he remained standing awkwardly before them, staring alternately at each, and evidently much struck with the beauty of Emily, who was equally amused with the oddity of his manner and appearance. He was short, and somewhat corpulent, and was dressed in black, with a waistcoat of white dimity, tamboured[1] round the edges. His knee-buckles were set with stone, in the fashion of twenty years back, and his shoe-buckles of the same pattern. His hair was plaistered back from his forehead, and powdered as white as snow; his face was round, and red,

---

1 Elaborately embroidered. Tambour embroidery can be beaded, sequined, or chain-stitched in ornate, raised patterns.

and his features remarkably small, particularly his eyes, which resembled a pig's, both in size and expression.

Having twinkled them at Emily for some time, he beckoned significantly for Charles to rise, and drawing him a few paces from them, said in a half whisper, "She's a nice little thing!—Who is she?"

"The youngest Miss Hammond," replied Charles.

"Oho!" cried the doctor, still looking at her, "one of the grand high-flyers!—I wonder if a body might speak to her?"

"Not without an introduction," replied Charles.

"Aye," said the doctor, "I know—I understand these matters.—You must first tell her my name, and then I'll have a little tea-water-chat with her.—You understand me?" nodding his head.

"I must first ask permission," replied Charles, and turning to Emily, informed her of the request, which she had overheard, together with the rest of the dialogue, but refused her assent, lest it should be disagreeable to Helen, who had heard it also; and knowing from experience it would be impossible to keep him at a distance much longer, informed her that if he had taken it into his head to converse with her, it would make no difference whether she consented or not, for he would have his own way at last.

"A good promising character, that, for a lover!" cried Emily. "I suspect, Helen, you intend to smile upon him at last, and that I am to be employed as a peace maker!"

"Hush!" exclaimed Helen, almost screaming. "Good heavens! if he has heard you, he will believe it!"

Emily laughed at the consternation of her friend, and when Charles presented the doctor to her, returned his profound bow with a smile that placed him quite at his ease, notwithstanding the frowns of Helen, to which he had been too long accustomed to regard them as impediments either to speech, or gallantry. However he durst not venture to address himself to her immediately, but smirking at Emily, said, "There's a most a grand collection of ladies here to-night, ma'am, and some of them very handsome, I think."

"I think so too," replied she, "but in my opinion the appearance of some of the gentleman is equally striking."

"He! he! he!" returned he, looking down with a chuckle upon his fine waistcoat, "I am no judge of that part of the business, ma'am; I leave that to such bright eyes as yours and Miss Helen's. When a man comes to a ball, ma'am, he never thinks of being looked at, he leaves that entirely to the ladies, but I don't know how it is, that we gentlemen do contrive to divide the admiration with them; for certainly they deserve the most, both as being naturally women, and educated to be upon the watch for it."

"Well faith," cried Charles, "that is one of the most singular compliments to the sex that ever I heard."

"Compliment! he! he! was it a compliment? I intended it for a little plain truth: but the truth should not be spoken at all times: however, we'll let it pass." Waving his hand.

"You are a great curiosity!" said Charles, laughing.

"A'n't I?" cried he, "devil a one to match me! But that's not the business: I was thinking about love; I have some small notion of writing a pamphlet on that subject."

"Pray sir," said Emily, very archly, "have you ever been in love yourself?"

"Hem! that is rather a home question, ma'am," said he, "but we'll not pursue it any further at present. A great deal might be said, to be sure, by a person of my observation, but we'll drop it for particular reasons. However that the discourse may not flag, I'll tell you a little story about myself."

"No not now," cried Charles, "we cannot stay to listen to it!"

"Not listen to it!" replied he, "why you don't think I'm going to tell any thing that's not fit to be heard."

"No, no," said Charles, "but we cannot stay—it is time for us to take our places."

"Reason is reason!" said the doctor, looking round him, "so we'll put it off to a more convenient opportunity."

The dancing now commenced, and Emily, and Lucy were led away by their respective partners, but Helen was obliged to wait a few moments for hers, and the doctor conceiving her to be without one, ventured to solicit her hand, "not as a partner for life" he said, "although such an honour would be the essence of happiness—but merely to do him the favour of tripping through a small dance?" Much offended with this allusion, she pettishly replied that she was engaged, and turned her back upon him; and he marched off in dudgeon to try his fortune elsewhere.

During this conversation, Mr. Walsingham, Lucy's new admirer, had been introduced to her by the British minister, who was now seated next to Mrs. Hammond whom he informed in answer to her inquiries on the subject, that his young friend belonged to an ancient, and respectable family, and was possessed of an independent fortune, and had visited America with the double view of seeing an only sister who had married there, and making the tour of the United States—"which," added he, "few of my countrymen from various reasons are inclined to do; but

Walsingham is so entirely at his own disposal, that he is limited in those respects by his wishes alone."

Mrs. Hammond listened to this transporting narrative with a joy which she could hardly conceal; and vowed within herself not to suffer the subject of it to escape for want of exertion on her part.—His very name carried a charm with it. She remembered sir Francis Walsingham who flourished in the days of queen Elizabeth, and thought it very possible this might be a descendant of the same family; in which case, the connexion would be doubly valuable. Soothed by these delicious reveries, she presently became unusually agreeable, and commenced her operations by flattering the national pride of the minister. She professed herself happy in the idea that her country was now considered worthy to be explored by judicious, and enlightened foreigners, and expatiated in liberal terms on the advantages which were to be derived from an intercourse of this nature with the polished inhabitants of Europe, but more particularly those of Britain. The sight of Walsingham, who refrained from dancing solely for the purpose of beholding Lucy, and stood gazing at her with an expression of rapture not to be mistaken, completed her satisfaction, and she continued to indulge herself in complaisant speeches, and silent prospects of felicity until the dance ended, and the young people returned to their places.

Walsingham instantly followed, and joined the party, but the increasing intentions of old Mr. Mangold, who seemed determined to admit of no competitor for that evening, rendered it difficult for him to approach the object of his regard; and he was obliged, in order to remain near her, to content himself with listening to the eloquence of her mother, who addressed to him the most flattering compliments; and as a certain mean of exalting herself and her family in his estimation, contrived to let him know that her late husband had been third cousin to the Duke of G—.

Walsingham cared nothing about the Duke of G—'s dead cousins. His own connexions had afforded him a sufficient knowledge of rank and high life, to enable him to distinguish the affectation from the reality. He willingly accorded to the sons and daughters of Columbia[1] genius and beauty; but of all pretensions to *family*, in the general sense of the word, he considered them utterly void; and was at once amused and disgusted to observe in many of the natives of this land of liberty and equality, where titles are unknown, and distinction arises only from merit, a

---

1 US citizens.

species of emulation which made them regard it as a mark of consequence to belong to the very fag end of any family that could
boast of a peer for its head.—This piece of information, therefore
produced an effect very opposite to what she had imagined; but,
as he thought Lucy the most elegant female he had ever seen, a
wish to ingratiate himself in her favour, induced him to listen
to her mother with apparent deference, until an opportunity
of escaping presented itself, when he instantly flew to her side,
and endeavoured by every possible attention to convince her of
his profound respect, and adoration. Lucy had early perceived
her conquest, and having learnt in a whisper from her mother
the merits of her admirer, she spared no pains to ensure it, and
before the evening had half past away, Walsingham had lost his
heart.

Dr. Blake had wandered about in search of a partner without
success, and after numerous applications to both young and old
ladies, who were all as they said engaged, he ventured again to
approach Helen and her companion, but found access to them by
no means easy; because they were now surrounded by gentlemen,
who although chiefly attracted by Emily, were magnified by the
doctor into his own particular rivals, and his ill humour became
extreme. He stood aloof, watching them with jealous anxiety
for several hours, and at last had the good fortune to perceive a
vacancy next to Emily, of which he took possession without any
ceremony, and sat in sullen silence, with his mouth pouched out,
and his hands placed on his knees looking on the floor.

Emily and Helen continued to converse with a gentleman
near them, without noticing the doctor, whose solemnity amused
the one as much as incensed the other; when suddenly changing
his position, and staring Emily full in the face, he said "Well my
noble lady, how are you now?"

"Quite well, sir," replied she, somewhat startled by the
abruptness of his manner.

"I wish I could say as much[,"] cried he, "but somehow the
air of *these here* places don't agree with me, for I've got the head-
ache."

"You had better have the head-ache, than the heart-ache,"
said Emily.

"But what is a fellow to do that has both?" replied he.

"That indeed would be distressing! but I hope it is not your
case sir?"

"Oh! Miss—Emily, I think your name is—I'm an unhappy
man, Miss Emily!"

"May I ask in what respect, sir?"

"Your friend there, uses me scandalously—See! She has gone off!—but it's all one for that; as I'm determined she shall have nobody else while I'm alive. You see I am candid, and above disguise?—["]

"Perfectly so;" said Emily, amazed at his folly, "and I think you seem remarkably resolute.["]

"Yes—I have made up my mind on the affair, and I'm none of your weathercocks, to be chopping, and changing about.—But the thing is this,—I have been making some small inquiries, and I find it is in the power of your amiable self to persuade her to whatever you please. Now if you would just give a poor fellow a lift out of a hobble, by speaking a good word, or so, at a convenient season—you understand me?"—

"Really sir, I cannot take so great a liberty with Miss Cathcart,—she has never consulted me on the subject; of course it would be improper for me to introduce it."

"Oh, if that is all, I'll soon put you in a way of introducing it!—let the doctor alone for contrivance!—Here's a small fraction of rhetoric, that will do the business for you"—taking a letter from his pocket, "Now if you would just hand her this, she could not help but read it, you know; and then you would have a fair opportunity of doing a poor crazy devil a christian office."[1]

"Excuse me, sir," said Emily, scarcely able to refrain from laughing, "Excuse me, I cannot take it."

"In the name of Christopher Columbus, I wonder why?"

"There are various reasons, sir," replied Emily gravely, "one of which is, that I am determined not to interfere in the matter."

"What! you wont, hey?—well—there's no judging people by their outsides, I see. Here did I suppose from your fair face, and your soft eyes that you were as mild as new milk; but behold! when I come to try, you are like the rest of the women, with a heart as hard as a crocodile's."

"And is hardness of heart the necessary inference of refusing such a request as this?" said Emily, resentfully, "I spare you, sir, by refraining to express what I think of your temerity in making it."

"My noble lady," cried the pliant doctor, "don't be angry!—I would not be the means of placing a cloud on your beautiful countenance for all the diamonds at the bottom of the sea—and its my soul's opinion if I had 'em here, there's not a woman in the room, except yourself that would not jump at me."

---

1 A good deed.

"Who is it that intends jumping at you in such a hurry?" said Charles Cathcart, who had now joined them.

"Nobody that I know of," replied the doctor, "more's the pity!—I was just giving a small touch on the evils of poverty, which I take to be the chief fault of a great many honest people besides myself.—It was an ingenious thing Charles;—I was just fancying myself the owner of a bushel, or so, of diamonds, all stuck about me from head to foot, as grand as the great Mogul;[1] and wondering what effect it would produce on the visual and mental organs of the body-politic, here assembled."

"A very astonishing one no doubt," replied Charles.

"Ah! it would be a glorious sight to see me mounted once into a great man!—But then, what would become of many a miserable mortal?—Providence was in the right, I find, when it made me a poor man; for if it had been otherwise that old woman would have lost her nose."

"What old woman?" cried Charles "who are you speaking of?"

"Why an old woman that I attended t'other day, with a devilish long, snuffy snout, and a cancer[2] at the end of it. Doctor, says she, can you cure my nose? Madam, says I, it's more than half gone, and I cannot promise to restore to you what you have lost, but I'll assist you to keep what you have left. So I clapt a plaister[3] on it, and in a week's time it was well, and the old woman handsomer than ever."

Both Emily and Charles now laughed so heartily, that the doctor imagined he had gained his point in removing the displeasure of the former; and he had just time to beg her in a low voice not to mention any thing about the letter, when Helen approached with Mr. Mangold, and informed her that they were all going home. She instantly rose, and they were now joined by the rest of their party, together with the enamoured Walsingham, who was employing the few precious moments which remained, in animated conversation with Lucy.

Mrs. Hammond had been so engrossed by the apparent success of her eldest daughter who was, in fact, her favourite, that she had scarcely attended to Emily during the latter part of

---

1 The legendary Great Mogul diamond, discovered around 1650, disappeared in 1747 when its owner, Persian ruler Nadir Shah, was assassinated.

2 A sore.

3 A healing compress, often to hold a paste-like preparation close to the skin.

the evening; but when she saw doctor Blake, whom she did not know, standing familiarly at her elbow, her indignation suddenly rose, and she gave him a fixed look of contempt which she fancied would have banished him instantly from her vicinity. But the doctor, who was conscious of no evil design, kept his post without shrinking; and supposing from her continued stare that she knew him, made her a very ceremonious bow. She drew up her chin, at this insult to her dignity, and bidding her daughters follow her, walked haughtily to the door, accompanied by Mrs. Cathcart, where they were handed their carriages; the doctor standing by the whole time, making offers of assistance, and bidding them all good-night, with an air of intimacy which highly incensed her.

"Pray," said she to Emily, the moment they arrived at home, "who was that strange looking creature whom I found on such mighty familiar terms with you?"

Emily felt disconcerted by her mother's manner, but answered that he was an admirer of Helen Cathcart's, and related the way in which he had managed to introduce himself to her acquaintance. The resentment of Mrs. Hammond was immediately appeased when she heard this, but, afraid he might take it into his head to pay them a visit, she charged Emily never again to take the smallest notice of him, on pain of her heavy displeasure; and after a few tart remarks on Mrs. Cathcart and her son for suffering Helen to be teized by him, and expressions of fond approbation to Lucy, whom she recommended to her sister as a pattern of propriety, they retired to their respective chambers.

Sleep, with its accustomed abhorrence of fraud, and ambition, long delayed to visit Mrs. Hammond and her eldest daughter, whilst Emily enjoyed on her pillow the calm repose of juvenile virtue, which, reviewing the past without care, looks with bright, untroubled eye towards the future, and finds in its own trusting visions a balm which practised hearts shall seek in vain.

CHAPTER IV.

THE next morning, Mrs. Hammond descanted largely at breakfast, on the occurrences of the preceding night, and predicted nothing less than a speedy proposal of marriage from Walsingham, whom she pronounced to be a perfect gentleman, worthy in every respect of her fullest approbation. Lucy coincided with her mother, and expressed herself in a style which convinced Emily that her next reception of her swain[1] would not be such as to leave him cause to despair.

It was late when they rose, and Mrs. Hammond hastened away the breakfast table, and sent Lucy to adjust herself, in expectation of a visit from her lover, but Emily excused herself from remaining to witness his devotion, because of a promise she had made to spend the day with Helen Cathcart.

Her mother readily acquiesced in her absence, as she was well aware that in the simplicity of undress, Emily was infinitely more attractive than her sister, and she dreaded the indecision which might possibly arise in the mind of Walsingham from having them both presented to his view in this early stage of the affair; and bidding her return in time to dress, as they were to have company to tea, she gladly dismissed her.

Emily found her friend Helen in great tribulation. She had just received a letter from doctor Blake, directed in a feigned hand, and not knowing from whence it came, had opened it, and in the anger of her heart, at his incorrigible obstinacy, had thrown it into the fire, and was now at a loss how to convince him that she did not retain it from motives favourable to the writer. "For that I have burnt it," said she, "he never will be prevailed on to believe, as it is the only one of the many he has sent me which I have not returned immediately, and I cannot sufficiently blame myself for destroying this."

Emily was sorry for her embarrassment, but declared, that were she in her place, she would keep no measures with him. She then related his behaviour at the ball, and concluded by advising her to apply to her father, or her brother. Helen replied that she had complained of him to them both, but as there was nothing disrespectful either in his letters or his conduct, her father had declined interfering otherwise than by treating him with marked coolness; and her brother, as an old acquaintance, was unwilling openly to affront him; and he had presumed in consequence of their forbearance, to continue his addresses for more than five years.

Emily agreed that it was very provoking to be the object of such ridiculous courtship, but could devise no possible means of terminating it, since all the usual methods had failed. Having diverted themselves for some time with remarks at the doctor's expense, the conversation at length turned on other topics, and after passing an agreeable day, she returned home, and found

---

1 Suitor.

her mother and sister in high spirits, preparing for company. Walsingham had called in the morning, and Mrs. Hammond, who was an adept in such cases, was convinced that the want of an opportunity had alone prevented a disclosure of his sentiments. She had requested him to take tea with her, and he accepted the invitation with undisguised pleasure.

The evening was productive of fresh assurances of success; and whilst Lucy read in the ardent looks of Walsingham, a confirmation of her ascendancy which seemed only restrained by the presence of surrounding observers from flowing to his lips; Emily amused herself with watching the rueful visage of old Mangold, whose frequent changes of countenance denoted his severe mortification on finding himself neglected in favour of a gay, young rival.

The day following, Walsingham, as was expected, declared himself in form,[1] and Lucy, with well dissembled airs of modest reluctance, referred him to her mother. Mrs. Hammond received his application with her usual finesse, and affected to yield her consent as a sacrifice to the happiness of her daughter; and after certain discussions, and preliminaries in which she carefully avoided the article of fortune, to the infinite surprise of Walsingham, who having satisfied her respecting his own circumstances, was too delicate to inquire into those of his future bride, it was decided that the wedding should take place in three weeks, as he intended within two months to return to England.

The prospect of leaving her family was but a secondary consideration with Lucy, who, exulting in the gay scenes which she believed awaited her, seldom bestowed a thought on the ensuing separation; but Mrs. Hammond with all her pride, was sometimes much affected, when amidst the hurry, and confusion of the nuptial preparations she reflected that she must soon part with her child for ever.

Walsingham was constantly at the house; and Lucy, although she treated him with distinguished politeness evinced none of those marks of refined regard, which flow involuntarily from the heart. Emily, who knew her sufficiently to view every action in its proper light, perceived with astonishment her real indifference towards this amiable young man, who seemed scarcely to live, but in her presence; and, blinded by her beauty, discovered not, that the splendid presents which he almost daily lavished on her, were of far greater value in her estimation than himself.

---

1 Proposed marriage.

One week now only remained of that tedious space which love's fantastic calender had magnified into centuries with Walsingham, when Helen and her brother were invited to an entertainment at the house of Mrs. S. a lady who had no acquaintance with Mrs. Hammond's family. There was a large collection of both sexes present, and among them Helen observed a young gentleman drest in black, whom she had never seen before. He appeared to be a stranger to the greater part of the company, and little anxious to extend his knowledge of them; but sat in silence, completely inattentive to the studied graces of some young ladies near him, who were displaying their whole stock of charms, both mental, and personal, to attract his notice. The abstraction of his fine, dark eyes, as he sometimes inconsciously threw a momentary glance on these industrious damsels, discovered him to be absorbed in reflections foreign to the scene before him; and Helen, who felt a curiosity, to know who he was, was prevented from inquiring by an innocent looking little girl near her, who said to Mrs. S. "Who is he?"

"Who is who?" replied Mrs. S. laughing.

"Why the man in black ma'am."

"His name is Kelroy, my dear. He is very handsome, as you see; he is also a man of fine sense, and a poet."

"Heavens! a poet! I never saw a poet before, in my life! How melancholy he looks! I dare say he is making verses now!" And away she flew, to tell what she had heard on the other side of the room.

Whilst this simple chit[1] was repeating to her companions the information she had just received, together with her own comments on it, Kelroy, who found himself somewhat annoyed by the exertions of his noisy neighbours, rose, and moved to a station near Mrs. S. with whom he wished to have a few moments conversation previous to his taking leave, which he resolved should be as early as possible. She rallied him on his want of spirits, and asked whether some good music would not assist in raising them.

"Perhaps not," replied he.

"What, not if it pleased you, sir?" said the pretty little girl, who had now finished circulating her intelligence respecting him, and seeing him engaged with Mrs. S. came back to listen.

"What pleases, does not always enliven," returned he, regarding her with a grave smile.

"True," said Mrs. S. "and I believe you are one of those, who would at all times prefer a pensive pleasure to a gay one; however,

---

1 Silly girl.

as we are seldom so fortunate as to have a choice the wisest way is, to take them as they come."

"And can you suppose me so great an enemy to myself, as to reject any rational pleasure, merely because it does not wear one peculiar aspect?"

"Oh! no; but I suppose that many things which are a source of gratification to others, afford very little to you."

"Allowing that to be the case, to what do you imagine it is owing?"

"To nature in part, I am afraid."

"Then nature only is to blame, as her decrees seldom admit of reversion. For instance, if she had denied me an ear for music, my utmost efforts would not enable me to relish the concert you have promised me?"

"But which your grave distinctions had like to have banished from my recollection. Are you a physiognomist?"

"Sometimes."

"Then look about you, and tell me if you perceive any musical countenances here?"

"Yes several; particularly the lady opposite to us, in a white veil, who has a most harmonious one."

"Yet she does not sing!"

"But her features do; they breathe the sweetest of all melodies—that of the heart."

"Then let me advise you as a friend, to listen no longer, for she is soon to be married."

"You are very good to apprize me of it, but I am in no danger."

"I hope not, for you would certainly be obliged to hang your harp on the willow."[1]

"And himself too in the end perhaps," said Charles Cathcart, who now approached them; and Helen saw, to her surprise, that he was acquainted with Kelroy. Mrs. S. soon after left them, and Charles took her place and continued to converse with him until the music began, which for the most part, was very fashionable, and very execrable; and as it is considered an unpardonable piece of neglect not to ask every body to play who has ever tried to learn, the ladies were handed to the piano one after another, and exerted themselves so effectually, that Kelroy who watched in vain for an

---

1 A reference to the King James version of Psalm 137, which begins, "By the rivers of Babylon, there we sat down, yea, we wept, when we remembered Zion. We hanged our harps upon the willows in the midst thereof."

opportunity of escaping, felt ready to hang himself without having experienced the pangs of despairing love. After they had all, as he thought, exhibited themselves, a figure was led forward by Mrs. S. whose appearance was so singularly awkward, and unpromising, that Charles Cathcart whispered to him, "here comes the *climax!*" and Kelroy with silent indignation beheld her seat herself at the instrument, from whence he now expected more horrible discords than any he had yet heard.—The first touch of her finger convinced him of his error; and after a very sweet symphony, performed in a style of superiority which rivetted the attention of all present, she accompanied with her voice the following song.

> To distant climes forbid to rove,
>> And doom'd to linger here,
> Alas! how shall I cease to love,
>> Whilst sooth'd by scenes so dear?—
> Each wood-crown'd hill, and lowly plain,
>> Where happy oft I've met her,
> Memorials sweet to me remain—
>> I never shall forget her.
>
> Though far from me her wishes stray,
>> My soul, to her so true,
> In silent anguish each sad day,
>> Its sorrows shall renew.
> With many a bitter sigh, this heart
>> Through life shall still regret her;
> Shall droop, the victim of her art—
>> But never shall forget her.

When she ceased the warmest applause was bestowed on her by every body except Kelroy. Her voice was remarkably soft and plaintive, and the melody of that simple kind which finds its way directly to the heart; which, added to his surprise, and the contrast between that and what he had been tormented with for the last hour altogether so powerfully affected him, that the tears sprang into his eyes, and finding it impossible in the present high wrought state of his feelings to remain a moment longer in society, he abruptly retired.

His emotion was observed by several persons amongst whom were Helen, and her brother, and Mrs. S. who forbore however to express themselves on the subject until they found it was the general topic of conversation.

"What an animal!" said one of the misses whose efforts to captivate him had failed. "Here he sat half the evening as stupid as an owl, and at last starts up, and runs out ready to cry."

"The man's a fool!" said another.

"There is something singular in it!" exclaimed a dowager of fifty, who had laid down her cards during the song, and was prevented by curiosity from resuming them immediately. "There is something singular in it! he appeared to be distressed!"

"Oh, quite so!" said her partner.

"But it is very odd," continued the dowager, "surely there must be some particular reason for it!—some attachment perhaps?"

"No, I believe not," said Mrs. S. "at least I have never heard of any."

"But surely there must be some uncommon cause for such behaviour?"

"Nothing more madam," said Charles Cathcart, "than that Kelroy possesses a brilliant imagination, and strong feelings, and is of course peculiarly susceptible to the power of music."

"The gentleman is a genius I presume?"—crowed a little old bachelor in one corner.

"He is generally considered as possessing superior talents," replied Charles.

"But of what description are his talents, Mr. Cathcart?" inquired the bachelor, "do they relate to algebra, or astronomy?"

"To neither sir," replied Charles, rather displeased at his manner of asking the question.

"The ladies," said Mrs. S. "call Mr. Kelroy a poet."

"A poet!" cried the old bachelor; "Oh, now the murder's out!—how could I possibly be so wanting in penetration, as not to discover it?"

"These people of *refined understandings* as they are called," resumed the dowager, "are in my opinion not much to be envied. They are constantly in search of a romantic sort of happiness which has no existence but in their own imaginations; and because they cannot find it, conceit that they are miserable. If these are the fruits of *genius*, commend me to *common sense*."

"Your remark is perfectly just madam," observed a sharp visaged matron, who was blest with a couple of sons stupid to a proverb—"and I think it a serious misfortune to possess a mind which cannot relish the common enjoyments of life. A celebrated authoress tells us, [']that the flights of poetic fancy are too wild for the exercise of subjects bound within the limits of rationality, fitness and convenience.[']"[1]

"Have the goodness madam," said Charles Cathcart without noticing her pompous quotation, "to inform us what you consider as the common enjoyments of life."

"Really, Mr. Cathcart, that is an extensive question. They differ with age, and climate; but are generally thought to consist in the possession of a fair character, a plentiful fortune, and a good understanding with the world."

"And yet madam," replied he "we have daily instances, in which the blessings you mention have failed to produce happiness, even amongst those whose well regulated minds scorn to entertain a single thought beyond the verge of mediocrity. It is neither riches nor honours, nor the smiles of the world which can afford us perfect enjoyment; for moralists tell us, and our own experience hourly confirms the truth of the assertion, that happiness is not attainable in this life."

"Bless us! Mr. Cathcart!" cried the bachelor interrupting him, "are you going to preach?"

"No sir, I have no such intention. I merely meant to observe, that since perfect felicity is denied us, and even health, one of our most valuable blessings, stands in constant danger of decay, those persons whose chief pleasures arrive from abstracted enjoyments appear to me to have the advantage of the generality of mankind in two instances. First, as approaching nearer to the nature of the divine essence, and next, as possessing a remedy against natural and unavoidable evils, which nothing, except the loss of intellect can deprive them of."

"As to their pleasures," said the bachelor "I will not pretend to decide, for if I may be permitted to judge from what I heard Mr. Kelroy himself say, they certainly differ from any that I am acquainted with; but with respect to their vast superiority, I must take the liberty of dissenting from you. As far as my observations have extended, they are usually persons of strong passions, and imprudent dispositions, who first render themselves miserable by their own conduct, and then quarrel with the world because it is not disposed to tolerate a parcel of wild freaks and fancies, which few understand and nobody cares for."

---

1 Catherine Macaulay, *The History of England from the Accession of James I to the Elevation of the House of Hanover, Volume IV* (London: Printed for the author, 1768) 8.

"But you surely will not contend that misery and imprudence are the necessary concomitants of genius."

"Aye will I, and add poverty into the bargain;—shew me one of these bright headed chaps that is rich if you can?"

"These bright-headed chaps, as you term them, are so scarce, that I cannot shew you any at present either rich or poor; but your own recollection will inform you that there have existed several whose portion of wealth was far from contemptible.— For instance, Swift, Johnson, Pope, Congreve, and many more whose names are equally familiar to you."

"Yes, I will put Shenstone on the list:—a fellow who cut up a handsome estate into a garden, and spent his time in planting flowers, and making rhymes, while he suffered his house to go to ruin over his head, and luckily died just in time to escape a jail."[1]

"All this may be true, sir, but it does not tend to strengthen your argument, unless you can prove that persons of every description have not been equally indolent and imprudent.—Error, and misfortune are common to us all, with this difference, that the man of plain sense, the blockhead, and the knave, sink together with their absurdities into oblivion; but those, whose powers of mind have been displayed to instruct, and delight us, must submit to have their failings recorded with their names."

"And a pretty high tax too, for a poor devil in his grave to pay for praise he can neither hear nor feel! what good would it do *me*, I wonder, to have my name handed down to posterity?—you may talk as you please, Mr. Cathcart, but I have always been of opinion that to be born a genius, is nine times out of ten, the greatest misfortune that can befal a human being."

"Their feelings are certainly much more acute, and of course their susceptibility of pain must be greater; but then, recollect that their sense of pleasure is equally great. Neither does it appear to me, that in proportion to their number they are more subject to misfortune than the rest of the world.—As a proof of this, visit the numerous public asylums of the poor, and I will engage that amongst the croud of miserable wretches which they contain, you shall not find one in a thousand who possesses a single trait of the quality which you consider as the surest passport to poverty and distress."

---

1 William Shenston (1714–63), poet and early practitioner of landscape gardening. He inherited an estate, The Leasowes, in Shropshire, England, and impoverished himself through his efforts to beautify it.

"That may be, but yet you know as well as I do, that some of the greatest men the world ever produced have died in such places. Besides, independent of this, my own experience convinces me that a limited capacity is by far the best adopted to our limited comforts; and that a larger share of it seldom answers any other purpose, than to enable the owner of it to see more clearly the evils of his situation, and to repine accordingly."

"You consider then as nothing the progress which they have effected in literature and the sciences?—Judging from these, I should imagine that heaven had created them for some wiser and better purpose than to repine at its decrees!"

"I do not speak of the benefits society may have received from them, but of their own exclusive happiness."

"And do you suppose that a being of refined intellect, and exquisite sensibility, to whom the universe abounds with endless objects of contemplation, can be without his share of enjoyment?"

"I can't tell how that may be, but at any rate, it is a sort of enjoyment very little to be envied. Would any body attempt now, for instance, to persuade me, that instead of sitting comfortably in the midst of my friends, I should be happier wandering about by myself, or gaping up at the moon?—I mean if I had a taste for such amusements, which certainly is not the case.—A reasonable understanding, that can be contented with less sublime matters, and go through the world without minding its rubs, is a much more desirable gift."

"Or to illustrate your meaning rather more forcibly, a coarse, common mind has in those respects the same advantage of one more delicately organized, that a hardy savage, who can bear the utmost inclemency of the seasons without shrinking, has of the native of a civilized country; yet there are few, I believe, who would wish to resemble him.—It is but justice, however, to Mr. Kelroy, to inform you that very little of what has been said will apply to him, for he does not belong to that despicable class who trust to their genius for support, but is preparing I have understood, for a voyage to the East Indies."

"So much the better!—I am glad to hear it! for it would be a pity so fine a looking fellow should waste his life in scribbling nonsense!"

Here the dispute ended, for the old gentleman was summoned

to a loo-table[1] which he very readily joined, and soon shewed by his eagerness to win, that he considered it as a matter of much greater importance than the subject he had been discussing. But this was not one of his lucky nights, and after several hours spent in losing and growling, he was at last worked up to such a pitch of rage, that he started from his chair, dashed the cards on the middle of the table with such force that they flew from it in every direction, and swore vehemently that the devil had invented them as a curse to society, and that he, of all mortal men who had ever touched them, was the most regularly unfortunate!

"Moderation! moderation, my good sir!" cried Charles Cathcart, who had been watching the progress of his disturbance; "these transports would be natural enough in a poor, imprudent scribbler, who had lost in a minute what he toiled for a month; but in a gentleman of your enviable circumstances, and very excellent, plain, reasonable abilities they are really surprising!"

"What do you mean by that sir?" replied he. "Do you expect a man to sit like an ass, and lose his money without opening his mouth?"

"Not I, sir;" returned Charles, "for if a man is ass enough to subject himself to the probability of it, I think he ought afterwards to be allowed the consolation of braying a little; but I am not quite so clear that it is the duty of others to listen to it, and shall therefore do myself the honour of wishing you a very good night."

And with these words he left the room to accompany Helen. On their way home, in answer to her inquiries respecting Kelroy, he said that he had seen him for the first time, and been introduced to him that morning by Walsingham at his lodgings, as a very particular friend. That they had spent several hours there together, and he was greatly pleased with the manners, and conversation of Kelroy, but knew no more of him than what he had learned from Walsingham, who had spoken of him in the highest terms, and mentioned that he contemplated a voyage to India.

"Why then, if you are not better acquainted with him, did you so strenuously espouse for his sake, the cause of his fraternity?" said Helen.

"Because I am certain he deserves it; and because I could not endure quietly to hear that old half-souled wretch congratulating

---

1 Loo was a trick-taking card game for five or more players in which the pot could grow very quickly, leading to high stakes, vicious gambling, and significant losses.

himself on his imaginary superiority to those, in comparison with whom, he is, in the scale of creation, even less than nothing.["]

CHAPTER V.

THE next morning Mrs. Hammond and Lucy went out early a shopping, and Emily, who was remarkably fond of flowers, took that opportunity of going to Mrs. Cathcart's to request that Helen would walk with her to some of the gardens on the outside of the town, and found her just preparing to go abroad also. Before they went, Helen gave an account of her evening's entertainment, in which Kelroy was of course included, and her description of the part which related to him, excited a considerable degree of curiosity in Emily, who said she had occasionally heard Walsingham mention his name, but that he always seemed to speak of him by mere accident, and never, when she was present, said any thing that could induce her to suppose he considered him superior to his sex in general.

"You will soon have an opportunity of judging for yourself," cried Helen, as they walked out of the house, "for if I am not much mistaken, yonder he comes with Walsingham, this moment!"

Emily looked up, and saw him coming down the street towards them, accompanied by a gentleman, whom he presented when they met, as Mr. Edward Kelroy. He then inquired where they were going, and having requested and received permission for himself and his friend to walk with them, they all went together; and as the weather was uncommonly fine for the season, strolled to such a distance, that the morning was almost spent before they thought of returning. Accustomed to admiration, Emily remarked nothing unusual in Kelroy's manner towards herself, but she was much struck with the elegance of his language, and the similarity of his feelings and sentiments to her own; and when contrary to his usual custom, Walsingham took leave of them at her mother's door, and carried Kelroy with him, she felt that she should have been better pleased if they had remained some time longer.

Dinner was on the table when she entered the parlour with Helen, which explained to her Walsingham's reasons for not coming in with them; and in describing to her mother and sister their morning's ramble, she did not omit to mention the handsome stranger. Lucy condescended to listen with some attention as Walsingham was included in the tale, and when it was finished, quietly observed, that she believed Kelroy was to be at her wedding.

Emily was surprised she had not heard this sooner. She was not in her sister's confidence, whose habitual reserve avoided those minute communications which form the delight of social dispositions, but she thought it singular that Walsingham himself should not have mentioned it.

When he returned in the evening, the first question he asked her was, "How she liked his friend?"

Emily expressed without scruple the opinion she had formed of him and inquired in her turn why she had never seen him before?

"Self-interest, my handsome little sister!" replied Walsingham, "you know I shall soon be in want of his services, and I was apprehensive if I suffered him to come within the reach of your fascinations, he might get to the altar before me."

Emily laughed, and said "she presumed he must be possessed of wonderful attractions, since his success was considered as a matter of course?"

Walsingham replied by an animated panegyric on the character of Kelroy, whom he described as amiable in the highest degree, but somewhat depressed at present, in consequence of a sudden change of fortune; and after much playful raillery on his own prudence in keeping such a paragon from her sight, informed her that he had been absent nearly two months from the city, to which he had returned but the preceding day. "My acquaintance with him," continued Walsingham, "commenced on board the packet[1] in which we sailed together from England, and I found in him a most entertaining and instructive companion. There is scarcely a part of Europe which he has not visited: and having gratified his wishes, and increased his knowledge by exploring the curiosities, and observing the manners and customs of other countries, he was returning, as he thought, to the enjoyment of ease and affluence in his own, but found on his arrival a melancholy reverse.—His father, whose only child he was, had been induced during his absence, to embark in a wild speculating scheme, which he fancied would at least double his property, but on the contrary it failed, and ruined him. He lost all he was worth except about two hundred a year which happened to be settled on his wife; yet he still continued to flatter himself with an idea he should be able to retrieve it, and kept the matter a profound secret from his son, to whom he regularly transmitted his usual allowance. Grief, and disappointment at length destroyed

---

1 A packet ship was a small boat designed to carry passengers, mail, and freight, usually on a regular schedule.

his health, and on Kelroy's return to America, six months ago, he found his father dead, and his affairs in the utmost perplexity and confusion. He directly instituted a suit for the recovery of a large proportion of the estate, which is fraudulently withheld from him, but although nearly certain of obtaining it in the end, such is the dilatory nature of the law, that years may pass before it is decided, and as he is not of a temper indolently to await the result, he is now preparing for a voyage to India."

Emily listened to this account of him with great attention, and then repeated to Walsingham what she had heard from Helen of the emotion he had shewn at Mrs. S's., and the conversation which followed.

"His feelings,["] said Walsingham, ["]were always quick, but latterly he has met with so much to excite them, that they are probably more irritable now than usual. Mrs. S. is his relation, which accounts for his being prevailed on to spend the evening there, for he is by no means fond of frequenting such mixed assemblies; but with respect to his claims to the title of a *poet*, you shall if you wish it, judge for yourself."

Emily replied that she should be much gratified to have it in her power to do so; and Walsingham took from his pocket book a paper which he presented to her, containing the following lines.

HYMN TO POETRY.

Benignant power! whose radiant form,
    With light celestial glows!
Bestow'd life's dreary waste to warm,
    And lessen human woes!

Thou, who art hopeless sorrow's friend,
    And pensive love's delight,
And with affliction's gloom canst blend,
    Visions serenely bright.

Oh! to sustain a sinking heart,
    And life's dull cares relieve,
To me that spirit now impart,
    Which thou alone canst give;

And o'er the space of bliss and woe,
    Which fate ordains for mine,
Bid thy soft song melodious flow,

Thy peaceful glories shine.

With thee, let me the rising day
Enthron'd in light behold;
With thee, view evening's purple ray,
Ting'd with refulgent gold.—

And, when the silent moon rides high,
In majesty serene,
And countless stars adorn the sky,
To crown night's solemn scene;

Let every thought and wish recede,
To regions bright and calm;
And o'er my soul divinely shed
Devotion's purest balm.

Let dewy spring her buds unfold,
Let transient summer bloom;
Let autumn fade, and winter cold,
Enwrap the world in gloom;

Since nature's boundless fair expanse,
Lies open all to thee,
Do thou each wondrous change enhance,
And each shall dearer be.

No gold have I, upon thy shrine
In glitt'ring heaps to pour,
But I a glowing heart resign,
And thou wilt ask no more.

Thou lovest not the pomp and pride,
From wealth and power which springs,
But turnest with delight aside,
To sweeter, simpler things.

Oh! let me then from thee receive,
Whilst through the world I stray,
Joys which that world could never give,
Nor e'er can take away.

For me still deck the morning's smile,

Still paint the mountain flower,
And, with thy soothing dreams beguile
Each solitary hour.

And when rude sounds of human strife,
My sick'ning mind assail,
Secure me from those ills of life,
Beneath thy mystic veil.

No earthly hand shall ever dare
To rend that veil away;
For death alone can enter there,
To quench thy beaming ray.

Yet soon, within its native sphere,
Thy lamp again will burn;
For thou from heaven wert banish'd here,
And shalt to heaven return.

"What is your opinion of it?" said Walsingham after she had finished reading it.

"It at least proves" replied she, "that he is not one of the people that Mrs. S's old bachelor talked of, who were born to repine at every thing."

She then returned him the paper, with sensations of stronger interest towards its author than she chose to express. She was passionately fond of poetry, and the enthusiasm of her disposition led her to believe that those who possessed the talent of composing it, were of a superior order of beings. The romantic person, and elevated character of Kelroy were not calculated to remove the illusion, and when, accompanied by Walsingham, he came the next day to Mrs. Hammond's, and was introduced to the family, he was received by Emily with a mixture of softness and timidity, which rendered her, in his sight, all that was attractively lovely. Her beauty when he first beheld her, appeared to his vivid imagination something more than mortal, and having learned from Walsingham, that the qualities of her mind were nowise inferior, he met her again with an increased disposition to admire and esteem her.

Mutually inclined to a favourable opinion of each other, and mutually gifted with whatever could tend to confirm it, a short space sufficed to remove the restraint which attended their first acquaintance, and Emily soon experienced in the society of Kelroy a pleasure wholly new. Without seeking to analyze her feelings, she thoughtlessly resigned herself to a novelty which extended its bewitching influence to every impulse and idea, until Mrs. Cathcart painfully awakened her to a sense of their real state, by relating somewhat that created in her a confusion, and uneasiness to which her happy heart had been hitherto a stranger.

Flying into the house with her accustomed busy importance, on the morning of the day previous to the wedding, she had scarcely seated herself, ere she began her story, which, illustrated by her remarks, and lengthened by her love of talking, seemed to Emily as endless as it was distressing.

"My dear ma'am," said she, addressing herself to Mrs. Hammond, "I have something to tell you. I called just now to see Mrs. C. I have owed her a visit a great while, and I was determined to put it off no longer. Well, who should I meet with there, but Mr. A. who is lately returned from France you know. Mrs. C. and I were talking about you all, and I happened to mention Mr. Kelroy as a very fine young man. They both agreed with me, and Mr. A. said he deserved to be more respected than ever, because of the dignity with which he bore his misfortunes."

"What misfortunes pray?" said Mrs. Hammond.

"Why he is not worth a cent, you know!"

"Indeed I do not know it," replied Mrs. Hammond. "I heard he was involved in a troublesome law-suit, but nothing further!"

"O dear! why then I can tell it all to you!" said Mrs. Cathcart, and she then repeated nearly the same particulars which Emily had heard from Walsingham, except with respect to the law-suit, which she represented as a hopeless thing, and his intended voyage as his sole reliance.

"Very astonishing!" said Mrs. Hammond. "I had heard a different story. What is his profession pray?"

"Oh, he was bred to none! The time that most young men spend in that way, he spent in travelling. He was gone four whole years!"

"No profession, and no fortune!" said Mrs. Hammond, gravely. "Bred a gentleman, and left to maintain the appearance of one the best way he can!"

"Aye! there's the misery of it!" said the compassionate Mrs. Cathcart. "I wonder for my part, it did not drive him crazy! But they say he did not seem to mind it on his own account, but tried to console his mother, who doats on him, and grieves as much at the alteration of his prospects, as if he was actually going to be starved. But Mr. A. said, if report was true, she might cease her lamentations, for he had heard from good authority that her son was engaged to Miss Emily Hammond!"

"Engaged to *my* daughter?" said Mrs. Hammond.

"Yes, and that they were positively to be married in a very short time."

"What stuff!" said Mrs. Hammond scornfully. "I hope you contradicted it immediately?"

"That I did! and told them that I was very sure it would never take place upon earth."

"That it most certainly never will, whilst I live!" said Mrs. Hammond, and having thus expressed as much of her mind as she thought expedient, she listened to the remainder of Mrs. Cathcart's harangue in silence, and at its close refrained from any comments; but it effectually revived in her that caution which in the hurry of business and pleasure, she had latterly almost forgotten; and she was no sooner alone, than she began to meditate very seriously upon what she had heard. She felt a considerable degree of vexation towards Walsingham for having been the means of introducing an accomplished beggar, as she now considered him, to her acquaintance; and was half inclined to suspect him of a scheme to assist Kelroy in attempting to better his circumstances, by depriving her of her youngest daughter, whom she now recollected to have appeared remarkably solicitous on every point in which he was concerned, and was astonished at her own inadvertence in not perceiving it sooner.

Towards Kelroy himself, she conceived a most sovereign dislike, but to despise him was impossible; and in place of the contempt which she usually bestowed on persons in his situation, she nourished from his acknowledged superiority a sentiment of fear which rendered him doubly hateful to her. Yet, to banish him from her house was impossible, as it could only be done at the risk of exposing herself, and offending Walsingham; and she blessed her lucky stars which had thus revealed to her the evil whilst it was in her power to remedy it by less violent measures.

To Emily, she said nothing, wisely remembering, that prohibition in such cases, frequently acts as an additional incentive to disobedience; but having noticed her silence, and the pensive expression of her face which ensued on hearing Mrs. Cathcart's narrative, she felt assured that some immediate precautions were necessary, and began to act on the defensive that very evening, by contriving, apparently without design, to separate her from Kelroy as often as they were placed near each other, and thus effectually prevented for the time, that exclusive intercourse for which, to her great dismay, she discovered them to be mutually solicitous.

CHAPTER VI.

THE nuptials of Walsingham and Lucy were celebrated with all the parade that the circumstance would admit of, and the satisfaction of Mrs. Hammond would have been complete, but for the sight of Kelroy, who was necessarily present, and whose assiduities to Emily, as bride's-maid, it was not in her power to impede. Her attention was much divided by the large company she had collected, but whenever the rules of politeness permitted her to relax from her exertions to entertain and accommodate them, her eyes wandered with restless anxiety towards Emily, who observed her mother's watchfulness, and, aided by her own feelings, failed not to divine its cause.

Possessed of infinite taste, and delicacy, and endued with powers of discrimination unusual to her age, she had hitherto beheld the whole sex with indifference; and in this calm, inexperienced state, her imagination had formed to itself a brilliant picture of felicity in the future disposal of her heart. Convinced that she could never bestow her hand except on distinguished worth and merit, she remembered not that she might discern those qualities only to lament them; and anticipated the period that should awaken her yet dormant affections, as one destined to place her in possession of every happiness.

That hour had now arrived—not drest in the gay colours which her fancy had painted, but arrayed by the hand of truth in hues of dull perplexity, whose gloom the bright spirit of Kelroy might lessen, but could not remove. In his character was combined all that appeared to her worthy of estimation, and she contemplated this living image of her own cherished standard of excellence, with indescribable emotions both of pleasure and pain. His learning, genius, temper, and understanding, were such as might silence the most fastidious critic; and she felt soothed by the consciousness that her preference, however misplaced in other respects, could only reflect honour on her judgment; but his depressed situation, and her perfect knowledge of her mother's views, convinced her that she ought, if possible, to banish him entirely from her thoughts. She endeavoured to turn her mind from these melancholy ideas to the happier lot of her sister, but the contrast afforded aggravated uneasiness, and she felt tempted, for the first time in her life, to arraign fortune of unkindness. She saw Lucy, cold, and heartless, in possession of the undivided affections of an amiable man, whose worth she was incapable of appreciating, and mistress of immense wealth which she would never employ to any better purpose than the attainment of luxury or fashion; and whilst Walsingham was thus cheated into a union with one whose deficiencies she feared would be too early displayed to him, Kelroy and herself might waste the bloom of life in pursuing hopes, which if unsuccessful, would embitter the remainder of their days.

Harassed by these reflections, her spirits sunk, and as she was not sufficiently accustomed to their desertion to have learnt to substitute the appearance of them for the reality, her dejection became evident. Kelroy, who perceived it without knowing its cause, soon grew equally thoughtful; for to be gay when Emily was otherwise, seemed to him impossible. Their mutual gravity drew some observations from part of the company which accidentally reached the ears of Mrs. Cathcart, and she resolved to put an end by her agreeable raillery to a species of deportment which she considered highly preposterous at a wedding, where all should be mirth and jollity. However, as no immediate opportunity offered, she presently forgot it, and it would probably have occurred to her no more, had she not been placed opposite to them at the supper table, where their grave faces, contrasted with those of Mr. and Mrs. Walsingham, appeared in her eyes to very little advantage.

"Lord! my dear!" said she to Emily, "what is the matter with you?—Why you look as solemn at the sight of our bride here, as if you were afraid you never would be one yourself!"

At these words Mrs. Hammond darted a scrutinizing glance at her youngest daughter, who blushed deeply, and attempted to laugh off the accusation; and Mrs. Cathcart next addressed herself to Kelroy.

"And Mr. Kelroy too, looks just as bad!—I declare, I wonder for my part, what can you be thinking of?—Its the strangest thing in the world to see a young gentleman wear such a long face, except when he is in love; and that can hardly be the case with you at present, I fancy?"

These ridiculous speeches, made without ill-will, and heard without suspicion, or emotion except by Helen Cathcart, Mrs. Hammond, and the two persons to whom they were directed, created a universal laugh, in which they each joined, though from different motives—for Emily would much rather have cried—Mrs. Hammond was enraged, yet chose to appear diverted—Helen was ashamed for her mother, and distressed for her young friend, whose embarrassment she feared to increase by seeming to notice it,—and Kelroy felt more disconcerted than he was willing to acknowledge even to himself.

He required not the remarks of the literal Mrs. Cathcart, to inform him, how improbable it must appear to the eye of common reason, that situated as he was, despoiled of his property, and preparing for a long voyage, from whence he might never return, he should suffer himself to become seriously attached to a beautiful young woman, whose accomplishments might justly challenge advantages superior to those he could formerly have offered her; but he was by no means conscious that his admiration had betrayed him into such unguarded sympathy, and determined to be more cautious in future.—Engaged during the life of his father chiefly in the pursuits of knowledge, and literature, but a small portion of his time had been devoted to female society, where few pleased, and fewer still interested him; and since his death, he had been unremittingly employed in endeavouring to collect from the wreck of his fortune a sum sufficient to enable him to aspire once more to independence, without either lessening the pittance of his mother, or having recourse to the assistance of others—an expedient which his lofty spirit rejected with abhorrence, whilst a single alternative remained. Wealth he had never despised, but he coveted not an excess of it; and regarding the circumstance which had secured his parent from distress as a providential alleviation of his misfortunes, he refrained from useless repinings at an evil which a few years might probably repair; and resigned himself to the prospect of labours untried, and climes unknown with the calmness of a practical philosopher.

These resolves, although meritorious in themselves, were adopted without much repugnance by Kelroy, who, uninfluenced by local views, scarcely considered his acquiescence in the light of a sacrifice, until Emily, rich in personal, and intellectual charms, arose like the vision of conviction, and taught him the value of that affluence which was his no more. To him, her beauty, eminent as it was, seemed her least attraction, since it exceeded not such as he had frequently beheld without receiving any permanent impression; but her luminous mind, and inimitable manner, adorned with all those touching graces, which from being rarely seen are believed to exist only in imagination, rendered her in his estimation the most perfect of her sex, and filled him with emotions which quickly resolved themselves into deep regret, and unalterable passion. She was all that he had wished or fancied, but more than he had ever hoped to meet; and his affection could only be equalled by his distress at the idea of being in a situation which precluded every hope of obtaining her hand, except on clandestine terms; for common report, and his own observations convinced him, that should Emily herself consent, Mrs. Hammond would reject such a proposition with disdain. Thus circumstanced, nothing could be less agreeable than the remarks he had just heard; and, to prevent a repetition of them, he assumed for the remainder of the evening an air of pleasantry utterly foreign to his feelings, and compelled himself to converse, almost without knowing what he said, until apprized of its inconsistency by the answers of those around him.

Abashed, and agitated, Emily longed to be alone, that she might reflect on his wild sentiments, and unconnected expressions, which bordered so much upon absurdity as almost to wear the appearance of intoxication; yet they lessened him not in her opinion, since she believed herself to be in a great measure, the cause of them; and she carefully treasured up every look and word to be retraced and examined in solitude. But Mrs. Cathcart discovered neither inconsistencies nor deficiencies in him, and without a thought of the pain she had inflicted, enjoyed his extravagant flights as the effect of her own ingenious remarks, and talked and laughed unceasingly until the company retired.

The two succeeding weeks were spent by Mrs. Hammond and her family in receiving and returning the congratulatory visits of their acquaintance; and Kelroy, who was frequently of the party, found too much pleasure in the society of Emily to be able to deny himself a gratification which must soon cease entirely; and refraining somewhat from his former pointed attentions, fancied that his attachment was unknown, even to its object. Having thus formed a compromise with his feelings which in some degree satisfied him respecting the propriety of his conduct, he no longer scrupled to indulge himself in seeking to be continually in her presence, since persuaded that he was to be the only sufferer by it. But a short time sufficed to evince the fallacy of such reasoning by creating in him a perplexity of mind, and confusion of manner which frequently displayed themselves in such a light as to give Emily just reason to imagine that she was far from indifferent to him; and the consequence of this was, such involuntary softness on her part, as had the ultimate effect of convincing them that each was equally dear to the other.

Delicious as this persuasion was to Kelroy, he hesitated to take advantage of it, to draw from her an avowal of her affection, lest he should involve her in an engagement which he might never have power to fulfil; and thus subject her during his absence to the displeasure of her haughty mother; whose dislike of him he discovered in innumerable trifling instances, where her malignity hoped to gratify itself unnoticed.

The patience of Mrs. Hammond with regard to Kelroy, was exercised in a degree which she had never been sensible of on any former occasion; and although in her cooler moments she entertained few serious apprehensions from a partiality, which his approaching departure, and her own management, would she trusted, render a transient one on the part of her daughter; she was nevertheless frequently so irritated with them both as to be compelled to exert herself to the utmost to avoid bursting into open anger with Emily, whom she considered as a romantic enthusiast born to torment and disappoint her.—Kelroy she perfectly detested; and the restraint in which she was held by Walsingham, whom it behoved her not to offend, enabled her to look forward with something like consolation to her separation from Lucy, after which she should be at liberty to act as she pleased, and drive from her presence this hated innovater of her repose.

But not all her art could conceal entirely from Walsingham the workings of her indignation, which although it escaped her not in words, was often visible in her countenance; and compassionating both Emily and Kelroy, whom he thought singularly adapted to each other, he lamented that they had ever met, since their acquaintance threatened to prove only a source of unhappiness. He could not censure as wholly unjust, the disapprobation of Mrs. Hammond, which in some respects was certainly excusable; but he was of opinion that much consideration was likewise due to Kelroy himself, whose merit bade defiance to any objection which arose not from pecuniary, or ambitious views; and if, as he believed both Lucy and Emily were entitled to a share of property which was withheld from them by the arbitrary disposition of their mother, he saw no positive reason why she should manifest such strong repugnance towards a union, which with her consent, might be productive of the happiest consequences.

But Walsingham judged only from appearances, and was a stranger to the hidden motives which actuated this selfish, imperious woman; who, surrounded by difficulties which had originated in her own false pride, suffered all the anxiety that she merited, without daring to venture on one decisive measure to extricate herself.

She easily discerned that Walsingham was desirous of a pretext for promoting the success of Kelroy, and dreading lest somewhat should occur which might authorize him to declare his sentiments openly on the subject, she several times repeated her injunctions to Mrs. Cathcart, to contradict the reports which were already in circulation; and contrived on various pretences, constantly to detain Emily near her at home, and as constantly to accompany her abroad; and whenever Kelroy was present, insinuated herself into every group where they were placed, and took a part in every conversation in which they were concerned, to the infinite chagrin of them both, who beheld themselves watched, and followed as if they had been engaged in a plan of high treason.—Yet so well did she manage her intrusions, that a very skilful observer would scarcely, without some previous clue, have ascribed them to any sinister motive; and whilst Kelroy and Emily were writhing under the restraint which she perpetually imposed on them, Mrs. Hammond appeared to indifferent spectators to be one of the most amiable, and affectionate of mothers.

Whilst she thus, by her unwearied address, prevented that explanation on the part of Kelroy, of which she lived in continual fear; Emily, shocked, and depressed, suffered intensely from her mother's want of confidence, and her own unfortunate predilection, which she now believed doomed to be confined to her own bosom.—Independent of other obstacles, she now fancied that she discovered one in Kelroy himself, whose gravity and reserve hourly increased; and resigning every hope of the happy result she had once promised herself, she endeavoured to submit composedly to a disappointment which seemed inevitable.

Unused to these internal conflicts, her appetite failed and her colour faded; and in the sorrow of her heart she would have shut herself up in constant solitude, had not pride prevented her, by representing the humiliating inference which might ensue from such conduct.—A severe cold with which she was attacked, afforded her an unquestionable excuse to indulge this melancholy propensity, and confined her wholly to her chamber; where, in a few days, indisposition and anxiety produced a change in her appearance that was seriously alarming. When she grew better, her physician so strictly urged the necessity of the utmost care to prevent a relapse, which might be attended he said, with fatal consequences, that she no longer had occasion to seek a pretence for seclusion.

Mrs. Hammond omitted no remedy or advice which might conduce to her recovery, but after her first terror had subsided, dedicated no more time to her than was absolutely requisite to save her own credit; and, except for Helen Cathcart, who frequently spent whole days with her she would have been left almost alone. But no sooner was she able to leave her apartment, and join the family below stairs, than the kindness of her mother assumed a different complexion; and engagements which had hitherto seemed indispensable, were now relinquished, that her evenings might be devoted to Emily, whom she said she could not bear to leave hovering alone over the parlour fire, whilst every body else was gone abroad.

Helen was frequently there, and would willingly have saved her this trouble, but Kelroy was frequently there too; and she did not choose to risk the chance, which might, perhaps, render all further precautions fruitless.—Night after night did this female Argus[1] sit at home, fretting inwardly at the deprivation of her darling amusements, yet resolved to continue it whilst a shadow of doubt remained; and in the vexation attending her self-imposed penance, she evinced towards Kelroy a species of indefinite neglect, and half suppressed scorn, which severely mortified him, and would have prevented him from ever again entering her doors, had not the pale figure of Emily, now become doubly dear from her recent danger, and altered looks forcibly recalled him.

Having occasion to leave town for a short time, Kelroy came one morning to Mrs. Hammond's in quest of Walsingham, whom he informed in her presence, that he was going out of town, and added, that he wished to speak with him.—Walsingham took his hat, and they went out together, leaving Mrs. Hammond highly gratified with the prospect of this unexpected respite from her task. In about an hour Walsingham came back, and finding Lucy and Emily sitting with their mother, mentioned to them that he had just parted from Kelroy, who had gone to Jersey and did not expect to return in less than five days.

Mrs. Hammond had the prudence to abstain from going abroad that evening, but having nothing to distract her attention, and make her lose her money, she solaced herself with a snug card party at home; but the next day, she discovered that Emily was so much better, that she might venture to leave her and go to the play.—Emily was well content to be left and she went accordingly.

The third and fourth evenings were also spent abroad by this tender mother; but when the fifth arrived, she was sadly perplexed what course to pursue, for Walsingham, Lucy, and herself were engaged to a ball and supper which she could hardly endure the thought of renouncing; yet as this was the night on which Kelroy

---

1 The hundred-eyed giant of Greek mythology.

was to return, she doubted whether she had not better be seized with a violent head-ache, and stay at home?—Remembering however to have heard him say that he also had received an invitation, she flattered herself that if he came to town, he would probably be there in hopes of meeting Emily; and after weighing the matter very seriously she at last concluded to go; but before she began to dress sent privately for her man Henry, and telling him that Miss Emily was sick, and must not be disturbed by strangers, charged him if any person came, to say she was not at home.

This Henry was a free negro[1] that had grown grey in the service of Mrs. Hammond, who with all her faults, was not a bad Mistress. He liked his *old lady*, as he called her, very well, but his two young ones much better; particularly Emily, whom he extolled as the perfection of beauty and good nature.—Having constant opportunities of observing what was going forward, he had found out that his old lady had more reasons than one for confining herself so much to the house for several weeks; and when family affairs were discussed in the kitchen, frequently gave it as his opinion, that "it was dam pity old Missus no let Massa Kelroy court Miss Emily."

When Mrs. Hammond was arrayed to her satisfaction she came down stairs, and having begged Emily to take great care of herself, and not sit up late, got into the carriage with Lucy and her husband, and drove off. After they had been gone about an hour somebody knocked at the street door, which was opened, as usual, by old Henry; and Kelroy, who had just arrived in town, inquired if Walsingham was within.

The negro hesitated a moment whether to disobey his mistress?—but his own notions of right, together with the spirit of intrigue inherent in his race, prevailed, and he answered, "No sir, Massa Walsingham not at home—but—old Missus gone out too sir; and Miss Emily in de parlour quite 'lone."

"Emily at home!—and Emily alone!"—The heart of Kelroy bounded at the news!—and without further reflection, he sprung lightly into the passage, whilst the negro returned grinning to the kitchen, where he related what he had done; and shaking his finger at the mulatto girl who waited on Mrs. Hammond, said "You Sal! when old lady ask who been here, don't you go tell now?—if you do, by jingo, next time I catch you stealing sweetmeats, I tell too."

---

1 Pennsylvania had passed a gradual emancipation law in 1780, under which no African American born in the state after 1780 could remain enslaved past the age of 28.

Left to pass the evening alone, Emily first had recourse to a book; but finding it impossible to confine her attention to aught that it contained, she threw it aside; and taking her harp, which she had not touched since her illness, began playing various favourite melodies, accompanying them at intervals with her voice; and when Kelroy knocked, had just commenced that pathetic little air,

"Forever fortune wilt thou prove,
"An unrelenting foe to love."[1]

Absorbed in the song, which was singularly adapted to her own situation, she had not heard him enter the house; and when he came gently into the parlour, supposed it to be one of the servants, and without changing her attitude waved her hand not to be interrupted.

Kelroy was about to advance, but on seeing the motion of her hand, shut the door, and stood looking at her in silence; and Emily concluding the person to have retired, continued singing, unconscious of an auditor.

She sat with her profile towards him; her white drapery was wreathed round her person in careless folds, her face turned upwards, and her eyes half closed; and in her countenance and whole air an expression of rapt melancholy, that seemed in perfect unison with the plaintive sounds which flowed from her lips.—Kelroy scarcely breathed, lest he should lose a note; yet felt concerned in what manner to intimate to her his presence without alarming her.

After the two first stanzas, she paused, and sighed heavily, and Kelroy was again going to advance, when the following verse, sung in tremulous tones, arrested his steps a second time.

"But busy, fortune, still art thou,
To form the loveless, joyless vow;
The heart from pleasure to delude,
And join the gentle to the rude."

Her voice failed as she pronounced the last line, and leaning her head against the instrument she burst into tears.

"Emily!" said Kelroy, in the utmost agitation.

---

1 From "To Fortune," by Scottish poet and playwright James Thomson (1700–48).

At the sound of her own name, she started from her chair in wild astonishment, and perceiving him at her side fainted in his arms.

"Emily!—dear Emily!"—said Kelroy, as he held her to his bosom.

When she recovered, he besought her forgiveness for the terror he had occasioned her.—Unable to speak, she endeavoured to escape from him, but he would not suffer her, and avowing his attachment in the most impassioned language, desisted not from protestations and entreaties, until he prevailed on her to confess that he was beloved in return.—Mutual inquiries, and explanations ensued, and neither of them thought of separating, until a time piece over the mantle striking twelve, informed Emily of the lateness of the hour.—Frightened lest her mother should return, she told Kelroy he must leave her; and conscious of the necessity of so doing he reluctantly departed.

Old Henry bolted the door after him, and then came into the parlour under pretence of mending the fire.—Finding that Emily did not notice him, he looked attentively at her to discover the cause, and observing no displeasure in her countenance, said "Miss Emily, you please be so kind not tell your ma' I let Massa Kelroy come in, else may be I get good scolding—cause Missus say, if any body come, I must say nobody at home."

Aware instantly of the full purport of this speech, Emily inquired why, if that was the case, he had ventured to disobey his orders?

"Ah, Miss Emily!—I understand well enough!—he pretty young gentleman, and you beautiful young lady!—what I tell lie, and shut him out for?"

Touched by this proof of sympathy in a creature whose familiarity seemed authorized by his long services, Emily attempted not to reprove him but merely saying "she should not mention it this time, provided he would be careful not to do such a thing again;" retired to her chamber, where the tumult of her thoughts long kept her waking, and she at last sunk to rest with tears of mingled grief and rapture stealing from her eyes.

CHAPTER VII.

WHEN Kelroy called the next morning, he found the family at breakfast; and as Mrs. Hammond who had risen very late, had not had an opportunity of inquiring whether he had been there in her absence, his visit was supposed to be the first since his return, by all except Emily; whose increased bloom at his approach was occasioned in part by again meeting him, but more by the consciousness of a mistake which she wanted courage to rectify.

Mrs. Hammond observed her blushes, and attributed them to the surprise of seeing him unexpectedly; but after her embarrassment had subsided, and the conversation became general, she fancied she discerned in Emily an air of placid satisfaction widely different from that which she had latterly worn, and in Kelroy a degree of animation for which she could account for in but one way. She thought too, that she saw some very intelligent glances pass between them, and her suspicions increased every moment.

"Pray, what time did you reach town last night?" said Walsingham to Kelroy.

"At about half past seven," replied he.

"So early!" said Walsingham, "I wonder then you did not join us at Mrs. N's?"

"You know I am not remarkably fond of dancing," said Kelroy.

"Oh!" cried Lucy, "how can you say such a thing, Mr. Kelroy? I must confess I did not expect that from a gentleman of your taste!"

"Our tastes are various, madam;" said Kelroy with a smile, "and in their diversity consists our happiness."

"Well then," cried Lucy with vivacity, "to convince us that your taste was more refined than ours, tell us where you spent your evening?"

"I had—some very particular—business," said Kelroy, hesitatingly.

"At *home* with a book, I suppose?" said Walsingham, laughing.

"Or perhaps *abroad* with a *belle*?" said Mrs. Hammond, fixing her penetrating eyes on his face.

He coloured; but not choosing to deny even by implication, an accidental circumstance, with the result of which he meant to acquaint her in due season, he bowed without speaking; and Emily hastily retreated to a window.

Walsingham looked at him with surprise, and Lucy with curiosity, but neither of them spoke; and Mrs. Hammond was too much confounded to utter a syllable.—Emily remained at the window; and a silence of some minutes followed, which was broken by the entrance of Mrs. Cathcart, and Helen, with several ladies and gentlemen who had joined them on the way.

Their presence was a sensible relief to Emily, who had never before felt herself so awkwardly situated.—She had acknowledged to Kelroy that his suspicions of her mother's determination to oppose him, were well founded; and when in the ardour of increased love, and newly acquired hope, he pleaded for a promise to suffer no future argument to influence her against him; she resisted from a sense of mingled modesty and duty; and all he could obtain, was permission to request her mother's consent through the medium of Walsingham, whose interposition was her sole reliance for obtaining it. But knowing that the disclosure had not yet taken place, she was apprehensive lest her confusion at these unlucky questions should be the means through which it might be made; and although in the certainty of being beloved by Kelroy, half her difficulties seemed to have vanished, as if by the touch of magic; she nevertheless felt extremely averse to encounter the sarcasms and reproaches which she presumed would inevitably follow, unless prevented by the mediation and good offices of her brother-in-law.

Helen, who had seated herself next to Emily, observed with pleasure the increased lustre of her eyes, and complexion; and Kelroy determined to be no longer checked except by Emily herself, glided round, and leaning over the back of their chairs, entered into conversation with them.

Mrs. Cathcart was in her usual spirits, and chattered away on the subject of Mrs. N's ball; describing not only the dresses of all the ladies, but also the position of every dish on the supper table, and the manner in which their contents were separately disposed of; repeating, at the same time as many of her own speeches, and witticisms as she could remember; and concluded with an account of her adventures at the card-table where she had won, she said, twenty dollars.—Here she ceased speaking to indulge herself in a hearty laugh; and Walsingham, amused with her loquacity, laughed also; but Mrs. Hammond, engaged in watching the trio on the opposite side of the fire, did not applaud her with so much as a smile.—This however was no discouragement to Mrs. Cathcart, who in common with all great talkers, spoke longer and louder, in proportion as she saw the attention of any of her hearers beginning to fail; and finding that Mrs. Hammond did not listen to her, she dashed into a fresh subject, and every now and then twitched her by the sleeve, saying "but observe now, my dear friend!—listen now! for this is the best of the joke."

Having pretty well exhausted all the usual topics, she rose to take leave; but finding that Helen did not immediately second her motion, she advanced to Emily, and began congratulating her on her mended looks.

"Why my dear, nobody could believe you had been sick, that was not an eye witness of it! why your cheeks are like two roses! you are a little thinner to be sure, but that will soon wear away."

Then turning to Mrs. Hammond, she continued "but I hope you dont intend to keep her moping in the house any longer? poor thing! she has had a dismal time of it already! Emily my dear did'n't you feel very lonesome here last night, by yourself?"

The roses which Mrs. Cathcart had been admiring, assumed a brighter glow at this question, which Emily affected not to hear; and Kelroy could scarcely repress a smile at the repetition of inquiries, which although purely accidental, were exactly such as were most calculated to confuse her and embarrass him.

But far different were the sensations of Mrs. Hammond, who became every instant more confirmed in her conjectures; and having accepted an invitation from Mrs. Cathcart to spend the evening with her, and consented that Emily should accompany them; she returned the parting civilities of her guests, and then, regardless of Kelroy, directly retired to her chamber, to deliberate on the methods necessary to be adopted in such an emergency, which threatened, she feared, the entire overthrow of all her plans.

The immediate impulse of her mind was, to assert her own authority, and forcibly prevent her daughter from ever again seeing Kelroy; but a little reflection convinced her of the folly of such a step; and controuling with a strong effort, every tempestuous emotion, she listened to the suggestions of her native caution, which pointed out a more difficult, but less perilous course.

After remaining alone near an hour, she sent for Emily, who hastily obeyed the summons, lest her mother should suppose her tardiness arose from her reluctance to leave Kelroy, who was still below.

She paused at the door of the apartment to recover herself, and then, timorously opening it, beheld Mrs. Hammond seated in an arm chair, busily employed in looking over a small drawer of laces and muslins, with a countenance so composed, that she began to hope she had mistaken the purpose for which her presence was requested.

Mrs. Hammond looked up, as she entered, and telling her she was glad she had come, gave into her hands some materials for a cap, which she desired her to make immediately, saying she should want it in the evening.

Emily sat down with a beating heart, to comply with this unusual request, and began sewing them together, wondering what would come next; and Mrs. Hammond, who was considering in what manner to commence her intended oration, enjoyed her agitation with malicious pleasure; but although she wished to refrain from severity, could not deny herself the satisfaction of tormenting her a little before she proceeded to business. Eyeing her therefore with a sort of dubious expression, she burst into a laugh, and said, "why Emily! child! your finger shakes as if you had the ague! What is the matter with you?"

"Nothing ma'am."

"Nothing, ha? well then since there is no particular reason for those very long stitches, I should be glad to see them made a little shorter."

Emily tried to pursue her work with more regularity, but the sarcastic tone of her mother discomposed her; and the stitches not only grew longer, but became crooked.

"Well," cried Mrs. Hammond with a sneer, "you improve in your operations! This said *nothing* of yours seems to be a powerful stimulant to some part of the system; on others, indeed, it acts differently; your tongue, for instance, which appears to have lost the faculty of motion?"

Unused to language like this, every particle of pride and spirit in Emily's composition flew to her aid; and losing all apprehension in her disgust at so rude an attack, she instantaneously recovered herself, and rising, replied with calm dignity, "I know not how I have offended you, mother; but there is no question you may think fit to ask me, on any subject, which I shall not immediately answer without reserve or prevarication."

Her lofty but respectful air, astonished Mrs. Hammond, who now first became sensible that her daughter inherited a portion of her own haughtiness; and feeling from her reply that further irritation would be dangerous, she hastened to repair her error, and take advantage of Emily's candour, by saying in a softened voice, "you mistake me my dear—I am not offended, but surprised; and that perhaps, may have betrayed me into some little quickness of expression.—However, let me cut short all useless preface, and take you at your word.—Was not Kelroy here last night?"

"Yes," replied she, "he came unexpectedly."

"And how long did he stay?" inquired Mrs. Hammond.

"Until twelve o'clock," said Emily, looking down, and blushing with shame, and vexation.

Mrs. Hammond coloured too at this plain confession; and fearing if she continued thus minutely to investigate the affair, she should lose her temper; she paused a moment, and then said with an affectation of generosity, "Well Emily, I will not urge questions merely because you have pledged yourself to answer them. I have for some time observed with regret the increased attachment of that gentleman, and, fearing the consequences, have exerted every means in my power to prevent any intercourse between you in my absence.—Accident, I find, has frustrated my intentions, but I hope—I trust, that you have not been prevailed on to form any engagement?"

"No mother," said Emily, her eyes filling with tears as she spoke, ["]I have not quite forgotten what is due either to you, or myself. Last night was the first—until last night I did not know"—

She hesitated, and stopt; but Mrs. Hammond seizing her meaning, exclaimed with energy, "and but for *last night* you never would have known it, and all would quickly have faded from your mind like a dream! but now! I tremble for the result.—But you will not, surely Emily, bind yourself with open eyes to poverty and distress?"

"I would do nothing rashly;" replied Emily; "I am very young, and in a few years perhaps his situation may be very different."

"My dear child!" exclaimed Mrs. Hammond, "is it possible that with beauty like yours, you are desirous of devoting the spring of life to hopes and prospects like these?—Answer me sincerely, are you, *can* you be surprised to find me averse to all this?"

"In some respects I confess I am not," replied Emily.

"Name them," said Mrs. Hammond.

"Want of fortune," replied Emily, "and the necessity of a long absence, which cannot be prevented; since my own expectations, as I have understood, would be insufficient for that purpose."

"True," said Mrs. Hammond hastily, ["]they are less perhaps than is generally imagined.—But what are the advantages on the part of Kelroy, that are to counterbalance these objections?"

This was a painful question to Emily, who had she dared to give utterance to her thoughts, could have described in him virtues enough to merit a kingdom; but the fear of appearing fond, and romantic, and incurring her mother's raillery restrained her, and she only said, she "had heard from Walsingham that there was every probability of his gaining the suit he was engaged in; but should he even fail there, his talents and industry would enable him to make his way in the world without much difficulty."

"But taking every thing into consideration, are not the chances both ways nearly equal?"

Emily acknowledged that it was the case.

"Very well," replied Mrs. Hammond, with infinite self-applause for having adopted this Socratic method of obliging her to furnish arguments against herself, "very well then, out of your own mouth shall you be judged."

She then began a fluent harangue on her own past sacrifices, and singular tenderness towards her children; and having rung the usual changes,[1] with variations and additions, she next proceeded to comment on Lucy, who she said, had fulfilled her every wish, and rewarded her every care; and after drawing a very ingenious parallel between the prospects of the two sisters, concluded by beseeching Emily to consult her real happiness, and discard Kelroy forever!—But happiness and Kelroy were one with Emily; and notwithstanding all that was urged of present objections, and probable disasters, she could not be prevailed on to say she would renounce him; and Mrs. Hammond having exhausted every argument, and tried every art of persuasion, was at last content to temporize, and granted her permission to see him in future only on condition that she entered into no promise or engagement whatever, without her approbation.

On these terms they parted, Emily half-pleased, and half-frightened; wondering at her own courage, and her mother's lenity, and Mrs. Hammond with apparent calmness, and a heart full of rage, grieving that it was not in her power to banish Kelroy to the ends of the earth.

When the family met at dinner, Walsingham mentioned that he had had a long conversation with Kelroy that morning; and Mrs. Hammond significantly replied, that she had had one with a friend of that gentleman on the same subject.—Walsingham stared, and Emily felt extremely foolish; and the moment the cloth was removed[2] ran away to her chamber, where she remained until summoned to accompany her mother and sister to Mrs. Cathcart's.

Meanwhile Walsingham had not been idle.—Kelroy had confided to him what had passed, and after Emily left the room, Mrs. Hammond, as he expected from her previous hint, opened the matter without much ceremony; and expressing her regret that circumstances were so unfavourable, affected to consider herself in a great dilemma, and requested his advice. Agreeably surprised to find in her a disposition so consonant to his wishes, Walsingham spoke with great candour; and after giving her a minute account of Kelroy from their earliest acquaintance, painted in strong colours his singular perseverance and address

---

1 Presented old and familiar arguments.
2 Signaling the end of the meal.

in wresting a small part of his property from the iniquitous grasp of the persons who had so deplorably misled his father; and urged the improbability that such a man would long remain unpossessed of competence at least, if not independence. He then dwelt with much feeling, and delicacy on his fine domestic qualifications, his affection for Emily, and her undoubted prepossession in his favour; and ultimately, recommended to her not to oppose the prospect of their union.

This, although precisely what she had prepared herself to hear, was gall and bitterness to Mrs. Hammond, but she carefully concealed it; and slightly adverting to what had passed between Emily and herself, talked very sentimentally of the uncertainty of life, and the perpetual change of human views, and wishes, but allowed, that at some future day, if the young people should both continue in the same mind, it was possible she might grant them her unlimited consent. At present however, she thought it her duty to guard against accident, by forbidding any engagement on the part of her daughter; and signified that she could permit Kelroy to continue his attentions on no other terms.

Walsingham pleaded hard for a more direct answer, but so far from complying, she insisted on the additional term that the whole affair should be kept a profound secret; and requesting that he would inform Kelroy of her resolves, which nothing, she said could induce her at present to alter, she retired to dress; fully determined to avoid any conversation on the subject with that gentleman himself.

When Walsingham reflected on what had passed, it appeared to him to contain very little encouragement for a lover; but as it was all he could obtain, he walked down to Kelroy's lodgings, and informed him of his partial success; adding, that as the old lady seemed rather more tractable than could have been expected, he thought it best to let the matter rest for the present. Kelroy was of the same opinion; and transported to have gained the privilege of seeing Emily without restraint, he forgot the future anxiety which the annexed restrictions might occasion him, and in a very gay mood, returned with Walsingham to Mrs. Hammond's, where finding the three ladies just ready to depart, they handed them into the carriage, and then walked together to Mrs. Cathcart's, where they found a number of persons already assembled, amongst whom were Mr. Mangold, and, to the amazement of Emily, Doctor Blake, whose very existence she had forgotten. But observing that he was quite at his ease and apparently not unwelcome to the family, she felt a curiosity to know the means by which he had obtained admittance, and took the first opportunity of asking Helen in a low voice to inform her.

"Oh!" said Helen, "he is not like any thing else in the creation, and the house never will be rid of him unless somebody breaks his bones!—When Charles took him to task after the affair of the letter of which you were to have been the bearer, he acknowledged his folly in such ludicrous terms, and was so humble, and so ridiculous, that it was impossible to be seriously angry; and after a long argument, he reluctantly agreed never either to speak, or write another word on the subject, provided he was still permitted to visit here sometimes; for he had no notion, he said of being turned out like a mad dog, neck and heels forever. Finding that nothing more could be done, without forcing a downright quarrel, Charles consented to try him; and he has been here several times since, without attempting to break the truce; but I suspect his presence this evening is accidental, for I do not believe he was invited."

"What is all this whispering for?" said Charles Cathcart, who now made up to them, together with Kelroy.

"Pray," said Helen, pointing to the doctor, "did you ask that comely creature to make one here?"

"Yes," replied Charles, "but I assure you it was because I could not avoid it.—He came to my office a few hours ago, and regardless of the number of genteel hints which I threw out from time to time, stuck to me like wax; and at last, when I told him I was engaged, put on one of his odd looks and said he was entirely at leisure.—What could I do but invite him?"

"Nothing I believe," said Helen, "but I hope since he has got here, you will take care to keep him in order."

"Who," said Mr. Mangold, approaching them, and catching her last words, "who can possibly be here that is so savage as to require any check except the presence of such angels of these?" looking alternately at Helen and Emily with a languishing air.

"What a happy circumstance it would be, Mr. Mangold," said Helen, "if your sex in general were thus willing to acknowledge our supremacy?"

"Oh they are!" cried he. "All mankind are sensible of your bewitching influence, except here and there a frigid soul that cannot feel, or is too proud to own it."

"Pardon me," said Charles bowing low with pretended deference, "few men my dear sir, possess either your gallantry or penetration."

"Penetration, Mr. Cathcart!" cried the ancient beau; "and

is it possible at your age you can think an uncommon share of that necessary, to discover the attractions of the beautiful race of beings which every where surround you? To me they are all lovely in a degree; and some so transcendantly irresistible, that but to inhabit the same orb with them is happiness supreme!"—

As he closed this flourish with another roll of his "*lack-lustre eye*,"[1] a newly imported Irish boy of Mrs. Cathcart's, whom she had ventured to employ as a candle-snuffer, stumbled in the execution of his office, and fell with the whole weight of his knee on Mangold's gouty[2] foot, which occasioned him such exquisite torture that he furiously roared out, "Murder! damn it! Murder!" but instantly recollecting himself, clenched his jaws together, and in silent misery, was assisted to a chair, where he sat amidst the condolences of the company, the most rueful looking object imaginable.

When the consternation, and bustle created by this accident had subsided, tea was brought in; and Emily, who happened to be seated between Kelroy, and Charles Cathcart, was very agreeably engaged, when a squabble near them between Doctor Blake, and a very prim old maid drew their attention.

He had spilt a cup of coffee on her dress; and although he made numerous apologies for the accident, which he said was owing "purely to his awe of *great people*," she rejected them with the utmost contempt; and when he offered to assist in wiping it off bid him "not dare to touch her, for she abominated Hottentots!"[3]

"Oh ho!" said he, "that's the way you begin to talk, is it?—I don't believe now after all, that you can tell where these same Hottentots are to be found?"

"Walk to the looking-glass," said she scornfully, "and you'll see one in perfection."

"And what shall I see," cried he, "if your ladyship should come there behind me?"

"Fie Doctor!" said Mrs. Cathcart, "how you talk!"

"Oh dear! it's of no sort of consequence!" said the lady, screwing her mouth, and fanning herself violently! "he may say what he pleases, for I shall make no manner of answer."

"Shant you? well, that will be a great grief to me,—I was in hopes now, that all would have blown over, and we might have had

---

1 Shakespeare, *As You Like It*, II.vii.21.
2 Gout is a painful type of arthritis that frequently affects the big toe.
3 The Dutch name (now considered derogatory) for the Khoikhoi tribe of southwestern Africa.

a little pleasant discourse together about these same Hottentots; for really, and in earnest now, they are not such silly people as you may think.—For instance if a body was to spill a quart of coffee over one of their women, she would not say a word about it."

"Sir," returned she, very angrily, "you are really—a very—strange person."

"Oh!" replied he, "you might have found that out before, if you had been cunning;—But remember one thing, my noble lady, for I'm going away, and I'll be bound you wont catch me near you again, in a hurry—always keep yourself cool when you've a mind to look beautiful."

He then got up and went to another part of the room, highly tickled with the diversion which he had created at her expense.

Card-tables were now introduced, and those who chose to play leaving their former seats unoccupied, a general remove took place. A few of the company prefered walking about, of which number was the doctor; and after examining separately every print, and ornament in the room, and feeling the paper on the walls in several places, as if to try whether the colours would rub off, he marched from one table to another, inspecting and applauding the different games to the great annoyance of the players.

Having pretty well satisfied his curiosity, and received a smart rebuff from Mrs. Hammond, over whose chair he had familiarly leaned to peep into her hand, he went up to Charles Cathcart, and seizing him by the arm, dragged him into one corner, where he began complaining of the affronts he had met with.

"Great people!" said he, holding up his hands, "grand quality!—tip-top gentry to be sure!—I'll be-hang'd if I hav'n't been at a husking-frollick in the country where they behav'd better!—I drop a spoonful of coffee on one ugly thing, 'you're a Hottentot,' says she.—I stand behind another old witch, and ask her a civil question, and she snaps my head off!—Oh! if these are your tea-drinkings, the mischief may take 'em for me!"

"Poh! nonsense man!" said Charles; "you must have done something amiss?["]

"I didn't though!—they both began at me for nothing!—as for that last one," pointing to Mrs. Hammond, ["]she looked so plaguy fierce, that I never even answered her. Oh, she's a clinker!—the devil himself wouldn't get the odd word from her, for a wager."

"Suppose you challenge her?" said Charles.

"Challenge her? why you don't think she'd fight?"

"If she is as angry as you appear to be, nothing short of a battle can settle the matter!"—

"My dear soul and friend!" cried he, taking Charles by the hand, "I am glad you put me in mind of it.—It's the most ridiculous thing alive to be in a passion at these small rubs from the women; so we'll say no more about it, and I'll just go by way of a change and attack some of your provender."

They then went to the side-board, where different refreshments were placed, and he began helping himself, and eating as he stood. Walsingham who had overheard the preceding dialogue, joined them in expectation of further amusement, nor was he disappointed, for the doctor began a whimsical disquisition on the opposite qualities of every different article he swallowed, which lasted till he could contain nothing more. Having demolished five ice creams, three jellies, and a pound or two of cake, and drank above a quart of lemonade, he said "it was poor washy stuff, enough to freeze a fellow's insides! a little brandy punch, and a *Spaniard*[1] after it, would have been as good again!"—He then complained of being very chilly; and saying loud enough for every body to hear, "that he would take a small bit of a walk to warm himself, and visit a patient or two yet to night," gravely made his best bow and marched off.

Emerging for the first time from a confinement of several weeks, and no longer watched, and interrupted by her mother, Emily enjoyed a degree of ease and pleasure to which she had long been a stranger. Yet frequently her thoughts reverted to the scenes of last evening, and the expressive eyes of Kelroy continually made her sensible how welcome such solitude would again be to him. He was convinced of her affection, and happy in her presence, but experienced a sort of vague discontent at the attentions which she received from several gentlemen, and felt as if every compliment they paid her was an infringement of his own rights.—"Yet thus," said he mentally, "must it ever be! thus would it be, even were she mine! for she is too lovely, too attractive to be seen with indifference in any situation! and can I complain that others should feel somewhat as I do? or that she should afford them the returns of common civility, whilst I am assured her heart is only mine?—Let me not be so unjust.—If I cannot behold this without pain, what must be my sensations when separated from her by a boundless ocean?—When *time*, and *space* shall leave room for possibilities, which absence may clothe with all the horrors of conviction?"

---

1 A Spanish drink, possibly sherry or hot chocolate, that was associated with the Spanish nobility.

Alternately buried in reflections like these, or forgetting them all in looking at, and listening to Emily, did Kelroy pass the hours, until the unwelcome voice of Mrs. Hammond announced to her daughters that it was "time to go home."—

When he retired to his chamber, the same train of ideas continued to haunt his imagination, and unable to rest he employed himself in composing the following stanzas.

> Vision of future woe, begone!
>> Nor thus thy troubled shade display,
> Dimming bright fancy's radiant throne,
>> And less'ning rapture's short-liv'd day!
>
> Ah! with the rose of hope, and youth,
>> Seek not thy cypress to entwine;
> But wait 'till age, or mournful truth,
>> Have chill'd this glowing heart of mine.
>
> Too soon arrives the fated hour,
>> Of with'ring grief and real care;—
> Then cease, reflection's gloomy power;
>> To man the *present* moment spare!—
>
> Unmix'd, oh! let him taste its bliss,
>> Since bliss on earth is seldom known;
> And evanescent joy like this,
>> Is all that he can call his own.

CHAPTER VIII.

SIX weeks had now elapsed since the marriage of Walsingham, and as the time originally appointed for his leaving America was already past, his departure could be deferred no longer, and the beginning of the following week was fixed on for that purpose.

He was anxious to return to his native country for many reasons.—Mrs. Hammond had appeared of late to be in a state of restless perturbation, which found no relief except in crouds of company. Sometimes too, she would be seized with fits of gloom entirely foreign to her natural character; and had begun to let fall hints of an intention to accompany her daughter, and settle in England, which was utterly distasteful to Walsingham, and not very pleasing to Lucy, who had her own reasons for wishing to be at a distance from her family; and she received not on these occasions the smallest encouragement from either of them. He had as yet discovered no other faults in his wife, than such as he thought very excusable in a beautiful woman who had been accustomed to flattery, and admiration from her cradle; and ascribing her trifling blemishes in a great measure to the improper management of her mother, congratulated himself on the power of removing her from such a counsellor, whilst her mind was sufficiently ductile to receive other, and better impressions. He had designed taking her to Savanna,[1] to visit his sister; but Lucy had understood that southern climates were extremely injurious to the complexion, and not choosing to risk hers for any such consideration, she created so many delays, and feigned so many difficulties, that he finally abandoned the scheme, and sacrificed his desire to her art and vanity; believing that in so doing he merely gratified her wish to remain as long as possible with her friends. A voyage to Britain presented no similar objection to this handsome icicle, but promised on the contrary, so much novelty and pleasure that she assented to the period of its commencement without a murmur.

Emily was much concerned at the approaching event, for although there subsisted little uniformity of sentiment between these sisters, the difference of their tastes and views had prevented any peculiar competition; and this great source of domestic discord thus obviated, natural affection supplied the place of well grounded esteem, and they had lived together in perfect harmony. But the radical defects of a character so opposite to her own, no partiality could altogether conceal; and sensible of Lucy's strange indifference towards the person who contributed so largely to the only species of happiness for which she appeared to have any relish, Emily feared that the time would arrive when Walsingham would no longer continue to be a blind, adoring husband, and lamented the possible consequences of such a change to her sister; whilst Lucy, in her turn compassionated Emily's attachment to Kelroy, as most unfortunate, both in regard to herself and her connexions; but although she pitied her weakness, inwardly rejoiced that she should not remain a witness of what she imagined would be its humiliating effects.

Kelroy made as frequent use as he could of the liberty he had obtained of seeing Emily, but such was the bustle and dissipation of her mother's house which was now increased by the hurry of visits, and preparations on Lucy's account, that he seldom saw

---

1 Savanna, Georgia.

her except in the company of others. Mrs. Hammond constantly treated him with politeness, but never with cordiality, and his dislike of her principles, and conviction of her intriguing temper hourly increased. She carefully avoided giving him an opportunity of conversing with her on the subject nearest his heart; and had repeated her injunctions to Emily, forbidding any promises as unnecessary, and cautioned her strongly against that exclusive attention of lovers to each other, that was indicative of their attachment, and disgusting to all beholders, who treasure up every mark of public preference, and should any accident prevent the intended union, fail not to adduce them afterwards to the ridicule and detriment of one or both parties.

Kelroy thought the latter part of the counsel not entirely amiss, could he have been assured respecting the purity of its motives; but the first appeared to him both absurd and tyrannical, and he argued strenuously against it to Emily, who could only reply that she was not at liberty to act otherwise, and entreated him not to urge her to a measure, which, if complied with, would inevitably produce some very positive, if not violent conduct in her mother. The visible regret which attended her soft, but firm refusals, seemed to him almost an equivalent to any vows that could have been uttered; and he would willingly have trusted to her voluntary fidelity, but for the apprehension of some contrivance on the part of Mrs. Hammond, to take advantage of it in his absence.

Helen Cathcart, whom Emily had made the confident of these perplexities, sincerely sympathized with her, but could offer no advice where the positive commands of a parent were in question. Having long suspected Emily's partiality, she had studied the character of Kelroy with scrupulous attention; and believing from the result of her observations, that he was in every respect calculated to render her happy, she had earnestly hoped that he might meet with the approbation of Mrs. Hammond, whose well-known opinions in similar instances, forbade her, nevertheless to expect it; and she received the account of her dubious conduct with regret, but without any surprise. Better capable of judging, because less warmly interested than Emily, she viewed each circumstance in its proper light, and argued from many of them much future uneasiness to her young friend; but finding Emily rather sanguine in her hopes of the event, she forbore to damp her expectations, and add to the tumult of her thoughts, by insinuations of which time only could ascertain the truth.

Two days previous to his departure Walsingham gave a large dinner, to which he invited indiscriminately every gentleman to whom he considered himself indebted for any particular civilities. In the evening an entertainment was made by Mrs. Hammond, as a final return for the attentions which had been paid to Lucy; and the few gentlemen who remained at table after the company had collected above stairs, were requested by Walsingham to join them in the drawing room.

One of them, Mr. Marney, was a stranger to the ladies of the family, and might have been considered handsome, but for an occasional scowl which crept over his features; disfiguring them by an expression of evil, which, although seldom analysed, generally lessened that prepossession in his favour which his first appearance had inspired.

This Mr. Marney was one of those beings who may be said to spring from nobody knows where; and rise in the world nobody can tell how; and spend the latter half of their lives in striving to erase from the minds of the community all remembrance of the former.—But rumour, which no efforts can compel to perfect silence, ascribed his birth to a distant spot, and very humble parents, by whom he was bred a mechanic of the lowest order; and after a few years application to his trade, acquired a little sum which prompted him to leave his native place in search of adventures; and aided by those unaccountable causes which frequently influence human affairs, he rose rapidly from a state of indigence to the possession of an immense fortune; and filled with ideas of his own importance and ingenuity, determined to commence a buck of the first order,[1] without delay.—Accordingly he removed to a part of the town where there was not much danger of his being incommoded by any of his old companions; dressed in the extreme of the fashion, talked sparingly where his ignorance was in danger of detection; and in a short time contrived to introduce himself to the notice of a few well bred individuals of his own sex, whose manners he copied with tolerable success, and whose favour he secured by an affectation of generosity and profusion; whilst his real avarice was such, as induced him to practise in secret the most disgusting meanness.

By degrees, as his wealth became known, his vulgar origin was overlooked, or forgotten; and conceiving himself thoroughly

---

1   A dashing fellow of a high social class. In its definition of "buck," the *Oxford English Dictionary* notes that "in the 18th c. the word indicated rather the assumption of 'spirit' or gaiety of conduct than elegance of dress; the latter notion comes forward early in the 19th century."

established in genteel society, he assumed all the airs of consequential fastidiousness, which toleration, and assurance could aspire—affected to be a complete connosseur in matters of taste—invariably lost his stomach whenever a speck was to be seen on his plate, or the flies presumed to soil the transparency of his tumbler—sung and cracked his bamboo[1] on his boots as he passed through the streets—met the people who had befriended him in the days of his humility with as much forgetfulness, and indifference as they if they had been so many posts—and never was known to be out of countenance, except when some allusion was made to his former mode of life.

He possessed a great deal of low cunning, which enabled him to discern and take advantage of the weaknesses of others, in numerous instances; and an immoderate share of curiosity, which extended itself to the merest trifles, and rendered him little better than a spy upon his acquaintance, whom he was in the habit of surprising with details of domestic incidents, and concerns which they had imagined an entire secret; and the confusion which he often created by the display of such knowledge was the delight of his heart; although had the methods by which he obtained it been known, he would, nine times in ten, have risked being kicked out of doors.—He had frequently seen Mrs. Hammond and her daughters in public, and was languishing for an opportunity of making himself known to them, when the invitation from Walsingham, whom he had most assiduously courted for the purpose, presented the desired opening; and having through his usual channels of information, the servants, heard of the plan for the evening, he resolutely kept his post, together with Kelroy, Charles Cathcart, and some others, until he was, as he had foreseen, requested to join the party above stairs.

He was recognised on his entrance by several of the company, and a whisper was circulated that Mr. Marney was there.

"Mr. Marney!" said Emily, "I have not the honour of knowing him."

Helen Cathcart who was near her, was slightly acquainted with him, and at her request pointed him out.

"He is very handsome!" said Emily.

"You will be of a different opinion half an hour hence," said Helen.

---

1   A bamboo cane was an indispensible accessory for a "buck of the first order" in late eighteenth-century Philadelphia.

"Why so?" inquired Emily. "Is his face like the moon, subject to changes?"

"His features may remain the same," replied Helen, "but he is such a vile scandal-monger, that his looks have become as odious to me as his stories."

Here, Walsingham who had gone through the ceremony of introducing him to Mrs. Hammond and Lucy, approached with him towards Emily, to whom he made his bow, in great form, and then retreated to that customary rendesvous of the gentlemen, the fire-place, where he found several quondam[1] friends of his own amidst the group, which had assembled, as usual, for the double purpose of warming their heels, and whispering their remarks on the surrounding circle.

"An extremely handsome woman, that Mrs. Walsingham!" said Marney conceitedly, "I do not think I ever saw a more complete Roman nose in my life!"

"Roman, my dear sir!" said Mr. Mangold in astonishment; "Why Mrs. Walsingham's nose is a perfect model of the Grecian!"

"Exactly so! that was what I meant to say!" replied he.

"She is certainly handsome;" said a Mr. Drayton, "but she has an air of *hauteur* which does not altogether please me."

"Dignity, sir," said Marney, "nothing but dignity! I like dignity in a woman, it serves to keep fops, and vulgar fellows at a distance."

"But what is your opinion of Miss Emily," said Mr. Mangold, "she is thought by many persons, to be much handsomer than her sister."

"Um!—why she is a lively, delicate little thing, but I don't like all that hair, dangling about her eyes.—Besides she appears to me to want the high fashionable polish of Mrs. Walsingham."

"In what respect is it wanting?" said Mr. Mangold, "Have you discovered her to be deficient in politeness?"

"Not at all sir!—quite the contrary.—But there seems to be a sort of easiness about her, which borders rather more upon familiarity, than is usual with persons in her style."

"So then, in order to please you, Mr. Marney," said Charles Cathcart, "a lady must season her manners with a good portion of wholesome scorn?—Nor is this the only particular in which you have the honour of being singular: you are the first man, I believe, who has ever taken exception to any thing in the appearance of Miss Emily Hammond."

---

1 Former (Latin).

"Apostates are frequently converted into zealous worshippers," said Mr. Mangold, "and the little blind god will, I doubt not, revenge as he ought, the wrong offered to one of the brightest auxiliaries of his power."

Not exactly comprehending this speech, he would not venture upon an answer, but began criticising the company at large.

"Do but look at Mrs. Clinton!—My God! did you ever see such a head in your life?—I'll take my oath the curls in that wig are made of iron!—And there's her husband, with his lanthorn jaws,[1] and tobacco-pipe shanks just behind her!—And there's Hayward's niece, with her long scrawny neck—zounds what a figure she is!—Well, I'm surprised that any body can admire Miss Thompson!"

"Why not?" said Mr. Drayton, "she is generally allowed to be a very elegant girl."

"Her feet are too big, she'd ruin a man in shoes."

"I perceive, Mr. Marney," said Mangold, "that there is a degree of economy blended with your refinement?"

"Oh no: I don't speak for that, either," replied he, "but who likes a girl with such a pair of stampers?—Why she covers a good half yard, every time she sets one of them to the ground.—But what do you think of her cousin, that great broad shouldered thing yonder?"

"I think her a lady," replied Charles Cathcart.

"That's more than I do!—I wonder who ever saw a lady with such paws?—Why they are as red as a couple of boiled lobsters!"

Unfortunately his gloves happened to be off, as he uttered this, which Charles observing, said with an arch glance, "if our claims to gentility are to be decided by the delicacy of our hands, heaven help some of the present company!"

He coloured like scarlet, and thrusting his own rugged hands hastily into his pockets, complained of the intolerable heat of the fire, which he said he could bear no longer; and, retreating to a distant part of the room, took a seat next to Mrs. Hammond, and began complimenting her on the fanciful style in which the drapery of her curtains was arranged; and finding his flattery well received, poured forth such a profusion of civil speeches, that they presently became upon the best terms imaginable.

"Lord! my dear!" said Mrs. Cathcart, running up to Emily,

---

1 I.e., with his thin face. Lanthorn is a corruption of lantern; lanthorn-jawed means having nearly transparent cheeks.

"what a fine, new beau you've got here this evening!—I've just been telling your mama all about him."

"To whom do you allude, madam?" said Emily.

"Why to Mr. Marney to be sure!—don't you see!—he's talking to her himself now.—He's one of the finest fortunes in town, and all the girls are ready to pull caps for him[1] except our Helen there, and she cares for nobody, gentle or simple. I often tell her she'll be an old maid, she's so hard to please—but I hope you will be wiser, and not let such a conquest slip through your fingers for want of a few smiles!—"

"You are very good ma'am," said Emily, laughing, yet blushing that Kelroy who was now at her side should hear such a proposition, "but I believe it is fortunate that I am not inclined to make the attempt."

"I think so too," said Helen, "for you certainly would have to contend with a formidable rival."

"And who is that, I wonder?" said Mrs. Cathcart.

"*The innocent Fidelio*,[2] who lives with his back against the wall," said Helen.

"Oh! you mean the looking glass, I suppose," said Mrs. Cathcart, "but la! what then? Can't people admire themselves and others too?"

"Aye!" cried Walsingham, who now joined them, and whose spirits were a little elevated in consequence of having presided as master of the feast, "that they can! And if any body doubts it, let them look there!—Yonder is Marney unlocking all the flood-gates of eloquence, to give vent to his violent admiration of Mrs. Hammond."

"And pray what is he saying?" cried Mrs. Cathcart.

"Every thing that is gay, and gallant," cried Walsingham, ["]and if he goes on as he has begun, it is impossible to say how matters may end.—Emily, how would you like him for a papa?"

"A papa indeed?" cried Mrs. Cathcart, "how you talk!—Why I've just been recommending him to her for a husband."

"That may be," said Walsingham, "but if you will step and listen, you will find that he is recommending himself elsewhere in a manner that will leave her small hopes."

"Why you can't possibly be in earnest?" said Mrs. Cathcart, with a look of amazement.

Walsingham nodded his head.

---

1 To choose him as a potential husband.
2 A reference to "The Transformation of Fidelio into a Looking-glass," *The Spectator* 392 (30 May 1712).

"I'll go and see, this very minute," cried she, and away she bustled, and before Emily had time to ask Walsingham what he meant, several persons approached, and he soon after left them.

Mrs. Hammond was possessed of very good sense, and no inconsiderable share of discernment, when it was not obscured by her reigning foible; but to that she sacrificed every thing, and by that alone suffered herself to be guided; and merit was depressed without remorse, and ignorance, and stupidity courted, and advanced without scruple, whenever her interest demanded it.—Having first learned from Mrs. Cathcart, and had her assurances of Marney's solid claims to approbation confirmed by Mr. Mangold, she would have been slow to observe his mental deficiencies, even had he refrained from seeking particularly to insinuate himself into her good graces; but when to her knowledge of his great riches, and disengaged situation, was added an obvious wish on his part to please, expressed in liberal encomiums on herself, and her numerous amiable qualities, interspersed with praises of her daughters, for resembling her, certain ideas presented themselves to her mind, and she no longer beheld him in any one point of view, as an exceptionable character.—Had she been younger, she would without hesitation have ascribed his language to the effect of her beauty; but though conscious that she was still remarkably well-looking for her age, she was too thoroughly versed in human nature, to suppose that a woman near fifty could excite any very tender emotions in a man of thirty five. Her understanding prevented her from being the dupe of her vanity in this particular, but she quickly consoled herself by fancying that her talents, and address, unaccompanied by personal views, would be sufficient to mould him to any purpose she pleased, and hastily arranging with herself a new scheme of politics, she listened to his trite remarks and borrowed witticisms with perfect complacency; and permitted him, unreproved, to assail her with the most extravagant compliments.

In paying his court to Mrs. Hammond, Marney was impelled, in the first instance, by the confusion into which he had been thrown by Charles Cathcart; and to free himself from some very unpleasant sensations, sat down where chance directed him, and uttered rapidly he scarcely knew what, such was his rage, and consternation at the moment; but by degrees, as his disturbance subsided, he observed the favourable ear which was accorded him by the mistress of the mansion, and having understood that she was remarkable for pride, and haughtiness to her inferiors, he immediately concluded from her manner, that she thought him a person of distinguished consequence. This notion exalted her at once in his estimation, and feeling his scattered ideas of his own importance return with every sentence which she addressed to him, his gratified conceit prompted him to talk to her in a style which opened to her busy imagination a field of future action; and instead of discouraging his unmeaning prate, she adroitly impressed him with a belief that she entertained the highest respect for his judgment, and had already devoted to him a much larger portion of time, than is usually on such occasions bestowed on one person.

Meanwhile, Marney grew somewhat tired of the long conversation he had held with her. He thought her a mighty agreeable old lady, and was charmed with having secured her approbation; but in the plenitude of his restored good humour, he recollected that there were others present, who might possibly deem themselves neglected; and desirous of dispensing his civilities as equitably as possible, he was anxiously awaiting an opportunity to escape, which she seemed, however, by no means inclined to afford him.

Mrs. Cathcart, who had sidled towards them, to discover what was going forward, was filled with wonder at the speeches she overheard; and her curiosity urging her gradually to advance, she at length stood almost before them, unnoticed by Mrs. Hammond, who was in the midst of an animated reply to something Marney had said in commendation of her. He waited until she had finished speaking, and perceiving that Mrs. Cathcart remained standing hastily rose and offered her his chair, apologizing for not having done it sooner, by saying "he was so agreeably occupied, that he did not see her," and without staying for an answer, walked away.

Mrs. Cathcart sat down in silence, and Mrs. Hammond reading in her countenance an expression of more meaning than it usually wore, inquired whether she had anything to communicate?—Poor Mrs. Cathcart longed to say "yes," and give vent to the doubts which oppressed her, but her awe of her *dear friend* was at all times very great, and fearful of offending her dignity, she answered in the negative; and having asked two or three questions on indifferent subjects, found that Mrs. Hammond scarcely heard her. Convinced from this that Walsingham's insinuation was just, she presently removed to the opposite side of the apartment, and pushed her way among a cluster of ladies, who to her great relief, happened to be discussing the propensity which widows generally have to marriage. She eagerly joined in the conversation, and not only advocated the custom, but enumerated various instances of elderly widows, who had married men much younger than themselves, and lived happily with them; and finding nobody inclined to agree with her, defended her opinion with pertinacious obstinacy and clamour against every argument to the contrary; believing that in so doing she probably advocated the cause of friendship, and might be entitled hereafter not only to thanks for her kindness, but applause for her sagacity.

After leaving Mrs. Hammond, Mr. Marney strutted up to Mrs. Walsingham, whose dignity was so much to his taste, but found that lady very little disposed to regard him.—She was talking with a gentleman lately from Europe, who was describing to her the brilliant spectacles he had witnessed in Paris; and as the subject was perfectly agreeable to her, as according in some measure with the expectations which she entertained for herself, she did not choose to relinquish it.—A few months earlier, he would probably have met with a different reception; but her fortune was now made, and she considered herself at liberty to act as she pleased. She therefore held his advances very cheap, and presently made him sensible that she considered his presence as an intrusion.—Piqued by her careless answers, he no longer felt inclined to admire her Grecian nose, but stalked off towards her sister, whose beauty, although he had affected to depreciate it, had always appeared to him peculiarly engaging.

Not one of the little party who were merrily enjoying themselves in a corner, were at all pleased at his approach. Helen disliked him; and Emily, from the account she had heard of him, was not ambitious of his notice.—Kelroy thought him a ridiculous compound of foppery and ignorance; and the others, a couple of very young girls, who had just entered into company, were too much intimidated by his known habits of mimicry, and ill-nature to utter a syllable.

"Miss Cathcart," said he, bowing to Helen, "I hope you are well?—I have not had the pleasure of seeing you, I believe, since the night we met at Miss Wilmer's.—What a time that was hey?—By Jupiter, I never saw so many fat women together in one place since I was born! there was no such thing as stirring for them!—"

"You contrived to stir, Mr. Marney, notwithstanding," replied she, "for if I mistake not, you danced with the fattest of them all."

"My God, yes!—so I did!—don't you remember my fat cotillion?—Faith I shall never forget it the longest day I have to live!—Ma'am," said he, turning to Emily, "I pitched upon four, the least of them double the size of a bale of cotton; and Harris, Ryland, young Wilmer, and myself got at them, and persuaded them to dance.—Heavens! what a piece of work it was!—we had to squeeze through the figure at the risque of being suffocated; and every time one of them moved a limb, the house shook to the very foundation."

"According to your description, it must have been rather a hazardous experiment, sir!—" said Kelroy.

"Hazardous?—By the lord Harry it was little short of an earthquake!—and then to see them rolling off to their seats after it was over!—Phoo-o-o! says one, I'm just ready to die!—Give me a fan, says another, for I never was in such a heat in my life!—Oh lord, says the third, I hav'n't danc'd a step since I was married, 'till to night!—and as for the fourth, faith! she could not speak at all, but she made it up in blowing!—you might have heard her a hundred yards off, like a race horse, after a four-mile heat."

"I hope," said Emily, "the ladies did not discover that they were selected because of their size?"

"No ma'am! no! not until we had got them into the middle of the floor, and then it was too late. But if you had only seen their astonishment!—there they stood, like so many tons of hay, wondering at one another, and hardly knowing whether to laugh or cry! By Jupiter, it was a capital sight! I would not have missed such a joke for the universe."

"If we are to judge from the value you place on it," said Helen, "it must have afforded you infinitely more amusement than it did any other person?—"

"Oh! Miss Cathcart! you know every soul there was in a perfect roar; and you yourself were as much diverted as any body, for I heard you say so!—But have you heard any news lately?"

"None, except what is contained in the public papers," replied Helen.

"Well ma'am, then I shall have the pleasure of telling you some.—Your friend Lætitia is to be married to night."

"Indeed?" said Helen, "pray how did you learn that?—"

"Why, I called there this morning, and happening to go in without knocking, found the whole house in confusion; the maids thumping away with mops and scrubbing brushes, and scampering about, as if old Nick[1] was at their heels; and the old lady seated in the back parlour with a pile of glass before her, as high as Christ

---

1 The devil.

Church steeple.[1] Presently a fellow brought in a basket, and put it on the table, and called his mistress out of the room; and while she was gone, I took a peep into it, and saw a cake big enough to feast the St. Tammany society.[2] After she came back, I tried to get out of her what was going forward, but she would not tell; and when I was going away, I met John at the door, just coming from market, with a wheel-barrow loaded to the brim. I stopped just to look at a devilish fine rock fish that was laying on the top, and John let the whole secret out in a hurry."

The astonishment of Kelroy, and Emily at this elegant detail was extreme, and they looked at each other with countenances sufficiently indicative of their sentiments; but Helen, desirous of trying how far he would go, said with pretended earnestness, "and is this all?—did you hear nothing more?"

"No, not much, only that it was knocked up in a great hurry, and her relations in the country were sent for, and they were to have a monstrous wedding, and a handsome supper, much against the will of the old man, who is cursed stingy.—But faith! they've contrived to squeeze his purse somehow; for I counted in the wheelbarrow four pair of ducks, six fowls, two turkies, a calves head, two tongues, some game, and a ham, besides the fish I told you of, and fifty other things I had not time to take notice of, for while I was standing, John saw his master coming round the corner."

"What a pity," said Helen, "that such an interesting conversation should have been interrupted!—If it had lasted a few minutes longer, John would have made you master of the whole arrangement of the affair, from the garret to the cellar."

Not altogether relishing the ironical air with which this was spoken, he made no answer, but affected to examine a small Italian painting which hung near him, and turning to Kelroy, said very importantly, "I never heard, for my part, that Adam had more than *one* wife, and here they have given him *three!*"

"Have they really?" replied Kelroy, with an involuntary smile.

"Yes faith!—and here they stand all in a row. But where's the snake?—I don't see the snake?—"

---

1 Philadelphia's Christ Church was built between 1727 and 1744; its steeple, completed in 1754, made it the tallest building in North America.
2 A Philadelphia patriotic society formed in 1772, the St. Tammany Society was named for the seventeenth-century Lenape sachem Tamanend. Dr. Benjamin Rush (1746–1813), Rebecca Rush's uncle, was a member.

"Perhaps," said Helen, biting her lips, "he has hid himself in the grass."

"But how are we to be sure of that?" replied he, staring at her. "In all the pictures I ever saw of the garden of Eden, the snake was placed full in view; and I think it a great fault in the painter to have omitted it here."

"I think not," said Kelroy, "for this piece is intended to represent the judgment of Paris."

"The judgment of Paris, hey?—" replied he; ["]Why then I suppose this fellow with the apple in his hand, is meant for Bonaparte?"[1]

This was almost too much for the self-command of them all; but although they refrained from open laughter, Marney saw enough in their countenances to convince him that he had made some blunder; and, ignorant of its extent, he stood looking like a fool, afraid to speak, and ashamed to be silent; until Emily, from a motive of politeness, tried to relieve him by inquiring if he was fond of paintings?

"Extremely fond of them, indeed ma'am;" replied he, deceived by the mild gravity of her manner into a hope that his error was a slight one; "few people more so.—I generally visit the academy every day, and amuse myself with listening to the different remarks that are made.[2]—I have a picture at home, which I have thoughts of sending there.—One that belonged to my father."

"Is it a representation of the old gentleman himself, or the family residence?" said Helen drily.

"Neither ma'am," replied he colouring at the question; and desirous of changing the subject, asked Emily whether she did not sing?—she replied in the affirmative, and he then requested to have the pleasure of hearing her.—Glad of any escape from his stupid conversation, she immediately complied, and sung with her accustomed excellence; and as he happened to have a tolerable ear for music, he ventured to compliment her without much fear of again committing

---

1 This conversation, in which Marney mistakes the familiar painting of *The Judgment of Paris* for a picture of Eve in the Garden of Eden, and then muddles the mythical figure of Paris with Napoleon Bonaparte, reveals Marney's ignorance of Greek mythology, the Bible, current events, and fine art.

2 The Philadelphia Academy of Fine Arts was founded in 1805, opened as a museum in 1807, and held its first exhibition of more than 500 paintings and statues in 1811.

himself. Her voice was greatly to his taste, but the readiness with which she had obliged him was infinitely more so; and ascribing it without hesitation to some impression in his favour, he warmly intreated her to sing again. The eager interest of his manner was by no means pleasing to her, and she politely, but positively declined; and Kelroy, far from aiding the request as others did, internally rejoiced in her resistance.—Marney however would take no denial, and continued to press her, until Mrs. Hammond who had observed with delight his approaches to Emily, chanced to overhear something of the contest; and having learnt from whence it proceeded, instantly laid her commands on her daughter to comply.

The second song was attended with a repetition of the praises which had attended the first, and enchanted with Emily, whom he now began to hope was not, as report said, attached to Kelroy, he persisted in following her wherever she went, and talking to her without cessation for the remainder of the evening. Kelroy, restless, and uneasy, endeavoured by every means in his power to obstruct his attentions; but neither his efforts, nor the taciturnity of Emily, who was both wearied, and disgusted, could avail against the united manœuvers of Marney and Mrs. Hammond, and she was compelled to support a spiritless conversation with him, until the company began to retire.

Kelroy still lingered with a view of outstaying him, but Marney was in no haste to leave a house where he had found so many attractions; and having waited until no one remained except the Cathcarts, Kelroy, and himself, they at length all took leave at the same time.

The night was remarkably fine, and Charles Cathcart having placed his mother and sister in the carriage, declined entering it himself, saying he preferred walking home.—Marney and Kelroy who were standing on the pavement, both heard this declaration, and the former proposed that they should all walk together; but Kelroy, determined to evince his contempt of the forward fool who had tormented him for the last two hours, no sooner saw the carriage drive away, than he very cavalierly turned from him in the midst of a question concerning Mrs. Hammond's age, and seizing Charles by the arm, went off in a different direction, leaving him to digest the affront at his leisure.

CHAPTER IX.

THE next day, which proved rainy, was spent at home languor on the part of Mrs. Hammond, regret on that of Emily, and by Lucy with a mixture of impatience, and indifference which accorded with her character. Her thoughts were occupied solely by her approaching voyage and its consequences to herself; and she was continually putting questions concerning the probable duration of it; wondering whether or not she should be sea-sick; and conjecturing the effect which the terrors of a storm might produce on her nerves.

Mrs. Hammond listened to her with the fondest attention, answered her without perceiving the extreme selfishness of her ideas, and frequently shed tears of bitter anguish at the necessity of parting with this darling, and fortunate child. The proud, fantastic notions which had supported her while the event was at a distance began to fail; and the recollection of certain private embarrassments, which now presented themselves to her imagination with augmented force completed her dejection. Yet, in the midst of feelings which were strong in proportion to the vigour with which they had hitherto been repressed, the native bias of her mind still prevailed, and she experienced a sort of satisfaction from being thus enabled to indulge a double sorrow at the expense of a single apparent motive.

Walsingham passed part of the morning with Kelroy, whom he found filled with disturbance, occasioned in part by Mrs. Hammond's cordial reception and artful encouragement of Marney, but more by something he had heard about an hour before in a grocer's shop, where he had called by appointment to receive a small sum of money from the man who kept it, a shrewd Scotchman. Whilst he was there, a tall boy came in, and going up to his master said, "Well sir, I saw the lady, and said what you ordered me."

"And have ye brought nothing back with ye?" said the grocer.

"No sir, she said it was not convenient for her to pay you now, but that in a couple of weeks she should settle with you."

"Settle with the de'il! she has lived in this toun *five* months, and I have supplied her with every thing in my line the whole o' that time, and it is not a little that has served her, but I have not yet been so lucky as to see the colour of her money, and what is far worse, am afraid I never shall, until I go to work roughly for it."

"These are accidents," said Kelroy, "to which men in trade are unfortunately always liable."

"Yes sir, yes—but this is a *take-in* that few would have expected, any more than myself. This is a person who has the credit of great riches, and I have been trusting her 'till the amount of several hundreds, without asking for a penny, and should have trusted her as many more in the same way, if I had not luckily had a brother-in-law who is a sort of a broker, and some time ago, talking with him of one matter or other in business, I chanced to mention that I had a smart payment to make up in a few days, but that Mrs. *Such a one* owed me *so much*, and I supposed it was only ask and have. I am not so sure of that says he. A'n't you? says I, and I should be glad to know why? So then he told me, that he had reason to think she was hard pushed for money, and wanted more than she had means to raise; and faith, I have good cause to believe him; for I have either called or sent almost every day since but the de'il a shilling can I get out of her. But this work will not do for me! money I want and money I will have, if not by fair means, why by foul! With her carriage and her servants stuck up behind her, stopping here like a duchess to leave me first one order and then another, and was served quick as hands could do it! But when I want to be paid, it is *to-morrow*, and *next day* and *next week*! augh! damn such doings I say!" exclaimed he in a rage, and running to the other end of the shop, began tying up some parcels in a great hurry, which having finished, he threw them into a basket, and going back to his desk, wrote a short note, and calling his boy, bid him take those things to the person who had purchased them, and, putting the note into his hands, told him it would be all in his way to call and leave that with mistress *Haimond*.

"Mrs. who?" said Kelroy off his guard with surprise, "surely you do not mean Mrs. *Hammond*?"

"Aye but I do sir!—I mean Mistress *Haimond*, the great Mistress *Haimond*, who has money enough for every thing but to pay her debts; and if you're a friend of hers, as it's like you may be, you will do both her and me a kindness by advising her to let me have my due as soon as possible."

Words cannot express the astonishment of Kelroy on thus learning that the proud, scornful Mrs. Hammond, who looked upon half the community as fit only to be trampled under her feet, should render herself liable to be sued for a demand of this nature; and after asking the grocer several questions, all of which he answered in such a way as to leave no doubt of the truth of what he had been saying; and advising him not to be too precipitate in forcing the discharge of a debt which had been perhaps accidentally delayed, he went home, and was walking the floor in a state of melancholy reflection when Walsingham came in, who observing his dejection, suspected it arose from an apprehension that Marney would endeavour to supplant him, and be favoured in his designs by Mrs. Hammond, and told him so.—Kelroy did not deny it, and in discussing her strange temper, and singular conduct, Walsingham mentioned as an instance of it, her treatment of himself, when applied to for her consent to his marriage with Lucy, and the circumstance of her withholding that young lady's fortune, "which," continued he, "although of little consequence to me at present, is certainly in itself a very unwarrantable proceeding, founded on a love of idle parade, and dissipation, which she will never be prevailed on to relinquish but with her existence.—However, as it must be ours at last, I shall not dispute with her the pleasure which the possession of it a few years longer may afford, but I am at once astonished, and irritated that she should act in the same manner towards Emily, and ungenerously protract, if not prevent a union which might, were she disposed to conduct herself as she ought, take place without delay.—Mr. Hammond left no regular will I have understood; and from his widow it is impossible to obtain the slightest knowledge on the subject—but that prating Mrs. Cathcart, whom I once sounded for the purpose, assured me he died immensely rich, and in his last extremity, bequeathed by a verbal testament one half of his property to be divided between his children, and the other to the entire disposal of their mother, who, feeling her consequence, chooses to retain the whole of it in her power—and there it seems likely to continue; for she avoids all conversation of the kind as scrupulously as if she dreaded furnishing me with information sufficient to commence a suit against her."

Kelroy, whose wishes to fathom the motives which actuated this tormenting woman, were quickened by the suspense in which she persisted to hold the dearest interests of his future life, and who had already begun to suspect there was "*something rotten in the state of Denmark*,"[1] could by no means reconcile such facts as these, and what he had learned from the grocer, with the belief of the independent fortunes which these ladies were said to inherit from their father. He listened to the account which Walsingham gave of her wariness on that occasion, and total silence since with unbounded surprise, and fancying himself possessed of a clue to all her measures, scrupled not to declare that he believed the report of her wealth to be merely an invention of her own, formed for the purpose of imposing on the world—adducing

---

1 Shakespeare, *Hamlet*, I.iv.90.

in support of his opinion, what he just heard from one of her creditors, together with her known ambition, her eagerness to dispose of her eldest daughter, at the price, most probably, of being removed from her forever; and the visible care with which she sought the acquaintance, and cultivated the regard of every monied man who could be supposed to entertain matrimonial views; doubtless with a hope of forming a connexion equally advantageous for Emily, which could she effect, the remainder of her task would be easy; since, having carried the deception to that point, she might, by residing with her children, continue it to the end of her days.

Walsingham, who amidst the variety of conjectures to which her reserve had given birth, had surmised nothing of this kind, was much struck with these inferences, and upon revolving in his mind all he had heard, became inclined to think Kelroy in the right—yet, when he reflected on the elegance in which she lived, the profusion she seemed to delight in, and the confidence with which he had heard her speak publicly of her possessions and resources, the thing appeared incredible!—But he also recollected that she owed him nine hundred dollars, borrowed on different pretences; and as the time had now arrived, when if she meant to return it before he left her, she must of course do so within a few hours, he thought that this circumstance might lead to some tolerably just estimate of her situation, and determined to conduct himself accordingly.—Waving [sic] therefore, any further conversation respecting the state of her affairs, until better qualified to judge of them, he asked Kelroy whether he had ever had an opportunity of speaking to her himself on the subject of his attachment?

"Never," replied Kelroy, "although I have repeatedly sought one. She shuns me with the greatest care, as often as she perceives me desirous of conversing with her; and the information I have gained this day not only explains to me the true ground of that obstinate, and ill-concealed dislike, which every endeavour of mine has proved insufficient to lessen, but leaves me without a hope that she will be prevailed on to relent in my favour. The promise she has obtained from Emily is held sacred by her; and I shall be compelled to leave her at last without consolation or security, beyond the strength of her own affection—and when I reflect on the uncertainty of my prospects, and the intriguing, determined spirit of her mother, my feelings are sometimes very little short of distraction."

"She is indeed," replied Walsingham, "a compound of pride,

and haughtiness, but whether wholly deficient in honour, and principle, remains to be tried."

"With you it may," returned Kelroy, "but I have long been convinced that she possesses neither, and would, without compunction, sacrifice her child to the veriest wretch in nature—aye, by heaven! Sell her to a Jew, or a Turk to grace his seraglio, provided she herself were to be exalted by the bargain!—"

"My dear fellow," said Walsingham, who could not help smiling at his vehemence, "do not be so bitter!—you have, I confess, no great reason to venerate her, but whatever her other failings may be, she has at least never shewn herself wanting in parental affection; and her opposition to you arises more, I should hope, from the caution of age, and a wish to ensure her child's happiness, than such infamous designs, as you imagine."

"And what," said Kelroy, with asperity, "are her ideas of happiness? To inhabit a spacious dwelling, and clothed in all the extravagance of fashionable attire, and furnished with the means of indulging in every modern folly, live only to create pity in the wise, and wonder, and envy in fools!—My soul sickens when I think of her!—She seems like my evil genius, scattering doubt, and frowning darkness wherever she moves."

"Well, I will endeavour to be your good one," said Walsingham, "and as I have some magic arguments at my command which you are unacquainted with, I would advise you not to despond until you hear the result of them.—I cannot promise you success, but I will do every thing in my power to promote it; and I trust you know me sufficiently to believe it would afford me infinite satisfaction to see you relieved from these perplexities before we part?"

"I have experienced your friendship too often to become a sceptic now," said Kelroy, "but you must deal in *real* sorcery, I think, before you can prevail on Mrs. Hammond to confirm the pretensions of a man in my situation."

"I will deal with her," replied Walsingham, "like one who finds his forbearance not only useless to himself, but rendered an instrument of tyranny to others.—My time is short, and my methods must be somewhat more coercive than I could wish,—but as there certainly has been something singular in her conduct towards us both, I consider myself fully entitled to exert them. Should they fail, your hopes must rest on the caprice of Mrs. Hammond; but if they succeed, you may give your fears to the wind, for I shall not proceed by halves."

"And what means can you possibly pursue, that will have any

weight with her?" said Kelroy. "She has told you already, that nothing shall induce her to alter her resolution!—"

"I cannot stay to tell you now," cried Walsingham, "for I have much to attend to, and not a moment to lose—but I will see you again at five o'clock, and surprise you, I hope with the history of my *generalship*."

They then parted. Kelroy went to visit his mother, and Walsingham employed himself in settling some business which had been unavoidably protracted to this late period of his stay in America, and when he returned home, found them waiting dinner for him.

"Oh! you are come, are you?" said Lucy, entering the room as they were about to seat themselves at table. "I began to suspect you had set sail without me.—Where in the world have you been, all this time?—"

"Very disagreeably engaged, my love, during the latter part of it, in persuading people to pay their debts."

"I hope you were successful?"

"Oh, yes—it was a case of necessity, and I was obliged to be positive.—I have a foolish facility in *lending* which deserves to be severely checked; but I have met with one or two impositions in that way lately, which I think will prove a warning to me."

He looked at Mrs. Hammond as he spoke. A faint colour tinged her face, which was naturally rather pale, and her eyes met his with a glance of keen inquiry.—Finding herself observed by him, she slightly contracted her brows, and almost immediately recovering her countenance, remained silent, and apparently unconcerned as before.

"You have found your experience a dear purchase, I apprehend?" said Lucy, after a short pause.

"Tolerably so," replied Walsingham, "but I am glad to have escaped so well. I have recovered all except about nine hundred, or a thousand dollars."

"And when are you to get that?"

"Never, I fancy; if I may presume to judge from appearances."

These hints were so plain, so direct, so unlike the usual delicacy of Walsingham, that Mrs. Hammond could scarcely credit her own senses. Knowing her inability to return the sum in question, and fearing to reply to his remarks, lest she should seem to suppose them meant for herself, she sat frying with indignation, which her utmost self-command could scarcely restrain within proper bounds.

"Well, it is mighty odd, I think," said Lucy, "that you should be so willing to throw your money away to accommodate strangers, who, most probably would never do the same for you in return."

Mrs. Hammond breathed again at this.

It was evident Lucy was not in the secret, and she began to hope she had mistaken Walsingham's drift also.—

"You are right Lucy," replied he, "neither of the persons whom I have obliged, would submit voluntarily, I believe, to the smallest inconvenience to serve me.—I am sometimes tempted to turn miser, that I may have my pockets picked, and my feelings imposed upon no longer."

"O fie!" exclaimed Emily. "Would you permit the meanness and ingratitude of a few individuals to deprive you of that disinterested generosity which places their turpitude in the worst light, and finds an unfailing reward in its own benevolent intentions?—"

"That is a fine speech sister," said Lucy, "but you forget that people may be led by such wild sentiments to part with every thing; and when that is the case, they seldom find the fame of their former generosity procure for them much consideration."

"Emily is an enthusiast;" said Walsingham, "she puts her head out of the question, and reasons only from her heart."

"Because," replied Emily, "I find it the best counsellor. My head sometimes takes half an hour to decide a question, and is often wrong at last; but my heart unerringly says *yes*, or *no* in a moment."

"It would be happy for you," said Walsingham, "if you could be translated to a world filled with creatures as innocent, and undesigning as yourself; for I fear there is many a hard lesson awaiting you in this rough, and crooked one of ours."

"I have frequently been told that," said Emily, "and I believe it, so far as relates to those inevitable misfortunes in which we all must bear a part; but, that I shall ever change my present mode of thinking, and adopt another, appears to me as impossible as that I should gain a new soul."

"You will at least gain new impressions," said Walsingham. "Experience will teach you the real characters of the beings who chiefly compose your species. You will find them a set of harpies, absurd, treacherous, and deceitful—regardless of strong obligations, and mindful of slight injuries—and when your integrity has been shocked, and every just, and native feeling severely tried, the sensibility which you now so liberally bestow on others, will then be absorbed in lamenting its own cruel disappointments, and inefficacious tenderness; and you will gladly consult the dictates of your understanding, to prevent being preyed on by continual depravity."

"You have drawn a frightful picture," said Emily.

"It is nevertheless a true one," replied he.

"Emily would perhaps incline to be of the same mode of thinking already, if she had paid the same price for her knowledge that you have done," said Lucy.

"I have gained it in many ways;" replied Walsingham, "but those which you allude to, are the last impositions of the kind that shall be practised on me, for I find myself unequal to contend with the callous effrontery which universally accompanies such conduct. I hate *dunning*,[1] and would almost as soon lose my money, as be compelled to ask for it."

Fortunately for Mrs. Hammond, whose wrath, during this dialogue, had been increasing until a vent had become absolutely necessary to prevent her from bursting, a servant happened here to break a dish belonging to a beautiful set of cut glass, and she fiercely poured on him such a torrent of vindictive reproof, as neither of her auditors had ever heard issue from her lips before.

Walsingham, who had hitherto remarked her moderation on similar occasions, well knew that the accident alone was not the cause of this violence. He beheld the effect produced by his studied comments with a mixture of wonder, and exultation; and leaving them, like uncle Toby's questions to the widow Wadman, "to work their own way,"[2] he waited until her anger had exhausted itself, and then introduced another topic.

Relieved in a measure, by what had passed, Mrs. Hammond presently recollected herself; and sensible of the imprudence of being thrown off her guard at a period which required the utmost circumspection, she apologized for her fit of passion, and added, "that she had indulged her servants, and overlooked their faults, until they had grown too careless for endurance; and that some appearance of displeasure, and authority had become indispensably necessary." She afterwards joined occasionally in conversation as if nothing of the kind had taken place; and Walsingham soon saw, that she either did not choose, or did not dare to appear offended with him, and his curiosity and impatience increased every moment.

Mrs. Hammond, whose pride and poverty were still smarting

---

1 Persistently demanding repayment of debts.
2 A reference to Tristram's Uncle Toby, a comic character in Laurence Sterne's novel *Tristram Shandy* (1759).

under his pointed inuendoes, watched him closely, and boding no good from his manner, was devising with herself how to avoid him for the rest of the day; but before she had settled the means of so doing, the servants had cleared the table, and left the room; and their mistress, no longer protected by their presence from the possibility of a demand which she dreaded, was preparing to retire also, when Walsingham, seeing her intention, rose and begged to speak a few words with her in private.

A thousand thoughts rushed upon her at this request; but instead of regretting the hardened folly that had reduced her to such a dilemma, she regarded him as a mean, sordid wretch, and herself as an insulted woman.—The money she had borrowed of him was still in her possession—she could return it if she pleased—and to do so, and overwhelm him with her disdain on the spot, was a temptation almost irresistible:—But, on the other hand, it had been procured, and painfully hoarded to guard against future exigencies, in the presumption that respect, and politeness would prevent him from mentioning a circumstance which she herself appeared desirous to forget.—After a short hesitation, she spitefully determined to hear him, and not relinquish it unless compelled; nor even then, without such expressions of contempt, and reproach, as she fancied he deserved for daring to require from her any thing that she wished to retain.

With these ideas she gravely answered, "that she could not imagine what he had to communicate, and felt herself ill-calculated to discuss a matter of any importance just then;" and followed by Walsingham, she walked into the adjoining parlour, when she sat down with an air of calmness that somewhat disconcerted him. Having collected herself to sustain a mortification which she could not evade, she was now only anxious that it might be quickly over; and, as he did not immediately speak, she said, "be so good, Mr. Walsingham, as to inform me what you wish, without delay.—My heart is oppressed, and my time precious.—Every moment ought now to be devoted to my poor Lucy, whom to-morrow I must lose, perhaps forever."

The tears trickled from her eyes as she spoke, and she drew out her handkerchief and wiped them away. Walsingham felt moved for an instant, but suspicion of her unworthiness checked his sensibility.—"What a Proteus,"[1] thought he "is this woman!—Last night she was all gaiety and animation!—This morning,

---

1 A minor god in Greek mythology who would change his shape to avoid answering questions.

the emblem of despondency:—next, raving like a fury!—then immoveable as marble:—and *now*, she is weeping like a fountain to disarm me of my purpose!"

"Be not so deeply affected, Madam;" said he, at length, "I mean not to add unnecessarily to your distress.—My views are friendly, and our interview will be short, and productive, I hope, of permanent peace to us all."

Involuntary surprise at the style of this address dried up the source of Mrs. Hammond's tears; and resting the hand which held the handkerchief on her knee, she listened with eager attention.

"When I had the honour, Madam," continued Walsingham, "to solicit your consent to my union with your daughter, it was accorded by you, and received by me unconditionally.—Easy in my own circumstances, I was not particularly anxious respecting those of my intended wife; but understanding from general report that they were highly favourable, I naturally expected to have had my ideas confirmed; and having afforded you every possible opportunity for the explanation, I confess it appeared singular to me that it should have been so pertinaciously withheld. However, as no pecuniary advantages could have increased my happiness, I concluded that your reasons for acting thus were justly founded, and feeling no inconvenience from them, presumed on no inquiries, but became a member of your family in the full confidence that Mrs. Walsingham was entitled to a share of an immense estate.—Subsequent events incline me to think I have erred strangely in my calculations on this subject—"

This last half sentence acted like a shock of electricity.—She started from her chair, and interrupted him by exclaiming "what is the meaning of this?—What cause have you for such an unwarrantable insinuation, sir?"

"Pardon me, madam;" returned Walsingham coldly, "if I am wrong, it is certainly in your power to convince me of it."

"I never said—I did not attempt—I never asserted my wealth to any one." Said Mrs. Hammond, reseating herself, and striving to recover the presence of mind, which this attack had suddenly dissipated.

"To me you assuredly have not," replied Walsingham, "and you will excuse my saying, I should be extremely glad to be favoured with a direct answer now."

"You shall, when you have proposed your question." Said Mrs. Hammond, in a voice which rage, and trepidation rendered nearly inarticulate.

"I am sorry madam," said Walsingham, "that you will understand none except the most explicit terms, but since it is your choice, I cannot too soon have recourse to them.—My request contains nothing which ought to offend you.—I merely wish to know the nature, and extent of the property left to Mrs. Walsingham by her father?"

The contempt, which notwithstanding his wish to suppress it, was visible in his countenance, stung Mrs. Hammond to the quick; but recollecting that it was not in his power absolutely to controvert any reply that she chose to make, she permitted herself to be governed in part by the implication contained in this last speech, and answered with a forced smile, "we have strangely mistaken each other, Mr. Walsingham, until we have both been betrayed into some little impatience.—Your request, as you have observed, is neither improper, nor unreasonable; yet suffer me, to apprize you that the view with which it is advanced, cannot at present be gratified.—Apprehensive of those fatal changes to which mercantile concerns are always liable, Mr. Hammond, soon after the birth of Emily, executed a deed entitling me to one half of what he was then worth, and vesting the remainder in his children, to be divided equally between them when the youngest should obtain the age of twenty one; and the event has justified his prudence, for upon the settlement of his affairs after his death, I found there was little else remaining for us.—You are right, perhaps, in supposing yourself deceived respecting the amount of it, which although considerable, is by no means such as to render it an object with *you*; and as Emily still wants nearly four years of the term in question, I really thought this information useless, previous to its arrival."

This story of the deed appeared highly improbable to Walsingham. He suspected its truth for many reasons; one of which was, that it differed greatly from the account he had received from Mrs. Cathcart, whom from her intimacy with Mrs. Hammond he thought not likely to be so materially mistaken in a point of so much importance. Believing therefore, the whole to be a fabrication of her own, varied at different times, as best suited her convenience, he determined to pursue his first design; and replied after a pause of a few moments, "but Lucy herself, madam, is also ignorant of this?"

"True," said Mrs. Hammond, "but it was incompatible with my system of education, that my children should be made acquainted with any thing which might incline them to dispute my right to direct their conduct beyond a certain period.—Yet my authority has never been exerted but for their welfare:—my life has been devoted to them; and the propriety of my maxims will scarcely be disputed by any who have a knowledge of the success with which they have been attended in embellishing the minds, and forming the manners of two elegant young females, who are, confessedly ornaments to society."

"I thank you, madam," replied Walsingham, "for having thus satisfactorily communicated to me all that I desired.— No person, I believe, can be more sincerely impressed with a sense of the merits of your daughters than I am, of which you shall receive an unquestionable proof.—Regarding myself as responsible, in some degree, for the attachment which subsists between Emily and Kelroy, I have regretted their mutual, and increasing unhappiness, without imagining it was in my power so easily to remove it; but since the real obstacle is now explained, I consider it my duty as the friend of both, to exert the means which a fortunate coincidence of circumstances have furnished me with, of making you the proposal to relinquish, during your life, Lucy's interest in this estate, and advance in Emily's behalf, a sum equal to her share of it, provided you consent to her immediate union with Kelroy, and grant me a bond for the repayment when Mrs. Walsingham becomes of age—and I flatter myself that to a lady of your good-sense, and discernment, the advantages which must accrue from a compliance, are too obvious to be detailed."

Anguish is too light a name for the sensations which Mrs. Hammond experienced on hearing this. Caught in her own snare, and entangled beyond escape, independent of the will of him into whose hands she had unwittingly resigned the springs which held it, she knew not whither to turn without encountering accumulated danger. To comply was impossible, and she feared to irritate him by a refusal, lest a demand for the nine hundred dollars, or a sight of the deed she had named should be the consequence; and to convert the zealous Walsingham into an enemy, or be compelled to pay him, would alike ensure exposure, and seal her ruin.—One expedient alone presented itself, by which she could hope to be extricated with tolerable credit; and, as in the choice between speedy and remote evils, the latter, although equally inevitable, are sure to be preferred, she endeavoured by pursuing a middle course, to avert his resentment, and its probable effects for the present; and after a distressed pause, replied with visible agitation, "before we proceed in this affair, suffer me to ask also a question.—Is it at the instance of Kelroy, and with the concurrence of Emily, that you have made me this proposition?"

"No madam, I give you my honour that Emily is wholly ignorant of it; and that Kelroy, so far from soliciting my assistance, will with difficulty, I apprehend, be prevailed on to receive it, even in this form."

She paused again for a minute, and then said, "you are very good and very generous, Mr. Walsingham; but I cannot permit your compassion for these romantic mortals to triumph entirely over my judgment, and lead us both into measures which we may perhaps repent."

"Good God, madam!" exclaimed Walsingham, ["]can nothing lessen your abhorrence of this amiable young man?—Have neither tenderness for your daughter, or regard to your own interest any weight with you, that you just persist—"

"Hear me!" cried Mrs. Hammond, interrupting him, "and let not the warmth of your heart prompt you to view my decision in a harsh light, because it accords not exactly with their wishes.— The terms which you offer are liberal, but I cannot, merely for the sake of benefitting myself, accept them, and thus accelerate a marriage which I have hitherto determined to retard until Kelroy is in a more eligible situation.—All that he could gain by my acquiescence would be insufficient to maintain them in that sphere of life to which they have been accustomed.—It must be *risked* before it can be enlarged; and it may be *lost*, and my daughter precipitated through my weakness into the greatest misery; for I have lived long enough to be convinced that love and poverty are seldom companions long.—Be assured, therefore, that my reasons for opposing Mr. Kelroy arose not from dislike to him, and that they still remain in their original force; augmented perhaps, by my fears for my child's happiness, but possessing, as you must be conscious, much truth.—This, however, is only viewing the question on the dark side.—I am well aware that a short time may be productive of such a change as may induce me to think my precautions were needlessly rigid; but still it is best to pursue the safest path.—Yet, that your philanthropy may not be—"

"Talk not of my philanthropy, my dear madam!" cried Walsingham, wearied with her prolixity, and interrupting her in his turn, "but have the goodness to acquaint me with your own resolves?"

"I am hastening to do so," replied she, with studied mildness, "and that I may not altogether defeat the kind intentions of a person for whom I have every reason to entertain the highest respect, and regard, I not only consent to an engagement on Emily's part, but now give you my solemn promise that she shall be united to Kelroy *at all events*, immediately on his return from India, provided they both continue to desire it.—Beyond this I cannot venture consistent with my duty."

"And is this, madam, your final determination?"

"It is, Mr. Walsingham."

"And can you, without even one hour's deliberation—"

"I entreat you, press me no further!" exclaimed she, with uplifted hands, "deliberation is not wanting here, for I have reflected upon every thing!"

"Well then," said Walsingham, after a short silence, "since it must be so, there remains nothing more for me but to go in search of Kelroy.—Yet remember, if any latent cause, any concealed motive has influenced this rejection of my offer, how severely you may be taught to accuse yourself hereafter, for not having openly confided in me?"

She turned very pale, and rising, replied in a hurried manner, yet with a sort of half smile, "your anticipations are really not very consoling, but an old woman, like myself can scarcely be led to repent having refused what she might not live to enjoy."

She was about to leave the room as she spoke, when Walsingham said, "but you will see Kelroy?—You will speak with him yourself?"

"To-morrow I will—but now I am engaged—I expect company."

"Company?"

"Yes, Mrs. Cathcart, and Helen."

"It is still early," said Walsingham, taking out his watch, "oblige me therefore by suffering him to see you before they arrive?"

"Let it be so!—Let him come then!—To-morrow, or to day on this occasion, will be equal in the end!"

And unable to endure these trying vexations longer without complaint, she rushed rather than walked out of the parlour, muttering a sentence between her teeth, of which Walsingham understood nothing distinctly except the word ["]*heart*."

"Ah! that heart of thine!" said he as she closed the door. "Could I but look into it, what a volume of deception I should behold! But despicable as thou art, I nevertheless pity thee, for the agonies of thy disappointed pride, and humbled ambition are equal to the utmost of those, which but for my intervention, thou wouldest without remorse have inflicted upon others."

He then went in quest of his melancholy friend, who was

impatiently expecting him, and related without disguise all that had passed.

The wonder, and detestation of Kelroy at the mean subterfuges of Mrs. Hammond, was lost in the contemplation of Walsingham's disinterested benevolence, and the transporting conviction that the object of his wishes had now obtained an indisputable right to preserve her faith, and his peace inviolate.— His gratitude, and delight was evinced at first only in unconnected exclamations, but when the violence of his emotions subsided, he poured out his acknowledgments in the most exalted, and energetic language that an impassioned mind, glowing with a sense of its own felicity, and another's worth could dictate. Nor did the almost actual confirmation that the mistress of his heart could bless him with no treasures except those which centered in herself in the least damp his joy. He continued to dwell on the services he had received, and regret that it was not in his power to shew how sensibly he was touched by them, until Walsingham, who coveted neither praise nor reward for what he had done, would hear him no longer; but bidding him "reserve a few of his extravagant encomiums for Mrs. Hammond, who was much more in want of such a *salvo* than he was," intimated that his happiness was presently to be increased by having it confirmed by that lady herself.

"This indeed, is completing her tribulation," said Kelroy, taking up his hat, and preparing to depart; "but you are resolved, I see, that her cup shall be an unsparing one!—"

"The ingredients are chiefly of her own mixing," said Walsingham, "and if she finds them unpalatable, it is too late to complain now.—The terms which I offered her, no one in their senses would have rejected, who possessed the means of doing otherwise; and she, I am convinced, would gladly have closed with them, had it been in her power; but I quickly found it was useless to urge the matter.—What her difficulties are I know not; for although she could not command her countenance, she was careful to guard her tongue! but doubtless they must be great to induce her to yield so readily a point which hitherto she would scarcely endure to name."

"Great indeed," replied Kelroy, "if she has wasted the inheritance of her children, in the supposition that their attractions are to repair the injury."

"Yet she cannot be poor!—" said Walsingham, musing— ["]The house she lives in, I know is her own, and she certainly has property to a considerable amount besides!—But that she has been guilty of some imprudence in the management of it, and is in want of money, admits of no dispute; and had I respected her feelings as little as she does yours, I might easily have wrung the secret from her."

"Let us be satisfied with the victory as it now stands," said Kelroy, "for you could have achieved nothing more, without acting like a most ungallant knight."

"And in gaining this," said Walsingham laughing, "I have not shone as the pink of courtesy!—But Don Quixote himself,[1] thus circumstanced, would not have scrupled descending from the heights of chivalry to rescue so fair a damsel, and so fond a lover."

They then went together to Mrs. Hammond's, whom they found seated in the parlour with her daughters.—The remains of inquietude were visible in her countenance, but she received Kelroy without any apparent increase of it; yet her erect form, raised, as it were, in perpendicular defiance; and the keen expression of her eyes, as she glanced them from one object to another in quick succession, seemed to him indicative rather of obstinate contention, than the compliance he had been led to expect.—He looked at Emily, to discover whether some disagreeable altercation had not preceded their entrance; but seeing her tranquil and unconscious,[2] he endeavoured to appear so too, although in pain for the effect which the intended explanation, if not managed with delicacy, might produce on her.

Some trivial conversation in which Lucy bore the principal share ensued, but Mrs. Hammond was quite silent; and Walsingham having mended the fire, and bustled about on various pretences with a view to give her time to collect herself, now sat down also, in some doubt whether she would not attempt to foil him at last.—In this, however, he was mistaken.—Having taken an accurate survey of Emily's demeanour from the moment of Kelroy's entrance, and discerning nothing to warrant a suspicion of that collusion between them which she had resolved should not go unpunished, she at length deigned to speak, and addressing herself to Kelroy, said, "I presume, sir, Mr. Walsingham

---

1 Eponymous protagonist of the early Spanish novel *Don Quixote* (1605/15) by Miguel de Cervantes (1547–1616). Don Quixote reads so many romantic medieval tales that he loses his sanity and decides to bring back chivalry by becoming a knight and traveling the land performing chivalrous deeds.

2 Unconcerned.

has acquainted you with the change in my determinations on a certain subject?"

"He has, madam," replied Kelroy, disgusted with her abruptness; "but sensible as I am of the honour, I scarcely dare return you my acknowledgments, until I am so happy as to learn that the consent of one by whom alone I am guided, is added to yours?—"

He looked at Emily as he spoke, and saw her colour with a dawning apprehension of her mother's meaning.—Mrs. Hammond looked at her too, and said coldly, "as for *her* approbation, I believe I may safely answer—since having shewn that she understands an intimation so slightly expressed, she cannot affect to be averse to it."

"It is not affectation," said Emily confusedly, "for I really do not know—"

She ceased speaking, conscious that her ideas had adverted to a point which another word perhaps might betray.

Mrs. Hammond maliciously enjoying her disturbance, replied, "do not be prudish Emily; you know that is a species of conduct to which I have a peculiar aversion.—I have altered my mind respecting Mr. Kelroy and yourself.—Various sufficient reasons induce me to think that in bestowing you on him I shall act for the best; and having given my consent that you shall be his on his return from India, I expect you will oblige me by confirming it."

Abashed, astonished, and delighted, Emily almost doubted what she heard—She blushed until her eyes filled with tears, and unable to articulate a syllable, looked timidly at Kelroy for an elucidation of this unexpected command; who divided between the emotions resulting from her soft confusion, and her mother's ungracious assent, caught her hand, and exclaimed, "thus sanctioned, you cannot, you will not refuse what I have so often sought in vain?"

Emily tried to answer, but her emotion was too great for utterance.

"Speak!" cried Mrs. Hammond, in a tone of authority.

"She cannot," said Kelroy, pressing her hand, "the suddenness of this scene has overcome her."

"So it would seem;" said Mrs. Hammond sarcastically, "but supposing the intelligence could not be very unwelcome, I was not particularly studious as to the manner of imparting it."

Cruelly hurt at the intimation which this speech conveyed, Emily now wept without restraint, and Kelroy, trembling with indignation was only withheld by the fear of adding to her distress, from repaying Mrs. Hammond's insinuation with interest;

but Walsingham, less delicately situated, replied with some asperity, "I am sorry, madam, that you should fancy the kindness by which you profess yourself actuated, consistent with such expressions as these."

"Emily, why will you persist in irritating me? This perverse reluctance is beyond any thing that I could have conceived possible!" cried Mrs. Hammond, affecting to disregard him, and wilfully misconstruing her daughter's agitation to excuse herself.

"Not from perverseness—" said Emily at length, speaking with difficulty—"not from reluctance are these tears—for I have none—however I may be censured for the confession."

Enraptured with the innocent candour which rose superior to the ungenerous reflections which sought to suppress it, Kelroy could scarcely refrain from casting himself at her feet; but the presence of her mother checked him, and he replied, "no words—no language, Emily could ever do justice to the feelings of my heart at this moment—but you, who know it best, can best conceive them.—And now—henceforward, you are only mine?—"

"Yours—never to be another's," faultered Emily, when a loud rap at the street door, announced the arrival of Mrs. Cathcart, and the next moment her voice was heard in the hall, bawling about some mud on the tail of her gown.

"Go quick!—go directly to your chamber, until you recover yourself!—you are not fit to be seen!—" said Mrs. Hammond to Emily, who hastily left the room at one door, as Mrs. Cathcart entered at another; and Lucy, speaking for the first time, told them "she was very glad they had come," which was really true, for she was heartily tired of what was passing, and thought that both her mother and her husband acted as if on the borders of insanity.

Emily returned in a short time apparently composed, and exerted herself to contribute somewhat to the entertainment of her friends; but it was a vain attempt, and the evening passed heavily away with them all. Walsingham was grave, Kelroy restless, and Mrs. Hammond piteously silent.—Helen was in tolerable spirits when she came, but the dullness of the party soon extended itself to her also, and nobody seemed inclined to talk but Mrs. Cathcart and Lucy.—The entrance of Charles Cathcart, who came to accompany his mother and sister home at length relieved them; and after a weary three hours, during which Mrs. Hammond scarcely spoke three sentences in reply to the many condoling speeches addressed to her by Mrs. Cathcart, that agreeable lady at last thought fit to utter her farewell harangue to Walsingham and his wife, and depart; and Kelroy, finding no probability of an opportunity to converse with Emily, went also.

CHAPTER X.

WHEN Mrs. Hammond retired to her bed, and was at liberty to indulge in unrestrained reflection, she felt that the past had been productive of no positive comfort, but much certain misery; and beheld in the future an accumulation of it, in the form which of all others was most appalling to her.

Buoyed up with hopes which Lucy's marriage had tended to confirm, she had forgot the restrictions by which she meant to be regulated, and yielding to the suggestions of that intemperate pride which blinds its votaries to all beyond the vain splendour of the moment, she had since her return to the city expended on a new equipage, and various modern articles of furniture and ornament which she deemed absolutely necessary, the sum of six hundred pounds.—Fourteen hundred was all that the purchase of her country place, and the expensive education of her children had enabled her to preserve.—The remaining eight was still in her possession, but she found that if her prompt payments continued, it would be quickly gone; and having already established a good reputation for the ready discharge of her debts, she resolved to stop her hand in that particular, and by large credit, and a little private economy, make it last to the end of her game, which she was convinced, would not be long.—In this, however, she was mistaken.—Dress, public amusements, frequent, and extravagant entertainments, and the current expenses of her family, together with a passion for cards, by which she oftener lost than won, had not only consumed the whole of her ready money, but plunged her so deeply in debt, as to compel her to mortgage her little farm for nearly its full value, to enable her to preserve appearances during the time that she proposed remaining in town.

Thus situated, teized perpetually by her creditors, some of whom she was daily obliged to silence by lessening her only remaining support, it might be supposed she would have become sensible of her folly; but contrition was a feeling which as yet she knew not. Believing her own talents infinitely superior to those of persons in general, she imagined herself born to elude dangers, and surmount difficulties; and so far were these embarrassments from weakening her infatuation, that they acted as a fresh incentive to urge her still deeper into the whirlpool upon which she had embarked her fortunes.—The attachment of Emily to Kelroy was the only obstacle which appeared likely to impede the accomplishment of her wishes, but she considered it upon the whole as rather provoking, than dangerous; and resolving to await a proper season to put a final period to a very silly affair, she borrowed on different pretenses from Walsingham as much as would support her in the country through the ensuing summer; before the close of which she hoped that Emily's beauty, and her own management would release her from all her cares; leaving her in possession of property sufficient to preserve with ease, after the mortgage should be paid, that apparent consequence, and independence, which she had been labouring for years to establish.

Full of these ideas, and the concomitant agitation of mind and nerve which they failed not to produce, she was alternately gloomy or gay as her expectations chanced to be heightened or depressed; when the accidental introduction of Mr. Marney to her acquaintance, and the admiration which he expressed towards Emily, afforded her a satisfaction that she could scarcely conceal.—He was precisely a man suited to the exigencies of the occasion; for he was very rich, not very wise, and seemed in a fair way of being, with a very little encouragement, as much in love as she could possibly desire.—Marking him, therefore in her own mind as her future prey, she treated him with that insinuating politeness which she so well knew how to practise; and before he retired, gave him a flattering invitation to renew his visit, which he as eagerly promised, and they parted mutually satisfied with each other.—Marney of opinion that she was a clever, sensible old lady, and her daughter a charming young one, whom he should have no particular objection to honour with his hand; and Mrs. Hammond fully persuaded that the foundation was now laid on which skill and prudence might erect a superstructure adequate to her wishes, resolved immediately on Walsingham's departure to commence her operations; when the unexpected attack from that gentleman demolished her plan, she feared, forever.

Compelled either to comply with his request in some shape, or reduce herself to greater difficulties than she could endure to think of:—her pride all up in arms, and her temper irritated, she forgot that if her calculations respecting Marney were just, her wisest course was to return Walsingham his money, and set him at defiance:—no such thought occurred to her, so great was her rage, and consternation at finding herself suspected.—Her property exposed to sale, her duplicity laid open to the world, and the remainder of her life embittered by the scorn, and pity of those over whom she had hitherto soared triumphant, was all that presented itself to her alarmed imagination; and to gain time to deliberate upon the means of emancipating herself entirely, she gave that hasty assent to receive Kelroy, which obliged her to declare her newly adopted sentiments, and pass her word beyond the power of retraction.

Solitude discovered to her these errors, and taught her, too late, the folly of confiding wholly in herself. Deeply did she now regret the precipitate extravagance with which she had squandered in a few months sums sufficient to have supported her for years in comfort, and competence. And more deeply still did she lament the fatal oversight of suffering herself to be controuled by Walsingham, and thus rendered the instrument of destroying effectually her own scheme; since with what colour of justice could she endeavour hereafter to depreciate Kelroy, and prejudice Emily in favour of another? Not only her attachment, but her understanding, and natural sense of rectitude, would, she well knew, revolt against any attempt of the kind, and procure for herself the contempt she might seek to excite towards him. Believing therefore, their union inevitable if Kelroy returned at the expiration of a twelve month, she grieved that she had not, in the first instance, promoted their marriage, and left them to their fate, by insisting on accompanying Lucy to England.

These, and a thousand other miserable reflections, contrasted with the single, yet mean consolation of not being necessitated to return Walsingham his money, tormented her nearly the whole night; and she at last fell into a profound slumber.

There is a something wonderfully restorative in sleep! Not only the languid frame is strengthened and refreshed by it; but the mind, which harassed, and torn by the bitter recollections of a day, places its events in every possible light, and sinks to rest exhausted by its own fruitless efforts to obtain consolation, awakes calmed, and invigorated by the healing oblivion of a few hours! Sorrow loses somewhat of its poignancy, and evils appear to have so much abated of their horror, that we condemn our late dismay, and prepare to encounter them with less reluctance; and Mrs. Hammond, whose strong constitution generally exempted her from the addition of bodily indisposition, awoke the following morning with the impressions of yesterday so much lessened, as no longer to experience those distracting sensations which had nearly overwhelmed her. She was unhappy, but it was no longer the turbulent wretchedness bordering on despair. Conscious that no immediate efforts could relieve her, she suffered her ideas to sink into willing imbecility, and continued lying calmly on her pillow, until her mulatto girl softly opened the chamber door, and perceiving her mistress to be awake, told her that Mr. Green was below.

"What, Green the grocer?" exclaimed Mrs. Hammond.

"Yes ma'am."

"Why do you not tell him I am asleep, and will not be disturbed?"

"I did ma'am, but he says he does not believe it, or if you are, he can wait 'till you get up; and he has been here above an hour, scolding like any thing."

"Go down and tell him I am ill in bed, and he must come another time—but no!—stop!" cried she, hearing Walsingham descending the stairs, "tell him I will be there presently!"

And fearful that Walsingham might hear from this man, (who was the same Kelroy had mentioned,) a history of the frequent contests which had latterly past between them, she huddled on her clothes, and flew down as expeditiously as possible, but too late to effect her purpose; for when she entered the parlour, he was standing with his hat in his hand, telling Walsingham his name, and the nature of his business.—Fired with sudden rage, she walked fiercely up to the sturdy little Scotchman, and said, "there is no occasion Mr. for you to trouble that gentleman with my affairs. I sent you word I was coming, and that was sufficient."

"*Faith* madam, not to give you an ill answer, if that had been sufficient, I should have been satisfied long ago. The gentleman asked me my business, and I e'en tauld him; but I rather think, madam, there is no need I should do the same to you?"

"I have mislaid your bill, and forgotten the amount of it, as I told you before; and as I do not choose to pay you 'till I find it, you must call in a few days."

"Thinking you might not have had time since last week to look for it, I have brought another, madam; so if you please you will settle at once, to prevent further trouble," said the grocer, who finding the note he had sent her was of no effect, had called once more, with a determination if he was not paid, to proceed directly to extremities.[1]

"Three hundred and thirty dollars!" exclaimed she, after

---

1 If Mrs. Hammond does not pay him what she owes, the grocer intends to sue her—a public proceeding that would expose her true financial situation.

opening the bill which she had snatched out of his hand; "a likely matter, upon my word!" then, looking over it, she again exclaimed, "what do you suppose I could possibly want with half that you have here charged me with?"

"I can't pretend to say what you might want with it; all I know is that you have had it, madam," replied the grocer.

"I don't believe it," cried she, "for it is an utter impossibility that my family could have consumed articles to this amount; and you may depend upon it, I will have the thing better ascertained before I pay you one single cent!"

"I'll tell you what, mistress," returned the grocer, now in as great a passion as herself, "this is but a poor sham and I'll let you know it!—what! send to my shop for better than four months for all you wanted? aye, day after day, for things that other folks would go to market for, and then tax me with being a rascal?—I'm an *honest man*, madam! an *honest man*!—but I'll waste no more breath *aboot* it; for I see there is but one way to deal with you, and so good morning."

And with these words, he waddled wrathfully out of the room; when Walsingham fearful that her violence would expose her to further insult, called after him to stop, and having desired him to remain where he was for a few moments, shut the door, and asked Mrs. Hammond whether she really believed him to be dishonest?

"You heard what I said to him!" replied she.

"I did," said he, "but if you have not every reason to believe that you can prove him to be either dishonest, or mistaken, you had better pay him at once; or he may, if he is so inclined, give you a good deal of trouble."

"He is an insolent old villain!" said she, "and I am sure I have never had from him what he charges me with!"

"But can you make that appear?"

"I don't know whether I can or not," replied she, chafing.

"Then let me advise you to discharge his bill at once—or, if it does not suit you to do it immediately, perhaps I can prevail on him to wait a little longer?" said Walsingham.

"No, you shall not prevail on him!—If it must be paid, it suits me, sir, to do it now," said she; and almost bursting with contending passions, she ordered the grocer to come back; and going hastily up stairs, returned in a minute or two with notes to the amount of the sum in question, which to the amazement of Walsingham, she paid into the man's hands, and ordered him to leave her house, which he did with more readiness than he had ever entered it.—At the close of this unpleasant scene, the two sisters entered, and Mrs. Hammond no sooner saw Lucy, than she burst into a passion of tears, and bewailed anew with helpless, infantine distress, the approaching parting.

Emily had been occupied during the night with a variety of feelings, which scarcely permitted her to close her eyes; but the sweet consciousness of being plighted to him she loved predominated, and at once increased her tenderness, and softened her regret.—After a melancholy breakfast, Walsingham took an opportunity to express his wishes for her happiness, which he told her, depended now on fulfilling her engagement with Kelroy, whose affection, and numerous good qualities rendered him doubly deserving of her, and whose enterprizing spirit, aided by the hope of obtaining her, could scarcely fail to remove the obstacle which had occasioned their mutual uneasiness.—He felt desirous also, to give her some intimation of the situation of her mother's affairs, lest by some further imprudence on that lady's part, they might become so perplexed as to extend their unpleasant effects to Emily herself; but not knowing how to impart it at such a period, he contented himself with charging her if any difficulties, or unforeseen embarrassments should arise, in which he could be of service, to make them known to him as early as possible, and depend firmly on any assistance in his power. But, should they be of a nature where his good-offices could be of no avail, to consult her own excellent understanding, and be guided by the purity of those principles which were her best safeguard.

Emily loved Walsingham like a brother; and there was something so unaffectedly sincere in his manner of expressing this, that although ignorant of the full extent of his meaning, she could not refrain from tears at the involuntary comparison which her heart made between his friendly solicitude, and the careless coldness of her frigid sister.

Engrossed with herself, and the contemplation of her good fortune, Lucy seldom bestowed a thought upon any thing unconnected with her own gratification; and, as Emily could contribute but little to that, she was in general overlooked, or forgotten.—Her preference of Kelroy, whenever she was compelled to notice it, excited in her a sentiment of scornful surprise; but knowing him to be a favourite with her husband, she had never expressed herself further than to regret his want of fortune, which was, in fact the only objection, short of absolute deformity, that she would have regarded in any man. Her notions of matrimony were not quite new, but they were singularly systematic. She thought it was, or ought to be the business of every woman to marry to as much advantage, and as early as she could, because marriage would make her of more consequence; and, as *pretty* women are presumed to have the most extensive choice, it was, in her opinion, incumbent upon every one of that description to select from among her admirers him who had it in his power most to elevate her, and then by unremitting complaisance, and a shew of respect obtain over him the necessary influence, to be resorted to as occasion might require. The beauty of Emily she did not consider equal to her own, but she believed it to be more than adequate to the purpose in question; and the contempt with which she had heard her consent to mar her prospects by binding herself to Kelroy can hardly be conceived; but she shewed it only by her silence.—Naturally unimpassioned, the example of her mother had contributed still further to render her an adept in dissimulation; and by the undisturbed serenity of her beautiful countenance, or a degree of softness which she could always assume where it was requisite, she easily concealed her disapprobation of whatever did not relate immediately to herself, for in no other instance was she sufficiently interested to interfere; and Walsingham, whose uniform complaisance had hitherto prevented the necessity of the slightest remonstrance, saw no deficiencies where he experienced constant sweetness, but fancied her possessed of every feminine grace, and virtue.— The time, however, was fast approaching when he was to be in part undeceived.

They were to be on board the vessel at twelve, and Walsingham, who had still an hour to spare, walked to the lodgings of Kelroy, whom he met near the door, on his way to render that farewell, which to persons of real sensibility is ever a most painful task.— There is a reluctance—a sense of unavailing suffering attached to a *last* visit from which the mind instinctively recoils; and these gentlemen, who entertained for each other a very uncommon regard, would gladly have been spared this interview; but as neither knew how to avoid it without incurring a suspicion of neglect, they both sought what each was desirous to shun.— Their intimacy had commenced on their earliest acquaintance, and quickly changed to mutual friendship—they had lived in uninterrupted harmony, and increasing confidence—they were now to separate, never in all human probability, never to meet again!—And so few, or so disproportioned are the friendships of this world, that seldom is such genuine regret felt, as was experienced on this occasion by them.

When they returned to Mrs. Hammond's, they found the

parlour empty, and in a few moments the carriage which was to convey them to the water side arrived at the door.— Walsingham went up stairs, and found her in a state of extreme distress, Emily weeping, and Lucy sitting in a desponding posture, with her handkerchief thrown over her face.—After viewing them silently a few moments, he approached his wife, and apprized her, as gently as possible, that their parting could be no longer delayed.—She neither spoke nor moved, but Mrs. Hammond, rushing towards her, caught her in her arms, and uttered such exclamations of passionate sorrow as not only extremely affected Walsingham, but caused this insensate being, who had covered her face to hide her apathy, to burst into a flood of unaffected, and even bitter tears. Desirous of shortening so painful a scene, Walsingham hurried her from the arms of her weeping mother and sister, and having carried her down stairs, was assisted by Kelroy to lift her into the carriage, which they entered after her, and quickly reached the place of destination.

Lucy's grief proved to be of short duration. She cried vehemently the length of two whole squares, and might probably have done so for two more, had she not unfortunately recollected, that crying sometimes inflamed the eyes. "Red eyes were horrible things!" and to avoid them, she instantly dried hers with the greatest care; her sobs ceased, and her strength had so far returned, that in leaving the carriage she required no further aid than usual; and the bustle which she encountered on the wharf, soon by its novelty dissipated the small remains of her distress.

Walsingham, who was exerting himself to console her, found that he had succeeded but too well. He could neither understand, nor tolerate such a total absence of sensibility; and for the first time began seriously to call in question the qualities of her heart. The investigation was painful, but a few minutes sufficed to render it decisive, and the disgust, and disappointment which he endured was sufficiently visible to Kelroy, who had been an attentive spectator of all that passed, and silently lamented that he was compelled to witness the dawn of a discovery, which he had hoped her beauty, and address might for a few happy years have protracted. Full of sympathy, and increased regret, he accompanied them on board the ship, when Walsingham presently had the mortification to see his wife busily engaged in talking with several of the passengers; and Kelroy, who attempted in vain to divert his attention from her, having lingered until he had no longer any pretext for remaining, at last bade adieu to

Mrs. Walsingham, clasped the hand of his friend in emphatic silence, and departed.

The trouble and agitation which Mrs. Hammond had undergone for the last two days, threw her immediately after Lucy left her, into a fit of hysterics so violent as to alarm the whole house. Her shrieks, and spasms were dreadful; and Emily, unused to such sights, fancied from her pale, distorted features that she was dying, and sent first for a physician, and next for Mrs. Cathcart, who presently came, together with Helen, and they both endeavoured to quiet her apprehensions of her mother's danger without success, until the physician arrived, when the usual remedies being administered, she at length became more composed, and Emily's terror subsided. Exhausted by her recent disorder, Mrs. Hammond now lay perfectly still, and the wondering servants having one by one retreated, peace once more prevailed; and Mrs. Cathcart seeing Emily through fright and fatigue scarcely able to support herself, advised her to retire with Helen and lie down for an hour or two; saying, she would remain with her mother to supply her place. Emily declined, but Mrs. Hammond to whom the sight of her was painful, motioned with her hand for her to go, and seeing her hesitate, said that she wished to be alone with Mrs. Cathcart, and was instantly obeyed.

It was now almost five o'clock, when one of the maids came in, and gave Emily a note which old Henry desired her to say had been left there three hours ago, but owing to his mistress's illness, he had forgotten it.—

"It is from Kelroy," said Emily after reading it.

"But why does he write to you?" said Helen; "you are at liberty to see him, are you not?"

"Certainly," replied Emily, "but this note is to inform me that he saw my sister safe on board the vessel, and hopes to see me this evening. Strange things have happened, my dear Helen, since yesterday morning—I have had much cause, since then, both to rejoice and to mourn."

She then related all she knew of what had taken place the day before, relative to Kelroy and herself, and after expressing much surprise at the contrast between her mother's prompt command, and ungracious manner, asked Helen what she thought could possibly have induced her voluntarily to announce her consent when so little expected?

"But are you sure she has given it?" said the astonished Helen; are "you sure you did not misunderstand her?"

"I am indeed sure of it;" replied Emily; "the painful recollection of the terms she employed, are a sufficient proof I was not mistaken and I fear I shall still have much of the same description to bear before Kelroy returns. But," continued she bursting into tears, "could I, ought I to renounce the only man I can ever love, when I am certain that by doing so I shall destroy my own happiness without adding to my mother's?—For never can I marry as she wishes me!—never, never while he lives can I be the wife of any other!"

Wonder, simple and unalloyed, is said to arise only in little minds; but Helen with a good capacity, and no mean judgment, was compelled in the present instance, to experience it almost without a mixture of any other sentiment. Familiar, from long acquaintance, with Mrs. Hammond's views and temper, and a repeated witness of her ungenerous treatment of Kelroy, whom she delighted in mortifying whenever she could do so unobserved by Walsingham, she regarded her opposition to him as originating in principle, and therefore unchangeable; and had frequently endeavoured to impress on the mind of Emily those useful truths relative to life and its destinies, which might contribute to prepare her for that disappointment of a first, and fond affection, which she believed her inevitably doomed to experience. How then to account for Mrs. Hammond's sudden consent to a measure which was evidently detestable to her she knew not; for that the mere advice or persuasion of Walsingham could have had that effect she was convinced was impossible; and with only such facts as she was possessed of, the whole appeared to her perfectly incomprehensible: and after innumerable questions on her part, and answers, and conjectures on that of Emily, she was more inclined to ascribe it to the sullen caprice which sometimes actuates haughty spirits, than to any just or powerful motives. Still there remained much room for speculation; but as she could obtain no clue to assist her in elucidating the mystery, she abstained from further comment, and warmly congratulated Emily on being at last so unexpectedly relieved from the dread of encountering during Kelroy's absence, the entreaties and commands of her mother in favour of another.—Emily assented to this with her whole heart, and soon after expressed a wish to return to her mother, of whom, notwithstanding the sarcasms she had latterly experienced from her, she was extremely fond.

They found her asleep; and Mrs. Cathcart who was amusing herself with looking out of the window, said she had been quite composed during their absence. In a few minutes she awoke, and in answer to Emily's inquiries said she was much better but extremely weak.

"Does your head ache?" asked Mrs. Cathcart.

"No," replied Mrs. Hammond, "not the least."

"Oh then you will soon be well," cried Mrs. Cathcart, to whom silence was purgatory; and conceiving this information to have restored to her the liberty of speech, began to hold forth upon the miseries and pleasures of sensibility, to which she simply imagined the recent agitation of Mrs. Hammond was owing, and after a long story, which nobody seemed inclined to interrupt, about a lady whose feelings were so delicate, that on hearing of a very cruel murder, she fainted in a room full of company, she suddenly exclaimed, "Emily! come here! quick!"

Emily went to the window, and saw on the opposite side of the street Mr. Marney, who instantly made her a profound bow. She courtesied ceremoniously, and very little pleased at having been called, gravely retreated. Mrs. Cathcart gave him a familiar nod, and said to her laughing, "Well I am glad I contrived to let him get sight of you at last! This is the fifth time he has passed since I sat here, and he gazes up at the window in such a manner!"—

"Who is it?" inquired Helen.

"Mr. Marney," replied Mrs. Cathcart, whose foolish mistake in supposing him to be an admirer of Mrs. Hammond's had been rectified by her children.

On hearing his name Mrs. Hammond sighed heavily. "Ah!" said she, mentally, "he may pass, and repass! it is all in vain now!"

"Emily, do not look so shy about the matter, child," continued Mrs. Cathcart, "Mr. Kelroy is not here to know it."

"Know what, ma'am?" said Emily.

"Why that Mr. Marney has been parading here half the day in hopes to get a peep at a certain young lady, and had like to have seen nothing but an old one for his pains!—Oh! if I was as young as you, and had your beauty—"

"Do Cathcart cease your nonsense! You will persuade her presently that the man is in earnest. I hate to hear people talk so ridiculously!" peevishly exclaimed Mrs. Hammond, who felt every word as if studied to torment her.

"So!" said the simple, good-natured woman to herself, "what is to come next, I wonder? My son fairly snubbed me for hinting that she had a notion of this Marney, but as sure as fate she is jealous?—I wish I had held my tongue!"

Notice was now given that tea was ready; and Mrs. Hammond saying her mulatto girl should remain with her, insisted upon their all three going down stairs, where they were no sooner seated, than a tremendous rap at the door made them almost start from their chairs, and in marched Mr. Marney.

"Ladies your most obedient; Miss Hammond I am happy to see you well. Upon my soul I have been contemplating this visit ever since dinner."

Emily bowed slightly but made no answer; and he familiarly seated himself next her, and with the ease of an old acquaintance, inquired for her mother.

"She is very unwell sir, and confined to her chamber," replied Emily.

"Upon my soul I am very sorry to hear it—more sorry than surprised.—Mr. and Mrs. Walsingham sailed this morning I understand.—They had a capital wind for it—they will pass the capes like a breeze."

Emily, to whom he was by no means a welcome visitor, felt displeased at the air of intimacy with which he affected to utter this. She thought his presence and his remarks alike unseasonable, and deigned no reply; but Mrs. Cathcart, who was glad of his company as a relief to the gloomy day she had spent, saw nothing objectionable in either, and seizing the first subject of conversation that presented itself, from the capes she proceeded to the ocean, whither she was accompanied by Marney, who had made two voyages to South America, and now displayed the treasures of his nautical experience to her infinite terror, and satisfaction. It is frequently observed in persons of vulgar habits, that they seek to force themselves into notice by creating some strong, or sudden sensation in the minds of those around them; but whether of pain or pleasure they believe to be of no consequence, provided they are acknowledged to be the exciting cause. Marney, dissatisfied with the quiet indifference manifested by Emily, began to relate the scenes he had witnessed, and the dangers he had escaped at sea; intermingled with such accounts of sudden squalls, unexpected fogs, hidden shoals, and furious breakers, that she involuntarily lent him her serious attention, and as she listened, thought of her sister with tears in her eyes, and almost fancied that she beheld Lucy and Walsingham struggling amidst such horrors as he described.—Charmed with the interest he had awakened, his eloquence increased every moment, and he was proceeding to recount fresh perils, and Mrs. Cathcart, with open mouth, sat ready to swallow them. But short are all human triumphs! The door opened—Kelroy entered—and the first sound of his voice instantly broke the chain of Emily's ideas, who awaking as from a disagreeable dream, wondered that she could have listened so long to the dismal croakings of this raven. After the customary salutations, which were distant on Kelroy's part, and sulky on Marney's, he attempted to resume his subject, but found that he must now be content with a single auditor, for whilst he was holding forth to Mrs. Cathcart, interspersing his narrative with eternal repetitions of *this here, that there, says I, and says he,* neither of the young ladies seemed to hear him, but turned all their attention to Kelroy, who although rather surprised at meeting him there, viewed him with perfect unconcern; for having no longer any thing to fear from Mrs. Hammond, he could not possibly entertain a moment's apprehension from a competitor so deficient in every quality necessary to please a woman of refinement.

Marney, although he had been in Emily's company but once, was already as much enamoured of her as it was in his nature to be. He valued her in proportion as others admired her; and resolving to waste no time in useless delays, meant that this visit should be considered as the commencement of his devoirs. He knew that she had many lovers, and had heard she was inclined to favour Kelroy, and that her mother particularly disliked him. Of the latter part of the intelligence he had little doubt, but with respect to the first he was not quite so clear; but had he been assured of its truth, it would scarcely have deterred him, so inveterate were his prejudices in his own favour. He had visited her this evening without any apprehensions with regard to his reception, but the non-appearance of Mrs. Hammond, and the coolness of Emily had at first rather disconcerted him, and he was just beginning to congratulate himself upon having conquered it, when the entrance of Kelroy, his visible devotion to her, and the softness of her manner towards him, operated in spite of himself as a confirmation of all he had been told. He had not forgotten the cavalier behaviour of Kelroy a few nights before, of which he easily discerned the cause; and hating him for his insolence, without remembering how assiduously he had laboured to provoke it, had determined the instant he again beheld him, to be revenged; and shortening his discourse with Mrs. Cathcart, he drew his chair nearer to Emily, and began anew to compliment her on her beauty, and her skill in music, but indifferent to his praises, she scarcely answered him; and when, fearing he had offended her by too large a dose of flattery, he modestly resorted to another topic, both she and Kelroy appeared so insensible to the many bright speeches by which he had hoped to delight the one, and torment the other, that at last he became quite silent, with a view to discover, if he could, the charm by which his rival was enabled to recommend himself. That Kelroy *ought* to have been jealous, he thought a matter of course, when he compared their respective merits; but that he *should* have been so, seemed somewhat enigmatical.—After listening for some time, he remained as much at a loss as before; and Mrs. Cathcart rising to leave the room, he recollected that his taciturnity might appear remarkable, and making an effort to conceal his mortification, turned to Helen and addressed her with his favourite question of "Well ma'am have you heard any news?"

"None since I saw you last Mr. Marney. I should rather suppose you had by this time collected some to tell me," replied Helen.

"No ma'am I have heard nothing—nothing at all. The town is so dull that I am sick of it. Every body grows stupid."

"Thank you," said Helen, "for our share of the compliment."

"Heavens, Miss Cathcart! I hope you don't suppose I intended it for any body here? that would be a reflection on my own judgment," said he, with a spiteful glance at Kelroy, who did not observe it.

But Helen did; and desirous of tormenting him, said "Will you call mine in question if I tell you that I strongly suspect you have met with something to vex you lately."

"Something to vex me? not I indeed; but there is such a universal stagnation prevailing, that I find it impossible to preserve my spirits so well any where as at my own fire side. But one cannot always be at home; air and exercise are necessary—and if I go abroad, I must not expect to escape the prevailing disease."

"What disease?" said Helen. "Is the yellow fever in town?"

"No ma'am; but there are two disorders raging through it that are nearly as bad. Stupidity ma'am and scandal."

"How much are the poor wretches to be pitied," said Kelroy, "who are afflicted with a tendency to both."

"Faith I think so!" replied Marney, "but what does that signify?—People will not be at the trouble of diverting each other, unless they can do it with a story at somebody's expense, and there is so much of that work carried on at present, that it is as much as your head is worth, to speak in some places.—There is a set now in my neighbourhood that cannot live apart, and yet they are eternally back-biting, and abusing each other; but if I happen to repeat the merest trifle, or make the least remark to either of them, she directly tattles it to the rest, and I have the whole squad upon me, like wild-fire."

"And how do you defend yourself on such desperate occasions?" said Helen.

"Oh! very easily, by swearing point blank I never said a word of the kind, and leaving them to fight it out among themselves."

"It is said," replied Helen, "that females when particularly incensed, are apt to resort to the use of their nails; and if this is true, I suspect, Mr. Marney, you have more reason to be afraid of their *claws* than any weapon they possess."

"Heavens, Miss Cathcart!" cried he, rising, "you are too severe on your own sex, upon my soul!—If *I* had said such a thing now, it would be half over town before to-morrow night."

"Fortunately for me," said Helen, "I am not of sufficient consequence to have my observations so extensively repeated."

"Why ma'am, some people *are* fortunate in that way. They can say any thing, and no notice is taken of it; but others again are so unlucky, that—"

"That when they choose to be ill-natured," said Helen, interrupting him, "they find *others again* inclined to be sarcastic; and thus the peace of these benevolent regulators of society is seldom in their own keeping."

He reddened at this, and neither Kelroy nor Emily could suppress a smile; but though his anger was evident, he would not give proof of his consciousness of its application to himself by making a reply; but turned to Emily, and after some insignificant remarks on the colour of a riband attached to her dress, said with studied negligence, "Miss Hammond, what coloured eye is thought the handsomest?—"

"There is no exact criterion I believe, sir;" replied she, "the beauty of an eye is not supposed to depend so much upon its colour, as form and expression."

"But a lady's eye cannot be pretty unless it is mild; and it cannot be mild unless it is of a soft colour—blue, for instance?"

"Or green, for example," said Helen, "come, I'll help you out, if I can."

"Blue is the only colour," continued he, pretending not to hear her; "there is no other worth looking at.—Brown, and hazel may do, but they are too common—still they are better than grey, or black.—A grey-eyed girl looks like a cat; and as for black, zounds! I would not have a wife with black eyes for the universe!—I would as soon be married to a hyena!—"

"Then," cried Helen with great good-humour, making him at the same time a profound reverence, "I here renounce forever all hopes of being advanced to an honour, of which *my black eyes*, if you will have the goodness to look into them, must convince you I have been particularly ambitious."

"I beg your pardon, ma'am," said he, assuming an air of recollection; "I did not advert to your having black eyes, or I should have been more cautious."

"Oh, pray let it pass!" said she laughing; "and as you have expressed your disapprobation of them in my presence, you may consider yourself released from the necessity of repeating it in my absence, you know."

"Miss Cathcart, you are too keen for me!" said he, forcing a laugh also, "you shave like the north wind!"

"Perhaps then, if you could contrive to see me every morning, I might save you the expense of a barber."

To this he made no answer, and much out of humour at the result of his attempts to shine, began to contemplate a retreat, for which the entrance of the physician just then afforded him an excuse; and having repeated his regrets, and left his compliments for Mrs. Hammond, whom he hoped soon to have the pleasure of seeing in perfect health, he at last went away. Soon after, Mrs. Cathcart came down with the doctor, who pronounced Mrs. Hammond so much better, that there appeared no necessity for her remaining there all night, and she was preparing to depart.—Emily begged, however, that Helen would stay, and Mrs. Cathcart went home accompanied by Kelroy.

Emily found her mother as the doctor had represented, infinitely amended, and desirous of being left alone, but to this she could not consent; and seeing her inclined to repose, ordered a small bed to be brought for Helen, and herself, who sat up together till twelve o'clock; and Mrs. Hammond remaining in a sound sleep, they then went to bed also; and had the pleasure of seeing her the following morning able to rise, but not to leave her chamber, where she continued three days longer; refusing to admit any visitors except Mrs. Cathcart and her daughter.

CHAPTER XI.

WHILST Mrs. Hammond remained in her apartment a prey to chagrin and dejection, Kelroy experienced the greatest happiness he had ever yet known.—The house during that time was free from the crowd of company which usually infested it, and thus afforded him opportunities of enjoying undisturbed the society of Emily, to whom, if possible, he hourly became more attached. Recent events had rendered her more pensive than usual, but what she lost in gaiety was more than recompensed in sweetness; and sometimes, as he gazed on her mild, and beautiful countenance, or listened to a voice whose softness gave new interest to sentiments which required no embellishments beyond their own innocence and truth, he thought to be beloved by *such* a woman, was in itself sufficient to counterbalance every earthly evil.—But these were a lover's dreams! such as spread their sunshine in early life, and play round the heart to add one more to those illusions of which time alike unfolds to the simple, and to the wise the fallacy.—Reason spoke a different language, and taught him that a continuance of such happiness was only to be purchased by relinquishing it altogether for a season; and, yielding to necessity, he had begun to form decisive arrangements for his voyage, which was to commence within a fortnight.

His mother to whom he had confided his inauspicious affection, had constantly sympathized with his distresses, although she secretly lamented the chance which had caused them to arise from a member of the Hammond family, whom she knew only from report; but believing that the daughters of such a mother, educated as they had been, could not fail to inherit a greater portion of pride, frivolity, and extravagance than the generality of their sex, she thought the first affliction would be the least, and rather wished that Mrs. Hammond's endeavours to separate them might be successful. Learning at length the change which had taken place in her sentiments, she calmly acquiesced in a measure which he declared requisite to his future peace, but expressed an earnest desire to see before his departure the person who was to influence so largely the happiness of a dear, and only son. Her health was such as seldom permitted her to go abroad, and when Emily was informed by Kelroy of his mother's ardent wishes to become acquainted with her, she readily promised to take the earliest opportunity of allowing him to conduct her thither. She had often heard him speak with delight of his mother, and she now waited with impatience for the time to arrive when she should see that parent of whose benign, and gentle goodness he entertained so high a sense, that his regard for her seemed almost to partake of adoration.

The fourth morning after Mrs. Hammond's indisposition, she resolved, by the advice of her physician to take a ride. The carriage was ordered, and she set out with Emily, and seemed as they proceeded to regain something like animation. She had not uttered a word relating to what had passed respecting Kelroy since the hour in which it took place, but she now introduced the subject herself, and spoke of it with apparent composure, to the infinite relief of her daughter, who from her rigid silence, had apprehended a storm of concealed displeasure.—Reduced now to place her hopes upon Kelroy, she was compelled for her own sake to wish him success; yet she still retained towards him her original dislike; and notwithstanding her conviction that she had erred in some points, pertinaciously adhered to the belief that but for his influence her schemes would all have prospered, and her old age been fortunate and happy. But the extent of her disappointment, and its distressing effects she carefully concealed, and merely gave her daughter to understand, that having no longer any inducement to live in an expensive style, she should rent her house in the city, part with her carriage and horses, and reside in the country as she had formerly done. Delighted to find her mother's wishes accord with her own, Emily expressed so strongly the pleasure she should derive from the change, that Mrs. Hammond having listened to her with a feeling of contempt, replied after a pause, "As you are so enraptured with solitude, and seem to consider the forms of polished society such a hideous restraint, I suppose it will be a matter of exultation to you, rather than grief, if Kelroy returns as poor as he went—for then you will have a fair excuse for hiding yourselves from the world, and trying to make up in love what you want in better things."

Emily smiled, and replied, "that she was not quite so romantic as to imagine that love could compensate for the total want of what was generally meant by *better things*; but as she was not of an aspiring temper, a very moderate share of them would content her; and from poverty, in the strict sense of the word, she had every reason to believe she should always be secure.—" She then mentioned Kelroy's mother, and his request that she would visit her, adding that she had promised him to do so. She could not, however, have chosen a worse time to impart it; for although Mrs. Hammond was conscious that their families must one day be familiarly connected, she could scarcely bear the sound of a proposal which seemed to accelerate it; and feeling further irritated by her daughter's avowed want of ambition, and her expectations of a competency, she answered with an air which was meant to convey reproof, "that it would be most proper when she paid a visit of that kind to be accompanied by her mother," and ordered her, whatever Kelroy might urge to the contrary, not to go without her.

Emily was mortified by her mother's manner, which seemed to imply that she had been guilty of an impropriety in consenting to go without asking her permission; but the truth was, that supposing she could have no possible objection, she had not thought of consulting her; much less did she imagine that she would propose to accompany her, and heard it now with a sense of disappointment which called a deep blush into her cheeks, for she feared that her visit would be protracted until after the departure of Kelroy; the apprehension of which was so painful to her, that she ventured to ask her mother, whether she would not go soon?—

"I can fix no time," replied Mrs. Hammond, "but will go as soon as convenient, which will probably be in a few days, until when, you must have patience; for I shall most certainly not incommode myself by going in quest of old madam Kelroy."

Much hurt by this speech, Emily remained silent, and regretted that she had mentioned her promise of complying with a request which she could not decently have refused, had she even been so disposed; and which she now saw her mother desirous to prevent her from fulfilling—yet for what reason she could not divine.

Little more was said by either of them during the rest of their ride, which was not long, and on stopping at their own door, they saw Mr. Marney just descending the steps.—He flew to hand them from the carriage, and accompanied them into the house, inquiring most solicitously respecting Mrs. Hammond's health, and was careful to be glad and sorry in the right places, until she had given such an account of her illness as she judged proper, and he then recommenced his gallantries to Emily, who received them very coldly.—The attention of Mrs. Hammond compensated somewhat for the neglect of her daughter, of whose beauty he now felt the whole fascinating power; and, as is not unfrequently the case, in proportion as she seemed to disregard him, became more anxious to obtain her favour. He had called repeatedly while Mrs. Hammond was indisposed, but Emily had constantly denied herself to him; and amidst the complimentary nonsense with which he now sought to entertain her, he mentioned her cruelty in refusing to see him, and the uneasiness it had occasioned him.—These, and a hundred implications of the same nature, uttered between jest and earnest, were truly afflicting to Mrs. Hammond, who beheld in them demonstrations of a passion which could now be of no avail; yet, so rooted were her habits in certain respects, that she could not prevail upon herself to abstain from giving him every encouragement in her power; and by explaining away some of

Emily's expressions, and misconstruing others, she contrived to send him home tolerably elated.

When he was gone, she took occasion to begin a lecture on good-breeding, the want of which, she asserted, few possible circumstances could excuse in any one—but least of all in a young lady towards those of the opposite sex, whose sensibility to her attractions rendered them peculiarly alive to the most trifling deviation from it.—"Politeness," she said "was the smallest return that could be made in such cases, and was what every gentleman had a right to expect, and every lady might safely practise, without being liable to unwelcome constructions."

Having uttered this, she rose and went to her chamber, where she sat brooding over her fallen hopes, and alternately projecting and abandoning plans for the revival of them until dinner, during which she obstinately resisted every endeavour of Emily's to cheer and amuse her, who fancying that her mother's dejection was occasioned in part by regret for having consented to admit Kelroy into her family, endeavoured to compensate for what she believed to be a voluntary sacrifice, by bearing with the utmost mildness and good humour the peevish impatience of which Mrs. Hammond this day discovered an unusual share.—As they were sitting silently together in the course of the afternoon, a smart rap at the door was heard, and in a moment after the sharp, shrill voice of a woman, exclaimed "Come, come, I'm tir'd of this old story:—I'm sure she is at home, and I will see her."

"No, Madam, you not find mistus at home," said Henry.

"Not find her, hey?—Well there's no harm in looking for her, any how."

And with these words she opened the parlour door, and presented to Mrs. Hammond the sour visage of her milliner, a vulgar, passionate woman, with whom she had in a very short time after her return to the city run up a bill to the amount of five hundred dollars, and then indiscreetly affronted by purchasing Lucy's bridal attire from a person who had opened some later importations. Enraged at receiving such a slight where she thought herself entitled to different treatment, she directly had recourse to the only means of revenge in her power, and sent in her account, accompanied with a rude demand to have it speedily discharged; which so nettled Mrs. Hammond, whose finances about that time were rapidly failing her, that she complained to her children of the insult which she pretended to have received; and charging them never to purchase another article from the author of it, took no further notice of the matter, until the frequent messages, and at length the repeated calls of the offended milliner convinced her that something must be done, and she then ordered her servants constantly to tell that woman she was not at home.—But this excuse failed at last, and being really in want of the money, she had called this day with a determination, as she said, of "either *seeing* her, or *suing* her."

Great was Mrs. Hammond's consternation on being thus required to discharge a debt which would sweep off so large a proportion of her cash; and after trying every art she was mistress of, to prevail on the woman to wait some time longer, she at last lost her temper, and made one or two insolent speeches which so incensed the other, who was before sufficiently irritated, that she replied in terms which enraged Mrs. Hammond to such a degree, that she with difficulty refrained from striking her. Emily, confounded at what she heard and saw, in vain attempted to interfere, and they were in the midst of a violent altercation, Mrs. Hammond vehemently asserting her right to be unmolested in her own house, and threatening to call her servants to her assistance; and the milliner raving with all the fury of exasperated ignorance about *warrants* and *executions* until she almost foamed at the mouth, when Kelroy, whose approach the noise of their dispute had prevented them from hearing, suddenly made his appearance.

The sight of him calmed Mrs. Hammond at once, and restored to her the perfect use of her reason.—She recollected not only the conclusions which must be drawn from her conduct, but also that the demand was a just one, and must ultimately be paid; and that by refusing to do so now, she subjected herself to additional expense, and perhaps, speedier exposure of her poverty.—These reflections flashed through her mind with the rapidity of lightning, and reading surprise in the looks which he alternately directed towards herself, and the passion-swoln features of the milliner, whom the entrance of a stranger had silenced likewise, she turned to her with an air that might have suited an angry empress, and said, "Your conduct has been so outrageous, and the unbridled fury of your insolent tongue, in consequence of my informing you that it was not perfectly convenient for me to settle with you immediately, so great, that if I were to punish you as I ought, you would find that you had forfeited a much larger sum than the one in question. But I scorn a contest with you, and shall make you feel that your impertinent threats were of little consequence to me."

She walked out of the room as she spoke, leaving her creditor somewhat at a loss as to the meaning of her expressions, but the scrutinizing eye of Kelroy kept her silent. She knew not who he was, and fearing from the recollection of her own violence, that Mrs. Hammond might have power to punish her for it in some way, determined quietly to await the event, and thus secure a witness that one part of her behaviour at least was governed by decorum.—In a few minutes Mrs. Hammond's bell rung, and sending for Emily, she gave her money, and ordered her to pay that *audacious wretch*, and take a receipt in full from her; which she did in the presence of Kelroy, wondering that instead of descending to a frightful quarrel, her mother had not done so at first.

After the milliner was gone, Kelroy staid with Emily, and Mrs. Hammond continued in her chamber, where latterly she had spent the whole of her time.—She came down when summoned to tea, and remained until Kelroy left them, and then returned to it, to deliberate what measures were most expedient for her to pursue now.—Of the money she had obtained on her mortgage, there remained but one hundred dollars; and of that she had borrowed from Walsingham only seventy. Of the first great part had been idly wasted, and the last she had unexpectedly been compelled to resign to save her tottering credit, and still owed at least two thirds as much more, which for aught she knew to the contrary she might be called on to pay at an hour's warning; and the bad success of her squabbles with the grocer and milliner had taught her the folly of seeking to escape such claims either by dispute or evasion.—In this emergency, without a human being in whom she durst confide, or one friend whose attachment to her was such as to warrant the expectation of assistance without adequate security, she was almost wild with perplexity; and for a long time could not decide whether to raise money by a mortgage on the house she lived in, or by sacrificing those expensive baubles and ornaments of which she possessed a great number, but feared to part with, lest the absence of them should create immediate suspicion.—To continue her present style of living another month, was, however, absolutely impossible; and after a long, and bitter parley with herself, the extremity of her situation convinced her that unless she voluntarily resigned the appearance of splendour, that of respectability would in a short space be torn from her for ever; and to prevent it she made the following wise resolutions:—To keep her house unincumbered—to part immediately with her carriage and horses—to announce that she intended residing in future wholly in the country, and to send to auction, as useless to her, the elegant new furniture which she had so lately purchased—and lastly, to dispose not only of all her own valuable trinkets, but of Emily's also, which she dreaded as the most difficult part of her task. Not because she feared her daughter's unwillingness to relinquish them, but because she foresaw the impossibility of assigning any plausible reason for depriving her of them; and she shrunk with horror from the idea of imparting to her the true one.—Yet, reflecting that her own diamonds were very valuable, and would probably with the sale of a few pieces of plate, in addition to that of the articles already destined to the purpose, produce sufficient for the discharge of all demands against her, she concluded to let Emily retain hers for the present, and subsist as long as she could upon the rent of her town house.—To adopt a plan of this nature required the whole force of her mind, but having once completely formed, she determined strictly to adhere to it; and resolutely bent on beginning to put it in practice the next morning, retired to rest with a spirit considerably humbled, yet upon the whole better satisfied with herself than she had been for a length of time, and after hearing the clock strike one, fell asleep.—The subject which had occupied her for so many hours was still present to her imagination, and she fancied herself struggling amidst innumerable difficulties, until they pressed on her with a heaviness like death, and she awoke nearly suffocated with smoke.—Without consciousness of the cause of her horrible sensations, the first impulse of suffering nature was to seek for air; and springing convulsively from her bed, she threw up a window, and leaned forward into the street to recover her breath, which the freshness of the morning breezes, for it was almost day-break, soon restored to her, and with it her recollection, and it now struck her that the house must be on fire.—Dreadfully agitated, she yet would satisfy herself of the truth of her fears, and groping her way to the door, opened it, and beheld the flames bursting up the stair-case to her very feet, but happily had sufficient presence of mind left to shut it, and return to the window, where her agonized shrieks for help caught the ear of the retiring watchman, and the alarm being given, a crowd immediately collected, and it was discovered that the first two stories were completely in a blaze. All was now noise, horror, and confusion. Nothing was thought of but to save the lives of the terrified family, who fortunately all slept in the upper part of the building, the height of which alone prevented several of them from precipitating themselves to the pavement below.—Emily slept in the same story with Mrs.

Hammond, but at a greater distance from the part which the flames had reached, and did not awake until roused by her piercing screams; but not being endowed with as much self-command as her mother, she had nearly fallen a victim to her fears, and was found by Kelroy, who with frantic affection persisted to risk his life in search of her, stretched motionless on the floor of a chamber remote from her own, and so enveloped in smoke and fire, that although she was still unscorched, he dared not entertain a hope of her revival, and carried her down the ladder, gone as he thought, forever.—The affecting sight of so beautiful a form, apparently senseless in death, and the frenzied exclamations of Kelroy caused every one to give way before him, and he bore her through the pitying crowd to the house of a gentleman in the neighbourhood, where every assistance being rendered that humanity could suggest, in about a quarter of an hour she began to shew signs of life, and before six o'clock, was safely placed at Mrs. Cathcart's with her miserable mother, to the inexpressible joy of her friends, and the agitated Kelroy, who never more had expected light to revisit those eyes from which he now imbibed such rapturous thankfulness, as made all former happiness seem poor.—Mrs. Hammond, who had first given the alarm, was the first who had been rescued from danger.—Her strength and fortitude lasted until she reached the ground, and she then fainted; but being assured on her recovery that her daughter and servants were uninjured, she seemed somewhat comforted, but asked no further questions, and was conveyed by old Mr. Cathcart and his son to their house, where she arrived before Emily, and soon after learned the entire destruction of all she possessed on earth; a blow so overwhelming, that she sunk beneath its pressure, and was carried to bed, where she lay in a state of alternate delirium, and insensibility, which soon made her life despaired of.

Emily was for some time severely indisposed from the effects of what she had undergone, but youth, and her apprehensions for her mother enabled her to surmount it; and from the moment her strength permitted, she was constantly in her chamber, where she waited in sorrowful expectation of receiving her last sigh.

CHAPTER XII.

Mrs. CATHCART, who had really a compassionate heart, did every thing in her power to relieve and console the afflicted Emily; but, although extremely attentive both to her and her mother, she found time at intervals to accomplish what every body else had failed in; and by repeatedly questioning, and cross-examining each of Mrs. Hammond's servants separately, at last prevailed on the cook to confess that she had been the cause of this shocking accident by going into the cellar to draw herself a draught of beer after the others were in bed, and letting the candle fall out of her hand upon a heap of dry rubbish.

The fire had got to such a height before it was discovered, that the first object of those assembled was to prevent any lives from being lost; and as the family consisted of seven persons, five of whom were females, so much time necessarily elapsed before they could be assisted, that it was too late to attempt saving any thing of value; and except a carpet which chanced to be rolled up, a small trunk containing papers, and a few chairs, not a single article of either plate, furniture or wearing apparel had been rescued from the merciless element; and before ten o'clock, of those splendid apartments where so lately taste had shone, and beauty triumphed, nothing remained but melancholy black walls and smoking ruins.

After lingering many days apparently on the confines of the grave, Mrs. Hammond's disorder suddenly assumed a favourable complexion. Her senses became clear, and her strength rapidly returned; and to the astonishment of all who had beheld her, she was able in a short time to walk about her chamber without assistance. But no ray of gratitude, no expression of thankfulness marked this escape from death, and restoration to reason. Stern, and ferocious, her nature seemed to have changed as much as her countenance, for the one had become as grim, and haggard, as the other was tempestuous. Her mind was of that stamp on which no excess of misery can effect permanent insanity; and the renewal of feeling and memory presented a prospect so fraught with wretchedness, that dissolution or madness would have been comparatively blessings. Of all she had ever possessed, not an atom now remained that she could call her own except her carriage and horses; and to render her self-accusation complete, the policy of insurance on her house and furniture had expired only one week before it was destroyed, and governed by some strange fatality, she had neglected to renew it, and was thus left a very beggar, without hope or consolation. Yet, cruelly as she suffered, her lips, since the return of her intellects, were obstinately sealed as to the true source of her distress, and what she had uttered during her illness was now forgotten, or remembered only as the ravings of delirium, by all to whom they had been repeated except Kelroy; and her present temper and appearance regarded as natural consequences of the alarming shock she had sustained. In this manner a week passed, during which owing to unforeseen causes, Kelroy's voyage was postponed for another fortnight; a circumstance peculiarly grateful to him at this period, when agitated with well-grounded fears as to Mrs. Hammond's probable situation in consequence of her losses, he hesitated whether it were not best to abandon it entirely, and remain to protect Emily from those trials to which her beauty, sensibility, and her mother's indigence, he believed must otherwise too surely expose her, who alike unsuspicious of his apprehensions, and her own impoverished state, mentioned with confiding innocence the loss of their clothes, and the active kindness of Helen in replacing them.—Touched by the affecting picture which he drew of the scenes that had passed, and his own distracting conjectures, his mother, anxious, if possible to assist his decision by her own observations, exerted the feeble remains of her strength, and voluntarily accompanied him to Mrs. Cathcart's; but when Mrs. Hammond was informed of her name, she angrily refused to admit her, and she saw only Emily, with whom she was so much charmed, that no longer wondering at her son's hesitation, she considered him from that moment entitled to the highest commendation for the self-government which had hitherto enabled him to consult the real happiness of this beloved object, in preference to his own impetuous wishes; for well she saw in the speaking eye, the trembling accent, and colourless cheek which accompanied the mention of his departure, that Kelroy was all-powerful in that heart where gratitude for the preservation of her life had imparted new enthusiasm to the fervour of youthful affection. Instead of the airy levity which her prejudices had taught her to expect, she beheld graceful beauty tempered with a sweet seriousness through which the vivid smile that sometimes broke for a moment, shewed a gaiety which could illumine happier days; and to the many regrets which attended her declining years, was now added that of seeing her son taste all the bitterness of his father's misfortunes in the endless perplexities which continued to cloud the prospect of his union with a woman, whom love and nature seemed to have formed for him alone.—Nor was Emily less pleased with her visitor, whose simple garb, mild, religious eye, and peaceful countenance, presented an image of evangelical purity and resignation in strict unison with the chastened feelings, and benevolent principles for which she was so eminently distinguished; and Kelroy learned afterwards with delight from them each, that the interview had been mutually gratifying to both. The regard which Mrs. Kelroy had conceived for Emily rendered her now equally anxious with her son that she should become his wife, but as Mrs. Hammond had refused to see her, she was still inadequate to judge of the truth of his fears; yet to her they appeared too extravagant to be entirely just; and believing them exaggerated by the feelings of a lover, she with her customary disinterested virtue sacrificed her powerful wishes for him to remain—wishes so consonant to his own, that a few words of pathetic entreaty would instantly have decided the contest, and advised him to pursue the course which he had previously allotted himself, and trust to a wise, and all seeing providence for the event. But it was utterly impossible for Kelroy to surmount the many evil impressions which he had received, and his horror of Mrs. Hammond was so profound, that the idea of leaving Emily exposed to her machinations was to his imagination appalling as the prospect of perdition; yet to remain thus upon an uncertainty would he knew prove equally fatal?—And after suffering innumerable doubts, and indescribable misery, he was still painfully irresolute, when something suddenly happened which determined him at once.

Tortured by the consciousness of the degrading exposure of her past deeds which approaching want and dependance must soon effect, Mrs. Hammond had become so horribly perverse and irascible, that her own daughter could with the greatest difficulty accommodate herself to the intolerable caprices of her humour; and Mrs. Cathcart and Helen who saw that all bodily indisposition was removed, both grew so weary of her, that had not regard for Emily, and compassion for what she must have endured with such a companion prevented them, they would not have scrupled requesting her to provide herself with another home. She was now down stairs yet would neither be a moment alone, nor suffer the approach of any stranger; and by her sharp, vindictive reproaches to the family whenever they presumed to go abroad, and obstinate refusal to admit of the society of any other person, the house soon resembled a perfect desert. If they attempted to amuse her by relating the little anecdotes of the day, she generally replied by ordering them not to torment her; and when they remained silent, would break out into doleful lamentations on the hardships of being condemned to such a state of gloomy penance; but if they ventured to converse apart with each other, as they sometimes did, she never failed to interrupt the harmony of their discourse by her ill natured remarks, or provoking contradictions; and the trouble and discomfort which she occasioned to them all in various ways from the mistress down to the meanest servant, was scarcely to be borne.—One morning as she sat loitering, and fretting over the breakfast table, from which, to avoid her, Charles and his father had of late voluntarily banished themselves by taking that meal before she rose; Helen, who was perusing the newspaper, suddenly exclaimed, "Ah! fortune has smiled upon some lucky mortal!"

"Some fool, I make no doubt!" said Mrs. Hammond.

"Perhaps so," replied Helen, "but as he has obtained a golden veil for his folly, it will hereafter be invisible."

"Oh true! I forgot to tell you that the fifty thousand dollar prize came out in the lottery yesterday; but Charles says they have not yet been able to find out who it belongs to," said Mrs. Cathcart.

"What is the number?" said Mrs. Hammond eagerly.

"Five thousand, three hundred and seventy," replied Emily, who now had the paper.

"Give it to me!" said her mother, snatching it out of her hand; and having glared on it for an instant she repeated, "fifty thousand!" and sunk pale, convulsed, and gasping in her chair.

All conjecture with respect to the *cause* of this sudden and violent emotion was absorbed in its terrifying effect; and not staying to inquire from whence it arose, they each endeavoured to administer to its relief. Helen flew to look for salts, which she could not find, and having in her haste broke, and overturned half a dozen different things, at last recollected that there was some hartshorn[1] in the next room.—Emily, although very much frightened, tried to open her mother's hands, which were clenched so tight that the nails almost penetrated through the skin; and Mrs. Cathcart endeavoured to prevent her from falling to the floor, but as she was not expert in her movements, and Mrs. Hammond rather heavy, she so managed the matter that she herself slipped, and struck her dear friend such a blow in the face with her elbow, that the blood gushed from her nose in torrents, and not only immediately restored her to herself, without the necessity of any other remedy, but most probably prevented her agitation from throwing her into an apoplexy. After streaming profusely for some time, it at last stopped of itself, but not until her clothes were almost covered with it; and she lay on the sopha apparently a most awful spectacle when Kelroy entered.

---

1 Smelling salts, or ammonium chloride, were made by distilling hartshorn oil derived from the horn of a male red deer.

"Good God!" exclaimed he, "what is the matter?"

"A fright! something about a lottery!" said Mrs. Cathcart, whose wits had begun to return; and who uttered this in a tone meant for a whisper, but her curiosity and alarm rendered it much more like a scream.

Kelroy looked astonished, and Mrs. Hammond who had now sufficiently recovered her recollection to be sensible of the part that it was necessary for her to act, turned to Mrs. Cathcart and said, "I am absolutely good for nothing!—My nerves are so weakened that the least surprise almost destroys me."

"Why!—What!—Is it possible that you have got this prize then?" exclaimed Mrs. Cathcart, with outstretched neck, and staring eyes.

"I have reason to think so, provided the paper is correct," replied Mrs. Hammond, striving to restrain her feelings.

"Oh! It's right!—I'm sure it's true, for Charles says they can't find out the owner, and I'm sure it's you!" cried Mrs. Cathcart, "but heavens! what did you faint for? If it had been me, I should have danced for joy!"

"Very probably," replied Mrs. Hammond disdainfully, "but for my part I am not so deeply interested."

"Then what made you faint?" inquired Mrs. Cathcart simply.

"I wish to God," replied Mrs. Hammond, whom suspense still kept in a state of fermentation, "I wish to God you would learn to talk like a person possessed of common sense! You know as well as I do, that of late the merest trifle has been sufficient to overcome me, and yet you can ask such a ridiculous question! Do you take me for a stock, or a stone, that ought to be insensible to every thing? I suppose the next news I hear will be, that you have entertained half the town, with an account of this affair, and the obligations which I owe to your own clumsiness?"

Poor Mrs. Cathcart, wholly unprepared for this rough attack, which although not worse than several which she had already sustained, mortified her so much from being made in the presence of Kelroy, that she burst into tears; but Helen incensed, and disgusted beyond endurance at such unbridled insolence, replied with spirit, "You forget yourself, Mrs. Hammond, and it is the duty of your friends to remind you that it is not incumbent on them to submit in silence to such language as this!—If my mother, madam, should feel herself disposed to speak of obligations, she will not be at a loss to recollect a sufficient number without having recourse to the accident which you think proper to term one."

This tart reply, the first that Mrs. Hammond had ever received from Helen in her life, immediately made her sensible that there were bounds to patience here as well as elsewhere; and she condescended to apologize for what she had said, by ascribing her irritability solely to the *disorder of her nerves*, and requesting that it might be pardoned as an involuntary, and unintentional offence; whilst Kelroy regarded her as the most inexplicable of all created beings, and silently wondered in what manner the scene would end. As for Emily, she began to fear that this sudden increase of wealth had turned her mother's brain in earnest, so much was she shocked at her treatment of Mrs. Cathcart, whose good-nature and respect for riches made her very readily accept the excuse that was offered; and wiping her eyes, she said "Well, well, it's over now and we'll think no more about it—yet I must say nothing was ever further from me than the idea of mentioning what has past, for I shall make a point of not breathing a syllable of it to any living mortal. People will no doubt be curious, but they shall never hear a single word about it from me—But such a fortune! good lord what a lucky soul you are!—Why you will have more money than you know what to do with!"

"I fancy not my dear!" returned Mrs. Hammond with a gracious smile; and anxious to have the matter fully ascertained before she indulged in full exultation, she gave Emily a key, and directed her to the little trunk which had been saved from the fire, in which she said were two tickets, and desired her to bring them both. When they were produced, one of them was found to correspond with the number announced in the paper; the other Mrs. Hammond seemed perfectly indifferent about, owing to its having been drawn a blank[1] the day after she purchased them, not a *year ago*, as she now pretended, but the preceding week, when half wild with perturbation, it occurred to her to try her fate once more in a lottery; for although she had latterly been a repeated, and unsuccessful adventurer in this frequent resource of desperate extravagance, it was possible the scale might still turn in her favour. Resolved to give it a trial, she borrowed money from Mrs. Cathcart, on pretence of wanting it for some other purpose; and secretly sending her mulatto girl to purchase two tickets, with strict orders not to mention it, under pain of severe correction, had the intolerable vexation to see one of them advertised as a blank the next morning, which so disheartened her, that despairing of relief, she gave herself little concern about

---

1 Not a winner.

the other, and had ceased to dwell upon it, when she suddenly received the account that it had proved fortunate beyond her utmost hopes.

Kelroy who was better informed than any one present of the source of the violent emotions she had shewn, proposed, in compassion to what he imagined were her feelings, to go and inquire whether or not she was entitled to the prize in question. Her pride had not suffered her to ask it of him, but her suspense, and anxiety made her gladly accept the offer, desiring him, however, not to mention her name, "for really," continued she, "people might fancy it wore a strange appearance for *me* to seem so very solicitous about the fate of one poor, solitary lottery ticket."— Kelroy smiled involuntarily as he went out, at this characteristic speech from a woman whom he had reason to suspect was reduced to straits which she could scarcely bear to think of, much less to acknowledge. She saw him, and the recollection of the sarcastic expression of his countenance added one pang more to the many which wrung her bosom, during the fifteen minutes of his absence, towards the close of which her internal restlessness was such as threatened to wear the appearance of unconcern no longer. At length he returned with the intelligence that number *five thousand, three hundred and seventy* was actually entitled to the highest prize; and Mrs. Hammond exerting every particle of energy that nature had gifted her with to remove the evil impressions which might remain from her having fainted, received his congratulations with considerable apparent composure, whilst her heart throbbed with convulsive joy.

The exhilarating effects of this piece of good fortune quickly manifested themselves in the disposition of Mrs. Hammond, whose only care, next to restraining her own transports, and accounting for her past disturbances, and sallies of temper in a plausible manner, was to prevent Mrs. Cathcart from spreading it, with all its attending circumstances, wherever she went. Of Kelroy and Helen she was not afraid, and therefore took no methods to school them; but when the immediate ferment of her mind had subsided, she conducted herself with such a shew of dignity and composure, and bestowed on Mrs. Cathcart such sage advice, and so many remonstrances on the impropriety, and even wickedness of making the private concerns of our friends the subjects of public conversation, that she flattered herself she should succeed in keeping her fainting-fit, and its disastrous effects a profound secret. Her face still bore the marks of the contusion she had received, so that it would not have been practicable for her to have gone abroad had she wished it; but to resume so suddenly her former level of company would have worn a very suspicious aspect, therefore she not only remained at home as usual, but determined not to go out until a day or two previous to her removal to the country, which she resolved should be as early as possible.—The only change which appeared in her was, that she seemed no longer morose, and when the blackness was removed from her nose, resumed her seat in the parlour, where she received with grave politeness the congratulations of her acquaintance, who flocked to her in crouds when they were informed that she was well enough to see them; and were one and all completely deceived by her specious manner, and fine moral reflections on the wisdom and equity of providence in dispensing both good and evil, of which she professed to consider herself a striking example. To Kelroy, whose fears for Emily were now at an end, she behaved with unusual cordiality, but took care to insinuate, that although it was now doubly in her power to remove the necessity of his voyage to India, she approved too highly of that measure to exert the means of preventing it. He heard her with disgust, but without surprise, for he had not done her the injustice to surmise that her generosity could possibly have extended itself so far; but Emily, whose imagination where he was concerned, sometimes outran her judgment, had ventured to encourage different expectations.—Whilst there appeared no reasonable ground to hope that their separation might be prevented, she had endeavoured to reconcile herself to the prospect of it without murmuring; but now, seeing her mother, as she imagined rolling in superfluous wealth, she learnt with bitterness of heart that no part of it was to be appropriated to the only purpose which could render the accession of it valuable to her. Sensible of the folly of having yielded too easily to the suggestions of her own fancy, she carefully concealed from Kelroy that such an idea had occurred to her, and found in the sympathetic melancholy which marked his every word and action, the only consolation which at such a period her mind was capable of receiving.

Among the many persons who had thought it incumbent on them to inquire after Mrs. Hammond during her illness, none had been more assiduous than Mr. Marney, who had called regularly once a day. He was not in town on the night of the fire, and therefore had no opportunity of exerting himself in Emily's behalf as Kelroy had done, whom he now hated worse than ever for the advantage which he supposed him thus to have gained; but knowing that he was soon to be absent, and believing all women to be naturally fickle, he resolved to continue his attentions, and wait a favourable opportunity for proving the result of them.— When Mrs. Hammond again saw company, he was one of the first to pay his respects to her, and she received him so graciously, and he was encouraged to repeat his visits so often, that Emily, dreading that consummate address in her mother of which she had repeatedly felt the effects when least expected, constantly made some excuse to leave the room when he was there, unless Kelroy was present also. But although Marney had by his assiduities highly ingratiated himself with Mrs. Hammond, those designs for the completion of which she considered him a fit instrument had ceased to exist, and she no longer intcrested herself in his progress in the favour of Emily, for whom his passion was so evident, that nothing but the most thorough conviction of her contempt for him, could have prevented Kelroy from becoming seriously jealous.

Thus passed the days until the arrival of that previous to Kelroy's departure, on the morning of which Emily accompanied him on a visit to his amiable, and respectable mother, with whom she remained several hours, and as they returned home, he informed her, that it would not be in his power to see her again before eight in the evening, when, as the ship was expected to sail early, they must meet for the last time.—She spent the afternoon alone in her chamber, and when night approached, was found fixed in the deepest dejection by Helen, who was engaged out with her mother and brother, but would not go until she had first seen, and tried to cheer the spirits of Emily, who in compliance with her intreaties, arranged her dress, and descended to the parlour, where sat at tea Mr. Marney, Mrs. Hammond, and a distant relation of Mrs. Cathcart's, Mr. Nesbit, an ancient gentleman with whom Emily was a particular favourite.—He was a sprightly old man, and as she was equally partial to him, and fond of his conversation, they seldom met without much gay raillery on both sides; but after accosting her on her entrance in his usual way, he presently discovered from her answers that *all was not peace within*, and in a whisper told her so. She smiled, and endeavoured by forcing herself to seem more animated to persuade him that he was mistaken; but the humid appearance of her eyes, and the unconscious sadness which diffused itself at intervals over her countenance were such as could not be misconstrued by any but the enamoured, conceited Marney, who having made his own observations, wisely concluded that it was impossible for a person in much distress to look as beautiful as she did.

After Mrs. Cathcart and her son and daughter had been gone some time, Mr. Nesbit took out his watch and told Emily that "he had just twenty minutes longer to stay, and that although *she* was not quite *in tune*, the *harp was*;" and pointing to one that stood near her, requested her to play him a song before he went. She begged him to excuse her, but he declared he could not, and said she might choose the most dismal ditty in her whole collection if she pleased, but that he must absolutely have one of some sort.—Little as she felt inclined to comply, she would most probably have sacrificed her feelings to oblige him, had not Marney, who had vexed her by inquiring whether Kelroy was not to sail the next day, and staring rudely in her face for several minutes after she had answered him added his intreaties, and she then positively declined; but they both expressed so much disappointment, that Mrs. Hammond, who busied in writing a note for which a servant was waiting, had scarcely attended to them, now came forward and said, "Bless me, child! what is the matter with you?—I am afraid you have grown affected?"

"*Affected* ma'am?" repeated Emily with a half checked sigh.

"Yes to be sure you have!" said Mr. Nesbit, "at least I hope so; for I should not be willing to suppose that such doleful humours are natural to you?"

"Miss Hammond is not *doleful*, but pensive and interesting," said Marney with a look which he intended for a very languishing one.

"My dear, pray end all this by doing as you have been desired," said Mrs. Hammond, "for you are not sick, and I know of nothing else that ought to prevent you."

Marney now renewed his importunities, and Emily still refused, until tired of hearing them, Mrs. Hammond at length ended the contest by telling him in an authoritative tone to reach her the instrument, which thus compelled, her daughter received in silence, but very unwillingly, and began a tune, determined to play as ill as she could; but her taste in music was uncommonly just, and as she had no natural perverseness to second her resolution, she pursued it no further than a bar or two, and before she concluded, had forgot it entirely.—She seldom appeared to so much advantage as when she performed on the harp; and owing to her resentment, which had somewhat heightened her complexion, and a few scarlet flowers which Helen had twisted through her glossy hair in a manner peculiarly becoming, she had never perhaps looked more lovely than at that moment; and Marney gazed at her with the most intense admiration, and listened to her sweet voice, and thought of the money her father left, and the prize her mother had just drawn, until he was wrought up to such a pitch of affection, that he felt ready to fall down and worship her.—When she ceased he gave a great sigh, part real, and part affected, and with eyes full of what was passing in his heart, thanked her for the pleasure she had afforded him, but Mr. Nesbit said she was a "perverse little baggage, who instead of being applauded for her charming performance, ought to be punished for having delayed it so long," and jumping up, bade them all a hearty good night, and was followed into the entry by Mrs. Hammond, who said she had a question to ask him, and after talking together a few minutes, he went away, and she called for a light and walked up stairs.

Provoked, and mortified at being thus left alone with a man she detested, and whom neither coolness or scorn seemed to discourage, Emily sat without uttering a word.—Marney too was quite silent for a time, being engaged in a hard battle between his understanding, and his wishes; the first of which hinted that it would be imprudent to risk a confession of his love at present; but the latter were so clamorous, and urged so strongly the frequent happy effects of boldness, and perseverance, that they ultimately obtained the victory; and determined not to regard a little reserve as such a formidable obstacle, he drew his chair as close to hers as he dared, and said awkwardly, "I am very bad company—don't you wonder at my stupidity, Miss Hammond?—"

"No sir," replied Emily shrinking away from him.

"You ought not," continued he, "and I am sure you would not, if you knew the cause."

"Perhaps so; but I have no wish to know it."

"That is cruel!—but you know your power—you take pleasure in tormenting me!—"

"Pleasure in tormenting *you*?" said Emily, her eyes sparkling with disdain;—"believe me, sir, I never yet associated the idea of pleasure with aught relating to you."

"How cold!—how severe!—but every change serves only to increase your beauty and my affection."

She turned from him with disgust, and was rising to leave the room, but he seized her hands, and had just thrown himself on his knees, when the door opened, and Kelroy entered the room, who stopping short on seeing how they were situated, exclaimed with an agitated countenance, "What is all this?—"

Marney started up in great confusion; and regardless of his presence, Emily flew towards Kelroy, who seemed rooted to the spot, whilst his eyes alone spoke the tumult of his heart; and catching him by the arm, said in a tone which struck instant conviction of her strong attachment to this envied rival into the soul of Marney, "I am glad you are come!—"

"Are you?" replied Kelroy, looking keenly in her expressive face; and reading there in unequivocal characters the truth of her words, he led her to a seat, and placing himself beside her, tried to restrain his indignation for the present.—Emily had never before seen his temper ruffled, and perceiving with alarm how much he seemed incensed, trembled for the consequences of the altercation which she feared would presently ensue between him and Marney, whose dumb silence she supposed to proceed from similar feelings. But the prudence of that gentleman, whose aversion to broils[1] with his own sex was such, that rather than engage in one he would have relinquished the finest woman in existence, soon quieted her apprehensions; for to her infinite relief and surprise, he at length addressed himself to Kelroy, and in an amicable voice inquired the state of the weather, and was answered with a sneer "that there was a fine cooling shower just begun." Not liking the air with which this was uttered, he staid to ask no more questions, but took up his hat, and with a silent bow sneaked away, with his love considerably lessened by the exercises which it had sustained of mortification from Emily, and terror from Kelroy, whose evident wrath had intimidated him so much, that he thought of nothing but escaping from it; and apprehensive that he might follow him, instead of returning home, went to an obscure tavern where he passed the night.

He was no sooner gone, than Kelroy requested from Emily an explanation of what he had just witnessed, and she endeavoured to divert him from it, as a subject unworthy of notice; but finding that this not only increased his anger towards Marney, but also induced a suspicion that she was not entirely averse to his addresses, she was obliged, as the only means of satisfying him, to repeat all that had passed.—She found no great difficulty in convincing him it was not from choice she had listened to Marney, but she had a great deal to obtain a promise that he would not seek to extort from him an assurance that she should no more be molested by him.—In vain she pleaded her contempt of him, and his own insignificance; Kelroy could not forget that he had had the presumption to aspire to the heart and hand of Emily, and to persist in forcing himself into her society in defiance of her

---

1 Disputes.

downright aversion; and stimulated by the natural abhorrence which every man feels at the idea of the object of his choice being addressed in the language of affection by any but himself, argued that a fellow possessed of so much impudent perseverance ought never again to be permitted to enter her presence.—But subdued by her tears, and mournful remonstrances against the cruelty of thus embittering their hour of separation by unreasonable jealousy, and inflexibility, he at last yielded his judgment to her intreaties, and forgetting Marney, and every thing on earth but herself, thought only of the claims and endearments of parting love.—A thousand times did he fold her to his bosom, and repeating the vows which he had already so often uttered, implore her never to desert him; and as often did she assure him that neither time, absence, or misfortune could have power to change her heart—he still lingered, unable to leave her, until the stopping of Mrs. Cathcart's carriage at the door reminded him that he must remain no longer, and he then gave her his last, passionate farewell, and hastily left the house; and with the dawn of the following day, bade adieu to his native land.

CHAPTER XIII.

THE uncommon pains and vigilance of Mrs. Hammond in restraining the tongue of Mrs. Cathcart with respect to the untoward circumstances which had ushered in the late fortunate event, kept her silent for a little while; but the concealment of such a prolific fund of discourse was too irksome to be endured long; and she ventured to relieve herself by whispering it to about half a dozen sage old dowagers of her acquaintance, accompanied with the strictest injunctions of secrecy to each, which they observed exactly as she had done, and the story was presently in general circulation, embellished with additions and alterations by the wits of the day, which rendered it truly laughable. Yet such was the commanding air, and lofty demeanor of the lady at whose expense they indulged their mirth, that wherever she appeared she constantly awed into silence those whose flippancy might otherwise have tempted them to rally her on the subject; and having been duly felicitated in her presence, and envied, and ridiculed in her absence, it died away in a short time without her having known, or suspected any thing of the matter.—Freed at once from all her difficulties, she felt as if in paradise; and having received her money, paid off her mortgage, satisfied all her creditors, and provided herself with every thing necessary to comfort and elegance, she retired with her daughter into the country, where she tasted in all its luxury the sweets of that tranquility of mind to which she had so long been a stranger; and taught by her past distresses the value of economy, no longer indulged herself in endless company, and expensive entertainments, but contented herself with the occasional society of a few of her most intimate associates, and behaved in every respect like a rational woman. The change was particularly suited to the feelings of Emily, whose regret for the departure of her lover was visible in her appearance, and for several weeks she confined herself to entire solitude; but at her season of life, grief finds too many sources of consolation to continue its excesses long. Her mother suffered her to dispose of her time exactly as she pleased, and this indulgence, added to the perfect quietude which every where surrounded her, soon exhausted the violence of her sorrow; and ceasing to dwell forever on the past, fancy began to paint the scenes that would attend the future, and hope touched the picture with such soothing colours, that yielding to their influence, she voluntarily returned to her friends, and her customary occupations with a soul unchangeably devoted to Kelroy, but a mind that had recovered its natural serenity.

From the specimens she had received of Marney's disposition, she had been led to apprehend, that notwithstanding what had passed, he would still have endeavoured to continue his addresses; but on the contrary he absented himself entirely from Mrs. Cathcart's whilst she remained there, and she saw no more of him until some time after their removal from the city, when he one morning unexpectedly paid them a visit. He seemed in very good spirits, and in answer to Mrs. Hammond's inquiries respecting his sudden desertion of them, replied that he had been indisposed with a cold and fever. His looks, however, were unaltered, and to Emily's great astonishment, he conducted himself towards her with a degree of civil indifference which she had supposed him incapable of. She had expected either whining servility, or insolent rudeness, and was most agreeably surprised to find that he had sufficient respect for himself to preserve a medium.—Nor did he from that day forward, although he regularly continued to visit them, ever manifest by a single word or action that he recollected having once been a humble admirer of Emily's; and as he ceased to torment her, her aversion to him abated by degrees into perfect unconcern; but she sometimes could not help wondering what had become of his vehement admiration, when instead of joining her and her companions in their rambles, he preferred remaining in the house among a circle of elderly people, or playing chess with Mrs. Hammond.

As the summer advanced, they received letters from England announcing the safe arrival of Walsingham and Lucy, who was delighted with the reception she had met with from his titled relations, and talked of Lords, Ladies, and Knights of the Garter without end, to the inexpressible gratification of Mrs. Hammond, who retailed it all to her envying visitors as a matter of course; and exulting in having it now in her power to convince Walsingham that she was unquestionably possessed of the independence which he had doubted, immediately wrote her daughter an exaggerated account of the destruction of her house, her own illness, and her prize in the lottery, which without the least compunction for the falsehood, she magnified *fifty* thousand dollars to *eighty*; telling Emily who wrote both to her sister and Walsingham, that it would be unnecessary to repeat that, for she herself had mentioned it already.

Mrs. Cathcart who was never so happy as when she was ranging about, generally rode out with Helen once or twice a week to Mrs. Hammond's, who although she seldom went to town, still kept up her former intimacy with them; and after the extreme heats commenced, Helen remained there altogether, to the infinite joy of Emily, who had become so attached to her, and habituated to her society, that the loss of it was in leaving Philadelphia the only deprivation which she lamented.

The grounds of Mrs. Hammond bordered on the Schuylkill,[1] near which her house was situated, but so surrounded with trees that it was not visible at the distance of an hundred yards; and on the banks of the river, which there were steep, and rocky, was a beautifully romantic walk, and among the many attractions it possessed, which induced Helen and Emily when alone constantly to prefer it to any other, was that of being so shady, that they could resort to it without being incommoded by the sun in the hottest weather.—One morning as they were sauntering there in silence together, they heard upon turning an angle of the path, persons speaking on the edge of the water below, and stopped to listen.

"He is certainly dead!" exclaimed the first voice, "He fell on his head, and I think his neck is broken!"

---

1 A river that flows through Philadelphia.

"I hope not;" said the second, "his heart still beats."

"We must have assistance," replied the other, "but I see no living creature, and do not believe there is a house within a mile of us!"

The girls now made their way with some difficulty to the extremity of the bank, which was formed of a rock that projected several yards, and saw on the margin of the river beneath, two gentlemen standing over a young negro, who lay on the ground apparently dead. Emily uttered an involuntary exclamation of compassion, which caused them both to look up, and the one who had spoken last gazed on her for a moment, and then taking off his hat said, "Ladies you see here my poor servant, who I am afraid has destroyed himself in endeavouring to obey the orders of his master."

"Does any person live near us?" inquired the other.

"My mother does, sir," replied Emily, "and we will send somebody to your assistance immediately."

They then ran back to the house, where they found with Mrs. Hammond, Charles Cathcart, who had just arrived, and when informed of the accident, said he had passed doctor Blake on the road not three minutes since, and would endeavour to overtake him. He then remounted his horse and rode off, and Mrs. Hammond sent her coachman down to the river with whatever she thought might be of immediate service to the sufferer; but no sooner had the news of what had happened spread through the house, than impelled by curiosity, the gardener, cook, and chamber-maid followed; and when Charles Cathcart returned with the doctor, Mrs. Hammond herself accompanied them to the place which Emily pointed out, where they found one of the gentlemen, whom Charles saluted by the name of Dunlevy, but his companion had walked to the nearest ferry in quest of a boat. When the doctor examined poor Sancho, who had recovered from his swoon, and was howling most piteously, it was discovered that he had dislocated one of his knees, and his right shoulder, and broken his left arm and collar-bone; and as the boat did not arrive, and he lay exposed to a burning July sun on the sand, where it was not practicable to render him any assistance, Mrs. Hammond was obliged in common humanity to propose that he might be taken to her house, and as he was a favourite servant, and his situation such as to render a further removal at present extremely hazardous, Dunlevy gladly accepted the offer, and he was carried thither in a blanket.

When doctor Blake had finished his operations, he told Dunlevy, who had looked on the whole time, "that his man must not be moved; for he would not be answerable for the consequences of it."

"But what am I to do?" said Dunlevy, "this lady is an utter stranger to me, and I cannot take the liberty of imposing on her family the trouble of nursing this poor fellow: he must be removed in a boat!"

"No such thing, I tell you!" cried the doctor, "it will be death to him, for the poor black devil is in a fever already!—These small accidents will happen occasionally; and if you don't know this Mrs. Hammond, why I do, and I'll just civilly let her know how matters stand."

"If he must remain here," replied Dunlevy, "I will inform her of the necessity of it myself."

"Not at all!" said the doctor, "you won't make out half as well as I shall; for I have a way of my own of managing these affairs; and she is a crabbed old piece, I can tell you!"

Dunlevy looked at him with surprise, but made no answer; and they went together to the parlour, where they found Charles and Helen Cathcart, Emily, and Mr. Marney, who had just arrived, and was eagerly listening to Mrs. Hammond's relation of what had happened. She had learned from Charles certain incidents highly in Dunlevy's favour, and received him on his entrance with such cordiality, and introduced him so politely to the rest of the company, that he no longer felt embarrassed at the idea of being compelled to trespass on her hospitality; but before he had time to speak, doctor Blake marched up to her, and spreading out his hands, said pompously, "The art of man has certain limits, beyond which it is impossible for the wisest, and most skilful of us ever to proceed in this world!—We have done all we can, but we are not able to stir after it!"

"Sir?" replied Mrs. Hammond, staring at him.

"I have known many instances, ma'am," continued he, "where want of candour in a professional man, has been attended with very ugly consequences, and I make it a rule on these occasions always to do as I would be done by.—This *nigger*, ma'am, has hardly a whole bone left in him, and the only chance for his life is to let him lie where he is."

"Most certainly," replied Mrs. Hammond, and turning to Dunlevy, who was expressing his concern for the trouble he was thus compelled to occasion her, assured him that so far from considering it as any inconvenience, she felt much gratified in the reflection that it was in her power to render a service to a *fellow-creature*; and insisting that he would not mortify her with further apologies, requested to know to what cause the accident was owing?

Dunlevy informed her that his friend Calhoun had prevailed on him to accompany him that morning in his favourite amusement of catching sun-fish in the Schuylkill; in drawing his line up too hastily, it got entangled in the trees above, and he ordered his boy to climb, and endeavour to extricate it, and having mounted to a considerable height, his foot suddenly slipped, and he fell with his whole weight on the rugged points of the rocky bank, which he struck repeatedly in his descent. He concluded by saying he regretted extremely having been the means of reducing him to such a state, but that he could not possibly conceive how he could have fractured his limbs so deplorably without being deprived of his life also.

"I can't tell how he managed to *break* his bones," cried doctor Blake, "but I know that *mending* them was plaguy hard work, for it has made me so dry, I am ready to choke."

Mrs. Hammond took no notice of what he said, and all at once, as if he had only that moment recollected her, he jumped up, and ran across the room to Emily, "Why God bless me!— why to be sure—it certainly is the noble lady herself!—"

And seizing her by the hand, shook it violently, crying at the same time, "Why God bless your beautiful little soul, how have you been these hundred years?"

Then turning around to Helen, "and Miss Helen too, by the immortal Moses!—well, it's most extraordinary that I should get among old friends all of a sudden so! but that's the way! a body never knows how matters will turn up in this crooked world!— try for a thing, and the devil a bit you'll get it!—run out of the way, and plump it comes in your face the next minute!—Charles, is there any body about here that sells small beer?—"

Charles, who knew that the slightest liberty taken by a person not altogether agreeable to her, was sometimes sufficient to irritate Mrs. Hammond, winked at him to be quiet; but the doctor was really, as he had intimated, very thirsty; and thinking her extremely rude in neglecting to order him a drink, took no notice of his hints, but kept talking away to Emily like an old acquaintance about the ball, and the party at which he had seen her, and finished with, "Charles, I say, is there no such commodity as spring water to be had in these parts?"

"The river is very near!" cried Marney, sneeringly.

"Then water your horse at it," returned the doctor, "and when he's done, you may take a sup yourself."

Very much provoked, Mrs. Hammond now rang the bell, and ordered some wine and water to be brought; but Dunlevy who apprehended that she was not quite pleased, thought as the doctor had been called there on his account, that it was incumbent on him to prevent him from remaining to give further offence, if he could; and rising, thanked Mrs. Hammond in very handsome terms for her good offices, and said he would send a person in the evening to take care of his servant; and having received a polite invitation to continue an acquaintance thus accidentally begun, told Blake that he was going, and would accompany him some distance.

"Well, but how can that be?" said the doctor; "you've got no horse, have you?—"

"No," replied Dunlevy, "but come, let us go, for I have something to say to you on the road!—"

"Something to say to me?—well, I should be glad to hear it;—but then there's no hurry.—Besides, I a'n't half rested yet; and more than that, I must have a small dish of discourse with the ladies before I go."

"You have had quite as much as is agreeable to them already, I suspect," said Charles, laughing.

"Faith, I think so," said Marney in a low voice to Mrs. Hammond.

The doctor overheard him, and replied to Charles, "What a fashion some people in this crooked world have of meddling in the affairs of others!—I don't mean *you*, for a body can allow an old friend to make a little free; but some folks the very first time they see one's face, think they have a right to be whispering their little two-penny remarks!"

"Come doctor," cried Dunlevy, who began to suspect he was somewhat crazy, "if you stay much longer, I must go without you!—"

"Patience! my friend, patience," said the doctor, "it will be all one a hundred years hence whether you take my way, or I take yours; but if you have any regard for your own comfort, you will never allow any thing to put you in a passion!"

"Do you always in that respect adhere to your own prescriptions?—" said Dunlevy.

"*Me?* why I'm the happiest fellow alive!—By the lord of Oxford! I've often thought I would not have the temper of some men for the universal world!—If the sun shines, they'll swear—if the wind blows, they'll curse—if the wife's abroad, they'll scold—if she stays at home they'll growl!—it's all one to them what happens, for they're sure to find fault every way, poor souls!"

A servant now entered with wine and water, and he said, "Aye, aye, here it comes at last! I knew I was waiting for something, but I couldn't for my life tell what it was."

He then filled a tumbler and said, "Mrs. Hammond, I wish you very good health!—Miss Emily, I wish you a husband!—Miss Helen, I wish myself a wife!"

"Dr. Blake, I wish you a little common sense!—"replied Helen.

"Come let's start," cried he to Dunlevy; "I've done for myself!—The fat's all in the fire now!"

And snatching up his hat, he affected to bustle out in a violent hurry, and at the door ran plump against Calhoun, who had returned with a boat and two men, but finding neither Dunlevy nor Sancho, presumed he had been removed to the house which he had heard mentioned, and ascended the bank in search of it.

"Zounds, and fury!" exclaimed Blake, stopping short, "I believe the world is coming to an end to day!"

But Dunlevy, afraid he would return to the parlour with them if he suffered Calhoun to enter, affected to be in as great a hurry as the doctor, and hastily bowing to the company, shoved them both off before him; and Blake having mounted his steed, the cavalcade proceeded leisurely along the road to a tavern two miles distant, where Dunlevy and Calhoun had left their horses.

"What a brute," exclaimed Marney, looking after him as he left the gate; "why the fellow deserves to be horsewhipped!"

"He is certainly a most extraordinary creature," said Mrs. Hammond, "but as Mr. Dunlevy's servant is under his care, it will be impossible to prevent him from coming here for some time at least."

"Well and who is this Mr. Dunlevy?" said Marney, "Is he the nephew of that rich old fellow with the red nose, who was so puzzled about knowing which of his relations he should make his heir?"

"The same," replied Charles, "except that I never understood there was any difficulty about the matter, for William has been his uncle's favourite from a boy."

"He has hey?" said Marney, "Well and how long have you known him?"

"Several years," replied Charles, "he is about my own age, and we were at college together."

"You were hey? Well and was he thought to be pretty smart there?"

"Ask him a few questions in Greek and you'll soon know," replied Charles turning on his heel.

To this he made no answer, but soon after addressing himself to Mrs. Hammond, said "Who is this doctor Blake? Where did he come from? Is he of a good family?"

"I really cannot inform you;" replied Mrs. Hammond, "Mr. Cathcart probably knows."

Determined not to gratify his curiosity, Charles remained silent, and Marney then said, "*I* know he is an impudent fellow, and if he ever gives me any more of his impertinence I shall take him down."

"Will you faith?" said Charles laughing, "Egad I should like to see you try!"

Marney now rose, and inquired whether he meant to return to town before dinner, and being answered in the affirmative, observed that he himself must be there within an hour, to meet three of his friends on business of great consequence, which could not possibly be transacted without him.

"In the name of wonder then," replied Charles, who loved to plague him, "what are you lounging here for? Don't you know it is almost one o'clock and you have six miles to ride?"

"Oh! I shall be time enough," replied Marney, importantly, ["]and I know they will be forced to wait for me at any rate."

"No no, it will be a pity to let them do that," cried Charles, who knew it was only said to make himself appear of consequence; and resolving to have a little diversion at his expense, ordered their horses to be brought, and when Marney who was a cowardly rider, mounted his, which was a very frolicsome one, and often occasioned him severe alarms, Charles rode up to him and saying "now for a race" gave his horse a smart stroke behind, and then whipping his own, they both sat off full speed, to the inexpressible terror of Marney, who quite unprepared, thought only of keeping his seat, and in a few minutes felt himself carried away with the swiftness of the wind. In vain when he recovered his presence of mind, did he try to check his horse and swear and bawl to his companion to stop, or his neck would be broke; Charles turned a deaf ear to all his outcries, and knowing the animal he rode would inevitably compel him to follow, mischievously kept on before him full tilt, until they reached the turnpike, when slackening his pace by degrees, he allowed Marney, who was by this time in a violent rage, to come up with him. He swore most vehemently at the trick which had been played him, and averred that he had been the whole way in imminent danger of his life; whilst Charles who was in reality ready to expire with laughing, affected to apologize for the mistake he had fallen into;

but declared he had entertained an idea he was doing him an immense service, by preventing the distress and displeasure of the friends who would otherwise have been kept waiting for him.

Dunlevy's servant became excessively ill in consequence of his fall, and his master who valued him highly, rode out to see him every day, and for a whole week flattered himself that in doing so he had no other motive; but at the expiration of that time doctor Blake pronounced his patient out of danger, and Dunlevy who was sensible there was no longer any necessity for such frequent visits, discovered that he had been drawn thither in part by compassion for Sancho, but more by his admiration of the beautiful Emily, who from the first moment he beheld her, as she stood looking down upon him, on the banks of the river, had made an impression on his senses, which their subsequent interviews converted into a more serious sentiment, and had not her affections been previously disposed of, he was perhaps, next to Kelroy, of all men the most likely to have gained them. The circumstance of his being avowed heir to an old, capricious, sickly uncle, who had sent for him from Virginia where he lived with his parents, who were people of the first respectability, and agreed to leave him his whole estate upon condition that he made Philadelphia his permanent home, had at once recommended him to Mrs. Hammond, who still retained all her original reverence for great folks, and contempt of little ones; and his politeness, good sense and vivacity procured him the approbation of her daughter, who was not one of those refined heroines who conceive that an engagement with one man obliges them to shut their eyes to the merits of all the rest of his sex. Neither was she apt to imagine that every gentleman who seemed disposed to converse with her, had a design upon her heart; and as she was too sincerely attached to Kelroy to experience the remotest sensation of tenderness for any other, she forgot as she listened to the diverting narratives, and sprightly remarks of Dunlevy, that he might not be equally indifferent with respect to her, when in fact the friendly unconcern which pervaded her whole conduct towards him, was all that prevented a declaration of his sentiments. He saw that so far from returning his attachment, she did not even suspect that she had inspired one, which as it was sincere, sought not like Marney's to obtrude itself upon her notice, but instinctively awaited some indication of reciprocal feelings in its object.

One afternoon he rode out to Mrs. Hammond's, and found Emily alone. On his entrance she hastily concealed a picture on which she was gazing, and he fancied that she had been shedding tears. His heart throbbed with jealous anxiety at the sight, but the sweet smile with which she received him imparted such bewitching loveliness to her features, already softened by the fond recollection of one who was far away, that Dunlevy, no longer master of his feelings, was impelled by an irresistible anxiety to know his fate, and seating himself beside her on the sopha, uttered some incoherent expressions of concern for having unintentionally intruded upon her so suddenly.—She looked at him with astonishment, for neither his countenance, nor tone of voice were such as she had been accustomed to from Dunlevy; but her mother at that instant entering, prevented both her answer, and a further explanation on his part; but he could not immediately overcome his emotion, which was so evident that Mrs. Hammond observed it, and inquired whether he was not well?—He made some trifling excuse which seemed to satisfy her, and hardly conscious of what he said, inquired when she had seen Dr. Blake!

"Not for some time;" replied Mrs. Hammond; "he is generally here once a day, but we are seldom in the way, and he comes, and goes without seeing any body but his patient, who I am told is so far recovered, that the doctor says he will require very little more attendance."

Dunlevy said he thought so too, and then relapsed into a silence very unusual to him; and Emily, who had walked to one of the windows, where she stood pondering with no very pleasant sensations upon his behaviour, informed her mother that Doctor Blake was then coming.—In a few minutes he arrived, and seemed uncommonly frisky, and full of his strange remarks; so much so, that he forced a hearty laugh from Mrs. Hammond, although the next moment she was vexed at herself for having indulged it; but Dunlevy, who was in no humour to relish mirth of any description, scarcely smiled, and saying he would accompany him to see how his man fared, took him almost immediately out of the room. They were no sooner gone than Charles Cathcart drove up to the house with his sister, who had been in town two days, and presently after them, Mr. Marney, in a fine new phaeton,[1] and when Dunlevy returned, they were all seated round a table examining a number of large coloured prints which Helen had brought with her. One of them was a representation of a romantic country scene, in the midst of which was a sportsman reclining in the shade with his spaniel, and his

1 An open horse-drawn carriage.

gun; and Marney no sooner beheld it, than struck with the resemblance, he exclaimed, *"Kelroy!"*—and held it out to Emily, who blushed excessively; and although her mother and the rest were eloquent in expressing their surprise that so complete a likeness should proceed from accident, she scarcely spoke, but examined it a long time with the most sedulous attention; and upon looking up, met the eyes of Dunlevy fixed on her with a gaze of such distressful solicitude, that impressed with instant sense of the pain she had been inflicting, an involuntary impulse of humanity caused her hastily to push the picture from her; but recollecting the inference which he might perhaps form, she as precipitately drew it back, and Dunlevy then said dejectedly, "Is that the resemblance of a friend, Miss Hammond?"

"Yes sir," replied she, still examining it, "a very particular one."

He sighed unconsciously, and withdrew to a distant part of the room; and as what had passed had been observed by all present, a silence of some minutes prevailed, which was broken by the entrance of Doctor Blake, who perceiving the additions which had been made to the company in his absence, paid his compliments very ceremoniously, and then sat down to amuse himself with the prints, over which he continued to preach, and dilate as if nobody there had ever seen such a thing before, and Charles, and Emily sat listening to him; but Helen walked out into the piazza, and Dunlevy followed her. Marney, whose curiosity was ever on the watch to profit by the slightest incident, moved silently to a window, the venetian blinds of which were closed, and unobserved by them as they stood near it, overheard the following short dialogue, "What a heavenly evening!" said Dunlevy, looking towards the setting sun, which had illumined with its brightest glow a sky of uncommon beauty.

"And yet, you do not seem to enjoy it?" replied Helen, observing that he had sunk into a fit of musing, "Do you know I am a witch," continued she, tapping him on the shoulder, "and can divine the subject of your thoughts?["]

"Can you?" said he starting; "well then try, and if you are right, I will tell you so."

"Emily!" said she.

"I confess it;" replied he colouring, "and now, since it ought to be the province of magic to remove perplexity, answer me two questions—Is—is not Miss Hammond engaged?"

"Yes," replied Helen, who would have thought it inhuman to attempt deceiving him.

"And to the person whose resemblance we have just seen?" said he, turning very pale.

"The same," said she.

He bowed without speaking, and leaving her, went slowly into the garden; and sincerely compassionating him, Helen returned to the parlour, where Marney had already sidled away from his window, and pretended to be occupied with the doctor, who was now expatiating upon the last print, which was a village church, surrounded by groups of peasants, who appeared to have issued from it; or at least he chose to think so; for holding it up before him he exclaimed, "Here's a sight now!—here's a lesson for wicked sinners to profit by! a parcel of innocent, pious country people going from church to their homes, where all is peace, and quietness—Not much like the Sodom and Gomorrah that we live in, Charley, where coaches, chairs, and every thing else fly about in such a manner that a body can hardly tell Sunday from Saturday!"

"But there is one way of making sure of the difference, doctor," replied Charles, "and that is by going to church yourself."

"Why that's true, if a fellow could once get himself safe landed there; but I've often thought, that when I set out to go, the devil throws temptations in my way on purpose, for I commonly get into a *flustrification*, and forget all about it 'till the business is over.—And then comes repentance, and the small affair we call conscience; and I have a great quarrel with myself, all to no purpose; for the same thing just happens over again."

"But do you never contrive to get there doctor?" said Emily.

"Oh yes! about a month ago I felt in such an excellent humour for the business, that not knowing how long it might last, I thought the best way was to strike while the iron was hot, and so took the grand rounds, and went to half a dozen in one day.—The first place that I got to, had but eleven people in it—I counted to be certain—and thinking there was not much good to be had there, I marched off to another, where the folks were so thick they were standing upon one another's heads; so thinks I, there must be something more than common going on here; so I wedges myself in among 'em and heard a grand discourse, setting forth that when mortals pursue riches, and worldly prosperity, however discreet their plans may be, a thousand unforeseen accidents can frustrate them; but in the pursuits of religion and virtue no such obstacles arise; for a man's success there depends upon himself, and if his efforts are sincere, they are sure to accomplish the desired end at last.—It fairly electrified me!—I felt every word the parson said down to the end of my little toe!—"

Dunlevy, who had ordered his horse, and was on the point of mounting bare-headed, until apprized of it by the man who attended, now entered in search of his hat.

"You are not going, Dunlevy?" cried Charles.

"Yes," replied he, and with a hurried bow to the ladies, left the house.

"Stop a little, man, and I will go along with you!" cried the doctor, bawling after him; but Dunlevy paid no regard to him, and vaulting into his saddle, in five minutes was out of sight.

"Did ever any body see the beat of that now!—" exclaimed the doctor; "Here have I been waiting for him all this time, and at last he gallops off without me as if the very old-boy[1] was behind him!"

"I know a secret!" said Marney, looking very wise.

"How long have you had it Marney," said Mrs. Hammond, "for you know the girls declare you can't keep one?"

"Do they? well I promise you I've got a famous one now, at any rate!—"

"And I'll promise you that if you have, it won't be a secret long!" cried doctor Blake.

"How should you know whether it will or not, squire Gallipot?"[2] returned he, contemptuously.

"How?—Why because I think you look as if you were ready to split with it this very minute!"

"*You* think, do you?—and who are you pray, that take upon you to wag your tongue on all occasions, whether you are consulted or not?"

"Who am *I*?" replied Blake, deliberately, "why, it's no hard matter for me to tell that, though it might puzzle some other folks to do as much for themselves.—I'm a gentleman, sir, if a good education, a genteel profession, and a little more brains than a certain person I could name are sufficient to make me one—not of the *mushroom* sort neither, that pop up in a night's time out of the dirt nobody can tell how; but come of a decent old stock, that has been a growing some time.—And now, since turn about is fair play all the world over, who the mischief are you pray?"

---

1 Devil.
2 A small glazed earthenware pot used to mix medicines; here Marney uses it as a contemptuous term for "apothecary" in order to insult Doctor Blake.

"I shall not condescend to answer any of your impertinent questions!" said Marney, swelling with rage.

"Like enough," replied the doctor, "for it's commonly the case that people that are so plaguy fond of asking 'em, want to keep the trade all to themselves.—But I should have thought that such a great count as you pretend to be, would have had a little more manners than to pick a quarrel before a parcel of women? But I suppose you have your own reasons for thinking it the best way!"

"What do you mean by that, you puppy?" said Marney.

"Puppy! puppy! Say that again if you dare!" cried Blake, starting up and shaking his fist almost under Marney's nose; which so terrified the female part of the company, who apprehended an immediate boxing match, that the younger ones flew out of the room, and Mrs. Hammond exalted her voice to a very unusual key in commanding them not to break the peace of the commonwealth.

"You are a couple of pretty fellows, are you not?" cried Charles, running between them, and seizing the doctor by the arms, who was now by far the most angry of the two, and replied "what the devil business had he to begin with me then?"

"Come, come," said Charles, "you are both wrong! But Marney was only joking doctor, and you have taken it all for earnest!"

"Upon my soul, I had no thoughts of any thing but a little diversion!—" said Marney, much alarmed at the enraged aspect of his antagonist, and eagerly pursuing Charles's hint.

"You hadn't hey?" cried the doctor, "Oh, ho! that's quite another part of speech!—but I must say, that for one man to call another a *puppy*, sounds in my ears like any thing but fun!"

"Never mind!" cried Charles, "you heard what Mr. Marney said, and that ought to be sufficient!"

"Why as to that matter," said the doctor, "I'm not fonder of quarrelling than my neighbours, and as he chooses to make an apology, I've no particular objection to taking it; but one of my standing rules is, never to suffer myself to be imposed upon; for when once a man gets into that way, by George he may make up his mind to be a foot-ball for every fool he meets with for the rest of his days!"

"Vastly true Doctor," said Charles, "and suppose now to end the affair, that you and this gentleman shake hands?"

"Oh pray do!" cried Mrs. Hammond, "for really it is not very agreeable to me, to be compelled to witness such disputes in my own house."

"When a lady commands, there should be no time lost in obeying!" cried the doctor, looking at Marney, who glad of an excuse for doing so, peaceably held out his hand, which the other as formally received, and then with a very dignified *congee*[1] took his leave.

"Is the battle over?" said Helen, peeping into the room.

"Oh yes!" cried Mrs. Hammond, "for one of the champions has departed!"

"Curse the fellow!" cried Marney, striving to put a good face on the matter, "I had no notion of kicking up such riot with him!"

"He did indeed appear to be a little refractory!—I am afraid, Marney, you will be obliged to give him another *taking down*?" said Charles.

"If I am," said Marney, "I will take care that it shall be where I can consider myself at liberty to act as I please."

And not much enamoured of a theme so little to his advantage, he began to talk about his phaeton, which he asserted was the handsomest in the United States.

"But your *secret*, Mr. Marney!" said Helen, "What has become of that?—I hope this little fray has not scattered it so that you will not be able to collect the fragments for our entertainment to-morrow?"

"Oh!" said Charles, "he is keeping it to entertain me with upon the road!"

"I would not have you be too sure of that!" replied Marney.

"I'll engage to have the whole of it out of you before we have gone a mile!" said Charles.

"You shall see!" said Marney, as they drove off; and for once in his life shewed that he *could* keep a secret, by resisting every art, which Charles, who found that he really was very full of something, put in practice to extort it from him.

CHAPTER XIV.

THE first resolve of Dunlevy on recovering a little from the shock he had experienced in learning that he had nothing to hope from Emily, was to see her no more; and that he might not have any excuse for imposing upon himself, he had his servant, who was now able to bear the journey, removed to town, and for some time adhered courageously to his resolution.—But *"absence, which extinguishes a slight attachment, adds new strength*

---

1 A ceremonious bow.

to a sincere one;" and instead of the calmness which he flattered himself would be the result of his efforts to forget her, he became daily more restless, and unhappy.—The scorn of insulting beauty, conscious of its own power, or the recollection of a mortifying refusal which might have roused his pride, were denied to him, who had experienced neither; and he in vain endeavoured to banish her from his imagination, which, as she was faultless towards himself, continued to present her as perfect beyond humanity; and his wish to see her remaining unabated, he at length began to doubt the utility of his present course of conduct. This idea had no sooner taken possession of his mind, than it was succeeded by innumerable arguments to prove its truth; and believing that it was impossible for him to become more wretched, after three weeks of painful self-denial, he in a morning ride ended the debate by turning his horse's head toward the abode of Mrs. Hammond.

He was received with great pleasure by the old lady, with whom he was a particular favourite; and he commanded himself so well, that Helen, who watched him narrowly, could discern in him nothing correspondent to what had passed when she saw him last, except that he had grown considerably thinner. Conscious that his being permitted to see, and converse as formerly with her he loved would rest upon the concealment of his feelings, he conducted himself so guardedly, that Emily, ignorant of the questions he had addressed to Helen, fancied she had mistaken the source of his emotion; and condemning herself for a suspicion which she now began to think had originated in her own vanity, determined in future to be less confident of her attractions, and behaved with such unaffected ease and good-humour, that Dunlevy went home consoled with the idea that he had at least not forfeited her friendship; and limiting himself to certain restrictions, again indulged in the happiness of sometimes beholding her, although every visit served but to increase the devotedness of his attachment; and his days when absent from her were consumed in wretchedness, and his spirits wasted by the unavailing regrets of hopeless passion.

In the neighbourhood of Mrs. Hammond lived a family of the name of Gurnet. Mr. Job Gurnet had begun the world in the humble occupation of a pedlar; and having by unwearied frugality and perseverance, scraped together a sufficient capital, opened a sort of shop which he styled a *wholesale huckstery*; and finding his business thrive beyond his expectations, cast the eyes of affection on Nancy Black, a likely servant-girl who lived opposite to him, and married her. Mrs. Gurnet was naturally good tempered, and her husband obliged her to be industrious, and economical. They had four children within five years after their marriage, but the youngest, a boy, died in his infancy; and the survivors occasioned little expense to their father, or trouble to their mother, for they ran about half-naked through the streets, whilst their parents were employed in the pursuit of amassing money to render them respectable at a future day. When the eldest arrived at the age of eleven, Gurnet found himself possessed of two hundred pounds, *clear gain*; and thinking he might then venture to afford it, clothed his children decently, and sent them to school. But whether their capacities had been obscured by early neglect, or whether nature had not gifted them with any, was a point which could never be exactly ascertained—yet after three years tuition Miss *Polly* could scarcely write her own name, and Miss *Katy*, and Miss *Nelly* found a difficulty in spelling out of book words of two syllables.

At this period the prospects of Gurnet were greatly amended. He abandoned the *wholesale huckstery*, and commenced salt merchant, and such was his success, that in a few years he became monstrously rich. It is the opinion of certain philosophers that *the mind always rises with the station*; and elated with this sudden flow of wealth, which he believed to have accrued solely from his own prudence and management, Gurnet now began to enlarge his views, and extend his intercourse to those better classes of society from which he had hitherto been altogether excluded. His daughters were placed at a genteel boarding-school, and no expense spared that might conduce to their improvement; but their manners had early contracted a vulgarity which nothing could eradicate, and instead of feeling an ambition to acquire the accomplishments for which their companions were distinguished, they preferred remaining in ignorance. They were obliged in some measure to conform to the rules of the establishment, but they did it mechanically, and went through their lessons without either understanding, or remembering them. The two eldest having some little voice, were at the mother's request taught music; but the youngest, Miss Eleanor declared that she hated every thing of the sort, and refused to touch the *"nasty piano,"* as she termed it. After remaining there three years longer, and having each a parcel of smeared-looking drawings, and a piece of embroidery to display as their own work, although more than half of it was done by their tutoresses, they were taken home, and considered by their parents as completely educated.

In appearance they were not remarkable either for beauty or ugliness. The eldest had rather a long nose, and the eyes of the second were somewhat large, and prominent; and the youngest although she had the best features, was coarse in her person. These trifling blemishes, which seemed scarcely worthy of notice to strangers, were frequently mentioned by them in angry reproach to each other. Old Gurnet was very proud of them, and desirous that they should appear well drest; but his habits were too inveterately low, and sordid, for him to be prevailed on to trust his wife and daughters with money; and when they asked him for new clothes, he would teize them for several days by saying he was sure they did not want them; and after worrying them into fits of crying, and sullenness, would march abroad, and without making known his intentions, purchase quantities of ill-chosen, gaudy finery, which was given to them to divide as they thought proper; and as it often happened that they all fixed their fancy on the same thing, the most violent quarrels ensued, which usually terminated in the entire destruction of the article in question. As to Mrs. Gurnet, she wore linsey[1] petticoats, and short callico[2] wrappers all the morning, and spent more of her time in the kitchen than the parlour, yet she was not without her share of ambition, which manifested itself in a passion for satin gowns, and caps trimmed with broad lace; beyond which she seemed to have few pretensions, and was generally considered as the most rational of the family.

The style of living in which they had embarked was so little congenial to their natures, that they were perpetually committing blunders which subjected them to unavoidable ridicule; yet their opulence shielded them from open derision, and their house abounded too much in the solid comforts of good eating and drinking for them to be in any danger of neglect. But Gurnet who had declined business, soon grew weary of a place where he no longer had any employment; and fancying that he should be mighty happy on a farm, about the time that Mrs. Hammond went to reside in the city, purchased one, and with his usual obstinacy compelled his family, much against their inclination, to remove thither in the fall of the year, where in a short time they were visited and laughed at by the whole neighbourhood. They knew so little of the rules of etiquette, that when Mrs. Hammond returned in a few months to the country

---

1 Coarse fabric woven of wool and linen.
2 Printed cotton fabric.

where she had been a resident for years, they took it into their heads that it was incumbent on them to pay their respects to her; and having ascertained her to be what they denominated "*a creditable person,*" one day to her infinite astonishment, made their appearance at her house in a body.—She had frequently heard them spoken of as a set of originals, and happening to be in one of her condescending moods, behaved so much to their satisfaction, that they were all quite charmed with her, and Gurnet on their way home, pronounced her to be a fine *discoursable* woman, and told his wife that he desired that they might be very sociable with her.

Emily and Helen were not at home when they called, but were highly amused with the description which they received of the visit from Mrs. Hammond, and Mrs. Cathcart, who also was present; but chancing soon after to meet Gurnet and his daughters at a little party in the neighbourhood, found report to fall so short of their merits, that they promised to take the earliest opportunity of spending an afternoon with them, which Miss Gurnet pressed them to do as earnestly as if her life had depended on it. When Mrs. Hammond was informed of their intention, she at first objected to it, but as she was not so untractable as formerly, she was persuaded by Helen not only to consent to their going but to agree to accompany them; a piece of complaisance which upon consideration she thought might be dispensed with; and on the day which they had appointed to drink tea with the Gurnets, was taken with a *head-ache*, which, as the girls well knew, meant nothing more than she did not choose to go.

Unwilling to take their new friends by surprise, a servant had been dispatched in the morning to give notice of their intentions, and Mrs. Gurnet returned for answer, "that she was proper glad to hear it, and hoped they would come soon."—Fearing if this intimation was not attended to, tea might be over before they got there, Emily ordered the carriage at four o'clock, and just as they were getting into it, Charles Cathcart and Dunlevy rode up to the door, and having learnt where they were going, expressed a wish to escort them; but Charles proposed that their horses might be left behind, lest the sight of such a number of them should alarm the old man into a stingy fit, and in compliance with his advice the gentlemen were permitted to accompany them in the carriage. On their way Helen entertained them with a description of each of the sisters, beseeching them at the same time, to guard their hearts against the formidable assaults of these three Graces.[1] In little more than half an hour they arrived, and found the whole family assembled in full dress in the best parlour, the windows of which were sprawled wide open, and the blinds drawn up in order to admit *fresh air*, although it was a sultry afternoon in August, and not a breath of air stirring.

Mrs. Gurnet inquired very earnestly for Mrs. Hammond, and being told she had remained at home in consequence of a headache, said, "she was sure it could not be very bad, or Miss Emily would not be abroad;" and Gurnet observed "that when he was sick, there was nothing he hated worse than to be left alone." He then turned to Charles and began talking to him about the price of scantling.[2]

Miss Mary who dearly loved a beau, fastened herself upon Dunlevy, whom she teased with her unmeaning prate almost into a fever; whilst Miss Catharine, sat on the other side of the room watching Charles and whenever he happened to look at her, signified her approbation by a grin.

Mrs. Gurnet undertook the task of entertaining Emily, and gave her a history of the disasters which had attended their removal from the city.

"If you'll believe me, ma'am, I packed up every morsel of glass and *chany*[3] my own self, and an ugly job it was for a lusty[4] body like me to go through!—I saw every thing put into the waggons too, safe enough, as I thought; yet for all that, the careless *creeters* of *gals* out here, broke four blue *chany* plates, and I don't know how many of my very best *ankeen*[5] cups and saucers; and cracked one of my new decanters, that cost the dear knows how much! and knocked the handle off of a tureen besides!—And Gurnet, he always gets so mad when any thing's broke, that I hate it like the mischief!"

The striking of the clock put an end to her detail by reminding her that it was time for tea, and her assistance would be necessary in preparing it.

The moment her mother left the room, Miss Eleanor ran and seated herself close to Helen, and told her in a sort of half-whisper "that she thought Charles a very pretty man."

---

1 The Charites of Greek mythology, goddesses of charm, beauty, and creativity.
2 Small wooden beams or joists used in building.
3 China.
4 Healthy.
5 Blue and white porcelain imported from Nanking, China; later copied by European artisans.

"Is he your brother, or your cousin?"

"My brother," replied Helen.

"I thought so, because he looks so much like you. And who is the other?"

"A friend of my brother's."

"I believe our Moll wants him for a sweetheart, she sticks so close to him; but I guess he'll not want her in a hurry!"

"Why do you think so?"

"Oh! because he looks as if she only bother'd him!"

A black boy now entered and said, "Master, mistress wants to speak to you, sir!"

"Where is she?" said Gurnet.

"In the kitchen, sir."

"What's the reason she can't come to me?"

"Mistress is busy a frying some gammon,[1] sir."

"Poh! you fool! you had no need to tell that!" said his master, as they went out together.

Unrestrained by the presence of either of their parents, the young ladies began to exhibit increased proofs of their talents for conversation, and Miss Catharine commenced an attack on the heart of Charles, equal in vigour to that with which her sister was besieging Dunlevy; who sat twisting his switch into a hole in the carpet, and pondering on the strange varieties of the human mind, and character, as he listened to the endless nothings which flowed from the untired tongue of the persecuting Miss Mary. He seldom answered her, and only then because compelled by good manners; yet she appeared perfectly unconscious that she either annoyed him, or neglected others.

Charles rallied Miss Catharine with a great deal of freedom, which she seemed to take in very good part, and told him, "she liked a funny man, of all things!"

Miss Eleanor continued to sit by Helen, and endeavoured to amuse her with an account of a quarrel which had taken place in the morning between black Ben and the hired maid, which she described as having been extremely diverting, for Ben had thrown some brick-dust in the maid's eyes, and she resented it by dashing a bucket of dirty water over him.—Helen made several attempts to change the subject, but Miss Eleanor seemed to take such a particular pleasure in relating the achievements of Ben, that it was a great while before she could effect her purpose.—

---

1 A cheap cut of meat from a pig.

Observing a very handsome piano forte in the room, she asked Eleanor whether she did not play?

"Not I indeed!" replied she, "I hate strumming and howling."

"Perhaps your sisters play?" said Helen.

"Oh yes," replied Miss Eleanor, ["]only ask them, and they'll give you enough of it!"—Then, bursting into a smothered laugh, she whispered, "Do set 'em agoing, and see what fine fun I'll make for you!"

Apprehensive of some unpleasant consequences, Helen declined making the request; but Eleanor was determined not to be disappointed, and she bawled out to her sister, "Molly! Molly!—why Moll, don't you hear?—Miss Cathcart wants you to play and sing for her!"

"Well, you needn't squawk so, if she does," replied Miss Molly; "I can hear without all that racket."

Rejoiced that an opportunity had at last presented itself of "escape from durance vile,"[1] Dunlevy instantly rose, and handed her to the instrument, expressing at the same time his earnest desire to hear her sing; and ascribing the sudden animation of his manner to the effect of her own charms, she capered up to the piano, and seating herself on a high stool before it, as erect as if she had been skewered, gave the keys a few prelusive thumps, as if to try their strength, and then began the hackneyed air of "*Life let us cherish*,"[2] which she got through without any material difficulty, except being obliged to stop several times to inquire the words.

When she had finished, she rose, and making a low courtesy, received the thanks of her visitors, and Charles assured her with great sincerity, that he had seldom heard any thing of the kind equal to it.

Without being requested, Miss Catharine next placed herself at the instrument, and after a vast deal of hawking and hemming, began *The blue bells of Scotland*[3] in a voice so loud and shrill, that Emily started with surprise, and Eleanor said softly to Helen "Now for it;" and slipped out.

---

1 "Durance vile" is a long prison sentence.

2 Ballad whose words are thought to be by Swiss-born poet Johann Martin Usteri (1763–1827) and set to music by Wolfgang Amadeus Mozart (1756–91).

3 Traditional Scottish folk song published in 1801 with lyrics by Dorothea Jordan (1761–1816), an English actress and courtesan who was the longtime mistress of the future English king William IV (r. 1830–37).

Miss Catharine continued to twist her head about, and squall with unabated vehemence, and Charles, who had stationed himself for the purpose, affected to accompany her with such ludicrous extravagance of voice and action, that his companions with the utmost difficulty preserved their gravity.—In the midst of the song, Miss Eleanor returned on tiptoe, with a small dog in her arms, and perceiving how matters stood, slily pinched both its ears until it sent forth such a horrible outcry as entirely overcame the little remaining self-command of the company, and the shrill voice of Miss Catharine was drowned in a peal of universal laughter.

The moment she heard the cries of the dog, she knew that Eleanor had hurt him on purpose; as it was a common practice with her when she was tired of music, to bring Florian into the parlour, and pinch him until he howled what she called *Indian base*.—She was vexed at the evident diversion of her visitors, but her rage towards Eleanor, who laughed until the tears ran down her cheeks, exceeded all bounds.

"Eh! you nasty, spiteful brat!"—said she, bouncing away from the piano; "an't you ashamed of yourself to behave like such a hog?—But I'll tell Pa', the minute he comes in!"—

"Don't wait 'till he comes in!" cried Miss Eleanor; "run out and tell him now, that you howled 'till the very dog set up his pipes to help you:"—

"It's no such a thing!" said Miss Catharine, ["]you brought him in and pinched him o' purpose; and for one single cent I'd pinch you the same way!"

"You must pinch pretty hard, I guess," shouted Miss Eleanor, "before you'll be able to make me yell as you do."

At this critical moment the father entered, and his presence silenced them both. Eleanor knew she had behaved amiss, and that if he was informed of it he would certainly punish her; and she forbore to offer further provocation to the irritated Catharine, who retired into a corner, where she sat swelling, and picking her fingers with shame and anger.

Compassionating her mortification, Emily approached with an intention of offering her some consolation; but instead of answering, she pouched out her mouth, and turned sulkily away.— Unfortunately her father happened to observe this ungracious piece of conduct, and he immediately called out, "Hey! day! madam Sour-krout! what's the matter with you?—you haven't been quarrelling with your company, I hope?—"

This rough interrogation was more than the feelings of poor

Miss Catharine in their present state could bear.—She burst into tears, and sobbed out, "It's all Nell's fault!—so it is!—she brought the dog in—and and—and—"

"*And* what?—" said her father, "what in the devil's name is it that ails you?—Has the dog bit you?—Molly!—Nelly!—what is it that ails her?"—

Miss Eleanor now looked very wild—Miss Mary feared to speak, lest she should increase the hurricane which seemed rising—and Miss Catharine continued crying with all the violence of an affronted child.

Finding that no explanation was to be obtained from his daughters, Gurnet turned in some consternation to Emily, and begged her to inform him what was the matter?—She hesitated, and looked at Charles, as if wishing to speak, but he was too much amused with the scene, to shorten it by uttering a word; and Dunlevy attempted to give an explanation of what had passed; softening it as much as possible by suppressing the circumstance of Eleanor's having pinched the dog, and ascribing his noise to the *sympathy* which those animals are sometimes known to express on hearing musical sounds.

Gurnet laughed heartily and bade Catharine "dry her eyes, and not sit there, roaring like a bull-frog before strangers"—and as her passion had now pretty well subsided, she felt too much ashamed to contradict him. Besides, she flattered herself with a hope that Dunlevy had represented the affair as he really believed it to have happened, and that nobody except Miss Mary and herself knew of Eleanor's mischievous design.—Consoled with this idea, her countenance cleared up, and she remained quiet.

A large mahogany dining table was now placed in the middle of the floor and covered with a cloth, and the tea-equipage stationed at one corner of it.—Mrs. Gurnet made her appearance with a face as red as scarlet, and the servants brought in a profusion of cakes, and relishes which she had assisted in preparing, and the whole party at her request, assembled round the table; as she said, "Ben was but a poor waiter, and apt to let things fall."

Every thing was excellent of its kind, for she had exerted her utmost skill upon the occasion; yet her husband growled without ceasing.—"The sausages were raw," he said, "and the cakes were heavy. The coffee was too strong, and the water that the tea was made of, did not boil"—yet he ate of all that was before him, and tormented his guests because they could not do the same.

The sisters were blest with admirable appetites, and devoured their favourite viands in such quantities as to excite even the observation of their father; who upon seeing Eleanor stretch herself across the table towards a plate of preserves, seized her by the gown, and with a jerk pulled her back, muttering in an under voice, "Let it alone, you greedy plague! you've eat till I'm ashamed of you already!"

When tea was over, Gurnet announced that he meant to have a sillabub;[1] but when the nutmeg-grater was called for, it could not be found; and after scolding his wife and daughters for having mislaid it, he at last recollected that it was in his own pocket. He mixed the wine and sugar himself, in a large bowl, and gave it to the black boy, ordering him to carry it to the maid, that she might milk in it, and then invited every body to walk into the garden; but Mrs. Gurnet said she must stay to wash up the tea-cups, therefore they went without her.

The garden was large, and ornamented with rows of box-wood, and square beds of flowers; and divided from the barn and stables by a board fence, in which there was a gate. After viewing various shrubs and fruit trees, and hearing from their owner a tedious history of each, together with their separate prices, they proceeded to a little summer house covered with bean-vines at the lower end of the principal walk, and Gurnet desired they would rest themselves while he gathered each of them a *posy*;[2] observing at the same time, that he suffered nobody to pull any thing in his garden but himself.

He had scarcely gone the distance of five paces, when a tremendous uproar of voices in the barn yard arrested his steps, and Eleanor, springing eagerly from her seat, ran to a small hole in the fence, which she peeped through; and hastening back with her eyes as large as saucers, cried out "I'll never stir if our Ben ha'n't broke the bowl, and spilt all the sillabub!"

"What! broke my big punch bowl!" exclaimed her father, "and wasted a pint of wine and sugar? I'll pummel him for it, a worthless black rascal!"

And snatching Dunlevy's bamboo cane,[3] he waddled as fast as he could into the barn yard, from whence the howlings of Ben were presently heard to issue; and Miss Catharine, who had now recovered her spirits, said "she hoped father would give him a good licking!"

---

1 Also syllabub: a drink made from fresh milk that is curdled with wine or cider and then sweetened.
2 Small bouquet of flowers.
3 Fashion accessory for a dapper young gentleman.

The gate was open and the sisters, leaving their visitors, walked towards it. The noise and confusion increased every moment, and the young ladies, who had a full view of what was going forward, appeared so much diverted, that Emily and the rest impelled by curiosity advanced also, and beheld old Gurnet, furious with rage, chasing Ben, who had escaped from his grasp, and taken refuge among the cows, where he dodged about, until his master in the heat of the pursuit, happening to tread on the edge of a puddle, slipped and fell sprawling at full length, with his face in the mire. The negro then jumped over the fence, and ran out of sight.

The Miss Gurnets, the maid who was milking, and the man who was feeding the horses on the other side of the yard, burst into a roar of laughter in which Helen, Charles and Emily joined, and had it not been for Dunlevy, the old man would probably have suffocated. He ran to him, and drawing him out of the puddle by one leg, assisted him to rise—but his visage, covered with filth, through which his little grey eyes, glaring with rage and fright, and twinkling to get rid of the dirt, were just visible, was a sight that might have excited the risible faculties of a hermit; and Dunlevy turned from him to hide the smile which he could no longer suppress.

Not so the sisters—they shouted with unrestrained mirth until their father had emptied his mouth of the mud which obstructed his utterance; and perceiving their shameful behaviour, roared out, "Hold your tongues, you hussies! or I'll box every one of your ears for you!"

The two eldest were immediately silent, but Eleanor continuing a sort of inward giggle, he shook his fist at her with a wrathful look, and then seeming to recollect himself began something like an apology for what had happened.

"I'm very sorry, gentlemen, that you and these ladies should be here to see such doings, but there never was such another family as mine under the sun! nothing but breaking, and destroying! By jingo it's enough to drive a man beside himself! but I'll pay that black scrub for all this to-morrow! Mr. What-d'ye-call-um, here's your stick—no, it's too nasty for you to touch—Nell, go and wash it at the pump."

Eleanor, instead of obeying him, began to titter; and her father again losing all command of himself, lifted the cane, and swore "that if she did not behave better, and do as she was bid, he would thrash her hide for her that very minute."

She looked frightened, and Dunlevy thinking it highly probable that the threat might be carried into execution, insisted on having his stick, which the old man, after wiping it with his pocket handkerchief, at last returned to him.

They now proceeded towards the house, and near the door met Mrs. Gurnet, who had heard of her husband's disaster and was coming in search of him.—The instant she found that he was unhurt, she began her lamentation for the fate of his clothes.

"The *laws a marcy*! was ever *sitch* a sight upon *arth*?—why your breeches are ruined!—and your new Sunday waistcoat all over nothing but mud!—I wonder how you could fall into that stinking truck[1]?—"

"The next time I fall," returned he, "I'll get you to choose the place.—I did it because I could not help it, Mrs. Fool."

"Well, well," replied the wife, "there's no use in getting angry, daddy!—come in and let me get you some dry things." She then seized him, and hauled him away.

As it was now nearly dark, the ladies expressed a wish to return home, which the Miss Gurnets vehemently opposed, but finding them determined, they reluctantly delivered up their hats and shawls, and whilst they were putting them on, Miss Catharine took the opportunity to drop a magnificent courtesy to the gentlemen, and tell them "she was very much obliged to them for their company."

Dunlevy bowed, Charles stuffed his handkerchief into his mouth, and Helen and Emily scampered to the carriage, where after a string of compliments from each of these accomplished damsels, they were at length permitted to drive from the door, and made themselves ample amends on the road for the restraint which they had suffered during their visit.—But the mirth of Emily, who was unusually diverted with what she had witnessed, soon experienced a melancholy reverse; for she had scarcely reached home, when she was informed by Mrs. Cathcart, who had arrived there during her absence, of the death of Kelroy's mother.

CHAPTER XV.

THE frosts of autumn began to tinge the leaves with many-coloured hues, and the soft winds of summer were succeeded by chilling blasts, and clouded skies which forcibly reminded Mrs. Hammond of the warm comforts of the social city; and to the

---

1 Mud.

great regret of her daughter, she commissioned old Mr. Cathcart to take a house for her near his own, which although less than that which she had lost, was sufficiently spacious, and elegant to answer her present purposes; and she removed to it fully resolved not to fall into her former error of allowing her expenses to exceed her income.—She had not yet forgotten the miseries produced by her folly, nor her almost miraculous escape from the severest poverty; and as the chief motive of all her feverish extravagance was now removed by the actual possession of that wealth, of which she had for so many years retained only the shadow, she found no difficulty in adhering to a determination which permitted her to indulge in a very ample share of all her favourite amusements. Her parties were no longer remarked for their splendour, but they were distinguished by a certain elegance, and sociability which rendered them peculiarly agreeable; and as her late distresses had never transpired, and Emily still continued to preside as the genius of the scene, her house was once more the resort of the fashionable, and the gay, and her hours again devoted, although in a more moderate degree, to the pleasures she best loved.

In the month of December, after many disappointments, and uneasy conjectures, Emily at last received a letter from Kelroy, announcing his safe arrival at Calcutta. He lamented his absence from her with all the warmth of genuine affection, and mentioned having written to her by three different opportunities which occurred in the course of his voyage, not one line of which had ever reached her.—He spoke of his prospects as favourable in the extreme, and anticipated with rapture the season of his return, which, as his business was now nearly concluded, he believed would be sooner than he had dared to hope, and bade her expect him early the ensuing spring.—Enclosed in the same packet was a letter for his mother, which Emily also opened, and perused with streaming tears his affectionate address to one whose cares for him were all at rest; and was here taught a new lesson of the imperfection of human happiness, as she reflected that the future meeting between Kelroy and herself, although fortunate in every other point of view, must be clouded with regret for a loss that he would severely feel, and of which he must necessarily until that period, remain in ignorance.

The winter continued to pass away, and Dunlevy unable to resist the temptation, was still a visitor at Mrs. Hammond's where the consolation of *seeing* Emily was literally all that he obtained; for the passion which in studied interviews he had found means to conceal, no longer submitted to the controul of his reason when subjected to the trial of the frequent, and accidental meetings which were the result of her residence in the city; and he involuntarily betrayed so much of it that Emily ceased to consider herself at liberty to treat him as she had formerly done. He was a young man of excellent natural abilities, although he had been somewhat negligent in the cultivation of them; spirited, generous, good-natured almost to a fault, and, previous to the commencement of his attachment to her, remarkable for his gaiety; and by his estimable qualities, and manly, amiable deportment, had possessed himself of so large a portion of her esteem, that it was with infinite regret she beheld the melancholy with which he appeared to be affected in consequence of her change of conduct. Yet he attempted not to lessen her reserve by the slightest remonstrance, and no longer made an offer of civilities which she seemed desirous to shun; but conscious of their propriety, although lamenting their necessity, tacitly acquiesced in the measures she chose to adopt, until the intercourse between them seldom exceeded the compliments required by common politeness. This was Dunlevy's first serious passion, and it had gained such an entire ascendancy over him, that his character became quite changed, and his dejection so evident as to be universally noticed, and not unfrequently ascribed to its proper source. Believing that it would never be in his power to love any other woman, he had ceased to consider his actions as of any consequence in regard to himself, and his sole remaining study was to preserve whilst he could, that claim to being admitted into the society of Emily of which for his own sake she would gladly have deprived him, until time, and absence had enabled him to see her with less pain to himself. And one of the happy effects to which she looked forward in her marriage with Kelroy, was the destruction of that latent hope, which notwithstanding his uncomplaining submission to her wishes, she fancied must still continue to nourish the affection of Dunlevy, who in beholding her as a wife, would of course be compelled to renounce it, and thus regain the peace of which she had so unintentionally been the means of depriving him.

Spring at length returned in more than its accustomed beauty, and as it advanced, the heart of Emily beat high with alternate hopes and fears, which received their completion, when on the nineteenth day of April, a day smiling in all the bright sunshine of the season, she learned that the ship in which Kelroy had sailed had anchored in the Delaware.

A new species of disturbance now took possession of her. She doubted not that he had arrived, but was apprehensive although she knew not why, of a diminution of his regard; and waited in anxious expectation of some tidings from him, which however came not until late in the evening, when she was cautiously informed by Helen Cathcart, whose brother had been on board the vessel to inquire for him, that Kelroy was still at Calcutta, from whence, instead of returning to his own country, he contemplated a voyage to Europe. There could be no possible mistake in the intelligence, for Charles had received from one of the passengers, whom he knew, and who had not only seen and conversed with Kelroy repeatedly, but previous to their sailing was intrusted by him with a letter for his mother.

"And none for me? not one for *me?*" said Emily.

Helen sorrowfully shook her head.

"Oh then," exclaimed Emily clasping her hands in agony, "if *this* is true there is no longer faith in man, nor honour in human nature!—But it is not cannot be so!" continued she, more calmly, "and I will not believe it, until I am better assured of its truth."

"It is at least too certain, my dear," said Helen, "that he has not arrived."

"O, but he has written!—I am convinced he has!" said Emily, "something has suddenly happened to detain him, and I shall hear from him still; for he would not be so inhuman as to desert me in this manner without a word! Helen, if you knew him as I do, you could not believe it possible!"

Mrs. Hammond, whose return home at that hour was rather unexpected, now entered the parlour, and observing the unusual agitation of her daughter, inquired its cause, and was answered by Helen, who unwillingly repeated to ears which she believed would greedily catch the sound, her account of the dishonourable conduct of a man, whom she grieved to be compelled to regard as a villain, yet was so thoroughly convinced of it, that she would not attempt to defend him, but simply repeated what she had heard, and then remained silent.

The astonishment of Mrs. Hammond seemed, if possible, to exceed that of Emily, but as her concern was not quite so great, she asked Helen innumerable questions, and learned in reply, that the gentleman from whom her brother received his information, had mentioned that Kelroy appeared to be in bad health, and complained that the climate disagreed with him; but had been so fortunate in other respects, that he meant not to leave India for a considerable time; after which it was his intention to revisit different parts of Europe; but this last Mrs. Hammond maintained to be an utter impossibility.

She readily admitted that there were many causes which might have rendered his return, at the period his friends had been taught to expect him, impracticable; but declared she was too confident of the sincerity of his attachment to believe for an instant that he could be tempted to act as Helen seemed to suppose; and saying she had not a doubt that the whole originated in some mistake, of which they would receive an explanation from himself, begged Emily to keep up her spirits, and not suffer herself to think that he would dare to treat her with such indignity.

The conduct of Mrs. Hammond, from the hour in which she gave her consent that Kelroy should be admitted into her family, had been, with the exception of a few trifling instances, apparently free from reproach in regard to whatever concerned him; and glad to have the suggestions of her own heart supported by the opinion of one on whose judgment she had great reliance, Emily tried to flatter herself that her mother's conjectures were just; but she could not extort one word of comfort of that description from Helen, who, convinced of the truth of what she had heard, would not mislead her with useless hopes, but left her full of pity for a delusion, which the pride of Mrs. Hammond, who could not brook the thought of insult to aught that pertained to her, had tended to confirm.

After a sleepless night, passed in suspense, and sorrow, as Emily was sitting the following morning in company with her mother, Marney, and Mr. Mangold; Dunlevy, who seldom visited there at that hour, suddenly entered.—He had learned from Mrs. Cathcart, who could sooner die than refrain from repeating all she heard, that Kelroy had chosen to remain in India; and irresistible anxiety to know in what manner Emily had received the knowledge of his determination impelled him, contrary to his usual custom, to seek her in the early part of the day.

She looked pale, and was rather silent, but hope was not yet quite extinguished in her bosom, and Dunlevy watched in vain for symptoms of wretchedness correspondent to that which preyed upon himself.—The forced composure of her manner deceived him; and as she replied from time to time with a calm smile to Mr. Mangold, who was speaking of England, where he had once been, and of her sister, he began to conclude that she either had never loved Kelroy, or must be very insensible.

He had not been there many minutes, when Henry entered with a letter, and delivered it to his mistress.

"It is for you, Emily," said Mrs. Hammond, significantly.

She took it, and perceiving the well-known writing of Kelroy, changed colour violently, and left the room.

In about a quarter of an hour Mrs. Hammond's visitors left her, and she then went in quest of Emily, whom she found sitting at a window in her chamber, in a state of stupefaction, with the open letter in her hand.

She did not notice her mother's entrance, nor had the sound of her voice any immediate effect upon her; but when, struck with the despairing anguish of her countenance, Mrs. Hammond tenderly, and repeatedly inquired its cause, her recollection seemed suddenly to be awakened, and flinging herself impetuously upon her knees, she exclaimed in tones that might have penetrated with compassion the soul of a demon.

"Mother, you warned, you besought me to renounce the man who has at last made me so wretched, but I refused to listen to you—and I am punished for it.—He has renounced *me*!—Left me with all the bitterness of contempt and scorn!—and—I am punished as I deserve!"

Tears of agony stopped her utterance, and shocked and alarmed at her distress, Mrs. Hammond became as much agitated as herself.

In vain did she express the fondest commiseration, and entreat her to exert her fortitude; the feelings of Emily were too much excited to be capable of reflection; and when Mrs. Hammond besought her to be calm, and remember what she owed to herself, she answered by pressing into her hand the fatal letter; and then, faint and exhausted, was assisted to her bed, where she lay with her eyes closed; and her bosom heaving with convulsive sighs which she had not power to suppress, whilst her mother perused the following farewell from Kelroy:—

TO MISS HAMMOND.

Madam,

There was a time when you permitted me to hope that I was honoured with your best regards, and, believing there could be no happiness for me except such as you condescended to bestow, the obligations which I bound myself to perform, were the dictates of a heart at that period sincerely devoted to you.

Upon what principle to account for the change which has lately taken place in my feelings towards you, I know not, unless you will suffer me to ascribe it to its real source, the *mutability of human nature*, but however censureable I may appear to you, I should be much more so in my own estimation, if I hesitated candidly to inform you, that although I still reverence your virtues, and remember with delight your attractions, the impassioned preference with which they once inspired me exists no longer.

After such an avowal you will not be displeased to learn that my return to America is uncertain—and I intreat you to believe that nothing short of the most perfect conviction of my inability to make you as happy as you deserved to be, could have induced me to relinquish a claim which thousands would consider themselves enviable in possessing.

That you may soon be enabled to banish from your remembrance the man who laments that his sense of honour should compel him to wound you by an act of justice to yourself, and that every blessing of life may attend you, is the ardent wish of madam, your very

Humble servant,

E. KELROY.

Calcutta, January 14.

"Insolent, abandoned villain!" exclaimed Mrs. Hammond, as she finished it, "he deserves to die a thousand deaths!—Heaven, and earth!—Ill as I ever thought of him, I could not have supposed him capable of depravity like this! that he should dare to treat a child of *mine* thus, an artful monster! whining and cringing to make interest for himself—and I like a fool, to suffer myself to be prevailed on in his favour!—But recrimination is vain now," continued she, pressing Emily's hand,—"yet I hope—I trust, that when the first shock has subsided, you will scorn to regret the loss of such an inhuman savage?"

"I trust I shall," replied Emily, with a faint voice, and a bitter smile.

"I am grieved at the manner in which you are released from him," said Mrs. Hammond, because I am apprehensive it will occasion you more uneasiness than it ought; but I should wrong myself if I scrupled to say that I rejoice in beholding you freed on any terms from one of whose specious villainy I had such an unaccountable presentiment, that from the hour in which I first beheld him, he has invariably been my constant aversion."

"Ah! if I had but listened to—if I had but believed you!" said Emily, every nerve writhing with suppressed anguish, "I should not feel as I now do!—But it is fit—it is just that all should have happened thus, and I have no right to complain."

"Say not so," returned Mrs. Hammond, deeply affected, "for we are all liable to error—and I myself am much more to blame than you, for I ought to have exerted my natural authority to prevent the evils to which your innocence, and inexperience have exposed you."

Emily made no reply, but continued to wipe off the tears that fell slowly from her eyes; and rejoiced to see her already so composed, where she had dreaded the utmost vehemence of grief, Mrs. Hammond said she would leave her for a little while, for she well knew that solitude was what she most desired; and again bidding her remember the worthlessness of the wretch who had deceived her, and learn, if possible, to proportion her regrets to his deserts, she at length rose to depart, when Emily said, "Suffer me, my dear mother, to spend this day alone—and to be seen by nobody—not even yourself until to-morrow—and you will find I hope that I shall have made a proper use of the indulgence."

"My child, I would willingly permit you to do so, did I not fear it might be injurious to you!"

"Oh no! no!" replied Emily; "I can neither talk, nor listen, nor receive consolation, except from heaven and my own heart; and it would be most gratifying if my wish could be complied with."

Mrs. Hammond soothingly expostulated with her for several minutes; but unable to resist her plaintive entreaties, and hoping that what she so earnestly requested might possibly be productive of some good effects, she at last, although unwillingly, consented, and left her, but not until she had made her promise to permit her door to remain unfastened, that a servant might enter occasionally to see whether she was in want of any thing.

In the afternoon Helen Cathcart called, and was informed of what had passed by Mrs. Hammond, who with quivering lips, and unusual agitation, repeated part of the contents of Kelroy's insulting letter. Helen lifted up her hands and eyes, in utter amazement at his baseness, and wept at the thoughts of what her friend must suffer; whilst Mrs. Hammond continued in language the most vindictive to reprobate him as the vilest of the creation, until overcome by sympathy, and various painful, and mortifying reflections, she wept also; and for some time they both remained silent.

"If Emily Hammond," observed Helen at length, "possessed as she is of every charm which renders her sex attractive, has failed to meet with constancy in a lover, who shall dare in future to think herself assured of faith, because it has been sworn to her?"

"Ah, who indeed!" replied Mrs. Hammond, recovering herself. "Some newer face, I doubt not, has caught his fancy, and he is amusing himself by repeating to her all that he has so often uttered to another!—But come again to-morrow," said she, seeing Helen about to depart, "for I am anxious that you should see Emily as soon as possible; as I am convinced she will be more benefitted by your society and advice than that of any person whatever—and I shall depend greatly on your influence to withdraw her from that state of seclusion and despondence to which I have ever observed her, when afflicted to be inclined.— And the present instance is so infinitely beyond aught that she has hitherto experienced, that I look forward with terror to the consequences of it."

The fears of Mrs. Hammond in this respect, however, were vain.—Left to herself as she had desired, Emily spent her time not in weak, and fruitless lamentation, but in reviewing her past conduct, and forming resolutions for the future.

Retrospection afforded her no cause for self-reproach, except having in a single instance, one in which she was authorized by the example of millions, acted contrary to the admonitions of her mother.—She could recal no word, no action relative to Kelroy which was not perfectly consonant with her own ideas of propriety; and thus acquitted by conscience of the only circumstance that could have been considered as an excuse for such conduct, she was compelled to regard him as fickle, unfeeling, and dishonourable.

Her affection for him had been equally strong and sincere, and her heart bled whilst she recollected the many happy hours which she had passed with him, when she believed him to be all that he appeared; but her pride, which was also great, had received as deep a wound as her love, and combined with her reason to teach her that it would be an unpardonable weakness to suffer her happiness to be destroyed by the remembrance of one who had proved himself worthy only of her scorn.

During the night she did not once close her eyes, but when morning came, she felt that she had acquired a share of serenity which was astonishing even to herself.

The unmerited insult which she had received, had excited a spirit of contempt and resentment, which together with her dread of incurring the ridicule frequently attached to persons in her situation, assisted her to repress with tolerable success the emotions of tenderness, whilst it encouraged those of an opposite nature; and resolving to conquer her passion, or perish in the attempt, she arose, and dressed herself at an early hour; and when Mrs. Hammond, anxious to know how she was, soon after entered her chamber, she had the unlooked-for pleasure of seeing her quietly engaged in finishing a piece of fancy needle-work, on which she had for some time past been employed.

"How are you, my dear?" said she, affectionately kissing her, "and how did you sleep last night?"

"I am well, and ready to go down with you to breakfast," replied Emily, returning her embrace, and trying to smile, as she evaded the latter part of her question.

"That's my darling girl!" said Mrs. Hammond, with exultation. "This firmness, Emily, is worthy of you, and if persevered in, will save both your heart, and your mother's, many a pang."

That it would be persevered in, Emily presently gave a convincing proof.

During breakfast Mrs. Hammond again commended her behaviour, and, encouraged by her composure, began to speak of Kelroy, and comment on those parts of his character and conduct which had been particularly offensive to her; nor did Walsingham escape without his share of censure, since to his interference she attributed in a great measure all that had happened. She finished by remarking, that owing to her own prudence, one of the most unpleasant consequences usually attendant on affairs of this nature, would be obviated by the circumstance of the engagement being still a secret to all except Helen Cathcart and her brother.

Emily listened to her in perfect silence, and when she had ceased speaking, replied with a collected voice, "Mother, I am, it is true, young in misfortune; but a few hours have afforded me ages of experience, since in that space I have acquired more self-knowledge than during the whole of my previous life; and it has enabled me to form resolutions, which if adhered to, cannot fail of restoring me to tranquility."

Her breath failed her, and she paused a few moments to recover it, and then steadily continued, "I am sensible that I have still much to suffer—but the severest trial—that of discovering him to be unworthy—is already past.—Whatever is to come, relates only to myself.—You were so kind as to comply with my request yesterday, let me not find you less so now—and—henceforward let us speak of him no more.—I feel that the lessons which I ought to teach myself will be best learned in silence.—Let his name no more be mentioned to me."

Pale, and trembling, she reclined her head on her hand for support, and her mother, who had regarded her with a look of distressful admiration, was apprehensive she would faint, and hastened to assure her that all should be exactly as she desired.— That the wish was an honour to her; and she would not only religiously observe it herself, but be careful, as far as it depended on her, that others should do; and she kept her word.

Nor did her solicitude to aid, and support her afflicted child end here.—Conscious that it was a moral impossibility for Emily to be seen as usual by her acquaintance without risking a discovery of the situation of her mind, she formed on every occasion plausible excuses for her absence, which entirely satisfied those to whom they were addressed, and for several days she refrained from going abroad except to ride, accompanied by her mother, and at home saw no person else except Helen Cathcart, with whom, conformably to the resolution she had adopted, she continued to converse on indifferent subjects.—Helen had learned from Mrs. Hammond what had passed between Emily and herself, and scrupulously shunned every topic which might lead to the revival of ideas unfavourable to the restoration of that calmness which she saw her young friend so desirous to attain. Emulous not only of avoiding the strictures of the world, but of evincing to the few individuals who knew her story, that she was capable of surmounting an attachment which she blushed even to have acknowledged, Helen beheld her with surprise in a short time again enter into society, where she maintained a sweetness, and evenness of deportment that effectually concealed the agitation of a bosom to which repose had become a stranger; nor was it until after many weeks that she ventured to trust herself for the first, and only time to advert to the past.—Helen had passed the morning with her in her chamber, from which just before dinner she was summoned by the voice of her mother, who had promised to call for her on her way home, and was then squalling, and vociferating in the hall about the lateness of the hour, as if the welfare of the universe depended on the circumstance of her reaching her own house within five minutes.

"Stay one instant!" said Emily, summoning up courage at last, to do what had occupied her thoughts the whole day.

She then opened her work-table, and took from thence a beautiful ivory box, the gift of Kelroy; in which she had placed his picture, a ring with his hair, a number of notes, and copies of verses, and the two letters which she had received from him, and putting it into Helen's hands, said, "Take this—you perhaps can conjecture what it contains, and if ever you should feel inclined to doubt of falsehood or dishonour where nature seemed to promise better things, let one look at what is here convince you that no appearances, however fair, can be a security against evils like mine."

Tears were in her eyes as she concluded, and her air, and countenance expressive of such heart-felt sorrow, tempered with innocence, and the dignity of conscious worth, that Helen thought she had never until then seen any thing human which so much resembled an angel; and unable to reply, stood wistfully gazing on her for a moment, and then descended to her noisy mother, who was bawling from the foot of the stairs that she was half starved for her dinner, and could wait no longer.

The fortitude with which Emily continued to bear what had befallen her, not only reinstated her in the good graces of Mrs. Hammond, but obtained for her from that lady a degree of respect, and consideration which contributed greatly towards lessening the perplexities of her situation. Possest herself of strong energies of character, she delighted to meet with similar traits in others, provided they were not exercised in behalf of what she was accustomed to term *weaknesses*; and when her own daughter exhibited such indubitable proofs of strength of mind so properly exerted, she discovered her approbation of it in many instances; and more particularly in leaving it to her own option whether to retire to the country, or spend the summer in travelling.

Emily chose the former, for her mind was not of that description which requires the aid of perpetual bustle, and change of scene to assist it in the performance of its functions; and she preferred retreating to the quiet shades where she had spent her happy childhood, to all the adulation which she might have commanded at the fashionable places of public resort.

But, although deserted by the man on whom she had placed her youthful affections, love, and flattery still attended her footsteps; and in addition to Dunlevy, she had now another professed admirer, Mr. Dorelle, a French gentleman, who had seen her at Mrs. Cathcart's; and finding she had deprived him of his heart, proceeded with the usual ease of his countrymen on such occasions to inform her of it; and, but little discouraged by her refusal, which he regarded in so young a lady as almost a matter of course, he thought proper to continue his devoirs after her removal from the city, and by his persevering assiduities, and open gallantry, excited the most indignant jealousy in the bosom of his rival.

From the moment he learned that Kelroy meant not to return, Dunlevy had watched with unceasing attention every movement of Emily, and the result of his observations was a suspicion that some misunderstanding had arisen between them.—Eager to catch at the remotest hope, he once more had recourse to Helen Cathcart, from whose candour he flattered himself he should be able to discover the truth; but, contrary to his expectations, he found her alike impenetrable to every method either grave or gay, that he could devise.

He next endeavoured to sound her mother, and brother; but Mrs. Cathcart knew no more of the matter than she had informed him of already, which was neither more nor less than that Kelroy had purposed returning at that time, and had always seemed very fond of Miss Emily, who appeared not to dislike him; and Charles, although of late better informed by his sister, affected equal ignorance.

In this dilemma he ventured to attempt hinting the subject to Mrs. Hammond, who although she had chosen not to notice it to Emily, had long remarked his passion for her; and no sooner saw his drift, than assuming an air of sincerity, she assured him he had been misinformed, and that her daughter was perfectly free from any engagement whatever.—She acknowledged "there had been a little sort of romantic flirtation carried on formerly between her and *a Mr. Kelroy*, which she presumed was the foundation of what he had heard; but she was happy to have it in her power to assure him that Emily had wisely relinquished every idea of so unpromising a union."

This did not exactly agree with the serious intimation given him by Helen, but it agreed much better with the wishes of Dunlevy's heart, who in exchanging despair for uncertainty considered himself the most fortunate of mortals, and felt animated with new life by the prospect of a possibility of obtaining her favour.—Yet, such was his awe in consequence of the reserve which she still maintained towards him, that his love would not have presumed so early to manifest itself in words, had not the extravagant behaviour of the Frenchman, who scrupled not to make publicly the most vehement assertions of his regard, urged him on.

Dorelle was a little, plump, merry fellow, upon whom the *belle passion* sat as easily as a half-worn shoe; and he would frequently in the presence of a dozen people express with apparent seriousness the most lamentable regrets for the cruelty of his fate; walk up towards Emily, sigh, strike his hand upon his bosom, mutter two or three unintelligible sentences, and end with a profound bow, and a roll of his eyes upwards, until nothing was to be seen of them except the whites; after which he would directly resume his usual manner, and join in conversation with the greatest sprightliness imaginable. These antics were generally a source of much amusement to those who witnessed them; and even Emily herself, although not much inclined to mirth, and but little pleased to be the subject of them, was sometimes compelled to smile at his grimaces. But to Dunlevy, every faculty of whose soul, although he scarcely presumed to touch the hem of her garment, was absorbed in admiration of her, they seemed like profanation, and his disturbance sometimes knew no bounds. It gave him pain insupportable to reflect that this Frenchman, whose frivolity evinced the lightness of his pretensions, should already have gained the privilege of uttering to her whatever his flighty imagination prompted; whilst he, who from the hour he first beheld her, had neither known a joy, or a sorrow unconnected with her idea, had never yet dared to permit one decisive sentence to that effect to pass his lips. In a fit of jealous agony with which he was one day seized, on accidentally overhearing Dorelle pleading his passion, whilst owing to her speaking rather low, and her back being towards him, her replies were so indistinct that he could not comprehend them, he sought the first opportunity of throwing himself at her feet, and avowing in language proportioned to his feelings, his ardent attachment, and the sufferings he had so long endured from it.

Emily was deeply affected when she heard him—his eyes, his voice, his manner, so tender, so impassioned, brought strongly to her recollection the image of one, whose love, together with his vows had faded like a vapour; and her agitation was such that for a moment Dunlevy was almost deceived into a belief that it arose from partiality to himself—But the instant she was sufficiently recovered to speak, the flattering delusion vanished, and she gave him a mild, but positive denial; assuring him in return to his supplications for future hope, that it neither was, nor ever would be in her power to regard him otherwise than as a friend.

Of all the lovers she had ever had, except Kelroy, Dunlevy was most agreeable to her; and so highly did she estimate him, that she would have considered herself particularly fortunate in being enabled to return his sentiments; but, conscious that this could not be, she thought she best shewed her sense of what was due to his merits, by endeavouring to convince him that further pursuit of her would be vain.—Yet, whilst she did so, her native gentleness, and the pity which she felt for sorrows which she now knew how to appreciate, gave a softness to her manner, that left him, notwithstanding all she had said to the contrary, in possession of a vague hope that this rejection could not be a final one. It was not probable that the man whose love had survived the conviction that she was self-destined to be the wife of another, would, now that he knew her to be at liberty, yield to arguments of this description from a woman whom he doated on to distraction; and equally unable, as unwilling to give her up, he persisted in a continuation of that humble attention and modest deference which he had hitherto seen so acceptable to her sex, but found them of little avail with Emily, who was particularly cautious not to create hopes and expectations which she meant never to fulfil.—The Frenchman too, still kept his ground, and having discovered that Dunlevy's views were similar to his own, with the difference that he was infinitely more of a favourite with Mrs. Hammond, became captious in the extreme; and as Emily made it her study to avoid them both as much as possible, their sole ambition next to pleasing her seemed to be to thwart and plague each other; and their mutual efforts for that purpose were a fund of unfailing diversion to Marney, who used to make a point of fomenting their disputes; and more than once his mischievous interference had nearly been productive of serious consequences between them.

At length, Dorelle was obliged to go to Savanna, and his absence proved an inexpressible relief to Emily, who considered it as no small aggravation of her unhappiness, that at a season when her mind was struggling to disencumber itself of whatever might tend to retard its approaches to that state of indifference which it behoved her to attain, she should have been unavoidably subjected to the addresses of two gentlemen, one or the other of whom daily, either by comparison or analogy, compelled her to recal scenes and expressions which it was necessary for her to forget.

Towards the close of the summer, Helen Cathcart, who had been with her mother on a long visit to some relations in a distant part of Maryland, went soon after her return to spend a week at Mrs. Hammond's, where she was received with unfeigned joy by both her and Emily.—As they were all three sitting at work together one wet dismal morning, in a little side parlour which they were accustomed to occupy when alone, Marney made his appearance at the gate, on horseback.

"Heavens!" cried Helen, who hated the sight of him, "here is that abominable Marney coming to disturb us!—I should really like to know what has tempted him to risk himself abroad in such weather?—Some fresh piece of news, I engage!—and he has rode off with it piping hot, to have the pleasure of being the first to tell the story."

"Whatever it may be," said Emily, "I could have wished he had waited until to-morrow, for I feel very little inclined to listen at present to such stories as his usually are."

"Fy girls!" said Mrs. Hammond; "I declare you are often quite ill-natured about that poor man, who means nothing in the world by his little anecdotes, but to amuse you."

As she spoke he entered, and having seated himself, informed them which way the wind blew, and settled the time when it might be reasonably expected to clear up, he ended with his regular question of "whether they had heard any *news*?"

"No," replied Helen, "we have no news here; but I am sure you must have gathered a little somewhere, or we should not, as I said before you came in, have had the felicity of seeing you such a day as this."

"Lord, Miss Cathcart! what strange ideas you seem to have of people!—Upon my word I do not recollect that I have heard any thing particular."

"So much the better," replied Helen, "for then we may suppose you were actuated solely by a wish to enjoy our agreeable company."

"Upon my word you may; and I would willingly ride three times the distance any day for the same purpose."

He staid two hours, and notwithstanding his assertion that he had *heard nothing particular*, related within that time various tales of wives quarreling with their husbands, husbands taking to evil courses, and servants cheating and insulting their employers; a subject upon which he never failed to be uncommonly eloquent. But the grand article of intelligence he thought fit to reserve to the last; and rising to take his leave, said in a careless way, "I saw a gentleman a few days ago, who arrived lately from Calcutta, and he tells me, ladies, that he saw there your acquaintance Mr. Kelroy, who expected to leave it shortly after him, and will probably soon be here."

"I had understood," replied Mrs. Hammond, looking surprised, "that he intended going to Europe first?"

"I believe not, ma'am," said Marney. "This gentleman mentioned to me, that it was supposed he had been detained in Calcutta by an attachment for a pretty English woman there, who, it is said, has jilted him at last.—But be that as it may, he will at any rate soon be here, unless he happens to get drowned on the way."

"And if he should," replied Mrs. Hammond coldly, "he will not leave many mourners behind him in this part of the world, for his old mother is dead."

"So I hear," said Marney, cracking his whip against the legs of a chair.

The complexion of Emily during this conversation changed to a death-like hue, and she splashed with deep purple the leaves of a delicate moss-rose which she was painting, whilst Marney stood observing her with malicious satisfaction, until checked by a glance of ineffable contempt and indignation from Helen, and then withdrew, leaving her perfectly satisfied as to his motive for riding so far in the rain.

The fancied philosophy, the painfully-earned resignation of Emily was severely tried by the apprehension of again seeing a person whom she had hoped and believed she should never meet more; and she continued so evidently perturbed and discomposed by the intelligence she had received, that the next day after Helen left them, as she was reclining in a desponding posture on a seat in a retired part of the garden, she was unexpectedly joined by her mother, whose approach she had not perceived, and rose up in some confusion, on finding her so near.

"Why so alarmed?" said Mrs. Hammond, with a smile; "Did you think it was Dunlevy?"

"No ma'am, but I thought myself alone, and the sound of a foot-step startled me, I believe.—Why should you suppose I thought of Mr. Dunlevy?"

"Because he has been with me for some time, and is just gone.—We have had an interesting conversation Emily, and I have promised him to be his advocate."

"I hope not ma'am," replied Emily with involuntary quickness; quite forgetting in her apprehensions, that she had not yet been informed of the subject on which her mother's good offices were to be employed.

"You ought rather, for your own sake, to hope that I may be a successful one," replied Mrs. Hammond mildly. "I have hitherto at your request, Emily, forborne touching on a certain subject, which from my latest observations, I nevertheless have too much reason to fear incessantly occupies your thoughts; but I should be greatly wanting in my duty if I remained silent after what I have just heard from Dunlevy—and I beg that you will try to listen to me."

"Oh mother! I know all that you would say, and I have wished and tried to think as you do, but it will not be!—Do not, for God's sake, urge me, for I can give you but one answer," cried Emily, as she reluctantly suffered herself to be reseated.

"I will not urge you," replied Mrs. Hammond, "but reason with you.—What, my dear, can you possibly promise yourself from seeking, as you have done of late, to renew in solitude the remembrance of a wretch every way unworthy of you?"

"I have not *sought* to renew my remembrance of him," said Emily dejectedly, "nor can I believe that my general conduct has been such as to merit the accusation; but as I do not affect to be either iron or marble, I acknowledge that the prospect of his return has occasioned me some disturbance."

"I know it;" replied Mrs. Hammond, "but can you suppose that by resorting to seclusion and the indulgence of melancholy, you are to fortify yourself against the trials to which there is reason to apprehend you will in that case be exposed?"

"My trials, if any, must arise from myself, not from him—for he will not dare to approach me. And, conscious of that, I have examined my own heart, where I find there is still much to be subdued before I can appear as I would wish."

"Then take the advice of your mother, who knows you better than you know yourself; and, instead of wasting your soul and spirit in conflicts like these, make a more effectual effort, and by accepting a worthy amiable man who adores you, convince that reptile Kelroy, that you are not at his disposal."

"It would be difficult for him to find me so," replied Emily with a mortified aspect.

"He will however think you so if he finds you still single; and as the lady for whose sake he left you has discarded him, he may probably honour you with his addresses a second time."

"Never!—depraved, and unfeeling as he is, his presumption cannot surely amount to that!"

"I am nevertheless of opinion that it will, if you remain as you are at present;" replied Mrs. Hammond; "and were this the worst, I could be content, since it might enable you to repay him some of the vexations he has caused you;—but I fear Emily—I very much fear, that such is the ascendancy, which unknown to yourself he yet maintains over you, that should he affect contrition, and repentance, you will forget all that is passed, and accept him still?"

"I will die first," replied Emily; and unable to bear another word, she started up, and walked precipitately towards the house, where she found on her entrance some company who had arrived from town, and their presence preserved her from further importunity for the remainder of that day.

But the ice once broken, Mrs. Hammond failed not to renew from time to time her efforts; alternately piquing the pride, assailing the principles, and flattered the self-controul of this now irresolute girl, who bewildered between an invincible repugnance to the proposed marriage, and the dread of being again misled by adhering to her own judgment, with difficulty withstood the solicitations of her mother, her lover, and her friend Helen, who with well meant earnestness joined in endeavouring to convince her that such a step was best calculated to restore to her that tranquility, which she now more than once despondingly declared was gone for ever.

Sick of remonstrance and weary of opposing where she wished, but dreaded to comply; but most of all distrustful of herself, and her own weakness, she at last yielded to their united persuasion, and six weeks after she had heard of Kelroy's intended return to America, became the wife of Dunlevy, whose uncle, charmed to see him united to a lady of such singular beauty and merit, settled upon him two thirds of his large annual income; and, could wealth and splendour have purchased happiness, Emily would have found herself on the high road to perfect felicity. But although the frequent exertions which she was obliged, perforce to make, had taught her the art of dissipating in a degree her gloomy reflections, and prevented her from being absolutely miserable, the restraint which it was necessary to impose upon herself, produced a torpor which rendered every scene alike tasteless and insipid; and whilst she was extolled, and admired as an object of envy to half her sex, her prayers were daily offered up to heaven for the restoration of her departed peace.

Happy in the full attainment of her wishes, Mrs. Hammond had now not a care on earth, beyond the preservation of her health, and the choice of her visits; and triumphing in having secured to her daughter the possession of all which she considered desirable, had promised to herself a long succession of joyous years; when in the midst of the festivities which succeeded the wedding, she received a stroke of the palsy, which deprived her of her speech, and the use of her right side.

She lived two days after it, in possession of her senses, and piteously anxious to be understood in some communication which she repeatedly tried to make to those about her; but as she could neither hold a pen, nor articulate a syllable, her struggles were without effect, and her signs quite incomprehensible, the consciousness of which seemed to rack her with horror and she expired at last in convulsive agonies too shocking for description.

She was sincerely mourned by Emily, to whom her considerate kindness in the season of her affliction had endeared her beyond example; but in losing her parent, she first began to be sensible of the value of her husband, whose tenderness prevented her from knowing a wish or want which he had power to remedy; and as time softened her grief, gratitude seemed to inspire her with something like affection for him and she had ceased to lament her marriage as a misfortune, when an accidental discovery revived at once the flames of her smothered passion, and fixed her fate for ever.

Mrs. Hammond left no will, and six months after her death, Dunlevy, who was engaged in making an equal division of her property, which he found very inconsiderable in proportion to what he had been led to expect, requested Emily to seek for some papers necessary to the settlement of the estate, which he had not been able to find. After searching in every probable place without success, she at last happened in rummaging, to touch the spring of a small unknown drawer in a recess of her mother's writing desk, which to her amazement opened, and displayed papers neatly arranged in parcels, the first of which contained those which Dunlevy wanted, and sending them to him immediately, she sat down to inspect the rest.— They consisted chiefly of letters of business, accounts, and memorandums, which were only interesting to her as having belonged to her mother, yet she still continued to examine them, until she came to a packet enclosed in a blank cover, and tied with a piece of blue riband,[1] and having opened it, found three letters, two of which were directed to herself, in Kelroy's hand; and believing them to be the same she had given to Helen, she let them fall as if a serpent had stung her. The third letter, in a different hand, was addressed to Mrs. Hammond, and anxious to learn wherefore it had been classed with those, she hastily unfolded it, and taking out two papers which it contained, read as follows:—

---

1 Ribbon.

Dear madam,

I shall not have an opertunity of speaking to you as soon as necessary, without giving room for suspicion, so think best to write. An unlucky cut in my thum hinder'd me from finishing at the time apointed, but that you may not be uneasy, I write to let you know that the captain told me he will not sale before Saturday, so there will be time enough. I am sorry any part was amiss, but will take more care in the next coppy, which will be given as soon as possible to your inspecktion; by your friend, and humble servant,

M.

P.S. I shall bring back yours, as you desired.

The writing she now recollected to be that of Marney, and a frightful suspicion crossed her brain, which the contents of the two papers that she next perused confirmed.—The first was a letter from a lady to a gentleman, containing a haughty, yet simple and impressive declaration of having withdrawn the sentiments which she formerly professed in his favour; the second an exact copy of the last letter she had received from Kelroy; and both unquestionably the hand-writing of her *mother*!!!

Cold drops of perspiration bedewed her face and trembling limbs, as she contemplated these cruel proofs of her own irreparable injuries; but their effect was not complete until she had read the intercepted letters from Kelroy, which were those he had written to her immediately subsequent to his departure.— The conviction which their affecting eloquence gave of his *then unchanged* affection, and the treachery which had been employed to estrange them from each other, supported her almost fainting heart until she had finished them, when hearing her husband's voice, she instinctively returned them to the place of their concealment, and when Dunlevy entered the chamber, he found her lying senseless on the floor.

CONCLUSION.

THE hatred which Mrs. Hammond had conceived against Kelroy in consequence of the share which he had unwittingly contributed towards the increase of her troubles, was such as no common vengeance could appease.

One of the bitterest hours of her life was that in which she had felt herself necessitated to consent that he should become a future member of her family; and the scene of destruction which followed, and the prospect of being compelled either to embark for England, and present herself in a state of abject penury to Walsingham, or remain dependant on the charity of Mrs. Cathcart, until Emily's marriage should transfer her to the bounty of the very man to whose intervention she attributed the greatest part of her misery, was attended with sensations which nothing could obliterate the remembrance of.

The relief she experienced from the prize which she gained, and the three-fold business of concealing her extravagant joy, placing her money to the best advantage, and furnishing herself anew with various necessaries, left her in the beginning very little leisure for any thing else; but when all was arranged to her satisfaction, the novelty of her situation was soon lost in the review of the events which had preceded it. Her regard for Emily had sensibly diminished, yet she still loved her too well not to scruple entering into measures which she feared might be the ruin of her happiness, although at the same time she despised her for her want of ambition; but the settled enmity which she felt towards Kelroy, was of a species that would have rejoiced in his utter destruction; and in the midst of unexpected prosperity, she secretly murmured that it was not in her power to punish him and gratify herself, by depriving him of her daughter.

This desire in the first instance was merely passive, for she saw not any probability of being enabled to carry it into effect; but the sudden change in Marney's manner towards Emily, the cause of which she suspected, and had the dexterity to draw from him by acknowledging her detestation of his rival, was productive of a freedom of opinion and advice between them, which ended in one of the most diabolical schemes that envy ever planned, or malignity executed.

The mortifying scene which took place the night previous to Kelroy's departure, had not only determined Marney never again to subject himself to a scorn which he now believed to be real, but converted the selfish preference which he had dignified with the name of love, into dislike, and rancour. In his sulky ruminations on the affronts he had received, it occurred to him that although Emily was no longer an object worthy of his notice, her mother as a lady of fashion who had treated him with uncommon politeness was deserving of some attention; and he resolved to convince Miss Hammond that the house had attractions for him independent of her smiles.

Luckily for him, who could never act as he ought, except from an express model, his conception of the deportment necessary for him to assume, in order effectually to convince the lady that she must not entertain hopes of breaking his heart, was assisted by his observations on the conduct of a gentleman, whose behaviour under circumstances somewhat similar he had heard universally applauded; and ambitious of appearing equally dignified, he regulated himself by this example so successfully as to occasion a pleasing surprise to Emily, and much astonishment to her mother, who had the address to make herself in a very short time mistress of all his motives.

Having mutually disburdened their minds, it became a favourite subject of private discourse with them; and Marney, although he affected to consider Emily's attachment as silly, and romantic in the extreme, repeatedly declared he had no longer a wish to supplant Kelroy, whilst Mrs. Hammond as often expressed her regrets that he, or some other had not both the wish, and the power. Beyond this neither of them ventured to advance until accident introduced Dunlevy among them, whose partiality for Emily, and her approbation of him were immediately remarked by them; and Marney declared that he thought it would be perfectly justifiable to have recourse to some means which might bring them to a better understanding with each other.

Mrs. Hammond inquired what he meant? and after some dark hints, which she either could not, or would not comprehend, he intimated in pretty plain terms that with her permission and assistance, he would engage to produce a letter which if left to his management, would probably prevent her from being ever again annoyed in her own house by the presence of Kelroy; but, intimidated by the obvious hazard of such a measure, and the censure to which she would become liable in case of a discovery, she recoiled from it at once, as a thing impossible.

Compassion too, had not quite left her bosom; and although in the frequent debates which they afterwards held together, Marney, whose malicious, undermining spirit longed for such a secret, sweet revenge as this would be, frequently pointed out to her the ease with which the whole might be contrived, she still had sufficient conscience left to refuse, until the pleasure which Emily seemed to experience in the company of Dunlevy, added to her peculiar embarrassment when questioned by him respecting Kelroy's likeness, suggested a willing belief that in preventing the return of her lover she should do her no material injury.

The next day Helen and Emily chanced to be abroad, and she was sitting alone, profoundly meditating upon the expediency of her confident's advice, a genteel looking young man rode up to the house, and having inquired whether Mrs. Hammond lived there, dismounted, and gave into her hands a packet directed to her daughter, which he informed her he had received at the Cape of Good Hope from Mr. Kelroy, and had promised that gentleman to deliver it himself.

She thanked him very politely for his trouble, and insisted upon his staying to take some refreshment, which afforded her an opportunity of learning that he had been employed formerly in the capacity of a clerk by Kelroy's father, but was no longer a resident of Philadelphia, where he had landed four days since, and had been prevented by indispensable business from fulfilling his trust earlier. He seemed of a very communicative temper, and as Mrs. Hammond had reasons of her own for wishing to know all she could of his affairs, she contrived to detain and interrogate him until she discovered that he had been rather unsuccessful in life, and intended shortly to go to New Orleans, where he had two brothers, and a sister, all married, and settle there also.—She then dismissed him, highly pleased with the civility that had been shewn him.

He had scarcely got out of sight, when Marney arrived, and finding the coast clear, hastened with eager importance to relate in exaggerated terms the conversation he had overheard between Helen and Dunlevy, which added to the packet she had received, and was debating with herself how to dispose of, proved a temptation irresistible to the malice, and restless intriguing disposition of Mrs. Hammond. She produced the sealed packet, and repeating what the stranger who brought it had said of himself, insinuated that it was in her power to act as she pleased. She then, at the instigation of Marney, whose curiosity was if possible greater than his unprincipled ill-nature, opened it.—After which half an hour sufficed for the arrangement of their whole plan.

The two letters from Kelroy which had been enclosed under one cover were left to the care of Mrs. Hammond, who wrote in her daughter's name the answer already mentioned, which Marney himself, who possessed the talent of counterfeiting with admirable dexterity, the most difficult hand, undertook to copy, but was so egregiously deficient in orthography, that his first attempt, although a most perfect imitation of Emily's writing, was spelt in such a manner as to be totally unfit for the purpose in question.

Mrs. Hammond sent it back to town, with a few lines intimating the defect, and requesting him to begin another immediately, lest the opportunity of forwarding it should be lost; but as they had agreed not to meet oftener than usual, and he had in paring some fruit cut his thumb across nearly to the bone, he excused himself in a note which she kept.

After the second copy was finished, and dispatched, their next care was to prevent, if possible, any letter from Kelroy reaching Emily, until they had learned the effect produced by the one they had sent to him.

The third he wrote her was lost on the way; but the fourth which she received notwithstanding all their vigilance, gave great uneasiness both to Marney, and Mrs. Hammond, neither of whom seemed to relish the prospect of being detected in such practices.

Many a long consultation did they hold during the winter, and many were their anxious conjectures respecting the success of their contrivances; which, if Kelroy neither wrote, nor returned at the appointed time, they concluded might be regarded *complete as to him*; and they prepared in concert a letter for Emily, to be held in readiness as occasion might serve.

Unhappily, every thing succeeded to their wishes, and it was conveyed to her by an artifice of Marney's, who hoped to have had the gratification of seeing her read it, and was sorely disappointed when she left the room for that purpose.

The remorse of Mrs. Hammond when she witnessed the distress, and self accusation of her unsuspecting daughter, was strong, but transient; for, upon finding that neither her health nor her intellects suffered from the disappointment, she buried every trace of compunction in the indulgence with which she made it a point to treat her.—Besides, she so thoroughly detested Kelroy, and was so averse to the idea of being subjected to the perpetual strictures of one whose pleasures and pursuits were so different from her own, that she easily persuaded herself she was very excusable. But, when the preconcerted, groundless tale of Kelroy's attachment to an English lady, and his intended return to America, together with her own incessant warnings, and exhortations at length combined to effect the marriage with Dunlevy, she was then at ease, for she had no longer any thing to apprehend from a discovery which she was well convinced Marney would for his own sake cautiously avoid. Applauding therefore the whole of her past conduct, which she so far imposed upon herself as to imagine could not be erroneous since nothing disastrous had followed it, she gaily prepared to enjoy the fruits of her ingenuity, when the hand of disease arrested her iniquitous progress; and the anguish of her dying hours was augmented by her inability to command the destruction of those papers which she had preserved lest circumstances should have rendered a reference to them necessary; and after they had become useless she was too much occupied with other concerns to attend to what she fancied might be accomplished at any time. But the obloquy which a discovery of them would throw upon her memory, and the misery and dissention which they might be the means of creating between Dunlevy and his wife, were the last, agonizing ideas of her departing soul.

The death-like swoon into which Emily had fallen, was succeeded by a fever which reduced her to the borders of the grave, and she recovered from it only to experience the pangs of a lingering decay. In vain was the kindness, and attention of a fond husband, and anxious friends, who ascribed her dejected languor to recent illness, exerted to relieve her; the blow was given which rendered them of no avail. Betrayed where she had believed herself cherished—sacrificed to the inhuman machinations of her own mother, who whilst employed in forging the chains of her wretchedness had appeared to be actuated by the warmest, and most disinterested wishes for her welfare, existence became a burden to her; and encouraged by the innocence of her past life to look with hope, and confidence towards futurity, she longed for the hour which was to dismiss her from a world, where of all of which was once so dear, nothing now remained but the friendship of Helen.

Two cares alone occupied her during her painful decline. One was to soften the affliction of Dunlevy, who unsuspicious of the cause which had reduced her to such a state, appeared totally unable to reconcile himself to the prospect of losing her; the other to be justified in the opinion of Kelroy. To this end she employed herself at intervals in composing a pathetic little narrative of her misfortunes, in which she omitted nothing except the name of Marney; and having burnt his letter, enclosed it together with those of Kelroy, and her mother under one cover, directed to Helen.

This she kept until the increase of her disorder forbade a hope of recovery, and when her weakness was such that she could no longer rise, she one day called Helen to her bed-side, and said, "I have something to confide to your care, my dear Helen, and a last request to make provided you will comply with the terms of it."

"I will do whatever you wish," replied Helen, in tears.

"Then take this;" said Emily, drawing it from under her pillow, "and promise me solemnly never to mention the contents of it to any person but one. That one I need not name—but if you ever should meet, it is my desire you will shew him these, that he may know I was not the faithless, heartless being he supposed me."

Helen received the sealed papers in speechless sorrow, whilst the dying beauty calmly continued, "You will not open them until I am gone, which now must soon be—and then, in the conviction that if I had survived, my life must have been spent in pining discomfort, you will learn to be resigned to our separation."

"What am I to think?" said Helen.

"Think," replied Emily, "that I have been injured, but have forgiven those who destroyed me.—Think, that situated as I now am, I regard my early death as a signal mercy.—And believe, that in this my last desire, I am actuated not by a spirit of unchristian resentment, but by a natural wish to stand acquitted in the eyes of one with whom I once hoped to have been happy; and who if left to the guidance of his present prejudices, may perhaps have cause to lament the consequences of them more deeply than I have done mine."

She survived this conversation but a few days; and, shortly after she had attained her twentieth year, all that remained of the once gay, and fascinating Emily Hammond was consigned to the bosom of the earth.

Her loss was unaffectedly deplored by Helen, whose sole consolation for her untimely end, arose from the perusal of the heart rending proofs that she had died a martyr to incurable grief; and whilst she shuddered at the perfidy of Mrs. Hammond, and her confederate, mournfully rejoiced that her devoted child was so providentially released.

Time, the softener of every sorrow, at length calmed the distracted regrets of Dunlevy; and when sufficiently composed to experience relief from dwelling on the past, he derived his greatest happiness from the society of Helen, whose strong attachment to his departed wife laid the foundation of that regard, which a more intimate knowledge of her excellent qualities converted by degrees into the tenderest friendship on both sides; and three years after the death of Emily, he paid his addresses to her, and was accepted; to the inexpressible delight of poor old Mrs. Cathcart, who had begun to entertain serious apprehensions that her daughter was to be an *old maid*.

Whilst these events were passing, Kelroy had become a gloomy wanderer, seeking to recover in distant countries, that repose of which one whom he in vain endeavoured to forget had deprived him.

The effect of the letter which he had received as Emily's, was heightened by the recollection of the familiar addresses which he had surprised Marney offering to her; and denouncing the bitterest curses on his own folly in having suffered himself to be thus deceived, he sternly, and solemnly swore never again to inhabit the same quarter of the globe with the woman who had rendered creation a desert to him.—

The wildest paroxysms of disappointed passion succeeded, and, to avert reflections teeming with horror, he madly plunged into every species of dissipation; hoping through means of that, and the ravages which misery, and the climate combined to make on his health, to be spared the guilt of that self-destruction to which he felt himself unceasingly inclined.

A knowledge of the death of his mother first awakened him to a sense of the pernicious courses he was pursuing; and remembering the grief which a consciousness of his lamentable departure from moral dignity would have occasioned to her, he left the scene of his excesses, resolved to renounce both that and them for ever.

After traversing almost every part of modern Europe, and dispensing with a liberal hand towards the relief of the wants, and weaknesses of his fellow beings, that wealth which was now of no other value to him, he at length bent his course towards England, and there learned from Walsingham, that both Emily and her mother were no more. There too, he heard of her previous marriage; and the morbid melancholy which had usurped the place of his former animation, prevented any inquiries on the part of Walsingham, whose wife had made him the father of three children; the second of which, a girl, was named after her deceased aunt, whom she so strikingly resembled, that Kelroy of whom she became extremely fond, was frequently scarcely able to command himself, as he listened to her innocent prattle.

Weary of himself and all the world, and absolved now from further observance of his oath, a wish to revisit the home which he had so long abandoned, impelled him to seek once more the land of his nativity, where he arrived a few months subsequent to the union of Helen and Dunlevy.

The total change in his character, and appearance gave rise to numerous conjectures, and remarks in those who had formerly known him; and such was the seclusion in which he lived, that although she had early been informed of his return, a considerable time elapsed before Helen could meet with him, which she at last did, at the house of his cousin Mrs. S.

The sight of her was painful to him, but his natural courtesy was not yet so far obscured as to render him capable of treating her friendly advances with neglect; but when, calling to mind the sacred promise she had given, she saw an opportunity of requesting to be favoured with a visit from him, he shrunk with involuntary disgust from the idea of entering the house of a man, whom he believed had been preferred to himself by the only woman he had ever loved.

His altered form, and the extinguished lustre of his eyes, were affecting evidences of what he had suffered, and Helen was grieved that she should be compelled to revive, perhaps, all the violence of his original distress; but her word, so solemnly pledged to one on the brink of eternity, was not to be recalled; and as the only method allowed her of fulfilling Emily's pathetic injunctions, she finally sent him the papers, accompanied with a written assurance, that except herself and one more, he was the only person then in existence who had the slightest knowledge of them, and requesting that when he had read them, they might be returned to her possession.

A fortnight passed away without her having heard from him, when one morning whilst Dunlevy happened to be abroad, she was informed that a gentleman below stairs wished to see her, and upon entering the parlour was surprised to find Kelroy there.

He seemed much affected when they met, and Helen too felt greatly moved; yet she sought to hide her own concern, and lessen his, by appearing to esteem his visit as a complimentary one.

A few ineffectual attempts at conversation followed, and he then rose, and taking from his pocket the packet she had sent him, said in a low voice, as he gave it into her hands, "What the perusal of these has cost me, can never be known, except to the Almighty."

He paused, and turned away his face, and Helen then said, "Believe me I regretted the necessity I was under of permitting them to be seen; but a promise like mine—"

"Oh! it was a just, and a kind one," interrupted Kelroy, "and the manner in which you have fulfilled it, demands my everlasting gratitude!—But who was the wretch whose name she has concealed?—The miscreant who stooped to be the tool of that mother, whom I will not execrate, since she is now where the punishment is proportioned to the crime?"

"I am ignorant myself," replied Helen, "except from conjecture; yet were it proper that you should know, I should not, in pointing him out to you, be apprehensive of accusing an innocent person."

"Then why hesitate to do so?" said Kelroy. "Fear not that any resentment of mine will cause you to repent your confidence; for rest assured I have no wish by entering into a useless contest with cowardice, and villainy, to expose to light secrets on which the grave has placed its seal."

"Since these are your sentiments," replied Helen, "you may be trusted, for providence has half avenged you already.—It was Marney—who by the bursting of a gun has not only lost his sight, but had his right hand so dreadfully shattered, that it was found necessary to amputate it."

"Damn'd, infernal, execrable scoundrel!" exclaimed Kelroy, a transport of ungovernable fury lighting up his emaciated features; "Oh! may he exist in helplessness and torment, until life is wasted to the very dregs!—Of such sufferings it would indeed be mercy to deprive him, who, if it depended on me, would endure them for millions of years, and even then, the expiation be incomplete!"

The entrance of Dunlevy prevented Helen's reply, and Kelroy, who in learning that he also had been a victim to Mrs. Hammond's artifices, felt every particle of animosity towards him extinguished, returned his civilities with cordiality, and soon after took his leave.

But the tortures he had sustained from his once-suppressed, and now-awakened sensibilities unhinged him for ever; and his approaches towards insanity grew so evident, that Helen, whom he had continued occasionally to visit, felt infinitely relieved when informed that he meant to take a voyage to Leghorn.[1]

Previous to his departure, he placed the following lines in a book, which he left with her:—

STANZAS.

Time, as it slowly wears away,
Can never take from me,
The memory of that mournful day
Which robb'd the world of thee.

---

1 The English name for Livorno, a Mediterranean port city on the western coast of Italy.

Regret, which hovers round thy tomb,
　　Now life and love are o'er,
Can never to its native bloom,
　　That wasted form restore[.]

Yet, thou shalt live within my breast,
　　An angel, bright and fair,
In youth's sweet early beauties drest,
　　Enshrin'd and worshipp'd there.

Three weeks after, the vessel in which he had embarked, perished, together with all on board of her, in a storm; and Kelroy
and his sorrows were hushed to rest in the depths of the ocean.

FINIS.

Appendix A: Early Philadelphia

1. "A Plan of the City and Environs of Philadelphia," Engraved by Willm Faden (1777)

[William Faden's 1777 "Plan of the City and Environs of Philadelphia" sketches the city's layout and shows the locations of family homes along the Schuylkill River, encompassing *Kelroy*'s city and country settings. Born in London, Faden (1749–1836) was a cartographer and map publisher best known for the maps he produced during the American Revolutionary War. In 1783, he was appointed geographer for King George III (r. 1760–1820).]

2. William Russell Birch, Introduction to *The City of Philadelphia, in the State of Pennsylvania North America; as It Appeared in the Year 1800* (Philadelphia: William Birch, 1800)

[Engraver William Russell Birch (1755–1834) produced numerous engravings of Philadelphia and its surroundings, some of which he collected in his beautiful full-color volume *The City of Philadelphia.* Birch's Introduction gives a sense of his volume's aim: to depict Philadelphia as a thriving city and to encourage further investment.]

PHILADELPHIA.

The ground on which it stands, was less than a century ago, in a state of wild nature; covered with wood, and inhabited by Indians. It has in this short time, been raised, as it were, by magic power, to the eminence of an opulent city, famous for its trade and commerce, crouded in its port, with vessels of its own producing, and visited by others from all parts of the world. Its situation on the bank of the Delaware, lies about 40 degrees north from the equator, and about 75 degrees west from London, on the west side of the river, about 40 leagues from the sea. Its plan was laid out by William Penn, and was confirmed by charter, on the 25th of October, 1701. This Work will stand as a memorial of its progress for the first century; the buildings, of any consequence, are generally included, and the street-scenes all accurate as they now stand; the choice of subjects are those that give the most general idea of the town; the scenery is confined within the limits of the city, excepting the first and last views: the frontispiece represents, with the city at large, a busy preparation for commerce, and the last plate, with the Swedish church, the exertion of naval architecture to protect it; each subject terminating at the opposite extremities of the suburbs, on the bank of the river.

3. William Russell Birch, "Plan of the City of Philadelphia," from *The City of Philadelphia in 1800* (1800)

[Birch's Plan of the City shows Philadelphia's development creeping past Centre Square (today's City Hall). Comparing Birch's Plan to Faden's 1777 Plan shows how much the city had grown in 23 years.]

4. William Russell Birch, "Bank of the United States, in Third Street, Philadelphia," Plate 17 in *The City of Philadelphia in 1800* (1800)

[Birch's cramped, crowded, building-centered view of the Bank of the United States presages the future of urban images. Appropriately for a volume aimed at solidifying Philadelphia's city status, in this image the bank's façade looms over the fashionable ladies and gentlemen who walk or ride through Philadelphia's streets. In the colored plate, bright yellow breeches adorn the man entering the posh brick house; *Kelroy*'s readers might imagine Kelroy, Walsingham, or the ever-fashionable Marney in similar attire. Birch emphasizes the size and architectural detail on the brick residence across the street from the bank, allowing the two structures to work in visual partnership; together, the elite domestic and financial worlds dominate the urban landscape.]

5. William Russell Birch, "Mendenhall Ferry, Schuylkill, Pennsylvania" (1809)

[This 1809 engraving did not appear in Birch's *City of Philadelphia*. The image shows villas along the river in the neighborhood of Mrs. Hammond's country retreat. The villa to the center-left of the image belonged to Joseph Sims, a prominent Philadelphia merchant whose city home on Franklin Row was one of the city's oldest brick town houses. To the right is Harleigh, the fashionable retreat of lawyer William Rawle, on what is now known as South Laurel Hill.]

Appendix B: Gender, Economics, and Marriage

1. From *Fidelity Rewarded, Or, The History of Polly Granville* (Boston: Young and Adams, 1796) 3–19

[*Fidelity Rewarded*, an anonymously published epistolary novel, gives voice to Polly Granville, one of the first openly rebellious teenage daughters in American literature. Polly's petulant complaints to her friend, Sophia; her lover, Mr. Danford; and her mother about her father's decision to force her to marry an undesirable suitor for his money, are resolved through the intervention of a benevolent uncle in Philadelphia and Mr. Danford's lucrative business dealings in Canton, China.]

FIDELITY REWARDED:
OR, THE
HISTORY OF
POLLY GRANVILLE

IN A SERIES OF
LETTERS;

Giving an account of her sufferings for her steadfast adherance to her promise; and also of her deliverance from her troubles, and her marriage, in consequence of her father's commencing a virtuous and religious course of life.

Boston:
FROM THE PRESS OF YOUNG AND MINNS,
STATE STREET.—1796.

TO THE PUBLIC

THE *credentials of Miss Polly Granville being only in the hands of the author, who, at first, threw the following sheets together, without any further design than for his own amusement: But, as they are founded on truth, and nature, and those who have perused them, have solicited the author to send them to the press, he now consents they may appear in public.*

For certain reasons, the names of each person in the following letters are false ones, and the place of their abode concealed: but Miss Polly visiting her uncle at Philadelphia, will plainly show that they were inhabitants of America, and lived within these United States.

The drift of the subject is to show the preference of virtue, to riches and grandeur; with some remarks on domestic regulations.

Perhaps some may think, in reading some of the first letters, that there appears too great a degree of contumacy in the heroine of the story; but if they will read the whole, with care, they will find, that her seeming obstinacy is founded on reason. As the author aimed to inculcate virtue, and discourage vice, he hopes it will be kindly received. And vice being so predominant in the present age; if it should be the means of reforming a single person from any of their vicious practices, he thinks he shall be richly repaid for his labour. That it may have a beneficial effect, and thereby obtain some degree of approbation from the public, is the wish of your humble servant,

THE AUTHOR.

LETTER I.

From Miss POLLY GRANVILLE, to Miss SOPHIA DANIELSON.

Dear Miss Sophia,

YOU know that Mr. Danford, of late, has paid his addresses to me; and you know, likewise, that he is a man worthy of any body's esteem. I am sure he had engaged all my affections; and we had got so far in our courtship, that we had promised marriage to each other: But my father, for some family convenience, hath engaged Mr. Stapleton to address me. Now Mr. Stapleton is very wealthy, but he is quite ill looking: I believe you never saw him. Well, I will try to let you know how he looks. He is a tall figure of a man; has very large coarse features, and a dead looking eye; with hollow cheeks, large irregular teeth, and a mouth no ways bespeaking approbation. Indeed he is a frightful looking man as to his person. He is, besides, of a violent temper, and hath no consideration in any matter whatsoever. He speaks quick, and talks much, without sense, or method; is quite a libertine; is very fond of company; and no company comes amiss to him. And, indeed, he is altogether a debauchee. Now could you think your Polly could be fond of such an alliance? No. What, to exchange Mr. Danford, who has every personal qualification, for such a creature as this? No, I won't! for I will die first! Besides, I would not break my promise, that is of such a nature, for all the world; and there is nothing shall tempt me to break it!

My mother and I have had a long discourse on the subject, and I find I am not to expect much favour from my father in this affair; and my mother seems to side with him, at present. I will send you the discourse I had with my mother; which was nearly as follows:

My mother called me to her, and upon my seating myself by her, said, Polly, do you intend to favour the addresses of Mr. Danford any longer, or have you dismissed him already? Dear mamma, said I, I have not dismissed him at present; and why should I? I hope you have no objections to his visits; have you? Yes, Polly, said my mother, I have: and if I should only tell you that it is disagreeable to me, it ought to be a sufficient reason for you to dismiss him. But I will give you some reasons why I wish you to break with him. It is high time that you knew your own importance. For prithee, child, don't you know that you are nobly descended; that our family is one of the oldest in the country; and that your father is very wealthy, having a large estate in his hands; is immensely rich in money and lands; and carries on an extensive trade at sea; and is called one of the first men on the continent? Now Mr. Danford's circumstances being but moderate, no ways equal to yours, it cannot be thought that you will stoop so low as to receive his visits; much less to encourage any further alliance with him. It is therefore your father's pleasure that you break with him; and so it is mine. For your sister Jenny married a man that was exceeding wealthy, and you was always looked upon above her, both in beauty and accomplishments of mind, and it is in your power to make the richest man in the country happy: So I hope you will not displease your father nor vex me, for I never had a child that I set more by than I do by you. Neither should try harder to make any child happier in a wealthy marriage, than I should you. And now, I think I have given you sufficient reasons, why I think it will be best for you to break with him. And I am sure I would not advise you to any thing that is not for your good.

Dear ma'am, said I, you greatly surprise me; for I had not the least thought that Mr. Danford was disgustful to you; for you never hinted a syllable of it to me before—and he engrosses all my attention. And my inclination is too strongly biased in his favour to admit of an alteration. Neither can I see why you should despise him: For Mr. Danford is every thing that I could possibly wish for in a man. He is of a noble mind, is above every little action—is of a kind and affable disposition, and has a heart not ungenerous. He seems to be formed both to defend and love the other sex; and indeed there is nothing of meanness in him: For he has acquired great honour in the service of his country, as a public officer; and is in possession of a good estate, his circumstances being quite easy. And indeed great riches never had such charms with me! 'Tis true, where there is riches, it enables one to be kind and benevolent to the poor and needy. But to love riches for the sake of grandeur, and that only, characterizes a low and little mind, and borders on selfish stupidity. But, ma'am, you know that I always was of a serious turn of mind, and I think I have some love for religion; nor do I confine my ideas of happiness to this world; but my schemes of happiness are chiefly beyond the grave. Now, Mr. Danford is of a consonant turn of mind, being a great lover of religion, which is beautifully mixed in all his discourse; and, in my mind, sets him above the richest man on earth, who is void of his qualifications. And then, when he talks of love, or marriage, it is with that open frankness, that ever denotes the noble mind. And from him, you never hear any of that frantic disorder of speech: but persuasion seems to dwell on his tongue, in a just and noble manner. And can you think, that such an alliance as this can be disagreeable to me? An alliance that will not end at death, but will endure when the sun and moon shall forget to shine? O what a rich thought is this; that we may be mutual helps to each other in this world, and then be removed to the realms of joy and happiness, never to be parted again! And would you deprive me of the anticipation of all this happiness, and sink me below the dust? For I never shall be happy with any other man; because we have pledged ourselves to each other. And as for Mr. Murfee, who married Jenny, 'tis true, he is in possession of a large estate; but then, he is altogether a man of this world. And indeed he is nothing more than a fashionable rake—a professed libertine. If she feels herself happy with him, it is well. But it is hardly supposable that she does? But if we may judge by appearances, she is very uneasy in her mind; and does not rejoice in her noble marriage: And now, would you have me tied to another, such as Mr. Murfee is? If I was, I should bid farewel to all enjoyments in this world; and must set down miserable for life: And then, what avail would riches and grandeur be to me? Why, they would only serve to heighten my misery, and augment the troubles of life to a greater degree.

Polly, said my mother, you seem to branch out very largely; but I hope you are not in earnest: for your father, of late, had some overtures made to him by Mr. Stapleton on your account; which I think cannot be disagreeable to you. For he is a very wealthy man, indeed; there is hardly any end to his riches. And he is a man well enough as to other qualifications. And now what objections can you have to him?

Dear mamma, said I, don't mention Mr. Stapleton to me for such an alliance; for he is a frightful looking man, and has nothing attractive in his behaviour; being quite void of that tenderness to be found in many others. And then there is nothing noble in his mind, or generous in his temper. And indeed, he seems to be formed by nature for a mere tyrant. For having a churlish ungovernable temper, and not having sense enough to know right from wrong; he is many times in a passion, without knowing what he is angry at. And, above all, he is a great libertine, caring for nothing but debauchery. Now, could you have a single thought of such a man for your Polly? Dear ma'am, you cannot! For I had rather live a single life all my days, or marry a man without any estate at all, provided he is endowed with personal qualifications, than to have him. For it is easier for a poor man, thus qualified, to attain an estate, than for a rich, selfish clown, to attain to those qualifications. So I hope you won't mention him to me any more.

Well, Polly, said my mother, you had better think seriously of the matter; for your father is determined that Mr. Danford shall not continue his visits; and has wrote him a line to forbid him our house. I think you had better encourage the addresses of Mr. Stapleton; for your father is set upon it, to give him all the aid in his power. For there is to be some exchange of property between your father and Mr. Stapleton, in consequence of your marriage, which will be very advantageous to our family. And so, I fear, he is too much set to be turned. For Mr. Stapleton being very wealthy, he thinks 'twill reflect great honour on the family. But I shall not say any more to you at present.

Dear ma'am, said I, let me just answer you before you withdraw. Then the matter is concluded already, I find. And I am to be sold to Mr. Stapleton, to be his slave. For if I am married to him, no other shall I be, I warrant. But I never will be neither his wife, nor slave! For if I cannot have a man of my own choosing, I had rather never alter my condition. But if I am ever married, Mr. Danford must be the man: indeed he must! Dear mamma, do stand my friend! And don't insist on my breaking with Mr. Danford, for my life depends upon it! and if you are not my friend, I am wholly destitute of any except Mr. Danford. And you say I am not to see him again. O shocking! Then I am to be plunged into distress and misery at an early age. And how can you say that you love me above any of your relations, when you do not care what befalls me? Which denotes you don't love me at all. But you will love your Polly yet, will you not? And will you not try to persuade my father to deal otherwise by me?—But if you will forsake me, I have no where to go but to a merciful God; on whose care and protection I will ever venture myself, hoping he will not lay more on me, than I am able to bear.

At this my mother withdrew, and now what have I to expect but hard treatment? Well, 'tis hard to disobey parents; but, as for my marrying Mr. Stapleton, I never will, let what will come of it. Neither will I marry any other man whilst Mr. Danford is living. For how can I, we having promised each other not to? which promises I hold to be sacred; and that no body hath a right to revoke them. And so you see, that I am stedfastly set, to hold my promise with Mr. Danford. But I cannot tell yet how it will be brought about.

By this time you will think it is time for me to conclude, which I do by sending you my kind regards.

POLLY GRANVILLE.

LETTER II.

From Mr. DANFORD, to Miss POLLY GRANVILLE.

My dear Miss Polly,

AND am I forbidden to visit you? Yes, I received a line from your father, which forbids me his house. On what account I cannot tell; but have heard, by the bye, that it is because my estate is not large enough. And I hear farther, that Mr. Stapleton is encouraged to visit you; and I suppose his estate is sufficient, and that is all he has to recommend him. But I should not think that my Polly (you see that I call you mine yet) would take up with such a wretch as Mr. Stapleton, who is void of every good quality. And then, my dear, what have I done to your father? For if I am guilty of any enormity that is offensive to him, if he will but hint it to me, I will amend; and shall be very proud to gain his affections at any rate, let it cost me what it will. And indeed, I should be willing to seek danger in the face of stubborn foes, if that would reconcile him to me. But I fear his disgust is of another nature. For I believe that nothing but money is wanting. As for an estate, I have enough of that to make us comfortable, and I don't think we ought to let the world engross all our desires.

And now, my dear, are your affections alienated from me? Or have you forgot me? You used to say that you had some esteem for me, and that I was delightful to you. And indeed you promised to be mine, let what would be the consequence. And may not I expect a line from you to inform me of the state of your mind towards me. As to myself, my love to you is, and ever will be, the same it ever was. Don't think that absence will, or can efface it. No; but if the sun should forget to shine, or the rivers forget to flow, then might I forget my Polly Granville, but not otherwise. Nor will the trials and troubles of this world make me unmindful of you. And I am resolved never to marry any other whilst you are living. But how you will behave yourself to me, is yet uncertain. But I always did depend on your word and promise, and think I may yet.

As for an estate, don't let that trouble you; for if your father should disinherit you, yet I have a competence of this world; and if I can but have your person, I do not care whether your father gives you any thing or not. For riches, abstractly of themselves, will never make a person happy; and I ever loved you more for the beauties of your mind than any thing else. Your being of an open temper, that ever sets the noble above the low minded, and having a love for virtue and religion, and not confining your ideas of happiness wholly to this world, greatly heightened you in my esteem, for I am myself, of a consonant turn of mind. How pleasing was the anticipation of these things to me; that we should be able to give advice and counsel to one another, which would mutually heighten the thoughts of heaven, even whilst in this state of change and vicissitude; and finally, that our friendship should not end at death, but that we should be partakers of that blessedness which is laid up for those who make virtue their chief aim.—But I cannot, and will not give you up as lost to me yet. For there are many intricate windings in life, which appear to us to be wholly against us; yet at the same time are working together for our good. And the person that puts his trust wholly in a divine Providence, is seldom disappointed. For Providence can overcome all these seemingly untoward obstacles, and make them all turn to our advantage; and then we can look back with delight on those seeming afflictions, and can see how they did work together for our good.

I shall depend upon a letter from you: and pray write whether your affections are unalterable to me or not; and at the same time you may assure yourself, that I am unalterably your's,

JAMES DANFORD.

LETTER III.

From Miss POLLY GRANVILE, *to* Mr. DANFORD.

Dear Sir,

IS it possible that you should distrust the love and fidelity of your Polly? No, I'll not harbour such a thought—I think you are not capable of such a thing. And do you ask whether my love is the same towards you? I answer, no; for the unthought-of trials that I have met with of late, have greatly heightened my love and affection to you. My esteem for you is altogether unalterable, and my heart is fixed. Neither is there any thing in this world that shall alienate my affections from you; and you may assure yourself that I am unalterably yours, and never will I marry any other man whilst you are living. Let the trials and trouble I meet with be ever so great, yet I will never break this resolution. For you cannot think that I set so light by the promise I made you as to break it, for any consideration whatsoever. But I have experienced great troubles, and heavy trials, since I saw you, which are on your account: and I expect they are not at an end yet. But this consideration makes them the lighter, that they are on your account: and I am willing to suffer greater trials for your sake, if I can but obtain your person. So you may see by this that you are no ways indifferent to me; but that you engross my whole attention, as to the things of this world; my worldly happiness being wholly centered in you.

I would give you, if I could, a sketch of my troubles. My father hath forbid my receiving your visits, and I suppose forbidden you his house, and hath likewise proposed Mr. Stapleton to me as a suitor; but I have utterly refused to have any thing to say to Mr. Stapleton on such an account. And have peremptorily declared, that if I could not be favored with an alliance with you, I would never alter my condition: which seems to raise great anger in my father: for it seems (tho' it is hard to say it of one's parents) that my father sets more by riches, than he does by the peace and quiet of his children. It seems that Mr. Stapleton is to pay me a visit; but it will be labour lost; I can tell them that: for I am determined not to have any thing to say to him on the subject; and I will warrant, he will get nothing but frowns from me. For if my affections were not fixed already, I could not think of Mr. Stapleton for a companion—indeed I could not; for he is no ways engaging to me, neither in person or behaviour. And then his mind is altogether naughty; and, in my view, he is not in possession of one good quality. So, if I was not biassed in your favour, you may see he would not be likely to make a conquest of me. But to return; my father hath not confined me to my chamber yet; though he says he will, if I don't comply with his proposal. But I have liberty of the garden, and to visit, having one of the family with me, to see that I am not in your company. I am also allowed to write; and my maid being wholly on my side, I can convey my letters when, and where I please: So you may leave your letters, and she will call for them.

Your letter to me revived my spirits greatly. To think, that you don't despise, nor forget me in this trouble, is a great consolation to me. And your hint, that "they who put their trust in Providence, will not be disappointed," gave me great encouragement; for my whole dependence is on a kind indulgent Providence; in whose hands I am willing to venture myself, and all my concerns. Ever praying that he will not lay greater trials on me than he shall enable me to bear, and that I may, in some measure, be blameless.

Sir, you may assure yourself I am your's, &c.

POLLY GRANVILLE.

LETTER IV.

From Miss POLLY GRANVILLE, *to Miss* SOPHIA DANIELSON.

Dear Miss Sophia,

I MUST write to you, because to my Miss Sophia I can write without the least reserve. Perhaps you will think that I write without sense or method. But then, when I write to you, I wish to unbosom my whole mind; knowing that you will make proper allowances for my imperfections. Well, I have a great many strange things to tell you, for I am used with great severity by my parents; who try all in their power to make me break with Mr. Danford, and favour Mr. Stapleton, but I utterly refuse to do either, which vexes them greatly.

Mr. Stapleton has paid us a visit, and you will wish to know how I behaved myself with my new lover, and how he conducted in the business. Why, I believe that we both behaved quite awkwardly. I am sure he did; and I have not much to say for myself. Well, as my mother and I were sitting in the parlour, who should enter but my papa, and Mr. Stapleton with him, which put me in a terrible flutter. My papa introduced him to my mother, and then to me; and I arose to receive him—but tremble, tremble, went my feet, so that I could hardly stand. I hope, said he, I see you well, Miss Polly: very well, Sir, said I; but did not say, at your service, you may well think. Well, he seated himself not far from me, and seemed as if his seat was uneasy to him. Now turning to this side, now to that; and seemed to be at a loss what to say. But my father and mother put him out of his pain, by withdrawing: my father saying, as he went out, well, Polly, I have engaged Mr. Stapleton to visit you, and I hope you will receive him kindly; and that you will be agreeable to him, and he to you. While my father addressed himself to me, I stood up, and when he had done, I courtesied, and down again; and was in hopes, that when I should tell Mr. Stapleton how the matter stood between Mr. Danford and myself, that he would relinquish all his pretentions to me, and would try to help me out of my present difficulty. But in this I found myself mistaken; for the more I expostulated with him, the more he would claim his right by my father's engagement; so I was resolved to use him very plainly, and to let him know, that I was determined to adhere to my promise to Mr. Danford. Well, as to our discourse; after I had seated myself, he moved his seat nearer to me, and accosted me as follows:

Well, Miss Polly, your father hath engaged me to address you, and I hope that my visits will meet with your approbation; for I should be fond of an alliance with your family; and I hope I shall make myself agreeable to you, as you are to me.

Sir, said I, if it were in my power to receive your visits, I should be very glad to on my father's account, who hath given you the trouble to call upon me. But as I have a prior engagement, I hope you will excuse me, Sir, when I tell you, that I cannot discourse with you on the subject. And I have more dependence on your honour, Sir, than to think that you will try to make a young defenceless creature break her promise with another man. For you know, Sir, that such an engagement is solemn, and ought to be held sacred. And I have great dependence on your honour, Sir, in this affair; expecting you will not insist on my favouring your pretensions; and hope you will say no more to me on that subject.

As I said before, he is quite an unpolite gentleman, wherefore breaking in upon me, he said, ma'am! ma'am!—if you are agreeable to Mr. Danford, why should not you be so to me? And no doubt, if Mr. Danford is agreeable to you, I can make myself equally agreeable. For we all know that affections are transferable. And besides, I am vastly above Mr. Danford in every point of view. So I am no ways concerned, but that you will like me, in a little time, as well as you do him.

But Mr. Stapleton, said I, what shall I do with the promise I have made to Mr. Danford? for I have pledged myself to him in a solemn manner; and if I should break that promise, I should be afraid that some thing uncommon would befal me. And what can you say to this?

Love-promises, said he, are nothing but words of course, and I have made a dozen of them in my lifetime; but never thought them binding. And if you have made a promise to Mr. Danford, you know the form now: and so you may make another to me, and I will do the same to you, and we will join our hands at the church, and then the matter will be settled, and who can call you to an account about it?

Mr. Stapleton, said I, you surprise me! Do you make thus light of solemn promises? If these are your sentiments, what security could a woman have with you? why you put me quite out of conceit of the other sex. But I hope they are not all of your turn of mind. And I am under the necessity of telling you, that you are no ways pleasing to me; therefore wish you to withdraw, and not disturb me with such discourse—for I must tell you, that I have no liking to you. And indeed, Sir, if I was not engaged, I could not think of a man of your sentiments for a companion—indeed I could not! And now, as I have been so plain with you, I hope you will give me no more trouble in this affair: for we being not of a consonant turn of mind, cannot be agreeable to each other.

Well, said Mr. Stapleton, I shall not give up my pretensions to you, for your father and I have settled the whole matter; and he having a right to command you, I shall depend upon his authority, and expect a speedy marriage. For I have engaged so far in the affair, that I cannot easily give it up: and so you may as well comply, as not.

Sir, said I, may not I depend on your honour, when I tell you, that I cannot love you, and that you are wholly disagreeable to me? If I should consent to give you my hand, what a life should we be likely to live together? For, where there is no love, there can be no confidence: and then we might both repent our proceedings when it would be too late.

I am, said he, not at all concerned about that. For it is a wife's duty, to obey her husband. And I shall take care of that in the first place, and then look out for your affections afterwards. And it will be strange if you cannot both love and esteem me—for I have a large estate; and, you know, where there is riches, there must be contentment of mind. So I have no doubt, but, in time, you will both love and respect me; and I am resolved to venture the consequence, and doubt not, that we shall be married soon.

Mr. Stapleton, said I, you may rely upon it, that I will never be your wife whilst I am living—neither do I intend to talk any more with you about the matter. Indeed, I did depend some upon your honour, but I find that you are void of that qualification. And to show you that I am in earnest in all that I have said, I shall this moment withdraw, and leave you by yourself, hoping you will make proper reflections on what hath been said, and that you will give me no more trouble.

And so I retired to my chamber. But my father and he had a long conference, after I withdrew. And, by what I can find out, by the bye, my father is determined to use all his authority, to make me comply with his proposal. And, I believe, he told Mr. Stapleton as much—for since that time, he uses me more like a stranger than a child: only with this difference, that he is not so polite with me, as he is with others.

When we sat down to tea, after Mr. Stapleton was gone—we having no company, his discourse was wholly about the above affair; and he said, I was altogether unpolite to Mr. Stapleton; but if I did not behave myself better to him, the next time he visited me, he would use his authority with me: and if that would not make me bend, he should take such measures with me, as would be very distressing, both for him to inflict, and for me to bear.

I thought it best for me not to answer him, so made no reply to what he said; but soon retired to my chamber again, and wrote you the result.

And now, ma'am, what must I expect? Nothing but hard words and angry looks from them that ought to deal most kindly and tenderly by me. But I did not think my mother capable of hard-heartedness: for she used to be very kind to me; indeed, she never gave me an angry word before this affair happened. But I intend to have another discourse with her. Pray, my dear Miss Sophia, write to me, and tell me how one ought to behave to parents in such a case as mine. I know one ought to obey parents in all things: But when Mr. Danford first addressed me, my parents seemed to encourage me in the affair; and now when my inclination has got strongly biassed in his favour, and we have promised marriage to each other—and all done, as it were, through their concurrence, they can have no right, I think, to insist upon my breaking with him, and admitting the visits of another, who is altogether disagreeable to me. Therefore, I think I shall not be altogether wrong, if I do disobey them in this point, for my worldly happiness does depend on it, and I fear it will go far in breaking my peace with heaven. For, dear ma'am, we should, in all our schemes of worldly happiness, make some provision for the better part; and not let the world infringe on the affairs of the soul and eternal happiness. But in my mind, to be joined to such an abandoned man, is, in effect, to bid farewel to all serious thoughts, and is forsaking religion entirely. But do, dear Miss Sophia, send me your thoughts on this subject; and if I am wrong, don't spare me; but give me your mind upon the matter plainly; for I am a young defenceless creature, and I seem to have no mortal to ask advice of but you at present. So I will conclude by sending you my best wishes.

I am your's, &c.

POLLY GRANVILLE.

2. From Mrs. Patterson, *The Unfortunate Lovers, and Cruel Parents: A Very Interesting Tale Founded on Fact* (New Haven, CT: Read and Morse, 1799) 1–12

[The unfortunate lovers of Mrs. Patterson's short novel, though clearly destined for one another, are separated by the cruel parents of the title. After a number of wild transatlantic plot twists, the newly rich Mr. Beaumont returns from Europe to marry Nancy, who is about to wed "Captain Sheldrick, of the East India Company." As in *Fidelity Rewarded* (Appendix B1), the younger generation's loyalties to their love interests are rewarded with both the marriages they desire *and* great financial success.]

INTRODUCTION.

PARENTS are either the dupes or tyrants of their children: Some parents keep their children at such an awful distance, that home becomes a prison; and they will flee to their neighbor's fire side for refuge, to screen themselves from the frowns of a turbulent parent. Others, soured by misfortunes, by their parents (not granting them the object of their wishes) are drove into a state of melancholy—languish and die. Mankind are not desirous of having their faults exposed to public view, but vent all their passions at the domestic fire side, where all should be calm and serene. Others will indulge their children from their infancy, until they arrive to a state of maturity, then check them for the same familiarities which they always indulge them in, and will not allow

*them to love for themselves, but they must love for them; which is many
times the cause of confinement, banishment and death, as will appear
in the following narrative.*

THE UNFORTUNATE LOVERS.

IN the year 1766, Mr. Benjamin Beaumont and Mr. Samuel
Gauze were partners in mercantile concerns in the town of
Boston. They were not related, but lived in perfect friendship.
They were men of the first characters in town, and had a rapid
run of business, both in wholesale and retail, by which they
accumulated great property. At length Mr. Beaumont married,
and his partner, Mr. Gauze, in the space of three months afterwards. Notwithstanding they lived in perfect friendship for
the term of three months, then by mutual consent of both parties, dissolved partnership; but still had a good understanding. However, at the end of nine months, Mr. Beaumont was
favored with a handsome boy; and on account of the love and
good will he owed to his friend, Mr. Gauze, invited him in (as
their houses were adjoining) to make merry with him on the
occasion. Dinner being over, Mr. Beaumont and Mr. Gauze,
retired into a private room for amusement. After conversing
upon different topics, Mr. Beaumont turns to Mr. Gauze with
a joyful countenance, saying, if it was so ordered by the Deity,
that your wife should bring forth a daughter, so that their tender minds might be filled with love and gratitude toward each
other, from their youth up to the age of maturity, and then be
joined in the hands of wedlock—with all my heart, replied Mr.
Gauze, God grant that to be the case.—With that, they renewed
it by a solemn vow, that nothing should be wanting on their
part, to endear them to each other. And they had their wish;
for scarcely had three months revolved, when Mrs. Gauze was
delivered of a handsome daughter.—Then Mr. Beaumont was
sent for to make merry on the occasion; where they renewed
their former promises, and confirmed it with a solemn oath. At
the end of a year, the children were baptized. The boy, Samuel Beaumont, and the girl, Nancy Gauze—in memory of Mrs.
Beaumont. And when old enough to go to school, were sent to
school together, and all the pains imaginable taken to endear
them to each other: Mr. Beaumont would often say, Samuel, if
you go any where to day, you must go with Miss Nancy:—And
Mr. Gauze would frequently say, Nancy, be sure and call for
Samuel, when going to school to day.

Thus a few years had elapsed, when they became attached to each other, to such a degree, that it was beyond the art of human reason to keep them apart for any length of time. However, Samuel was sent to college at the age of fourteen, which proved very grievous to Nancy, and brought her immediately into a state of despondent melancholy. But their parents indulged them as much as possible, by the privilege of frequent visits, and by unfolding their minds to each other by letters.

During the time of Samuel's collegiate life, his father (Mr. Beaumont) was deeply engaged in the East India trade, which proved so unfortunate, by storms at sea, that he lost all his shipping, and in less than one month after his son took his degree, his creditors called upon him and found him unable to pay ten shillings on the pound. Notwithstanding this sudden and unfortunate change, he bore it with the greatest fortitude.

Now let us turn to the young lovers, who were encouraged by indulgent parents.

By this time their passions became more strong. As they increased in years, Cupid's arrows were implanted strongly in both their breasts; and they lived in so much love and unity, save the nuptial bed, as though bound by the tenderest ties of nature. But pride, rank pride, the destroyer of peace and happiness, soon made a separation: For Gauze, finding his intended son-in-law (Mr. Beaumont, as his age gives him the title) reduced to poverty, by the misfortunes of his honored father, then denies him the privilege of coming to his house, or paying any further respects to his daughter. This refusal was so sudden and unexpected, that he remained speechless for some minutes—at length exclaimed with a loud and bitter cry: In the name of justice! from what motives have you altered your mind? This is beyond my conception, to have an open denial of the privileges you always indulged me in, even from my infancy. Oh! good heavens! is it possible for us to part, who have been so long united, and have been taught by indulgent parents to accent the first words of our utterance, *love.*—By this time his courage began to return, and he addresses himself to Mr. Gauze in the following manner:

Sir, I beseech you to take a retrospective view of your past conduct respecting this unhappy affair, which appears to be so at present. Don't you remember the solemn promises that passed between you and my father, that Nancy and I should be bound by the bands of wedlock, provided we were agreed, which you know to be the case? And not only so, but you confirmed it with an oath. I am not ignorant of this matter. This was not done in a corner; for the lowest class of people in town are well acquainted with it. Now, Sir, please to let me know what you ever observed in me, or my conduct, to give you any reason to treat me with neglect, and deprive me of the object of my wishes, which you ever indulged me in. Mr. Gauze remains speechless—at length replies: I have ever observed your conduct to be good, but do not wish to have my daughter go to the arms of a beggar.—Your father was in good circumstances when I passed my word, which I don't consider binding, since he has been reduced to poverty.

The young man replied: Your riches perish with you—and departed with a heavy heart. Miss Nancy was then in her apartment, and knew nothing of the conversation; but no sooner had Mr. Beaumont retired, than her father entered the room and said, I'm determined to break up a scene that has been so long in agitation, both to your ruin and the dishonor of your father.

Nancy replies with a look of wildness—good God! Father, what scene? what scene? The scene between you and Beaumont, that has been so long brewing. Don't you know that his fortune is not adequate to yours? But still you keep his company to the injury of your credit, as it will throw you into the meanest company in town. I look upon him no better than the offscouring of humanity. Nancy cries, forbear, I pray, forbear, with her eyes brim full of tears. She could not utter more—at length recovering, says: Father, were not the first seeds of love sown in my tender breast by your own hand, and cherished by your insinuations, and have budded and blossomed, and arrived at such a degree of perfection, that they are past removing? Oh! father, how often have I heard you say, be sure and go with Samuel to school to day, when I was incapable of comprehending your meaning? And now must I tell you, with tears in my eyes, that nothing can part us but death. On hearing of this, her father interrupted her and said: You are under my commands, and to them you must submit.

3. Susanna Rowson, "The Power of Affection" (1802) and "The Choice," *Miscellaneous Poems* (Boston: Gilbert and Sons, 1804) 137–40

[Both of these poems on the topic of friendship and marriage—"Affection" and "The Choice" by Susanna Rowson (1762–1824), an actress, writer, and teacher best known today as the author of *Charlotte Temple*—appear in Rowson's 1804 collection, *Miscellaneous Poems*. A version of "Affection" reproduced here appeared anonymously on page 3 of the *Philadelphia*

Gazette's 22 June 1802 issue; an edited version appears in *Miscellaneous Poems* under the title "Affection," but without the epigraph.]

AFFECTION

"Trifles in themselves,
Are to the feeling heart of greater worth,
Than India's richest gems."

TOUCH'D by the magic hand of those we love,
A trifle will of consequence appear;
A flow'r, a blade of grass, a pin, a glove,
A scrap of paper, will become most dear.

And is that being happy whose cold heart
Feels not, nor understands this source of joy;
To whom a trifle can no joy impart,
Who lose them, cast them by, deface, destroy?

Yes, they are happy, if the insensate rocks
On which the ocean beats or softly laves,
Rejoices that its lustre comes from him;
And glows with rapture to reflect its rays.

Not else. Though hearts so exquisitely form'd
Feel agony a thousand different ways;
Yet when by love, or friendship's power charm'd,
One moment's bliss, an age of pain repays.

One kind approving look, one cheerful smile,
Can from the mind each painful image blot;
The voice that charms us can all pain beguile,
List'ning, the world beside is all forgot.

Tho' sharp the pang, which friendship slighted gives,
Tho' to the eye, fond tears may force their way;
The cause removed, when hope again revives,
Light sits the "bosom's lord" and all is gay.

True, when obliged to part from those we love,
'Tis like the pang, when soul and body's riven;
But when we meet, the spirit soars above,
And tastes the exquisite delights of heaven.

Be mine, the feeling heart; for who would fear
To pass the dreary vale of death's abode;
If certain at the end they should be near,
And feel the smile of a benignant God.

THE CHOICE.

I ASK no more than just to be
From vice and folly wholly free;
To have a competent estate,
Neither too small, nor yet too great;
Something of rent and taxes clear,
About five hundred pounds a year.
My house, though small, should be complete,
Furnished, not elegant, but neat;
One little room should sacred be
To study, solitude, and me.
The windows, jessamine should shade,
Nor should a sound the ear invade,
Except the warblings from the grove,
Or plaintive murm'rings of the dove.

Here would I often pass the day,
Turn o'er the page, or tune the lay,
And court the aid and sacred fire
Of the Parnassian tuneful choir.
While calmly thus my time I'd spend,
Grant me, kind Heaven, a faithful friend,
In each emotion of my heart,
Of grief or joy to bear a part;
Possess'd of learning, and good sense,
Free from pedantic insolence;
Pleas'd with retirement let him be,
Yet cheerful, midst society;
Know how to trifle with a grace,
Yet grave in proper time and place.

Let frugal plenty deck my board,
So that its surplus may afford
Assistance to the neighb'ring poor,
And send them thankful from the door.
A few associates I'd select,
Worthy esteem and high respect;
And social mirth I would invite,
With sportive dance on tiptoe light;
Nor should sweet music's voice be mute,
The vocal strain, or plaintive lute;
But all, and each, in turn agree,
To afford life sweet variety;
T' keep serene the cheerful breast,
And give to solitude a zest.

And often be it our employ,
For there is not a purer joy,
To wipe the languid grief-swoln eye,
To sooth the pensive mourner's sigh,
To calm their fears, allay their grief,
And give, if possible, relief.
But if this fate, directing Heaven
Thinks too indulgent to be given,
Let health and innocence be mine,
And I will strive not to repine;
Will thankful take each blessing lent,
Be humble, patient, and content.

Appendix C: Entertainments in Early Urban America

1. Thomas Rowlandson, "A Gambling Table at Devonshire House" (1791)

[The image is a detail from Thomas Rowlandson's *A Gambling Table at Devonshire House* (1791). This pen-and-ink and water-color drawing by the renowned caricaturist shows Georgiana Cavendish, the Duchess of Devonshire (seated, with arm raised) and her sister the Viscountess Duncannon (standing) at the gaming table in Devonshire House, London. Scenes like these represent and exaggerate the urban entertainments Mrs. Hammond frequents in the first half of *Kelroy*.]

2. From Sarah "Sally" Sayward Barrell Keating Wood, *Dorval, or, The Speculator: A Novel, Founded on Recent Facts* (Portsmouth, NH: Nutting and Wheelock, 1801) iii–vii, 27–35

[In this excerpt from gothic novelist Sally Sayward Barrell Keating Wood's 1801 novel *Dorval, or, The Speculator*, the narrator encounters the shocking figure of the female gamester. *Dorval*'s horrified description contrasts with Rush's comparative acceptance of card games as an appropriate female pastime. Wood was born in York, Maine, in 1759, and her most familiar work today is *Julia, or, the Illuminated Baron* (1800). She was known to her readers as Madame Wood.]

PREFACE.

WHILE every library is filled with romances and novels, some apology is perhaps necessary for adding to the number, and introducing a similar work to the public. Wishing to avoid the imputation of arrogance, I will only say, that while society is so fond of literary amusements, some, and I believe, a large number, will be tempted to devote a part of their time to the perusal of the works of fancy and imagination; and while reading is so much in fashion, romantic tales will be read with avidity, and the works of the novelist will claim their station in almost every library. Hitherto we have been indebted to France, Germany, and Great Britain, for the majority of our literary pleasures. Why we should not aim at independence, with respect to our mental enjoyments, as well as for our more substantial gratifications, I know not. Why must the amusements of our leisure hours cross the Atlantic? and introduce foreign fashions and foreign manners, to a people, certainly capable of fabricating their own. Surely we ought to make a return in the same way. I should indeed be vain, if I indulged for a moment an idea that any of my productions were worth transporting to another climate, or that they could be read with any satisfaction, where the works of a Moore, a Burney, a Kotzebue, or a Rowland, had originated. But the attempt will be forgiven where the design is good; and it may possibly call forth the pens of some of my country women, better qualified to instruct and amuse. I hope no one will suppose that I entertain ideas so fallacious as to imagine it necessary for a female to be a writer: far from it. I am sure

"That Woman's noblest station is retreat;"[1]

and that a female is never half so lovely, half so engaging or amiable, as when performing her domestic duties, and cheering, with smiles of unaffected good humor, those about her. But there are some, who, forgetful of those sacred duties, or viewing them all in a circle very circumscribed, devote a large portion of time to dissipation, and such fashionable occupations, as waste many hours that might be devoted to better purposes. If a small share of that time were attached to the pen, I am certain no future author would agree with the Abbe Raynal, "That America had produced but few persons

---

1 George Lyttelton, "Advice to a Lady" (1733).

of genius:"[1] *Envy would be banished from society: and while a woman was drawing a picture of virtue and amiableness from imagination, she would imperceptibly follow the example and copy the portrait.*

A small, a very small portion of praise, will, I am sure, be awarded to the Novelist. The philosopher will turn with disgust from the pages of Romance; and the prudent will think the time lost that is spent in perusing fictitious sorrow and fictitious joys; the gay and the giddy will prefer the ball room or the card table; and the idle cannot find time or inclination to read. But there are some, who, retiring from domestic occupations, and whose time is not wholly spent in the city, will open, with pleasure, a volume which is meant to convey a little instruction, while it amuses an idle or a leisure hour; who can enjoy the well meant fiction, and "shed a tear on sorrows not their own."

The following pages are wholly American; the characters are those of our own country. The author has endeavored to catch the manners of her native land: and it is hoped no one will find, upon perusal, a lesson, or even a sentence, that could authorize vice or sanction immorality. It has been her wish to shew by example, the evils that have arisen from speculation, and which have fallen upon the virtuous and the good, as well as the wicked. She cannot help saying, in her own vindication, that the most vicious character is not the creature of imagination, "the vagrant fancy of a woman's brain." With regard to the other characters, it is left to the world to determine whether they are visionary beings, or copied from real life. It is hoped, however, while they acknowledge the possibility of the existence of such a being as DORVAL, they will believe it more than probable that an Aurelia, a Burlington, and many others, are still inhabitants of the world.

When the following pages were written, it was the warmest wish of the author's heart to dedicate them to a lady, whose goodness and virtues had deeply impressed her heart. But that lady's modesty has forbidden that public tribute. To admire in silence those qualities, which must create and rivet the esteem of all that know her, is all that is permitted.

The volume will of consequence appear without a patron to protect or acknowledge it. The author has only to beg that candor instead of criticism may be extended towards it. Not expecting that it will meet with applause, she only hopes it will not be too severely condemned.

THE AUTHOR.

YORK, *MARCH* 26, 1801.

---

1 Here Wood is paraphrasing French enlightenment writer Guillaume Thomas François Raynal (1713–96), better known as Abbé Raynal.

AURELIA TO ELIZABETH

July 1st.

YESTERDAY several ladies called upon my Mamma. They had been previously informed that we were to be here on Tuesday. We have walked through the principal streets in this town, with which I am very much pleased; but as you have heard Boston described, I shall not pretend to give you an account of the size or magnificence of the houses, the width of the streets, or the appearance of gaiety, opulence, and business of the shops. The truth is, I do not pay half the attention to things that I do to persons; and I have passed by some elegant buildings without observing them, when my eye has been arrested by a countenance that has charmed me, and I have in imagination looked into the heart, and found the features corresponding with the lovely ones which I beheld in the face.

Were I to judge from those I have seen, I should imagine that Boston had a large, a very large majority of handsome women. Indeed, I have seen but very few who might not lay claim to beauty.

Last evening we were at the Federal-street theatre. Of the performance I am not perhaps a judge; but my feelings were wrought up to a very high pitch; and the evening was so agreeably passed, that I was astonished at the rapidity of the hours.

When we returned, we found a number of invitation cards; so that we are engaged every day for a fortnight. This afternoon Mrs. Selkirk has a party, which she has put off for some time on account of our coming. To-morrow I will give you some description of the company; but I must now attend my parents. Adieu.

A.M.

CHAPTER VI.

Ah! From a female gamester heaven defend me.
Her smiles are most deceitful;
And her good humour all depends on cards,
The throw of dice, a lucky hit, or trumps;
Not on a husband's smiles, a daughter's virtue,
Or parent's happiness or health,
Or brother's honor; all these are risk'd.
For infamy and ruin, woes and sorrow,
Must and will follow such a life of folly.

AURELIA TO ELIZABETH.

LONG, very long since, my dear Eliza, from circumstances that convinced me of the destructive effects of play, I resolved never to risque a single sixpence upon the turning up of a card. Though I have frequently been rallied upon my forbearance, till last evening I was never very strongly tempted; but I here came off victress. I had much rather be laughed at for my peculiarity, than sacrifice so large a share of my own peace, as I must have done, had I been prevailed upon to become a female gamester; for such I must have considered myself, had I played for money. Not having any good humor to lose, I could not squander it away in so trifling a manner. My dear father supplies all my wants in a most bountiful manner; but were I once attached to cards, I should often have to call upon him with a draw-back that I never yet experienced; for I should indeed be ashamed to inform him to what use those supplies were appropriated. I was, indeed, last evening, flattered by the approbation he expressed of my conduct; but was really sorry, when I saw so many fine and lovely women with gentlemen, who were qualified to bear a part in conversation, fixed at the card table, and every idea annihilated but such as concern the worthless bits of paste-board which they held in their hands, and the white and yellow metal that glittered on the table, and which seemed to absorb every faculty.

I did not, however, sit alone. A Mr. Stewart, perceiving I declined playing, came to that side of the room where I was sitting, and addressed me in that easy and familiar way, which bespeaks an acquaintance with the world, and a finished education; and also with that good sense and agreeable manner, which discovers fine abilities and a benevolent heart. He is, I think, one of the most pleasing young men I have seen. His person is really engaging; and every sentence he utters forces its way to those feelings he wishes to address. I am told he is accused of coquetry; but am half inclined to think some one, who has attributed his attention, which is at once polite and friendly, to the power of her own charms, has, in a fit of disappointment, charged him with a folly of which he is innocent.

It is indeéd very difficult for a man so pleasing, to conduct in such a manner as to stand the test of criticism: he is either accused of indifference or coquetry. I acknowledge I can more readily pardon the latter than the former; and when it is productive of evil, I think the fault is rather in ourselves than in the other sex.

Why may not a sensible and refined man, converse with,

and pay attention to a young woman without any thoughts of courtship? Why may he not single out one, as a friend and acquaintance, when she possesses some quality which strikes him, without being considered as aiming to gain a place in her affections, since all he wishes for is her friendship and esteem? I think the attention must be pointed, and continue for a considerable length of time, and the most open and candid professions made, before a young lady has any right to suppose herself the object of his affection. Let us, my dear Elizabeth, be upon our guard.

Mr. Stewart gave me a most enchanting character of one lady, whose ill health obliged her to retire as soon as tea was over. "She goes," said he, as she left the apartment, accompanied by her excellent husband, "attended by the good wishes of every individual, not only here, but every where. She is, Miss Morley, a most amiable woman! an acquaintance with her would give you pleasure. Her heart is ever ready to pity, her purse ever open to relieve the afflictions of mankind. Her husband is her kindred spirit, and has, like her guardian angel, hovered over her, during a long and painful illness—she is now upon the eve of a voyage to Madeira, for the recovery of her health. They have one child, who is equally dear to them both; and their domestic happiness can know of no increase but her entire restoration."

You may believe I breathed an ardent wish for so desirable an event. Such characters, I am afraid, are not so common as we could wish; and, when met with, how ought they to be prized? Providence seems to have been particularly lavish of its bounty to this charming pair; for they are blessed with liberal and open hearts and an ample fortune.

The company did not separate till it was late: and I retired, pleased, though fatigued, to my chamber; and as it was rather late when I arose, I must at present resign my pen; for I am summoned to the breakfast table. Adieu, and be happy.

CHAPTER VII.

The groves of Eden, vanish'd now so long,
Live in description, and look green in song.
These, were my breast inspir'd with equal flame,
Like them in beauty, should be like in fame.
Here hills and vales, the woodland and the plain;
Here earth and water seem to strive again,
Not, cheese-like, together crush'd and bruis'd;
But, as the world, harmoniously confus'd.

Pope's Windsor Forest.[1]

---

1 Alexander Pope's "Windsor Forest," started in 1704, was completed in 1713.

AURELIA TO ELIZABETH.

July 10th.

A THOUSAND thanks, my dear friend, for your kind minuteness, and indeed for the endearments of your charming epistle. I rejoice to hear Miss Barton has at last named the period which is to connect her with your family; yet am sorry it is so distant. But we have often heard that the days of courtship are very pleasant; and if they are followed by a happy marriage, your brother, notwithstanding his present regrets, will look back upon them with the same pleasure that we all experience, when, after reaching the end of a delightful journey, we sit down with those we love, and take a retrospective view of the fine roads, flowing meadows, and enameled plains, through which we have passed. I do not blame Miss Barton: I think with her, that twenty-two is quite young enough to assume the important character of a wife.

We yesterday dined at a Mr. Enscott's, who has a very elegant and delightful seat about three miles from Boston. I wish I was acquainted with the rules of architecture, or the terms which are used to describe the beauty or magnificence of buildings: I would then endeavor to give you some idea of this superb and delightful mansion.

From the front of the house, you have a fine view of Boston. Charlestown lies upon the left hand; Cambridge and the colleges upon the right. The prospect of well cultivated fields, a rich and fertile country, interspersed with gentlemen's seats, rural cottages, lofty hills, and romantic vales, arrests and delights the eye. This charming spot is almost surrounded by water. The bridges, which unite Boston to Charlestown upon one side, and Boston to Cambridge upon the other, have a very pleasing appearance. The grounds around the house are highly cultivated; the balm of Gilead and the Lombardy poplars flourish, with a variety of other trees in almost every part, and are interspersed with fish-ponds, gardens, and green-houses, which are ornamented with every flower and shrub of almost every climate, and at once display the taste and wealth of the owner.

When we entered the court, the carriage drove round a little hillock covered with a soft verdure, and surrounded by a light green railing. This may surely be termed the mount of Cupid; for the little god stands upon a pedestal in the midst of it. This court is secured from the inclemency of the weather, by small buildings on each side, and a rising ground covered with trees, on the back.

We were introduced to a large hall, in which are two stair-cases, which meet before you arrive at the top, upon one large stair; and then dividing, you ascend by three different flights to the second story. Upon looking up the eye is arrested by a gallery, which runs round to every apartment in the third. The top of this ceiling is painted blue, and has a very pleasing effect. Opposite the door we entered, is another, which leads into the oval room; and as the front opens upon the flower garden, from this apartment, we are enchanted with a view of various beauties, both of art and nature, of the town and of the country; and also of the noble river of Charlestown, whose clear and lucid streams, running peacefully along, lave the banks at the extremity of the garden. This apartment is nobly furnished. As a great part of the walls, which are plaster of Paris, are covered with mirrors, and the residue adorned with elegant prints, every person must be pleased with the object that is presented, either with the works of the artist in sculpture and painting, or with his own form, which is more or less pleasing to all, and which is reflected from every part of the room.

> "For every soul finds reason to be proud,
> "Tho' hiss'd and hooted by the pointing croud."[1]

Upon the left hand of the hall, are two apartments for summer, the one a drawing-room, and the other a dining parlour. They are both furnished with tapestry, the one silk, and the other worsted, done with great neatness and taste in tent stitch.[2] The pictures and glasses in this room are superb. Upon the right hand is a keeping parlor, and a room devoted to the servants. The first is certainly the pleasantest room I was ever in; it is furnished most magnificently. The chambers are equally tasty and elegant; and the saloon, which is over a part of the oval room, is enchanting.

If I was delighted with the situation, the house, and ornaments, I was charmed with the owner, who is certainly one of the handsomest, and most pleasing men I have ever seen, and his wit and humor kept all his guests in spirits and perfect mirth. And indeed, my dear Elizabeth, we here met with some of the loveliest and most engaging women in the world.

We did not return to Boston 'till evening, when a full moon had illuminated this terrestrial paradise, and with its mild and silver rays danced upon Charlestown's clear stream, and displayed every object to the best advantage.

---

1 Edward Young, "Satire II," *Poetical Works* (London: Curll, Tonson, et al., 1741) 183.
2 A slanted needlepoint stitch.

Upon our return, my father received a letter from yours, and read us part of the contents. I own I am a little curious to see the bearer. I find you have not seen him. When I am favored with an interview I will obey you, and give you my opinion of this Mr. Dorval. We have generally thought alike. Good night.

A.M.

3. A Lady's Invitation to the Philadelphia Assembly (1785)

[In *Kelroy*, the Hammond women attend one of Philadelphia's grandest social events, an annual ball sponsored by the Philadelphia Dancing Assembly in honor of George Washington's birthday (22 February). This image shows a 1789 invitation to the Assembly. As the rules in the following entry reveal, subscribers were entitled to invite two ladies to each event.]

4. Rules of the Philadelphia Assembly, Season 1812 & 13 (1812)

[The rules for the Philadelphia Assembly were clearly codified and enforced by managers, who wore white ribbons at the dances. Though these were very urbane affairs, Philadelphians followed the latest British dance trends—in this case by dancing reels known as "country dances." The rules were reprinted in Thomas Willing Balch's history, *The Philadelphia Assemblies* (Philadelphia: Allen, Lane and Scott, 1916) 106–08.]

RULES
of the
PHILADELPHIA ASSEMBLY
Season . . . . . . 1812 & 13

1. The Assembly shall consist of forty subscribers.
2. The subscribers shall be under the direction of five managers, who shall have the entire management of the assembly.
3. Each subscriber will be entitled to two ladies' tickets.
4. The treasurer shall exhibit a regular account of receipts and disbursements, which account shall be open to the inspection of the subscribers.
5. No gentleman's ticket transferable except by consent of the managers.
6. The assembly rooms to be open at six o'clock, and the dancing to commence at seven, and conclude at one.
7. No refreshments admitted in the assembly room, but by order of the mangers.
8. No subscriber admitted in boots.
9. Ladies or gentlemen shall not leave their places after dancing down a country dance until the end of the dance, except in cases of absolute indisposition; and if they dance again during that dance, they are to take their places at the bottom.
10. The managers, and the ladies who dance with them, may stand up and take their places as second couple, and may retire when at bottom.
11. The managers will be distinguished by a white ribbon.
12. Should any improper person be introduced, they will be compelled to quit the room and the subscriber introducing such person will be expelled the assembly.

Lastly. These rules and regulations shall be printed and placed in the rooms, and every subscriber is expected to subscribe his name in a book prepared for that purpose. Any member acting contrary to them will render himself liable to be expelled the assembly, and forfeit his subscription.

5. "The City Dancing Assembly Honors Washington's Birthday with a Ball," *Philadelphia Gazette* (24 February 1794)

[President George Washington did not always attend his birthday balls in Philadelphia, but in 1794 he and his wife Martha were the guests of honor. Toasting was a common feature of public entertainments in the Early Republic; newspapers like the *Gazette* frequently reprinted significant toasts.]

The City Dancing Assembly Honors Washington's Birthday
with a Ball.

Saturday the 22nd instant, being the Birth Day of our beloved President, the managers of the City Dancing Assembly gave a ball in the evening.

They were honored with the company of the President and Mrs. Washington, several of the Foreign Ministers, a number of the members of Congress, the Secretaries of the treasury and of war, the Governors of the state and of the Western Territory, and the most brilliant display of beauty, perhaps, ever exhibited in this city. The countenances of all present, appeared perfectly congenial with the happy occasion.

The following toasts were drank, the last after the President and Mrs. Washington had left the room.

1. The day—may it always be illustrious in the annals of time, for the civil and military virtues it gave birth to.
2. May the hand of liberty always entwine the brow of patriotism.
3. May the light of Liberty illuminate the recesses of despotism, and all the world be free.
4. May our Republican virtues in peace, equal our military exertions in war.
5. May the fetters of slavery be broken on the head of Tyranny.
6. The *Fair* of America—may they be protected and embraced by the arms of Freemen.
7. The United States, the colony of the world, the assylum of unmerited distress, and persecuted virtue.
8. May the turbulence of Faction be trod under the feet of Liberty.
9. The President of the United States—long may he live an example to magistrates, and a blessing to his country.

6. Thomas Wilson, "The Five Positions of Dancing," *An Analysis of Country Dancing* (London: J.S. Dickson, 1808; 3rd ed. 1811)

[This image, "The Five Positions of Dancing," comes from the 1811 edition of English dancing master Thomas Wilson's influential instruction book, *An Analysis of Country Dancing*. Wilson attempted to codify the art of calling country dances (known today as contradances or contredanses) in his books, so that rural dancing masters could keep up with the newest dance steps and teach them to dancers in far-flung locales.]

THE FIVE POSITIONS OF DANCING.

Engraved for Wilson's Analysis of Country Dancing.

The Figures shew the positions of the Learner,
and the Feet that of a finish'd Dancer.

Appendix D: Gambling and the Lottery

1. From Caroline Matilda Warren, *The Gamesters: or, Ruins of Innocence. An Original Novel. Founded in Truth* (Boston: Carlisle for Thomas & Andrews et al., 1805) iii–vii, 215–27

[This excerpt from schoolteacher Caroline Matilda Warren's 1805 novel *The Gamesters: or, Ruins of Innocence* will remind *Kelroy*'s readers of Mrs. Hammond's late-night reckoning of her assets and debts. Like other anti-gambling tracts and fiction, *The Gamesters* revolves around a young man's futile struggle to resist the allure of drinking and gambling. Though it will strike readers today as highly moralistic and sentimental, it was reprinted in many editions in Warren's day.]

PREFACE.

THE author of the following work is sensible it will not bear the test of criticism. As the production of a youth, whose education has been limited, whose opportunities have been penurious, she hopes it will be viewed with that candour, which is ever an attendant of discernment.

She presents it to the public, not as the laboured production of erudition, but as the efforts of a mind rather of the contemplative turn, whose principal amusement is derived from such pursuits.

At a period, when the novelist is seldom greeted with a solitary smile of approbation from the whole regiment of literati; when even "the house is divided against itself," and *novel writers* attribute many of the fashionable foibles of the day, to *novel reading*; it may argue a degree of temerity to produce a work, which bears this "image and superscription."

While she cordially agrees with the objector, that *some* novels have exhibited too highly coloured portraits of life; and have, like an *ignis fatuus*, too frequently led the young mind astray; yet the writer believes, that were novels devoted to the cause of moral virtue, they might become as *useful*, as they are thought to be *pernicious*. The light, unthinking mind, that would revolt at a moral lesson from the pulpit, will seize, with avidity, the instruction offered under the similitude "of a story."

To blend instruction with amusement, and at once to regale the imagination, and reform the heart, has been the writer's object; how far she has succeeded, a candid public will determine.

Though the writer is confident the work would not pass unscorched through the firy ordeal of criticism; yet if it possess sufficient merit to meet a smile from the brow of candour; or, (what is infinitely dearer to her heart) if it gain one soul to virtue, or lure one profligate from the arms of dissipation, or snatch from the precipice of ruin, one fair fabric of innocence, she will deem herself amply compensated for every studious effort she has made, to throw the following sheets into their present form.

Perhaps no vice is more seemingly *venial*, or more *really* destructive, than gaming. Many a lost, despairing son of pleasure, will attest the truth of this observation.

What was at first practised to amuse a leisure hour, "grows with their growth, and strengthens with their strength," till it becomes a fixed and rooted vice; and when the husband, the father, and the friend, can find attractions in a gaming table, superior to those offered by the domestic fire side, virtue herself is eradicated from his bosom, and *feeling* is exchanged for inhumanity. The writer has attempted to discourage the practice of this too fashionable vice, and should the attempt prove unsuccessful, and the work be justly condemned,

"One secret voice, at least, shall sooth my heart,
Nor will I tremble at the critic's dart,
While conscience sweetly whispers this applause,
Thou hast not injur'd virtue's sacred cause."[1]

Of the ill judging and censorious hypercritic, who views with the jaundiced eye of prejudice, "every production from a *female pen*," she has nothing to ask, confidently believing, that the really learned and virtuous, will approve the *intention*, though a want of merit should oblige them to censure the *execution of the work*.

THE AUTHOR.

Sutton, September, 1805.

---

1 T.S. Surr, *George Barnwell* (Boston: Joseph Bumstead, 1800) vi.

CHAPTER XXVI.

"Nor think
"That virtue, in sequester'd solitude
"Is always found. Within the inmost soul
"The hidden tempter lurks nor less betrays
"In the still seeming safety of retreat,
"Than where the treacherous world delusive smiles."
                    More's "SACRED DRAMAS."[1]

SOMERTON proposed retiring to a public house, and Leander unwarily consented. Already had the sophistry of Somerton considerably weakened his objections to the indulging of his favourite passion for play. As yet he had never strayed from the path of rectitude; but he had begun to think very differently of the fashionable follies of the times. He had too implicitly followed the maxims he had drawn from books, and too fatally neglected the study of the human heart. Human nature he knew only in theory. Suspicion was a stranger to his bosom, and when the language of kindness vibrated on his ear, he looked not for a heart of adamant; when virtue sat upon the tongue, he fought not for a "soul black with treachery."

Edward and Evander were *professional gamesters,* in the confidence of each other; and this was so artfully concealed from Leander, and so great was Somerton's ascendancy over him, that one might as well have attempted to shake the earth from its centre, as to persuade him of his insincerity. What a magic charm is there in a gaming table, that can outweigh the dictates of reason, and even the precepts of religion? That the eye which has often glistened with the dew of sensibility, can gaze with anxiety on a set of *figured papers,* and the mind where science has shed her effulgent ray, can feel as much interested in a *deal,* as in the fate of a nation? Much more mysterious, that the heart that is guarded on all sides by principles the most inviolate, which beats in unison with religion, can so far debase itself, so far forget the dignity of its nature, as to stoop to the mean arts of base dissimulation. Tell me ye men of science, ye, who pretended to shew the causes of the actions of men, ye philosophers, who can trace every action to its purest source, through as many intricate mazes as the famed labyrinth of Crete; tell me, what is this potent magic that

---

1 *Sacred Dramas* is a 1782 collection of plays by Hannah More
   (1745–1833).

can work such astonishing changes; this irresistible attraction so much superior to reason, virtue, and domestic happiness? For at present all is conjecture, all is vain enquiry.

If the passions of Leander were already inflamed, his reception at the tavern was calculated to add fuel to the blaze. The neat apartment, sparkling glasses, and cheerful countenances of his companions, all conspired to facilitate his progress in the love of dissipation. Cards were introduced, and Leander felt compelled to join his companions; but he did it with repugnance, for, though his objections to play were weakened, they were not overcome.

An unfortunate succession of winnings, made it *ungentlemanlike* not to give his antagonists opportunity to recover their losses. Too polite to refuse (if politeness be not dishonoured by the use) and too unskilful to be long successful, his winnings were soon reversed. He then would gladly have withdrawn; but the same courtesy he had shewn to others was now shewn to himself. Somerton too, was his partner, and appeared unwilling to retire. Thus situated, Leander found it impossible to disengage himself, and Edward and Evander now thought their prey entirely in their power; for they knew full well, that "every indulgence of a vicious inclination, renders a second indulgence more easy."

The midnight bell had rolled through the silent air ere Leander left the tavern, and for the first time in his life, felt the stings of remorse. His heart suffered severely from a consciousness that he had *done wrong*. Sleep long refused him its wonted consolation, and when tired nature, at length overcame with watching, sunk in the arms of Somnus, mysterious visions haunted his imagination. Long and painful were the intervals between the broken slumbers of the night; alas! his conscience denied him its usual approbation.

While affairs were thus circumstanced at W—, Edward was constant and assiduous in his visits to the Herbert family. Eliza now indulged fair dreams of happiness. Hope scattered her fair flowers over the landscape of life, and whispered fond, delusive stories of tomorrow. To the fascinating charm of an engaging exterior, Edward added all the graceful polish of the gentleman. Eliza's vivid imagination had annexed virtues, to which his heart was a stranger; and conscious that her attachment was founded in virtue and cemented by friendship, she blushed not to consider how essential his presence was to her happiness. With him

"Not undelightful was the haunt
"Of wood, or lonely grove, or russet plain,
"Made vocal by the muse;"[1]

and without him

"Neither the breath of morn, when she ascends
"With charm of earliest birds, nor rising sun,
                    "Nor herb, fruit, flowers,
"Glistening with dew, nor fragrance after showers,
"Nor grateful evening mild, nor silent night,
"Nor walk by moon was sweet."[2]

Lorenzo too, found in his heart a growing passion for the lovely Harriet; not esteem, nor friendship, but warmer and more tender than either.

CHAPTER XXVII.

"Virtuous and vicious, every man must be,
"Few in th' extreme, but all in a degree;
"The rogue and fool, by fits, are fair and wise,
"And e'en the best, by turns, what they despise."

POPE.[3]

THE morning of prosperity was too bright to last. The machinations of Somerton succeeded, and Anderson was no longer himself. He had exchanged the soft peace of conscious innocence, for the restless inquietude of remorse. His brow was clouded with anxiety; the voice of love was no longer music in his ear; his youthful cheek no longer wore the crimson flush of health; his eye no longer beamed the serenity of his soul. He frequently spent whole nights with Somerton and Ebbert, in such pursuits as it pains humanity to think of, and over which charity would cast her celestial mantle. By degrees his mind became so familiarised to the society of his vicious companions, that the spark of virtue was stifled, if not entirely eradicated.

---

1   [Warren's note:] SACRED DRAMAS. [Warren is quoting from More's play "David and Goliath."]
2   [Warren's note:] PARADISE LOST. [Warren loosely quotes Book IV of Milton's *Paradise Lost*, lines 646–52.]
3   Alexander Pope, *An Essay on Man* (1733–34).

Amelia saw this change with keenest anguish. She had entered into life with him, with the brightest prospects of futurity, and when she saw those prospects fading away, when she saw his brow constantly clouded with care, she would have administered the balm of consolation; but she knew not the depth of the wounds she essayed to heal.

By a strict economy, in domestic concerns, she endeavoured as much as possible to avert the wide ruin she saw impending over their heads. The birth of a son, however, recalled Anderson awhile from his mad pursuits. It was, alas! but a momentary respite. The subtle arguments of the treacherous Somerton again drew his wandering footsteps from the paths of peace. His fortune was wasting rapidly; yet he had not sufficient courage to extricate himself from the snare, into which he had fallen. Yet there were hours of reflection, of serious, painful reflection. He still felt all that a father can feel for his little Alonzo; he still almost idolized his Amelia; and he still revered the shades of his departed parents. To drown the recollection of the past, and the dreadful anticipation of the future, he plunged still deeper in the scenes of dissipation. Herbert felt for Leander all the affection of a parent. How keen then must have been his anguish, when he saw the wide cloud of ruin, which was gathering, and almost ready to burst upon the head of a once promising youth, dear to him as a child, and the only remaining branch of a family once near his heart; when he saw that indigence and misery must inevitably ensue, unless some speedy means were devised, to deter him from the rock on which so many thousands have perished.

But Eliza, hapless Eliza, her's was the heart that felt, most exquisitely, the weight of anguish! She had formed many flattering presages of future happiness; but her hopes were now all blighted; the roses of happiness were withered, and love was left to prove the torment of her future life. To continue a connection with an unprincipled gamester, was repugnant to every feeling of delicacy, and every principal of virtue. She strove to cast him from her thoughts, but strove in vain. Vain, indeed, was the struggle between the cool dictates of reason, and the impetuosity of love. That a form so engaging should conceal a heart so depraved, both surprized and grieved her. She determined to think no more of a connection which, were it prolonged, must wound her delicacy, as well as her reputation. Eliza's sensibility was exquisite, and her heart, naturally generous and affectionate; and when she was compelled, at length, to withdraw her esteem from Somerton, she would not disengage her affection. She was a prey to silent anguish, and concealed misery. Her frame was too delicate to support the struggle, and the rosy hue of health no longer graced her cheek; the cheerful smile no longer sat upon her countenance. "Medical aid" was called, but physicians cannot cure the wounds of the heart. Observing the pain she created, she reasoned with herself, she remonstrated with her heart, and resolved, if possible, to conquer its feelings.

With a faint hope that Leander was not irrecoverably lost, Herbert resolved to separate him awhile from the fascinating society of Somerton, by accompanying him on a journey to visit his friends at Philadelphia. Fortunately, Leander was at home, (or rather at his own house, for of late the tavern had been his home) on the afternoon which his uncle had chosen to make the proposal. Leander received him with confusion; he knew that he was making an ill return for the guardian cares of his uncle, and his embarrassment was extreme. His countenance was pale, his eyes sunken, and his deportment bashful and timid; not the timidity of modesty, but of guilt and remorse. To some observation of his uncle, he attempted to reply, but the accent died upon his lips. Not appearing to notice his too evident embarrassment, Herbert began to caress and play with Alonzo. "What a lovely child!" said he, "how prettily he smiles. See, Leander, how strongly he resembles his mother; do you not think that he will possess her virtues? I should suppose similar features to be indicative of similar virtues." Leander's native sensibility was rising; it had been long repressed; for in the circles he frequented, sensibility was known, only to be ridiculed. Herbert made the proposal, and urged his nephew to a compliance. "Indeed," added he, "I cannot be denied; the plan is arranged, and my girls shall domesticate with Amelia till we return." After a variety of objections had been obviated, and Leander could no longer find a pretext to deny, he reluctantly acceded to the proposal, and the following morning was fixed for their departure.

The affection of his uncle had aroused Anderson from his lethargy, and though the good man had studiously avoided to mention his late irregularities, Leander could not help imagining that there was an uncommon earnestness in his manner, and a look of pity, he fancied, was often mingled with his earnest gaze at himself. "Alas," thought Leander, "I have forfeited his esteem forever, and now he pities, as he condemns me." He gazed on Amelia and Alonzo in succession, and his feelings were most exquisitely agonizing.

Amelia saw the struggle in his soul. She would have soothed

him; but her heart was too full for utterance. She gently touched her guitar, and calmed the tumult of his soul with the soft strains of melody. Leander was not yet so hardened in guilt, as to stifle the voice of conscience. He had tried, in vain, to quiet its murmurings, and lull its pangs; and when he retired this night to his chamber, he made the heroic resolution to hear its accusations. Multiplied, indeed, were his transgressions, and his heart pronounced sentence against him; yet he felt still a pleasing hope that he was not irrecoverably lost. He resolved to confess his errors to his uncle, and entreat his counsel. He was even pleased with his intended journey, as it might contribute to the recovery of his diseased mind.

Having made this resolution, he was led to an examination of the state of his finances. He had contracted many debts, which, in the dialect of the gamester, are called *debts of honour*, and which the writer supposes *are debts of infamy*; and his affairs were in a state of embarrassment. The duties of his profession had been for some time totally neglected; but he resolved to apply to them with industrious assiduity. These resolutions were made in the serious hour of retirement, when he was not surrounded with temptation, and saw not a party of his companions at a gaming table. Happy, thrice happy, would it have been, had he been enabled to perform his virtuous resolutions; but he knew not how deeply the poison was infused into his mind. The love of gaming was coeval with his existence, and outweighed even the love of virtue.

2. From Mason Locke Weems, *God's Revenge Against Gambling: Exemplified in the Miserable Lives and Untimely Deaths of a Number of Persons of Both Sexes, Who Had Sacrificed Their Health, Wealth, and Honor at Gaming Tables* (Augusta, GA: Hobby & Bunce, 1810) ii, 11–14

[The title suggests that this tract by Mason Locke Weems (1759–1825), also called Reverend Weems, will be a freewheeling, evangelical, sermon-like exhortation, and it does not disappoint. Weems was the author of a number of similar tracts, including *God's Revenge Against Murder* (1807), *God's Revenge Against Adultery* (1815), and *God's Revenge Against Dueling* (1820). He was also responsible for circulating—and perhaps even inventing—the myth of George Washington chopping down the cherry tree with his little hatchet.

The frontispiece image of the repentant gambler, as well as the recommendation by Rebecca Rush's father, Judge Jacob Rush, appeared in the second edition of *God's Revenge Against Gambling*

(1812). In endorsing Weems's book, Jacob Rush proposes harsh penalties for gamblers, exhorting lawmakers "to put an end to gambling by a law, declaring a person who shall play at cards, or any game of hazard, for money, or other article of value, shall not receive the benefit of any bankrupt or insolvent law, for seven years, and be incapable, for the same space of time, of voting at an election, or of being elected or appointed to any post of honor or profit, under the government." Compare these punishments to the fate of Rush's inveterate gambler, Mrs. Hammond. A short but typical excerpt from the main text of *God's Revenge Against Gambling* follows Jacob Rush's "Recommendation."]

He writhes, he gnashes his teeth. On bended knees, he curses the Authors of his [?].
Page 19

RECOMMENDATION.

However painful it may be to observe, yet nothing is more certain, than that the practice of gambling, with its train of pernicious consequences, is rapidly spreading through all classes of people, and daily producing the most destructive effects on the souls and bodies of its votaries. The truth of this remark is confirmed by the melancholy experience of every person. In this awful situation of our country, any effort, however feeble, to stem the torrent, is entitled to public attention. To Mr. Weems, however, an uncommon degree of merit is due—he has nobly come forward to check the progress of an evil, that threatens our country with ruin. In his observations on gambling, he has combined every thing that can be said against it, by wit, genius, and piety. With every species of argument that can reach the head or heart, enforced by striking examples, and adorned by flashes of eloquence, he has powerfully pleaded the cause of humanity and virtue. Of a gambler, who can read this pamphlet, and not be the better for the perusal, it may be truly said, he is incurable by any thing from the pen or tongue of an individual. If he be not convinced by Mr. Weems, he would not believe Moses and the Prophets, nor be persuaded though one rose from the dead. I can not however, avoid expressing my fears, that the moralist will dogmatize, and the pious man exhort to little purpose, unless they can prevail upon our Legislatures to afford *their* benevolent aid. It is in their power to lay the axe to the root of evil. It is in their power to put an end to gambling by a law, declaring a person who shall play at cards, or any game of hazard, for money, or other article of value, shall not receive the benefit of any bankrupt or insolvent law, for seven years, and be incapable, for the same space of time, of voting at an election, or of being elected or appointed to any post of honor or profit, under the government.

JACOB RUSH,
Judge of the Court of Common Pleas, Penn.

Philad. January 20th, 1812.

★ ★ ★ ★

Now, coming more nearly to the point, what is sin but violation of law? And what is God's law?—His *Royal* law?—the *end* of his law? And the *fulfilling* of his law? What is it all but LOVE. That divine sentiment, which, beating first with strongest pulse towards wife and children, thence swells on to neighbours and relations, to country and to all mankind, feeling for all a brother's solicitude, and with a brother's joy striving to do them good. Since then love is, thus, the source of all the virtues and the sweetest charities of life, and thereby the *"very bond of perfection,"* and "life of the world," no wonder God so strictly enjoins love; no wonder he so narrowly watches our observance, and so severely chastises every violation of it.

The modes of violating this great law are various: but they may all be thrown under the general term of *cruelty.* Of this, also, there is a numerous family: but I will confine my present speculation to *one* only, but that a gigantic one, and the fruitful parent of ten thousand others, I mean the Giant-Cruelty—GAMBLING.

It is not easy to conceive any vice more hateful to God than Gambling, because none can be conceived MORE DIAMETRICALLY OPPOSITE TO THE VERY END OF OUR CREATION!

God created the human family to be as one great *social body,* whereof every man is a member, and to which every man is bound to contribute his part of *service,* and in return to receive from it his portion of *safety* and comfort. Hence that sublime and sweet doctrine of the Apostle, "no man lives for *himself only,*" but in and for his brethren also; and hence too, that Golden saying, "live and *let live;*" implying that in his dealings with others, no man should take any thing from his brother without giving him an *equivalent* for it. This is the dictate of man's *necessities,* which require gains rather than losses; and this is the dictate of *love,* which finds it *"more blessed to give than to receive."*

But alas! the Gambler is blind to all such beautiful ideas, and stupidly insensible to all such divine impulses. Sordid, groveling wretch! Himself, Himself is all that he cares for; provided he swims, no matter who sinks.—Hence his life is a shameful discordance from the universal harmony. The sun rolls on in his light and life-giving glory; the winds breathe their refreshing gales; the tides heave their fish and commerce-laden floods; the trees put on their gay green robes, or bend under their luscious fruits; in short, all nature, like the springs of a Heaven-framed machine, rolls on harmoniously for the general good: but alas! the Gambler bears no part in the divine concert. Far, far he lives below the dignity and worth of the poorest animal.

See how patiently yon little Quadruped submits to the harness! How cheerfully he bends forward to the plough, heaving the deep black furrows behind him! See how quietly stands yon Cow, chewing her cud, at the pail of the Cottager's wife, whose little half-naked Children, hovering around with noisy delight await their wonted breakfast of milk and cakes. Sweet little favorites of Heaven! You may look to the nobler brutes for assistance, but not to your brother man, if he be a Gambler. Your angel faces touch not him, awaken no pity in his savage breast.— Without regret he can take away your Father's horse, and drive your Mother's cow to auction: and, provided he can but swallow your substance, and chuckle over his accursed gains, he cares not though you should mourn your loss of milk, and cry every morning for scantiness of bread—he cares not though your poor bankrupt Father, returning home, should feel a hell within him at sight of you, once his dearest delight, and after cruelly repulsing your caresses, and abusing your beggared mother, should then, torn with anguish intolerable, rush for relief to a razor or a pistol.

Poor Gilmore! Never shall I think of thee without mingling with thy memory my bitterest execrations against Gambling. Gilmore was a young man of as noble a soul as ever inhabited the manliest form. His countenance, at sight of his friends, was always brightened with a joy which they can never forget. Too much elated by an estate left him by his Father, and counting largely on the generosity of a widowed Mother, he ran into excesses. His excesses created debts; debts begat duns; and duns begat sorrow. To rid himself at once of his wretchedness, he went to a Gaming-table, which quickly swallowed up his estate, and reduced his young Wife and little son to poverty. An Uncle appointed him collector of his debts, which, being numerous, threw large sums of money into his hands. This welcome piece of news soon reached the ears of his Gambling acquaintance, who instantly formed a plan to fleece him once more.

Near his Uncle's house was one of those sinks of sin, where whiskey is sold by the half pint, and where the worthless and idle meet to drink, and swear, and hatch mischief. 'Twas here that they watched for him returning from a collecting tour with saddle-bags well lined with cash; and as he passed, with looks of brothers they ran out and seized him by the hand insisting that he should alight. He begged hard to be excused, saying he must positively see his Uncle that night. They replied that they had no objection to that neither, but still insisted that he would take *one* bowl with them, *"surely you won't refuse one bowl* to our *old friendship."* So after much intreaty they at length got him down. One bowl prepared the way for another, that for a third, and so on, till getting him half-drunk they easily fixed him down, like a young bullock, to the ring-bolt of their gaming table, where they soon *stripped him to the skin.*—he, during great part of the time, nearly insensible of what was passing, often let his cards fall, and at last, overcome with wine, fell himself under the table.

Wretched young man why couldst thou not have died in thy sleep! Oh! why did the Almighty suffer thee to awake to the agonies of the morning? But, perhaps it was that thou mightest exhibit to the whole world of youth, a dreadful example of the dangers of Gambling.—Poor fellow! Language was never made to tell what he felt next morning when he opened his eyes on the hated light. Unable to meet his Uncle's frown he skulked to his own home, where the sight of his injured wife and little beggared boy filled up the measure of his wretchedness.—The melancholy looks of the one, and the trembling cries of the other, overcame him; and the next morning while his wife kneeling at the fire was toasting a crust for his breakfast, and his boy was weeping on the floor, he took down his gun, placed it against his forehead, and touching the trigger with his toe, scattered his brains over the ceiling and fell by the side of his child half drowned in his father's blood.

3. From *The Wonderful Advantages of Adventuring in the Lottery!!!* (Philadelphia: B. & J. Johnson, 1800) 2–10

[Alas, the "advantages" referred to in the title of this anonymously published anti-lottery tract set in England include the death of John's virtuous wife from a broken heart, the orphaning of his son, and John's sentence to death by being drawn and quartered.]

JOHN BROWN was servant in the family of a respectable Merchant in this city. He had lived there for several years; and from his regular honesty, sobriety and diligence, possessed the confidence and affection of his master. While in that family, he married a fellow-servant, a young woman whose name was Mary Coates, and they lived for more than seven years very happily together. They had one child living, a fine little boy about six years old, whom they maintained at a school, kept some miles from town by Mary's father. This was thought better than putting him to school in London, as he was under an affectionate relation, and less exposed to the company of wicked children. John and his wife got leave from time to time to visit their child, and were always able to take him one little article or other of clothes, as well as a small present to the grandfather.

Thus comfortable were John and Mary, and had John been religious like his wife, they would have had a very fair prospect of continuing so. He, like many others, thought Religion rather an unnecessary thing for a man who made it a rule to be sober, and honest, and diligent, and kind. Besides the other very important considerations against which he shut his heart, he did not reflect that without religion his good conduct to his family and his master stood on no solid foundation.

One unfortunate day as he was going on a message, he received a hand-bill from a man standing at the door of a Lottery Office. This hand-bill set forth many wonders, and invited all who had a mind to be rich in a hurry, to seize the lucky hour of adventuring in the wheel of fortune; shewing them how many thousand pounds they would be sure to get for one guinea! Casting his eyes over the advertisement, the thought struck him that he would *try his fortune.* "Why may not I get a prize as well as any other?" said he to himself; "and if I get the twenty thousand pound prize, or *even* one of the ten thousands, I shall be as great a man as my master?" It was a woeful moment for poor John, when this imagination fastened on his mind. Full of the notion of getting rich, John returned home, and appeared all that day unusually thoughtful. At night, as he was not used to conceal any thing from his wife, he told her his intention. "Molly, (said he) we have just got our wages, and the drawing begins to-morrow; suppose we *try our fortune* in the Lottery." "Not with my consent, (she replied); I think we are rich enough as we are, and ought to be thankful to God that we want for nothing." John was obliged to acknowledge this; but observed that it would do them no *harm* to have something *more.* "Indeed, something but it might, (said Molly) for you know, John, God is the best judge of what is good for us, and it is his Providence that has placed us in our present situation. If he saw that more riches would do us good, I believe he would send them to us in an honest way: but I am sure you and I know some people, that are not at all the better for their riches, no nor the happier either." "But what harm (said he) can there be in *trying our fortune*?" "I know there is harm, (replied his wife, who was well read in the bible,) I know there is harm in covetousness; for the word of God says, *Be content with such things as you have; and he that maketh haste to be rich shall not be innocent; and the love of money is the root of all evil.* For my part I am very well satisfied as I am, and when I think of the poverty and distress our blessed Saviour submitted to, I find great reason to praise him for the abundance we enjoy. Besides trying our fortune, as you call it, is no better than tempting God, who is the real giver of what men say fortune gives them. Our blessed Saviour refused, you know, when he fasted in the wilderness to act in an extraordinary manner, in order that God might give him riches and other things, for he said that would be tempting God: and what would going into the Lottery be but tempting God, for would it not be taking an extraordinary course in order to try whether God would make us rich? But, my dear, what has put this matter into your head?" John pulled the hand-bill out of his pocket, and explained to her as well as he could, all the wonderful advantages which it promised. This did not satisfy his wife: and she wisely observed, that if there were so much to be got by these same tickets, it was strange that the people who sold them would not rather keep them for themselves. "But do you not see there before your eyes," said John, "the number of prizes that were sold last year at the *Lion's Office*?" "Well, replied his wife, I wish they had published the number of *blanks* that were sold too."

"But ah! John, there are a great many lies in print: and to tell you the truth, I fancy it is all a gambling trick, and that the people who sell these tickets are little better than *knaves*, and the folks who buy them no better than *fools*. And you know, my dear, our little boy wants clothes, and this is the time that you generally take something to his old grandfather. Sure," (said she), while a tear stole down her cheek, "you will not forget our dear Johnny." But all her arguments were in vain; and he concluded the conversation rather peevishly, with declaring. "It is a folly to talk; I am resolved to try." His wife wiped her eyes, and only said with a sigh, "I am sorry for it." He had never grieved her so much before.

That night John slept little; he was anxiously debating which of the various modes of adventuring was to be preferred, and laying a thousand plans as to what he would do upon getting his expected riches. Early next day he got from his wife some money which he had given her to keep; and making a false excuse of business for leaving home, he hurried to the Lottery Office. There, looking at various tickets, and shares, and policies that were shewn, out of several numbers that he was informed were peculiarly *lucky* he selected one ticket. But as he was returning with it home, beginning to think that it was foolish to spend *all his luck* (as he called it) upon *one* number, he went back, and changed the ticket for six policies, which he got at a guinea a piece. "Well (said he) as he put them in his pocket, they can never be all drawn blanks." Upon hearing that the ticket he had taken first was drawn the next day a prize of ten pounds, he thanked his *stars* that he had parted with it, as he should by no means be satisfied with gaining so little as two or three pounds by his venture.

John now became hourly anxious to know whether his numbers were drawn or not, and often neglected his business to enquire after them. He appeared thoughtful and gloomy in the house; and sometimes gave his master a very short answer, if he found fault with him. All in the family wondered at the entire change in his conduct;—his poor wife alone guessed at the cause. To her he now observed an entire silence up on the subject, as he had found her so decided against his venturing in the Lottery. But one day, when he had come home after hearing that two of his numbers were drawn blanks, and the third drawn a 10l. [£10] prize, (from which he of course got nothing,) she affectionately seized his hand, and with a flood of tears asked him why he had been for some days so peevish to her. "My dearest husband, (said she), it was never so with you before since our marriage. If I have done any thing lately to offend you, I am ready to go on my knees to ask your pardon. Only do not break my heart by behaving as if you did not love me."— "Pugh! Woman! (replied he sullenly)— don't make a fool of yourself." "Alas! (said she) is it a folly to be grieved at seeing you unhappy, or at the fear of having displeased you? But, ah! I fear the Lottery is the cause. I thought no good would come of it." Molly perceived that his mind was in a state of vexation; and therefore did not press the subject then. But in the evening she took an opportunity of tenderly entreating him to rest satisfied under any loss he had already suffered, without venturing farther; observing that he might thus learn a lesson which might be useful to him all his life; but that in the course in which he was he could not expect the blessing of God.—"And surely (added she) we shall be richer with that blessing and a few worldly comforts, than if we had all the world without it. Ah! John! there is indeed, as our Saviour says, but *one thing needful.* What matter whether we be rich or poor in this life, if we get to heaven at last? And truly God is so gracious a master, that his service brings peace and comfort with it even here: while on the contrary, those who set their hearts upon the world, do not even find in it *now* the enjoyment which they seek; not to say, *that if they gained the whole world, and lost their own souls,* they would make a fool's bargain."

Works Cited and Recommended Reading

Allibone, Austin. *Critical Dictionary of English Literature and British and American Authors, Volume III.* Philadelphia: J.B. Lippincott and Company, 1897.

Balch, Thomas Willing. *The Philadelphia Assemblies.* Philadelphia: Allen, Lane and Scott, 1916.

Bannet, Eve Tavor, and Susan Manning, eds. *Transatlantic Literary Studies 1660–1830.* Cambridge: Cambridge UP, 2014.

Barth, Gunther. *City People.* New York: Oxford UP, 1982.

Birch, William Russell. *The City of Philadelphia, in the State of Pennsylvania North America; as It Appeared in the Year 1800.* Philadelphia: William Birch, 1800.

Bowers, Toni, and Tita Chico, eds. *Atlantic Worlds in the Long Eighteenth Century: Seduction and Sentiment.* New York: Palgrave Macmillan, 2012.

Breen, T.H. *The Marketplace of Revolution: How Consumer Politics Shaped American Independence.* Oxford: Oxford UP, 2004.

Crane, Gregg. *The Cambridge Introduction to the Nineteenth-Century American Novel.* Cambridge: Cambridge UP, 2007.

Davidson, Cathy. *Revolution and the Word: The Rise of the Novel in America.* 2nd ed. New York: Oxford UP, 2004.

Derounian, Kathryn Zabelle. "Lost in the Crowd: Rebecca Rush's *Kelroy* (1812)." *American Transcendental Quarterly* 47–48 (1980): 117–26.

Dillon, Elizabeth Maddock. *New World Drama: The Performative Commons in the Atlantic World, 1649–1849.* Durham, NC: Duke UP, 2014.

Ezell, John Samuel. *Fortune's Merry Wheel: The Lottery in America.* Cambridge, MA: Harvard UP, 1960.

Fidelity Rewarded, Or, The History of Polly Granville. Boston: Young and Adams, 1796.

Gaul, Theresa Strouth. "Recovering Recovery: Early American Women and *Legacy*'s Future." *Legacy* 26.2 (2009): 262–83.

Herman, Bernard. *Town House: Architecture and Material Life in the Early American City, 1780–1830.* Chapel Hill: U of North Carolina P, 2005.

Klimasmith, Betsy. "*Kelroy*'s Parlor Games." *Early American Literature* 49.2 (2014): 467–97.

Loughran, Trish. *The Republic in Print: Print Culture in the Age of U.S. Nation Building, 1770–1870*. New York: Columbia UP, 2007.

Meserole, Harrison T. "Some Notes on Early American Fiction: *Kelroy* Was There." *Studies in American Fiction* 5 (1977): 1–12.

Nelson, Dana D. "Introduction." *Kelroy*. By Rebecca Rush. New York: Oxford UP, 1992. xi–xxi.

Mrs. Patterson. *The Unfortunate Lovers, and Cruel Parents: A Very Interesting Tale Founded on Fact*. New Haven, CT: Read and Morse, 1799.

Richards, Jeffery H. "Decorous Violence: Manners, Class, and Abuse in Rebecca Rush's *Kelroy*." *Over the Threshold: Intimate Violence in Early America*. Ed. Christine Daniels and Michael V. Kennedy. New York: Routledge, 1999. 202–16.

Rowson, Susanna. *Charlotte Temple*. 1794. New York: Oxford UP, 1987.

——. *Miscellaneous Poems*. Boston: Gilbert and Sons, 1804.

Rush, Rebecca. *Kelroy*. 1812. New York: Oxford UP, 1992.

Sartain, John. *The Reminiscences of a Very Old Man*. New York: D. Appleton and Company, 1899.

Shapiro, Stephen. *The Culture and Commerce of the Early American Novel: Reading the Atlantic World System*. University Park: The Pennsylvania State UP, 2008.

Simpson, Henry. *The Lives of Eminent Philadelphians, Now Deceased*. Philadelphia: William Brotherhead, 1859.

Stout, Janis. *Sodoms in Eden: The City in American Fiction before 1860*. Westport, CT: Greenwood Press, 1976.

Teitleman, S. Robert. *Views of Philadelphia 1800–1960–1982: A Comparative Record*. Philadelphia: U of Pennsylvania P, 1982.

Tennenhouse, Leonard. *The Importance of Feeling English: American Literature and the British Diaspora, 1750–1850*. Princeton, NJ: Princeton UP, 2007.

Upton, Dell. *Another City: Urban Life and Urban Spaces in the New American Republic*. New Haven, CT: Yale UP, 2008.

Warren, Caroline Matilda. *The Gamesters: or, Ruins of Innocence*. Boston: Carlisle for Thomas & Andrews et al., 1805.

Weems, Mason Locke. *God's Revenge Against Gambling: Exemplified in the Miserable Lives and Untimely Deaths of a Number of Persons of Both Sexes, Who Had Sacrificed Their Health, Wealth, and Honor at Gaming Tables*. Augusta, GA: Hobby & Bunce, 1810.

Weyler, Karen. *Intricate Relations: Sexual and Economic Desire in American Fiction, 1789–1814*. Iowa City: U of Iowa P, 2004.

——. "Introduction." *Kelroy*. By Rebecca Rush. San Antonio, TX: Early American Reprints, 2014. iv–xvi.

——. "'A Speculating Spirit': Trade, Speculation, and Gambling in Early American Fiction." *Early American Literature* 31.3 (1996): 207–42.

Wilson, Thomas. *An Analysis of Country Dancing*. London: J.S. Dickson, 1808. 3rd ed. 1811.

The Wonderful Advantages of Adventuring in the Lottery!!! Philadelphia: B. & J. Johnson, 1800.

Wood, Sally Sayward Barrell Keating. *Dorval, or, The Speculator: A Novel, Founded on Recent Facts*. Portsmouth, NH: Nutting & Whitlock, 1801.

From the Publisher

A name never says it all, but the word "Broadview" expresses a good deal of the philosophy behind our company. We are open to a broad range of academic approaches and political viewpoints. We pay attention to the broad impact book publishing and book printing has in the wider world; we began using recycled stock more than a decade ago, and for some years now we have used 100% recycled paper for most titles. Our publishing program is internationally oriented and broad-ranging. Our individual titles often appeal to a broad readership too; many are of interest as much to general readers as to academics and students.

Founded in 1985, Broadview remains a fully independent company owned by its shareholders—not an imprint or subsidiary of a larger multinational.

For the most accurate information on our books (including information on pricing, editions, and formats) please visit our website at www.broadviewpress.com. Our print books and ebooks are also available for sale on our site.

On the Broadview website we also offer several goods that are not books—among them the Broadview coffee mug, the Broadview beer stein (inscribed with a line from Geoffrey Chaucer's *Canterbury Tales*), the Broadview fridge magnets (your choice of philosophical or literary), and a range of T-shirts (made from combinations of hemp, bamboo, and/or high-quality pima cotton, with no child labor, sweatshop labor, or environmental degradation involved in their manufacture).

All these goods are available through the "merchandise" section of the Broadview website. When you buy Broadview goods you can support other goods too.

broadview press
www.broadviewpress.com

The interior of this book is printed on 100% recycled paper.